CODE BLUES

by Melissa Yi

Melissa Yi (signature)

D1598614

CODE BLUES

by Melissa Yi

Olo
books

Published by Olo Books
http://olobooks.wordpress.com/

In association with Windtree Press
http://windtreepress.com/

Dedicated to Matt Innes

CHAPTER 1

I pictured the city of Montreal as a woman with bleached blonde hair and a cigarette jammed in the corner of her mouth who turned around and bitch-slapped me.

At least, that's what it felt like. Even before I got mixed up with murder.

Last night, it took me seven hours to drive here from London, Ontario. When I hit the Quebec border, I could hardly make out the blue and white sign declaring *"Bonjour!"* and the *fleur-de-lis* flag fluttering against the dusky, grey-indigo June sky, but I noticed that my Ford Focus began bouncing over more frequent potholes. Although the maximum speed was still 100 kilometers per hour, there was also a minimum speed: 60. I decided that the roads were natural speed bumps. Everyone slowed down to about 110. Not me. I cranked up the On the Rocks's cover of Lady Gaga, gave my cinnamon gum an extra-hard chew, and zipped by them—

—only to pull up at a dead stop at a red light, one of many in two little towns, Dorion and Île-Perrot. I thought these must be the suburbs of Montreal, but no. Some planning committee thought it was a good idea to run Highway 20 through the heart of little bergs advertising *musculation* and *rénovation*. I knew the second one, but the first was intriguing. I could use a guy with some *musculation*.

I crossed the bridge over to the island of Montreal. Strange to say, as a girl from nearby Ottawa, but I hadn't realized Montreal was an island. Or how big a city it was, with the billboards lining the Ville Marie expressway, advertising everything from "Cuba, *sí*" to cell phones. Skyscrapers loomed above me, including one topped by a white searchlight that revolved around the city.

By the time I took a left up the steep hill of University Avenue, it was after 8 p.m. I felt very small and tired, but at least I'd arrived. I cashed in the last of my good karma by finding a parking space, avoiding the $10 parking lot at the top of the hill. It would all be strawberry daiquiris and whipped cream from here.

Except that the next morning, my alarm didn't go off. Like the white rabbit, I was very, very late.

I didn't panic. Being late was a habit of mine. Even though I was now a doctor, or at least a resident doctor, I often spared a moment to brush my teeth or dab on some lip gloss. Then, suddenly, there was no time, and I was hopping around, pulling up my socks after barely yanking on my underwear.

Today, I was late for my first day of orientation at St. Joseph's Hospital in Montreal. After four long, hard years of medical school, earning my M.D., I was in for two years of a residency in family medicine, mostly based at St. Joseph's.

I'd stayed the night at the Royal Victoria Hospital, in a cramped, pink call room with peeling paint, because it was free for visiting students.

Or not so free. When I ran down the hill, my keys clutched in sweaty fingers, my silver car was one of a chorus line sporting a $52 parking ticket under its windshield wiper.

After multiple red lights, one-way streets, and a guy flipping me the bird, I finally managed to drive up the right street, Péloquin.

I hit the brakes when a moving van shuddered to a halt in front of me. WTF? It reversed and angled left to obstruct all traffic on a diagonal.

The van's doors popped open. Two men leapt out. One pulled down the rear ramp while the other ran into the open door of a nearby apartment and began loading boxes into the van.

Heart hammering, I took a hard right into a parking spot. Even as I locked my doors, a city bus tried to nudge its way around the van, failed, and began honking. Two more cars joined the chorus.

The moving men continued loading the van. They were still smiling.

I did not understand this city.

However, I swiftly recognized St. Joseph's concrete block architecture, typical of hospitals and 19th century prisons. It looked like something my eight-year-old brother, Kevin, might build out of Legos. The only fancy bit was the limestone front entrance way declaring, *CENTRE HOSPITALIER DE SAINT JOSEPH*, and underneath it, in smaller letters, the English version. Taxis idled in the semicircular driveway with a widened lot for parking and drop-offs. A straggly-haired patient in a wheelchair, an IV still hooked up to her arm, took a drag off her cigarette.

I held my breath against the smoke and pushed open the glass door, ready for the Family Medicine Centre. Only the receptionist told me the FMC wasn't part of the hospital, it was in "the Annex." Great. Like Anne Frank's hiding place.

Finally inside the correct building, even I couldn't miss the orientation room immediately across from the Annex entrance. Its wooden doors were flung open to reveal a room full of people staring at me instead of the man saying, "...any time. I don't mind. That's why I get paid the big bucks."

The speaker stood at a podium to the left of the door. Dang. I tiptoed past him with an apologetic smile.

"Hi, I'm Dr. Kurt Radshaw." The speaker, a good-looking guy in his late 30's, held out his hand. His smile seemed genuine under his dark, Tom Selleck-style moustache. "Welcome to St. Joseph's."

"Thanks." I shook his hand. His grip was firm but not crushing. Bonus.

The skin crinkled around the corners of his eyes. "I was just saying, if you have any problems, page me. Sheilagh's handing out my numbers and e-mail address in the orientation package."

"Great. Thanks."

"I know what it's like to have problems," he said to the group. "I have Type I diabetes myself. So don't be afraid to speak to me anytime. My pager's always on." He tapped the small black plastic pager clipped to his belt.

I surveyed the room, looking for a place to sit. The room's two couches and two armchairs were full, and everyone else was sitting on cheap orange plastic chairs.

I got the hairy eyeball from a milky-white, twenty-something guy who was wearing a tie, his suit jacket neatly folded on the sofa arm. Clearly, my tardiness, tank top, and board shorts failed to impress this fellow resident.

I picked a plastic chair across from him and smiled, showing a lot of teeth. Nothing to do but brazen it out.

Beside Mr. Bean, a guy with slightly long, messy, chestnut hair smiled back at me. A real smile, his eyes glinting with amusement. He sat with his knees sprawled apart, but his ankles hooked together. He was wearing a shirt that reminded me of blue milk paint, dark instead of flashy, but fitted enough for me to see that he had some *musculation*.

Maybe Montreal wasn't so bad after all.

At the break, everyone made a run for the refreshments table against the wall, next to the entrance. Dr. Radshaw chewed on a croissant as he talked to the tie guy and an Asian woman.

I didn't rise. I tilted in my chair so I could peek around an East Indian woman. The milk paint shirt guy and I smiled at each other again, across the room.

"Hello." The white woman on my left held out her hand. Her square-jawed face might have been pretty, if she hadn't been forcing her smile. She wasn't fat, but big boned, and her grip was worthy of a wrestler. "My name is Mireille." Her chin-length brown curls were the only bouncy thing about her.

"Hope," I said, belatedly returning the metacarpal-crushing handshake. She didn't wince. I pulled my hand away, smiled, and said, "Boy, those drinks look good."

I was contemplating the mystery meat sandwiches when a male voice behind me said, "Don't do it."

I spun around, empty-handed. It was the milk paint guy. He was even better-looking up close. His grey eyes looked straight into mine. He was shorter than I expected, maybe half a foot taller than my own five-foot two. I didn't mind. The nice thing about being short is that guys of all size feel comfortable hitting on you.

I found myself focusing on his lips as he said, "I think they put something in those sandwiches so that you never want to leave Montreal."

I had to laugh. "Oh, yeah? Don't worry, I've already been immunized. In about twelve hours, I've gotten lost, got a $52 dollar parking ticket, and almost ran into a moving van with moving violations." I explained my morning while he snagged a bottled water and offered it to me. I took it.

He broke open another bottle for himself. "Don't worry. Everyone gets parking tickets when they move here. It's like losing your virginity."

He watched me blush. Silent laughter danced in his eyes. I tossed my head. "What about the moving van?"

"July first is moving day in Quebec. It's the default date when all the leases expire."

"On the same day? For the whole province?" My organized, Ontario head spun.

He laughed and crunched on a carrot stick. "Pretty much. It's chaos here for the week before and after. Where are you from?"

"Ontario. Ottawa, originally. Western for med school." I held the water bottle up in a silent toast.

He nodded. "Poor little Ontario girl."

"Hey. Ain't no such thing." I gave him an arch look. Mireille bumped into me on her way to the refreshments table and muttered, "Sorry."

Alex and I gravitated toward the windows at the opposite end of the room. He leaned against one of the carved oak windowsills. I drank some water and asked, "So. Are you a poor, little Quebec boy?"

He bent toward me and lowered his voice. "Sort of. I've been here for years. Undergrad, med school. But originally—" He whispered, his lips only two inches from my ear, "Kitchener."

I giggled. Not that there's anything wrong with Kitchener-Waterloo, a town famous for its university and its Oktoberfest, but it's not exactly cosmopolitan. In answer, he held his index finger so close to my mouth that I could almost feel the heat from his skin against my lips.

I stopped laughing, suddenly shy.

A smile grew across his face. He lowered his finger and intoned, "Not one word. I have a reputation to uphold." He held out his hand. "Alex Dyck."

His hand was warm and strong, and felt right in mine. I held it for an extra beat. "Hope Sze."

We let go slowly. I could hear the chatter around the room and sense the sun's rays on my shoulder and arm, but nothing felt as real as his fingers sliding away from mine.

He cleared his throat and dropped his hand back down to the windowsill. "Did you get teased as much about your name as I did about mine?"

I shook my head. "More." My voice sounded a bit rusty.

He laughed. "It can't be worse than Dyck-head, Dyck-face, Dyckie-Dee..."

"Hopeless," I countered. "I *hope* not. Sze-saw. Sze-sick. Sze-nile. Sze-nior. Sze—"

He held up his hand. "I surrender."

I tucked my hand into the shape of a gun and blew across the barrel that was my index finger.

Alex nodded slowly. "I like you."

I couldn't hide my smile. "Likewise."

When we headed back to the little circle, he abandoned his spot on the sofa to sit in the hard plastic chair on my right.

The program director, Dr. Bob Clarkson, tapped at the top sheet on one of those things that look like easels. "Ahem. Now that we're all here—"

A few eyes swung in my direction. I shrugged and smiled, but with Alex at my side, I was tempted to take a bow. Alex smothered a laugh into a cough.

Dr. Clarkson frowned at me. "Why don't we introduce ourselves and say why we chose family medicine? Let's start with—" His eyes moved to my right. "Alex, you've been here a while."

"Sure have," said Alex in a fake-jaunty voice. "I'm Alex Dyck. I'm doing family medicine because no one else would have me. Oh, and because it's what I've wanted to do ever since I was a little kid."

A small, relieved laugh rippled from the crowd. I glanced sidelong at him. He smiled back at me.

My turn already? I cleared my throat. "I'm Hope Sze. I like long walks on the beach, candlelit dinners, and family medicine."

Alex laughed out loud.

Dr. Radshaw's eyes twinkled at me. He'd taken Alex's place on the sofa.

The program director, Dr. Bob Clarkson, rotated his upper body from side to side like a perturbed puppet. "Yes. Well. I was hoping for a little more explanation of the reasoning, the process behind your selection of family medicine and our program in particular, so..."

I smiled again, but added nothing. Neither did Alex.

"All right then." Bob Clarkson cleared his throat and tried the other side of the room. "Uh, Tori?"

Tori was the other Asian woman. She wore an indigo dress with tiny blue flowers. She folded her hands in her lap, and I noticed her long, artistic-looking fingers. "My name is Tori Yamamoto." So her background was Japanese, not Chinese like me. Her voice was clipped and low-pitched, with no accent. "My aunt is a family doctor in Edmonton."

Next was the tie guy. "Robin Huxley." That explained a lot about him. "I chose family medicine because I like the continuity of care." He looked at the floor and straightened his tie. Not a big talker.

John Tucker was a white guy with a shock of wheat-coloured hair. I wondered if he dyed it, while he said in a baritone voice, "Call me Tucker. Everyone does. You can call me Tucker, Tuck, Turkey. I'll answer to anything." He winked at me.

I wrinkled my nose. He was trying too hard. Not my type.

Anu Raghavan had a single, long, braid of hair behind her back and several gold and silver rings, but none on her engagement finger. She said she was interested in doing obstetrics and family medicine.

Mireille's chair squeaked. She kept shifting, impatient for her turn. When it came, she wouldn't shut up. "Before medical school, I went to Kenya, and since then, I've been to Thailand and Guatemala, but I'm most fascinated by the plight of the native people of Canada. The conditions on the reservations are appalling."

I glanced at Alex. His eyelid barely twitched, but I knew we were on the same page. Although I'm interested in those issues, I don't bash people over the head about it.

While Bob Clarkson sounded off about the joys of family medicine, Dr. Radshaw's pager beeped. He leapt to his feet and rushed over to the phone in the corner. Bob Clarkson frowned and raised his voice over Dr. Radshaw's murmurs. Mireille kept shooting glances at Dr. Radshaw.

While everyone was distracted, I tugged the top sheet out of my orientation package. It was my schedule for the year.

I'd be starting with emergency medicine. Cool. That's what I wanted to do when I grew up.

Although I could've done without the first shift on the first day of residency: Saturday, July first, at 7:30 a.m. Tomorrow.

I tilted the schedule so Alex could see it.

"Sucks," he breathed, and tilted his schedule toward me: palliative care. I didn't even know that was part of our residency program. I rolled my eyes at him.

Alex scrawled on his envelope, "Want to go out tonight?"

I scrawled back, "Yes." And for the rest of orientation, my Spidey-sense was tingling.

Code Blues

CHAPTER 2

Alex laced his fingers together on the white linen tablecloth. "So what did you think of the clinic?"

"Honestly?" I sipped some jasmine tea out of a blue and white china cup. "It was scary."

Alex laughed. He'd taken me out for sushi, which I'd only had once before, in Toronto, for a friend's birthday. All I remembered was eating a piece covered in orange sacs of oil called roe eggs. It was disgusting. The meal had also cost me $40, and two hours later, I was so hungry that I ate a bowl of Bran Flakes. I wasn't eager to repeat the experience, but Alex had insisted, "I didn't like sushi either, until I came here. Come on. It's baptism by raw fish."

I had to admit that the ambiance was great. Elegant ebony furniture, white floral linen napkins that matched the tablecloth, and tinkling music in the background. We didn't sit on tatami mats, though. That was Alex's one concession to my bourgeois upbringing.

The tea was fragrant, but had a subtle flavor. I set the cup back on the table. "You know, I didn't bother to tour St. Joseph's at the interview. So I'd never seen the clinic before."

Alex raised his eyes. "You didn't like the duct tape holding down the carpet? Or the examining rooms with no running water?"

I shuddered. "I've heard of 'shabby chic,' but that was just shabby." The upstairs rooms were much more run-down than the conference room had been. "And that nurse who made us stab ourselves—"

He laughed. The nurse had insisted that in order to check diabetics' blood sugar, we should practice on ourselves. I had to jab my left pinky with a needle and drip the blood on a paper strip. My finger still ached. Plus Tucker had taken the opportunity to point out that my post-cookie reading of 7.5 was higher than his own 4.9. "I guess you're sweeter," he'd said. Yuck.

Alex tapped the tablecloth just next to my hand. "Dr. Kurt is awesome, though. You'll love him. Everybody does."

I hoped Dr. Kurt was awesome enough not to mind me interrupting his speech. I squirmed.

Alex didn't seem to notice. "The whole thing with the pager? It's true. You can call him anytime. I think he clips it to his bedpost. Seriously."

I found it a bit weird, but Dr. Radshaw had certainly seemed delighted to answer his page during Bob Clarkson's speech.

A slender, Japanese woman appeared at our elbows and laid an enormous china platter in front of us. My eyes widened at the neat bundles of rice topped with shrimp, fish, caviar, and other items I couldn't identify. Alex had ordered octopus, eel, and all sorts of goodies. "*Bon appétit*," the server murmured and withdrew silently.

Alex laughed at my expression. "Are you not in Kansas anymore?"

I looked across the table at him. His bangs were long, and he tossed his head, flipping them out of his eyes. I was on a date with a guy who intrigued me, for the first time in two years, and it felt damned good. I grinned back at him. "Yeah, but now I don't miss Kansas as much." I picked up my wooden chopsticks, which did not come in a paper wrapper and have to be snapped apart. "Do you miss Kitchener at all?"

He frowned. "What about it?" He looked away, focusing on the boisterous birthday crowd in the corner.

I tried to ignore the foot-in-mouth feeling. He was the one who'd mentioned his roots. "I don't know. Your family? Oktoberfest?" I paused, trying to dredge up more memories of the area. "The Mennonites?"

His fingers tightened on his chopsticks before he carefully laid them back on the tablecloth. His eyes didn't quite meet mine. "Have you been talking to people?"

I shook my head. I'd hardly had a chance. After orientation, I'd zipped to my new apartment, moved in a few boxes—the rest were coming via the Zippy Moving Company—showered, and slipped into a strappy silver top and a black miniskirt. My hair had barely dried before Alex had buzzed my apartment. "What's wrong?"

He picked up his chopsticks and arranged a smile on his face. "Nothing. Do you want wasabi or pickled ginger?"

"Uh—" I was still five steps back.

"I find that people are either into one or the other, not both. What's it gonna be?" He gestured at the triangular green mound in the centre of the dish. "I bet wasabi. Because you're a *very hot chick*." He waggled his eyebrows with the last three words.

I giggled. Tucker could take lessons from this guy. You can say cheesy things, as long as you're funny. "Well, I've never been into the ginger."

"See?" He picked up the soy sauce and poured a black puddle into a porcelain dish in front of me.

The sushi turned out to be delicious. No oily roe eggs. When some wasabi shot up my nose and made my eyes water, Alex handed me his napkin and watched me in concerned silence. I had to laugh as I wiped my eyes. "I'll live, doctor."

"Yeah, but I don't want you to hate sushi from now on. First the roe eggs, and now, attack of the wasabi."

"I don't hate sushi," I said softly, to my porcelain plate.

"Good." He took my hand. His hand was bigger than my ex's and definitely paler, with blunt-cut fingernails.

No. This was not the time to think about Ryan Wu. I smiled at Alex instead. He smiled back.

For dessert, I would have been happy with green tea ice cream, but Alex said, "I want to take you downtown, show you the action. There's a nice café on Ste-Catherine."

"Sold." I squeezed his hand before I reluctantly dropped it.

I would have split the bill, but Alex waved my MasterCard away. He wouldn't even let me see the final tally. "You can get the next one," he said, as he scrawled his signature.

I had to admit, I was relieved not to know the damage. I'd be getting my first paycheque in two weeks, but my student loans and moving costs cried out for repayment. "Thanks."

He reached out to run his thumb up the delicate inner skin of my wrist. I had to catch my breath. He said, "You're welcome."

As Alex ordered dessert at the café, I watched the passers-by on Ste-Catherine through the glass windows on its south wall. Just walking down the street seemed to be a Friday night party. A guy stumbled along in a green-sequined miniskirt, fishnet stockings, and high heels. His friends bellowed and laughed and shoved him down the street, probably on their way to a stag party.

I realized, too late, that Alex was handing the cashier a ten for our slice of Black Forest cake, coffee for him and papaya juice for me. I unzipped my purse, but he shook his head and faked an accent. "Your money no good here!"

A group of college kids lounged at the back near the bathroom. They seemed to be playing some sort of game, not checkers, but using the same board. A middle-aged man read the newspaper and nursed a coffee near the front of the café, ignoring the Ste-Catherine pedestrian party.

Alex chose a small table on the west wall, facing a quieter side street, away from everyone else. He slid our cake and drinks off and dropped the tray on an empty table behind him. When he put away his change, he ended up flashing a pack of cigarettes tucked away in his pocket. He caught me staring and said, "They don't let us smoke inside anymore, but we can hit the sidewalk if you want."

"You smoke?" I stalled.

"Sure. They're clove," he said, as if that made a difference.

Code Blues

I had taken a drag or two of clove cigarettes during medical school and enjoyed posing and flicking the ash. But first I had to be a nerd. "You're a doctor."

He laughed. "Yeah." He plucked a cigarette out of the packet and held it expertly between his teeth while he still managed to speak. "And you're Little Miss Muffet."

"Shut up." Just for that, I wasn't going to smoke. Peer-pressure booted me in the opposite direction. "But I thought you said they didn't allow smoking in restaurants anymore."

A red lighter appeared in his hand. He flicked it on, and brought the flame to the end of the cigarette.

I glanced around to see if anyone was watching. The counter girl shot me a worried look. I pointed at her. "See?"

Alex mimed astonishment. "Hey, you're right! My bad." He pocketed the lighter and held the cigarette out for me to inspect. The end hadn't caught.

I didn't understand him any better than this crazy city, but both of them were growing on me. "So where are we going after?"

"There are a few clubs downtown. But it's still early. They don't start rockin' until after midnight."

I struggled to keep a deadpan expression. "Rockin', huh?"

"Rockin'," he repeated firmly. "You probably don't know what that means, after living in London for four years."

I raised my eyebrows. "Have you ever been to clubs in London?"

"Yes." His lips quirked.

I believed him. "Dang."

We both laughed. He said, "You like frosting?"

I nodded. "It's the best part."

He spun the plate around so the cake's frosting end pointed toward me and the tip toward himself. I toyed with the cool metal handle of my fork and dug in. Thank goodness, they used real whipped cream. I'm a real snob about that. In short time, we polished off the cake.

Alex's cell phone played a tinny, Bach riff. He held it up to his ear and almost immediately, his eyebrows drew together. "Yeah."

I sipped my too-sweet papaya juice. Maybe we could hit the Jazz Festival. Place des Arts was probably within walking distance, and I'd heard that there were lots of free shows. It was almost ten, so we still had two hours to kill before midnight.

"So?...Uh huh. Yeah." Alex was half-turned away, his shoulder hunched. "Yeah. Okay." He jerked his chin at me, then at the door. He was going outside to finish the call.

I reached for my purse. He shook his head, gestured at me to stay there. He held up his index finger.

I got it. One minute. Well, that would give me a chance to go to the bathroom.

The bathroom was small, with cobalt tile walls and a terra cotta floor. More importantly, it was pretty clean except for a twirl of toilet paper in the corner of the stall. An ad mounted on the door warned me about sexually transmitted diseases. Nice.

I washed my hands and combed my close-cropped black hair. I'd cut my hair during clerkship, on my surgery rotation, and kept it short because I liked it. My eyes were a bit red, from smoke and from my contact lenses, but I looked good. My skin was a clear, smooth tan, and my smile was genuine.

I refreshed my burgundy lipstick, winked at myself, and sashayed back into the café.

Alex hadn't made it back, but his unused cigarette lay on the plate. I sat back down and crossed my legs. The college kids behind me burst out laughing, but not at me, I hoped.

The Ste-Catherine traffic ground to a standstill. A bunch of girls in skimpy club outfits shrieked and pushed their way through the cars. A Camaro played dance music with such a heavy bass that my chair vibrated with it. Behind it, a Mercedes broadcasted rap, while the little, white driver and his buddies nodded along. How could Alex hear anything out there?

Alex. I scanned the crowd. He wasn't in front of the café.

No. That couldn't be right. I half-stood, craning my neck. He must have gone around the corner, to get away from the mob.

Why did he go out there, anyway? It was louder out there than it was in here.

Better reception? But that was lame.

I crossed to the front of the café. Across the street, I caught sight of a guy with brown hair, his head tipped down. He held his shoulders like Alex. I rapped on the glass.

The guy turned west and disappeared into the crowd.

"Wait! Alex!" I called.

Beside me, the old man with the newspaper cleared his throat.

I muttered, *"Excusez-moi."* I shoved open the glass door and sprinted out on the street.

"Watch it, lady!" hollered a guy on the pavement. I barely registered him and his blanketful of necklaces and earrings.

"Sorry," I called over my shoulder, and I started running after the guy. I nearly knocked down an elderly couple who were arm in arm, taking up most of the sidewalk.

I stopped at the blue and white metro sign near the Paramount theatre. Herds of people pushed past me, intent on seeing *Twilight* or *Despicable Me*. I scrutinized their faces until I realized that I was, to stretch the movie analogy into retro territory, on my own mission impossible.

Alex had vanished.

"Worst. Date. Ever," I muttered, but it had been great until the phone call. "So his dismount needs work."

A guy who was passing by gave me a strange look and hugged his girlfriend closer.

Okay, now I was talking to myself. I joined the crush of people and snagged a lobby pay phone. I dug in my purse for Alex's numbers. The phone rang once, twice, three times.

Click. "We're sorry. The Bell Mobility customer you have reached is not in service."

It wouldn't even let me leave a message. What the hell? Was he still talking on the phone?

On my last quarter, I tried his home phone number. It rang four times. A recorded female voice, the phone company default one, intoned, "You have reached 555-2431. Please leave a message."

I wouldn't have figured Alex for such a vanilla message. Was this even the right number? I said, "Alex, it's me. Hope. What's up? I lost you at the café. I don't have a cell phone"—I'd planned to buy a new one in Montreal—"and my pager's back at the apartment. So I'll check for you, and then I'll, uh, head home, I guess. Call me." I left my apartment number and hung up.

One last try. I walked back to the café. A breeze raised goose bumps on my arms. I rubbed them.

"I'll keep you warm, baby!" a guy yelled. He was standing with a group of friends outside Club Sexxxy's drawings of chesty *danseuses nues*.

I gave him the finger. It made me feel better, even though he just cackled.

In the café, the old man was still reading his paper, a couple perused the display case, the college kids played on, and a server was wiping down the tables. No Alex.

My heart sank. I headed outside to ask the guy on the pavement with the necklaces. He looked like a middle-aged hippy, with a graying brown ponytail and a Guatemalan poncho even though it was a warm night. He smiled. His teeth were crooked. "Wanna buy something? I got the best beads."

Chunky plastic beads and some silver rings. I tried to look interested. "Hm. Maybe." I paused. "Did you see the guy with the cell phone who left the café? Brown hair, about five-seven, black T-shirt and jeans?"

He shrugged and smiled some more. "Wanna buy something?"

"Did you see him?" I countered.

"Yeah, I saw him." He gestured at his blanket ware. "I don't have all night, you know."

He did have all night. And silver doesn't complement my coloring as well as gold, but better that than plastic beads. I pointed to a plain silver ring. "How much?"

"A steal. Six bucks." He grinned, displaying nicotine teeth with a gap between his incisors.

Cigarettes reminded me of Alex. Something had to be really wrong for him to leave without a word. I shook three toonies out of my change purse. Before I handed them over, I prompted, "The guy with brown hair?"

"Yeah," he said. "I saw him." He grabbed the money. "He went that way." He gestured north, up the little cross-street.

"But—" I should have seen him. I'd been sitting right alongside—I checked the name—Ste-Alexandre. But then I'd gone to the bathroom. And north of here was McGill University. Alex had said he lived in the student ghetto. Had he chucked me and gone home?

"Here." The street guy held up the ring. His eyes were soft with—was that pity? I was now being pitied by a guy who sold chunky beads?

I snatched the ring away and headed back to the metro.

"Hope!" A guy's voice.

My head snapped up, my heart drumming at hummingbird speed. Then I saw the white-blond hair and more angular face. It was Tucker coming down the street toward me. Tori raised her hand in a cautious wave, and Anu beamed at me.

Shit. The last thing I wanted to do was face my new classmates. Clearly, Montreal wasn't *that* big a city.

"Hey guys," I said, adjusting the purse strap on my shoulder.

Tucker said, "Hey, we tried to call you. We're going to grab a bite to eat and check out the Jazz Fest. Wanna come?"

I shook my head. "I'm beat. Gotta unpack, and I've got the first emerg shift tomorrow." I bared my teeth in a cheery grin. "But have fun, okay?"

Tucker opened his mouth, but Tori said, "Sure. Some other time" and towed him off. Anu waved.

Once on the metro's orange and white plastic seats, I closed my eyes and tried not to feel like a disaster. My feet hurt, my eyes felt dry beneath my contact lenses, and I didn't know whether to worry about Alex or strangle him. The metro car was almost deserted. An electronic board flashed the names of the next stop and bus numbers for transfers, as well as ads and tidbits of news. My main companion was the recorded woman's voice that announced, *"Prôchaine arrêt..."* Everyone was heading downtown for the night, not partying in Côte-des-Neiges.

Actually, that was something else to worry about. When Alex picked me up, he told me that my neck of the woods "wasn't the greatest area."

At my expression, he tried to back peddle. "You probably don't have to worry. The real low-income housing is on Van Horne." Right by my neighbourhood grocery store. After I freaked out more, he said, "Look. It's probably just a bad rep, because Côte-des-Neiges has a lot of immigrants. And some students, because it's near the U of M, *l'Université de Montréal.*" Then he smiled and said, "Don't worry. I'll protect you."

He wasn't winning any gold stars right now. The *Université de Montreal* metro stop was only a five minute walk from my new place, but his warning had me jumping at every shadow behind a tree. I didn't dare cut through the university. I stuck to the poorly-lit streets. During the day, the maple, ash, and birch trees were pretty, but at night, they could hide a family of rapists. The sound of my own steps beating on the sidewalk, the wind in the leaves, the shadows in the apartment balconies—all of it spurred me, until I was almost running down Mimosa Avenue. My keys were clenched in my fingers, pointy side out, ready to take out someone's eyeball.

At last, I dashed up the concrete walkway to my three-story brick apartment. Only two dim torches lined the path. As soon as I opened the building door and stepped into the well-lit front hallway, I felt safer. Even silly. No one had attacked me. The silver mailboxes and buzzer system inside the entrance looked perfectly innocent.

Like St. Joseph's, the apartment had probably been beautiful when it was first built, but it had fallen into disrepair, from its overgrown, dandelion-fiesta lawn to the cracked glass in my balcony door. It was really two buildings, with an arched wrought iron sign between them that read, MIMOSA MANOR. Still, there were Art Deco squares of glass on either side of the outer door and I had real hardwood floors in my apartment.

I unlocked the inner building door, ambled up the staircase and turned the key in my apartment lock. I half-expected Alex to be there, saying, "Boo." But it was empty. I could hear the silence. Only a tap dripped in the kitchen.

Code Blues

I marched down the hall, to the kitchen, and tightened the faucet. I'm an environmentalist. I'd hate to end the day by wasting water, too.

The phone rang. I nearly jumped out of my skin. I had to race back to my bedroom to pick it up. I'd only brought one phone. The rest were on their way, in the moving van. The phone had rung four times before I snatched it up. "Hello? Alex?"

"Who's Alex?" said my mother.

"Are you making friends already?" said Dad. "That's good."

"Oh." I sunk into bed. "Hi guys. I was going to call you."

"I miss you!" said my brother, Kevin. He's only eight. My family makes weekly phone calls with everyone on a different extension.

"I miss you, too, bud." My throat tightened. I felt perilously close to tears. Ridiculous.

Dad said, "You sound like you have a cold!"

I cleared my throat. "I don't have a cold."

He tsked. "Well, you sound like you're getting one. It's a long drive from London. You should have let us help you pack!"

"It's too far. And you have Kevin." I took comfort in our old argument.

"I could have helped!" Kevin protested.

"I know, bud. But then you might have missed your violin lesson."

"Good," he muttered. My mother started scolding him.

I felt almost normal again. No matter what, my family was always there for me. I told them I was starting with an emerg shift at 7:30 a.m. Not a word about Alex, even though his name was throbbing at the back of my brain.

"Wow. We'd better not keep you up too late, then," said Dad immediately. "You need your rest."

"Wait, I wanted to tell you Grandma still has that cough, but she's feeling better." Mom went on at some length. My grandmother is very healthy, but we all need up-to-the-minute bulletins about her few vagaries. Especially me, the family doctor. I thought I heard a noise in the front hall, but turned back to hear, "Kevin is going to start summer school, but we could still go on a trip in August—"

I sighed. "Mom, I told you, I don't want to take a vacation at the beginning of residency."

"Right, right, right, I was just going to say, or we could come visit you. Maybe spend a week. What do you think?"

I looked around. My one-bedroom apartment was littered with a handful of half-unpacked boxes. "You guys would sleep in the living room?"

"Sure, sure. Why not? We could bring sleeping bags."

"It's like camping!" crowed Kevin.

"Uh." I held my head. It felt like the beginning of a headache. I massaged my temples.

"You think about it," Mom insisted.

"She should go to bed," Dad said.

Kevin piped up. "You're going to bed earlier than me!"

"Good for you." After some more last-minute news, I hung up. I had to smile. There was only one more thing to do tonight.

With an Exacto-knife that had been lying by the front door, I slit open a box labeled "Misc." Right at the top, wrapped in tissue paper, lay my faceless, jointed wooden man. I'd bought him for a long-ago art class, but didn't really have any drawing talent. I just liked this guy. Some of my friends called him my imaginary boyfriend. I called him Henry.

The previous tenants had left behind a black veneer desk, topped by a bench-shaped piece of wood that made a second level. Carefully, I placed Henry on top of the bench. I made him sit with his legs dangling down and his right arm bent, hand to his head. Not sad, but pensive.

Beep!

I definitely heard something that time. I tracked the noise to my backpack in the front hall. My little black pager read DUPLICATE. I pressed the button to read the number. Alex's cell phone.

Hot dog! I picked up my phone and heard the rapid beeps that meant someone had left a voice mail message.

"Hope. It's me. I'm so sorry." Alex's voice, a bit muffled.

I bit my lip.

Code Blues

"Listen. Something...came up. Something important. I know this sucks. I'll make it up to you. Maybe tomorrow." A noise, like he covered the mouthpiece, and he said, his voice far away but irritated, "In a *minute*." His voice got loud again. "Hope, I'll call you." And then he hung up.

I tried the cell phone number he'd left on my pager. Still out of service. He must have turned it off before and after calling me at home and on my pager. But why?

I bent Henry's other arm, so now both hands were pressed against his face, like in *The Scream*.

I slept fitfully that night.

Alex never called back.

CHAPTER 3

At 7:25 a.m., I stepped through the ER's automatic doors on the east side of the hospital, near the bike racks. I promptly spotted ten people on lime-green plastic chairs, dozing or watching the TV in the waiting room on my right.

Ten people already. Happy Canada Day to me.

On my left stood one black-uniformed security guard in a cubicle. Beside him sat two women behind desks with computers, supposedly registering patients, but really chatting with each other. Triage was a little Plexiglas alcove straight ahead, empty except for an examining table and a stray BP cuff machine, but even so, I didn't feel right cutting through the triage room.

I turned left, down a little hallway, hoping it would lead to an alternate entrance.

"Excuse me, miss," called one of the receptionists. "You're not supposed to go in there. That's for stretcher patients."

People never thought I worked here. I turned and smiled. "Hi, I'm one of the new residents."

"Oh. Sorry," trilled the middle-aged receptionist. Her mascara had smudged under her eyes, giving her a Goth look.

"It's July first," the older one muttered. "All the new residents."

"Oh." They giggled together. Way to make me feel welcome.

At the end of the hallway, I saw the ambulance bay, and took a right, pushing open the teal emerg doors. Made it.

Two people bent over charts at an extra-long desk on my right. On my left was an examining room with an eye chart and then two empty resuscitation rooms, their monitors off, oxygen masks and tanks hanging unused on the wall, and the stretchers covered in clean white sheets.

Nurses in pink uniforms chatted at the large, octagonal nursing station in the middle of the room. Along three walls surrounding the nursing station, blue-gowned patients sat in beds or rooms clearly labeled from one to 14, and more patients lay stretched out on beds beside the station and along the wall.

I took a cautious sniff. People often complain about the smell of hospitals, but unless it's bloody stool, pus, or a newly-disinfected room, I don't notice much anymore. St. Joe's smelled fine to me.

I walked up to a nurse with snapping brown eyes and a big smile. She looked to be about my age, and although she was wearing pink scrub pants, she had a blue and brown striped top. I said, "Hi, I'm Hope. This is my first day here."

She shook my hand. She had quick, bird-like movements. "I'm Roxanne. Let me show you the residents' room." From the windowsill, she plucked a two-foot long yellow stick with a key dangling from the end of it. It looked like a potential weapon. I stared. She laughed. "That's so we don't lose it."

Behind the nursing station, she showed me a small hallway with a kitchen, a bathroom, a conference room, and two little call rooms, one for the residents and one for the staff doctors. "The staff one has a shower. Yours is the one on the left. Have fun."

I shed my bag in the residents' room, which was a basic white box with a bed, a desk, and a few hooks for jackets. I wound my stethoscope around my neck and jammed a pen, a pharmacopoeia, and my trusty navy notebook into my pockets. It was just past 7:30.

Dr. Callendar turned out to be one of the guys I'd passed at the desk when I came in. I now knew that this was the ambulatory side of the emerg. Dr. Callendar looked fifty-something, with a black crew cut, beat-up Nikes, and a white coat over his greens. When I plopped into a chair beside him, he kept on writing a note on a brown clipboard.

After a full minute, without looking up or putting down his Bic pen, he grunted, "Who are you."

"Hi, my name is Hope Sze, I'm a first-year resident, and this is my first emergency shift—"

He glanced up, wearing extra wrinkles across his forehead. His nose was too blunt-tipped and his lips too thin for him to be handsome "You got oriented?"

Not really. "Well, we walked through the ER yesterday—"

He handed me a clipboard. "Start seeing patients."

Automatically, I took the clipboard, but my brain had stalled out. As a medical student, they took pains to orient me and make sure I was comfortable before I worked. As a first year resident, a.k.a. an R1, it was obviously sink or swim. Not to mention the fact that Alex told me my shift didn't really start until 8 a.m., so I was here voluntarily early.

Dr. Callendar had already turned back to his chart. I took meager comfort in his stereotypically atrocious handwriting. While I watched, he grabbed a giant rubber stamp, pressed it in a blue inkpad, and stamped his chart with headings for a complete history and physical, from "ID" to "Extremities" on his chart. At least that was legible.

I glanced at my own chart. A twenty-year-old woman, six years younger than me, who'd complained of burning, frequent urination. It sounded pretty straightforward. The triage nurse had even written, "Feels like UTI," or urinary tract infection. Still, it was cool to knock on the door of room 2 and introduce myself as Dr. Hope Sze for the first time.

By the time I returned, Dr. Callendar had disappeared. All that remained of him was his rubber stamp. I found him in the nursing station, rifling through green slips of paper. He scowled at me, and shoved them in the pocket of his lab coat, but not before I saw the patient names and numbers printed on the slips. He was doing his billing for the night shift.

I pretended not to notice. "Dr. Callendar, did you want to review the UTI before I send her home?"

"Of course!" he snapped. "All your patients have to be reviewed. You're a resident!"

Thanks for sharing. And then he went on to share some more. Did I ask about risk factors? Was she sexually active? Had she had UTI's in the past? How recently? Did she wipe from back to front or front to back?

I had asked some of these questions, but not others, so I felt stupid but also annoyed; I doubted he was this thorough when he was the one on the line. If pressed, he'd probably just say it was a UTI for reasons NYD, not yet diagnosed.

At last he waved me away. "Go back and do it right. You can follow up with Dr. Dupuis afterward. He's the one coming on at eight."

Good news: Dr. Hardass was leaving. Bad news: maybe Dr. Dupuis was Dr. Hardass II.

Granted, I was here to learn as well as serve, but some doctors really like to put you in your place at the beginning. I didn't look forward to playing *Who's the Boss* for the next two years. Good doctors, secure doctors, don't need to belittle you.

Sometimes I feel sorry for the patients at a tertiary teaching hospital. You may have to battle your way through multiple layers: med student, junior resident, senior resident, staff. But it's all learning, and as a community hospital, St. Joe's had a thinner hierarchy than most. I headed back to the twenty-year-old to play another twenty questions.

When I came back, Dr. Callendar was doing "sign out" with a thin, blond, stork-like man in glasses and greens. They strode around the room, talking about patients' results and what needed to be done.

When I got within a five-foot radius of them, Dr. Callendar flicked his fingers at me like he had water on them. "Go see more patients."

The blond doctor laughed and shook his head. "Wait a minute. You're a new resident?"

I nodded and held out my hand. "Hope Sze. R1."

He shook it. "Dave Dupuis. Welcome aboard."

"Thanks." At Western, once you were a resident, and therefore, a fellow M.D., a lot of the staff physicians let you call them by their first names. It sounds like a small thing, but after four years of undergrad and four years of medical school, I was ready for a tap on the shoulder.

Dr. Dupuis smiled down at me as if he were reading my mind. "Are you interested in working the ambulatory side or the acute side?"

Runny noses vs. potential heart attacks. No contest. "Acute."

Of course, Dr. Evil had to step in. "Dave, she's already started on the ambulatory side. She's ready to review a UTI." Dr. Callendar gestured at the chart in my hand.

I opened my mouth to object, but Dr. Dupuis was already on it. "Good. If you know that case, you can review it. But if a resident wants to work the acute side, she should." He turned to me and added, "Are you interested in emerg?"

"Yeah. I'm thinking of doing the third year."

"Good woman," he said.

We grinned at each other. Dave Dupuis was on my side. There was a hierarchy here, and Dupuis trumped Callendar. Good to know.

Some people, you just know you're on the same page. Like me and—Alex, I remembered, and my smile dimmed. But for only a second. If he didn't call back and beg my forgiveness, it was his loss. I had a job to do.

After sign-over, Dr. Callendar glared at me like I needed deodorant and a brain transplant. "So what do you think. Yeah, yeah, yeah. What do you want to give her? Okay." He scribbled his signature after my note, tore out the green slip, and stood up to go.

A mere 45 minutes after I first saw her, I handed my patient her prescription. It was the first time I'd written a script without getting it co-signed, and it felt good for about 60 seconds. Then Dr. Dupuis handed me a chart for a seventy-five-year-old woman with abdominal pain. "Have fun."

I drew the dirty pink curtain around bed number 11 before I began the interview. The patient's son helped swish it around his side of the stretcher. My patient turned out to be a tiny, white-haired, half-deaf woman who only spoke Spanish. Her family spoke a little French, but not much. I found myself yelling and playacting a lot.

Code Blues

"Do you feel nauseous? Are you vomiting?" Grab stomach, pretend to retch. "Do you have pain in your chest?" Hands to heart, with tormented eyes raised to the acoustic tile ceiling, like I was Saint Hope at the stake. "Do you have diarrhea?" That one was hard. I made shooing motions around my rear end. Even the patient laughed.

During the physical exam, my hands traversed all over her abdomen, while I asked if it hurt. "*Dolor? Dolor?*"

The family enjoyed this demonstration of fifty percent of my Spanish vocabulary (the other word I knew was *si*, or yes) and praised my excellent command of the language. "*Très bien!*" The patient beamed at me. She didn't look too pained. I was in the middle of asking her to turn over for a rectal exam when I heard a flat woman's voice from the speakers overhead, "CODE. BLUE. OPERATING ROOM."

I froze.

"*CODE. BLEU. BLOC OPÉRATOIRE.*"

The pink curtain ripped open, revealing Dr. Dupuis' flushed face. "Come on!" he yelled.

We flew around the nursing station and past the X-ray light boxes. He slammed the side door open with the heel of his hand. We dashed down the narrow back hallway.

He punched open another teal door. As we sprinted up two flights of stairs, one of my black leather clogs almost went airborne. I jammed my foot back into it. Dr. Dupuis ended up a half-flight ahead of me, but I caught up to him on the landing.

We dashed left, and then another left past the elevators, and then we were at the T junction of a hallway and Dr. Dupuis was yelling, "Where is it?" at a guy in a white uniform and a blue bonnet-cap.

The guy pointed back over Dr. Dupuis's shoulder. "Men's change room!"

Dr. Dupuis doubled-back a few steps and shoved open the door to a small, jaundice-yellow room.

Should I follow him in a men's room?

The door nearly swung shut again. I thrust it open.

Beige lockers lined the four yellow walls and made a row down the middle of the room. A wooden bench stretched lengthwise in each half-room.

In the far half, wedged between the bench and the lockers, I spotted a pair of men's leather shoes. The feet sprawled away from each other. The scuffed gray soles of the shoes pointing toward me.

Dr. Dupuis crouched at the man's head, blocking my view of the top, but someone had yanked the man's charcoal T-shirt up to his armpits, exposing his white belly and chest, above his brown leather belt and khaki pants.

A black woman in a white coat pressed her fingers against the side of the man's throat. "There's no pulse."

"I'll start CPR!" I yelled, running toward them. I'd only ever seen one code blue, on a sick patient in the emergency room who didn't make it. I'd never heard of a code in a men's room. We didn't even have gloves. Mouth-to-mouth wasn't my first choice.

I knelt on the cold tile floor, my arms extended, hands laced, and braced to do CPR. Then I finally saw the man's face.

His features were mottled purple, his filmy eyes fixed half-open, his jaw hanging open under his moustache.

The man was dead. Long dead. Cause NYD.

Dr. Dupuis lifted his stethoscope from the man's hairy brown chest, his face grim. "I'm calling it. Eight twenty-four."

He was calling the time of death. I had only seen that once, after the code. After we had tried intubation, CPR, drugs, and even a pericardiocentesis to try and remove any blood from around the heart. It was too late to try, for this man.

Dr. Dupuis pressed his fingers against the man's cheekbone. I flinched, but the purple color overriding the face didn't blanch. "Livor mortis," he said.

I took a deep breath. I remembered that from my forensic pathology course. After someone dies, gravity makes the blood pool and discolors any skin that's not under pressure. I'd just never seen it up close and personal. Now, avoiding the man's staring eyes, I could see that his anterior flanks were also blotched purple. He had died on his stomach.

I poked my index finger against his mottled flank, indenting the cool skin. As I pulled back, the flesh slowly rebounded, but still didn't change color.

Dr. Dupuis voice was loud and sudden in my ear. "Let him go."

I recoiled, wiping my finger against my scrub pants, but he was talking to the black woman who still had her fingers on his throat. "He's too far gone, and this may end up being a crime scene."

Crime scene?

Dr. Dupuis's voice shook only a little when he said, "It's Kurt."

She nodded, dropping her eyes. She withdrew her hand from his throat and crossed her arms, hugging herself tightly.

Dr. Dupuis stood. "He was one of the doctors here," he said, his head averted.

Oh, my God. I scanned the face again. The moustache. Was this the guy whose speech I'd interrupted?

Slowly, I reprogrammed the brown eyes, the broad forehead, the slightly hooked nose, and the moustache in my mind. Yes. It was him. I closed my eyes.

I heard Dr. Dupuis's steps thumping around the room. He called, "Did you see anything? Evidence of foul play?"

It sounded like something out of a movie. Maybe it was. I doubt Dr. Dupuis had ever found a colleague dead in the men's change room before, but he didn't let it faze him. He lifted the white plastic lid of the soiled linen cart by the door. "Look for needles," he said, peering inside. "Anything to do with drugs."

I glanced at the black woman. She lifted one shoulder in a shrug.

I said, "But wasn't he diabetic? Maybe he'll have his own needles."

"Even so," Dr. Dupuis replied, his mouth a grim line.

"You think we should search his pockets?"

Before he could answer, the door burst open. "Where's the—" Two nurses manhandled a scarlet crash cart into the room. "My God!" exclaimed the plump, blond one.

The black woman said, "It's not a code now. Dr. Dupuis already called it."

While she explained, I checked Dr. Radshaw's pockets. His wallet was still in his right pocket. I didn't open it. I found an Accucheck, the machine to check the glucose for diabetics, along with a few test strips, in his left pants pocket. Nothing in his shirt, and he wasn't wearing a jacket.

I hit the bathroom for evidence. Something was bugging me, but I couldn't put my finger on it. Dr. Dupuis was already in the bathroom, nudging a pile of clothes under the sinks with the toe of his running shoe. The room smelled of urine, mold, and I didn't want to know what else.

I held my breath and flung open the door of the first toilet stall. The last customer hadn't flushed, and the toilet was balled up with paper and worse, but the floor was clear. I slammed the door and opened the next one.

An empty white toilet bowl ringed with rust, the black toilet seat pointing toward the sky. Dr. Dupuis materialized over my right shoulder, banging open the stall door. "Don't touch anything!"

"I didn't." I didn't see any needles or drug baggies. I backed out slowly while he yanked back a beige shower curtain in the stall at the end of the room.

"Dave!" The plump, blond nurse appeared in the doorway, looking tearful. "It's Kurt—"

"I know," said Dr. Dupuis. "I know."

Behind her, I heard a flurry of voices arguing in the main room. Dr. Dupuis pushed past me. I hurried on his heels.

A freckled woman in glasses and a white coat barked orders, her brown flats parked inches away from Dr. Radshaw's hair.

A man in greens tried to fit the mask of an ambu bag over Dr. Radshaw's open, rigid mouth.

The black resident started CPR.

A nurse knelt beside Dr. Radshaw's arm while two more nurses, plus the blond nurse, yelled at her to stop.

Two men in black uniform gawked from Dr. Radshaw's feet.

And then a very thin woman in purple scrubs, standing by the main door, fisted her hands and started to scream.

CHAPTER 4

"Vicki!" called the woman in glasses, the doctor who was running the belated code, but I could barely hear her above the scream. It rose and filled the tiny room, until I struggled not to cover my ears.

Everyone else froze and fell silent, except Dr. Dupuis, who grabbed the screaming woman by the arm and jerked her toward the door. "Get her out of here," he snapped at the guards in black uniform, and then, to the blonde nurse, "Give her some Ativan. One milligram sublingual to start." The nurse rushed out of the room.

The other resident stopped doing CPR. She stood, wincing as she straightened her legs after kneeling on the floor, and backed away from the body. The resp tech lifted his head from his ambu bag. And the two staff doctors started arguing, literally, over Dr. Radshaw's dead body.

Dr. Dupuis said, "I already called the time of death. And this is a coroner's case. Any suspicious death in the hospital—"

"Did you make any effort to resuscitate him at all?"

"Courtney, he was dead."

Her eyes slitted in contempt. "You didn't even *try*. Did you check his glucose?"

"He. Was. Dead. You know that as well as I do." Dr. Dupuis turned to the rest of the group. "We're all upset. We all knew Kurt and want to give him our best effort. But it's too late. We can't bring him back."

After a few seconds, the group backed away from the body, including the resp tech, who stood and let the ambu bag dangle in his hands.

Dr. Dupuis released his breath. "The people who were first on scene need to stay here—" His eyes flicked at me, and passed on through the crowd. "—and we'll probably all need to make statements to the police and the coroner. Please don't move anything if you can help it."

The other resident's low voice rang through the room. "You think he was murdered?"

The crowd's murmur stopped. We all held our breath, waiting for Dr. Dupuis's answer.

He ran a hand through his hair. His blond bangs were dark and spiky with sweat. It was sweltering in this locker room stuffed full of people. And was I imagining it, or behind the sweat and deodorant and hairspray, was there the faint, sickly stench of death?

Sweat prickled in my armpits.

At last, Dr. Dupuis said, "I don't know. It could have been an accident with his insulin. But we have to treat it like a worst case—"

The door burst open. Two men in black, bulletproof vests, baby blue shirts, and dark navy pants shouldered their way into the room. They wore guns and walkie-talkies on their belts.

The police.

I never wanted to meet the *Sûreté de Québec*. The only time they make the national news is when they shoot young black men for no defensible reason. When I got my match results, that I'd be doing family medicine in Montreal, one unbidden thought was, *I hope they don't shoot me.* They didn't regularly mow down young Asian women, but I figured, once unbalanced, always unbalanced. And here they were.

A stocky, sandy-haired officer pushed his way to Dr. Radshaw. The white badge on his arm said Police. I wasn't sure if that was the same thing as the *Sûreté.* "Who is in charge here?" His English was good, laced with a moderate French accent

Dr. Dupuis said, "I am."

"You were the one who found the body?"

Everyone tensed. It was the first time someone had called Dr. Radshaw a body out loud.

"No. That was Jade." Dr. Dupuis pointed to the other resident, who was standing by the bathroom doorway, her arms crossed over her chest. "Dr Jade Watterson, one of our second-year residents."

The officer looked from Dr. Dupuis to Jade Watterson, and exchanged a look with his brown-haired colleague. "I have to talk to you. Both of you." He turned back to Dr. Dupuis. "I'll start with you." He raised his voice. "In the meantime, nobody touch *nothing*. You understand?" He repeated it in French.

His colleague, the brown-haired guy, ushered us all out of the room. "Let's go. Into the hall. No one leave until I say so." He turned to the woman doctor who'd started running the code. "Who are you? What's your name? Did you go in the room? Did you move anything?"

He scribbled things into his notebook. It seemed like anyone who hadn't entered the room or touched Kurt was free to go after he took down their name. The officer spoke on his radio, but too low for me to hear anything.

I made my way over to Jade's side. I had so many questions, I wasn't sure where to start, but I had to strike before they took her out of the room. "You were the one who found him?" Now that I thought about it, it was kind of weird that she stumbled into a men's change room and happened to find Dr. Radshaw.

She shook her head. "Maintenance did. I heard the code, same as you. But I got here before you and Dr. Dupuis, because I was on the second floor. ICU."

No wonder the pockets of her white coat bulged with notes. "At least you were prepared for it, I guess. I mean, if you were doing ICU." What a stupid thing to say.

She looked at me out of the corner of her eyes. "You're never prepared. Never."

"Yeah. I guess." I shifted my weight from foot to foot. "Anyway, I'm Hope Sze."

She shook my hand. "Jade Watterson."

We smiled a little at each other. I rotated my shoulders, which I belatedly realized were stiff with tension. "Who was the woman in purple? You know. The screamer."

She shuddered and bent toward my ear. "Dr. Radshaw's girlfriend."

He had a girlfriend. Jesus. "But what was she doing here?"

She glanced uneasily at the people milling around the room. The other staff doctor was talking to the resp tech. Jade said, "She's a nurse in obstetrics."

Good Lord. She happened to be working when they found her boyfriend's body. And she came to see. I struggled to get my mind around that, while the brown-haired officer positioned himself beside Jade. "We have some questions for you."

She gulped and left with him, sketching a goodbye in the air.

I heard a sob from one of the nurses. I turned. She had her hands pressed to her face, and she was shaking her head. A second nurse wrapped her arms around her. The ICU doctor, Courtney, spoke softly. She, too, had tears in her eyes.

I had liked Dr. Radshaw, from my brief contact with him yesterday. I was sorry he was dead. But my sorrow was nothing, nothing compared to what these people were feeling. They had lost a colleague, a friend, and a lover.

In mystery books, it's usually someone unpleasant who gets offed. That way, there are maximum suspects. But today, we had lost one of the good guys.

When I got matched to St. Joe's, I didn't think much about it. Like I said, I never even toured the place. But I was starting to realize that it wasn't just a hospital. For these people, it was a second family. And I was like a girlfriend who'd been invited to Thanksgiving, only to stumble upon tragedy. Theoretically, I belonged, but I didn't, really. Not yet. Not this way.

More officers arrived. One of them stood in front of the door, guarding it. Two more started quizzing people and letting them go.

The sandy-haired officer returned and asked me to come with him. Dr. Dupuis joined the tight circle around Dr. Radshaw, and I followed the officer into a conference room at the T-junction of the hallway I'd first encountered.

It felt unreal. Here I was, sitting at a blue plastic chair and a fake wood-grain desk, as if I were going to take notes on cervical dysplasia, but instead a police officer was interviewing me about a potential homicide. He pulled out a bunch of forms and a navy notebook. "What's your full name."

"Hope Sze."

He wrinkled his nose. Not a very *québécois* name, I guess. I had to spell both names out for him. And my address and home phone number, which was also surreal, since I'd only moved in yesterday. It was like a variation on a nursery rhyme. First comes parking ticket, then comes murder. Then comes—what? Not the baby in the baby carriage. I was on the pill, thanks.

The officer's voice pulled me back. His eyelashes were dark blond, with darker roots. "What did you see, when you came in the room." He had a flat way of talking. His question ended with a downward flick. It sounded almost like a German command. You will speak. Now. *Schnell.*

I did my best to describe the man lying on his back, on the floor, Dr. Dupuis crouched over his head, the resident, Jade, checking his carotid pulse—

His thin lips pressed together. "What does that mean."

I stared at him. Didn't they do first aid as part of their training? "Well, when we want to check if someone's heart is beating, we have to check the pulse. So she was checking the pulse in his neck. The carotid artery."

The corners of his mouth turned down. "Are you certain she was checking his pulse?"

I raised my eyebrows. "It sure looked like it."

"If you do not know for certain, I prefer..." He shifted in his chair. It creaked. "I prefer no...interpretation. You are to describe exactly what you see. If you see a woman with her hand on his neck, you say that. Do you understand me."

"Of course." What a lame brain. For a second, I was worried they'd try to pin in on Jade. But no. That was just paranoia. Just because they shot black guys didn't mean they'd frame anyone black. Right?

I went on to describe the scene as best I could, with "no interpretation." Sunlight fell in the conference room, across my legs. I was getting baked in my stiff, green, poly-cotton blend scrubs. I angled my legs out of the way of the sunshine.

He frowned when I said Dr. Dupuis had shifted the bundle of clothes in the bathroom, but really lit up when I remembered I'd gone through Dr. Radshaw's pockets. "You must never touch anything! This is a suspicious death. You should leave everything alone. If you disturb a hair, make any marks, we could lose the case! You must never move anything! Just call the police!"

I felt bad. I'd just been following Dr. Dupuis, but I understood the police's point. "Sorry."

He shook his head, mumbling, "Nev-er, ne-ver."

"So, you think it's was murder, then?" My voice was too loud.

He shook his head and stared at his navy spiral-bound notebook. "We have no evidence for that right now. It is only a suspicious death."

"But you think—"

His hazel eyes met mine. "I will contact the sergeant. If the homicide team gets involved, we will interview you. But right now, we have no evidence."

Then it struck me, what had been bothering me about Dr. Radshaw's relatively empty pockets and belt. "Wait a minute. He wasn't wearing his pager."

The officer pursed his lips. "Should he have been?"

"I'm not sure if he was on call. We could check. But the thing is, Dr. Radshaw wore his pager, 24/7. Even to bed. He wanted to be available all the time. For him not to have his cell phone or pager on him—that's wrong. I think—" It sounded preposterous, but I pushed it through. "I think he was murdered."

The officer heaved his shoulders. "You remember what I told you. No interpretation."

"Yes, but you don't understand. It was like his trademark. Ask anyone!"

42   *Code Blues*

The officer looked at his watch. "I must talk to my colleagues and the sergeant again. We will be in touch if homicide gets involved. But for a known diabetic, if his insulin was low, the other doctor told me, he might be confused and not know his own mind. He might forget his pager."

But he'd wander around St. Joseph's in hypoglycemic shock? It didn't add up. The OR change room was a funny place, too. I heard you needed a numerical access code for the elevator, although the stairs were open if you knew how to cut through the halls, as Dr. Dupuis and I had done this morning. A confused hypoglycemic would have a hard time navigating the stairs or a coded elevator.

Plus, a doctor should know how to regulate his insulin and recognize symptoms of hypoglycemia early on. He probably injected himself and checked his sugar four times a day. Why would he suddenly make a fatal error in the hospital, in the middle of the night?

No. The more I thought about it, the more it rang true. Dr. Radshaw was murdered.

The policeman studied me. "If you remember anything else..." He tapped the notebook with his pen. I noticed the pen cap had been chewed into a well-nibbled point. Gross. I folded my hands in my lap so I wouldn't accidentally brush the pen.

He handed me his card. J. Rivera, *Inspecteur*. I tucked the card into the front pocket of my shirt, next to my own navy notebook.

My throat was dry, and I felt a little light-headed. I'd seen a few dead people in medicine, but none of them had been murdered. As far as I knew, anyway. I turned blindly to the right, down a dim hallway, away from the men's change room.

I found a water fountain embedded into the wall. The white porcelain felt cool against my palms. The water was a thin stream, barely arching above the metal drink spout, but I wet my lips a little.

"Hi."

It was a low female voice. I spun around, pain streaking into my neck. "Ow!"

Jade Watterson took a step back. "Sorry. Didn't mean to scare you."

I rubbed my neck. After a long drive and a tense morning, my muscles had relatively seized. "It's been a lousy day."

She smiled wryly. "Tell me about it. I'm post-call."

"Ouch." I checked my watch. Getting on 10 a.m. She'd probably been going for 26 hours straight.

"At least I get to go home." She smiled. It made a huge difference on her. Her eyes were bloodshot, her face wide at the cheeks, her eyes a little close-set for classic beauty, but when she smiled, she jumped up a few points on the Richter scale. Her teeth shone toothpaste-commercial white against her brown skin. She asked, "Are you an R1? What a way to start!"

"Yeah."

She flipped her hand at me. "Gotta go. See ya."

She was already halfway down the hall when I mustered my voice. "Wait! Did you notice he didn't have his pager?"

She stopped, but didn't turn around. She jammed her hands in the front pocket of her lab coat.

I said, too loud, "Do you think someone killed him?"

She started to turn. Opened her mouth to speak. But up ahead, the door to the change room drew inward. She tucked her head down and strode past the change room, away from me, without another word.

Chapter 5

My backpack cut off my circulation from the shoulders down. Maybe I shouldn't have bought four liters of milk and Sherpa-ed them home. I snaked my arm around my own back, fumbling for the keys I'd left in the front pocket of the bulging pack, and managed to unlock the building door. After a strenuous emerg shift, plus shopping, my eyes ached, my feet were tired, and I was ready for an untaxing supper. Say, a bowl of Cheerios.

The concièrge must have been by, because the hallway floors glistened and a few shallow puddles were still drying along the wall. Good. At least they kept the apartment halls clean, even if Alex had dissed my neighborhood.

My pack was so heavy that I had to bend forward to counterbalance it as I mounted the relatively minor stairs to my apartment. I felt like an unlucky donkey.

I was two steps away from the landing when I heard the phone ring inside the apartment. I rolled my eyes. What a time for Alex to call, when I was in danger of toppling like the Titanic. Still, I sped up.

Mistake. My foot slipped off the last step.

I grabbed the wooden banister. It wobbled.

Dear God, I was going to die. I had a fleeting vision of falling backward and cracking my head on the fake granite floor, pinned in place by the weight of my backpack. The firefighters would have to cut me free with the Jaws of Life.

The banister held, but my keys dropped with a clang and slithered down a few steps.

The phone rang on.

I slipped the straps from my shoulders and heaved my backpack around to my front stoop. Newly freed, I fetched the keys, unlocked the door, and bumped the backpack inside.

As I locked the door behind me and kicked off my shoes, the phone stopped in mid-ring.

The air seemed to vibrate with sudden silence.

I wanted to curl into my sleeping bag until tomorrow's evening shift. But I was hungry. One of my classmates once said, about our work life, "You have to decide if you're too tired to eat or too hungry to sleep." This time, hunger won.

I wouldn't bother with my voice mail. If Alex was now feeling contrite, he could stew, simmer, and even boil in his own juices until tomorrow morning.

I unzipped my backpack and started toting groceries down the hall to my little galley kitchen. What had possessed me to buy two economy-sized cans of spaghetti sauce? I could do weights with these things.

The phone rang again.

Maybe something was wrong with my family. Or maybe Alex was extremely intent on kissing my ass. Either way, I thunked the cans of zesty Italian on my kitchen's black and white tile counter. Then I ran to my bedroom and caught it on the third ring. "Hello?" I brushed the hair out of my eyes. I needed a bang trim.

"Hello. Is this Hope? Hope Sze?"

It was a woman with a French accent. A telemarketer? How had they gotten my number so fast? And why wasn't it Alex?

"Yes," I said, wary.

"This is Mireille Laroque. From St. Joseph's."

It took me a minute to place the butchy French resident. "Ah, yes. How are you?"

She paused. "How are *you*?"

I wouldn't admit that I was exhausted and hated Montreal so far. "Just peachy."

Pause. "I heard that you found Dr. Radshaw this morning. It must have been very...traumatic."

"Kind of. They called a code, and Dr. Dupuis and I ran up from emerg, but a second year on ICU found him first."

Her voice hushed. "It was definitely Dr. Radshaw?"

The face reared in my mind again, with its open mouth and filmy eyes. I focused on the beige plastic telephone cradle, trying to propel the image away. "Yeah. It was him."

"But you didn't know him. You only met him once."

"That's true, but it looked like him. Dr. Dupuis, the nurses, the other resident—everyone else said it was him. You can talk to them if you want."

There was a long silence. At last she said, "That sounds definitive."

I felt bad. It wasn't Mireille's fault that I'd had a rotten day. "Yeah. Sorry. I know it's hard to believe. He seemed like a nice guy."

Another pause. "Yes." Pause. "What an experience for you."

"Yes. Well."

"It must have been horrible. Just terrible. We must do something. I was speaking to the other residents and everyone is in shock. In shock," she repeated. "No one should be alone tonight. It would be cruel. I am inviting everyone to my house for a potluck dinner, so that we can support each other."

Eesh. Tonight, I needed that support like I needed control top pantyhose. "Well, that's very kind of you. I'm sure everyone will appreciate it, and you'll feel better afterward. But it's been a long day for me—"

"Hope." When she said my name, she nearly dropped the H, shortened the O, and emphasized the P. Not Ope, as it Grand Ol' Opry, but close enough. "Please. It will be for your own good. You need to process the experience. I think it would be very healthy for you."

I should have pleaded exhaustion from the very beginning, setting up a graceful exit. "Thank you, Mireille, but—"

"Have you eaten yet?"

I hate to lie. I closed my eyes. "No, but—"

"There you go. You have to eat. Come and eat with us. Of course, I do not expect you to bring anything to the potluck. You will be our guest. I am making pasta for everybody, and Alex will probably bring a cake from *La Première Moisson*—he always does, it's an excellent bakery—and I asked Tucker to bring appetizers, but he will probably bring beer."

My hand tightened on the receiver. "Alex is coming?"

"Oh, yes. I just spoke to him. He said he wanted to see you." She paused to let that sink in. I remembered his phone message. *I'll make it up to you. Maybe tomorrow.* Tomorrow had arrived.

Mireille was still talking. "Tori is making a Greek salad and garlic bread. Anu was not home. Neither was Robin, but his wife promised to give him the message. I hope they will come."

My stomach twisted with longing. I adore good food. All Chinese people do. This potluck sounded a lot better than Cheerios. And Alex—well, I was still mad, but the fact was, Dr. Radshaw had appeared hale and hearty yesterday, and today he was dead. That shook my anger a little. In high school, we'd studied that poem, "To His Coy Mistress," which began, "Had we but world enough, and time,/This coyness, lady, were no crime." Back then, I thought that poem was pathetic blackmail. But today, I thought he might have a point. Alex was the first guy I'd dated in two years who gave me some zing. I could stave off sleep for a few more hours and delay my grudge long enough to hear him out.

I cleared my throat. "I don't have anything to bring." Except the econo spaghetti sauce.

"No, no, no! Don't bring anything! I will be very angry if you bring something. I will give it back to you. You should rest. We will take care of you."

Another of my secret weaknesses is that, although medicine is very take-charge and kick butt, deep down, when I go home, I like to be cosseted. "Well..."

"Seven o'clock. I am on Côte-des-Neiges, near the corner of Queen Mary. Across from the cemetery. You know the two apartment towers covered in black glass?"

I found myself agreeing to drive over. Have stomach, will travel.

CHAPTER 6

Refreshed by a mini nap, I landed on Mireille's doorstep and compared her building to mine.

My three-story apartment building was built in the 1930's, and its security consists of a buzzer above each mailbox, with everyone's box clearly labeled according to apartment. The outer door is unlocked and the inner door has a single key lock. Windows made of Art Deco glass rim the outer door, and plain glass borders the inner doors, so a thief could easily smash a way in. But he or she wouldn't bother, because half the time, both building doors are propped wide open. The easier for people to move in and out, my dear. It hadn't bothered me, except that I'd wished they'd left them open for me and my groceries this afternoon. Alex's warnings about my neighborhood seemed much more ludicrous in the daytime.

In contrast, Mireille's building was a sleek, shiny, black skyscraper. She had a real, live security guard, and a call-in buzzer system where the buzzer codes didn't match the apartment numbers. High tech stuff. The lobby had a lounge with a sofa, two love seats, and a mirrored wall. I bet she had a pool, too. At least my apartment had a mirrored lobby, I consoled myself. And my rent was only $550 a month, whereas hers might hit four digits.

Mireille buzzed me up, and I rode a swift black elevator to the 23rd floor. The hallways were carpeted in maroon paisley. The wall sconces were dim, imitation candlesticks. Even though the walls were painted white, it felt very somber, like a funeral home. I took two wrong turns before I rapped on apartment 2308.

Mireille threw open the door almost before my knuckles had left the wood. "I'm so glad you came!" She bent forward, pushing her face in mine, her burgundy lips pursed.

I froze. She was so close, I could see the pores on her face. She pecked me on each cheek before she drew away, her curls bouncing. Her perfume left a light citrus scent in the air.

In Ontario, we hug. And I only hug my friends. So I didn't clue in before she had already pulled back. "This is for you," I said, covering my awkwardness with a bottle of wine wrapped in a brown paper bag.

"No, no, no!" She flushed a dark red, like her lipstick, very noticeable against her simple black T-shirt and matching knee-length skirt. "I told you not to bring anything. And Tucker brought beer, as I said he would."

I wondered if she'd been dipping into it. She was so animated and bright, almost careless, compared to the tightly-wound woman from orientation. I liked this version better. "It's okay. The Metro was on the way."

The Metro is a grocery store chain with the same name as the subway. The grocery and corner stores here sell wine and beer, which makes it pretty convenient. I didn't want to show up empty-handed. Bad enough that I'd donned a pair of jean shorts and a white tank top while the hostess had picked funeral black.

Mireille accepted the bottle, but said, "I'll give it back to you when you leave!" She headed down the narrow white hallway.

"Hi, Hope," said a guy's voice, as I kicked my shoes into the pile by the door.

My heart thudded. I looked up, only to see Tucker dressed in a white shirt with aquamarine pinstripes, sleeves rolled up to reveal lightly tanned forearms.

At least he wasn't dressed in mourning, except for his black pants. And he held a beer in his right hand. I gave him a half-smile.

He returned it with a sly grin. Then he swooped down so close that his stubble brushed my cheek.

I tipped back on my heels.

Undeterred, he pressed a hearty, wet, smacking kiss on my left cheek. I ducked away from contact on my right.

He laughed and backed off, saluting me with his beer. "You're from Ontario, right?"

"Yeah." I glowered at him.

"You'll get used to it." Still laughing, he shook his head and strode into the next room.

I wiped my left cheek. Mireille swept back in, rolling her eyes. "Oh, that John. He thinks he's something."

"He's something, all right." I didn't know her well enough to say what I really thought of him, but I hoped that the food made up for him.

She towed me by the arm to the living room on the right. A bunch of residents on the sofa yelled, "Hi, Hope!" while Tucker leered at me from a bright red La-Z-Boy by the window. No one else was wearing all black, and I relaxed slightly. Pachelbel's Canon tinkled on the stereo. I started to reach for a handful of chips from a robin-egg-blue bowl on the low, black coffee table, but Mireille's hand tightened on my elbow. "You must be thirsty. I'll get you a drink first, all right?"

I waved goodbye to the people and the chips, and let her haul me to her cheerful yellow kitchen.

Mireille gestured at the array of bottles on her granite counter. "What would you like? Some of your wine?"

I winced. My temples throbbed at the mere mention of wine. "No, thanks. Just water."

She poured some water out of a Brita pitcher on the counter and handed the tumbler to me. "I'll be back in a second. Don't leave."

Hurry up and wait. I sipped the lukewarm water, grimacing.

"Hi, Hope," came a quiet, male voice behind me. It was lower than Tucker's voice, and it electrified the skin on my arms.

Alex. I spun on my heel, ready to tear a strip off his back and another off his testicles, but then I saw his wan face and the dark circles under his eyes. Compared to the charming guy who had treated me to sushi, he looked like the older brother who'd gone to war and ripped his soul on the battlefield.

He gripped a beer bottle in his left hand. Uneven stubble lined his face. His eyes were red. He was wearing a crumpled, '70s style striped shirt, and corduroys with shredded knees. His bare feet looked vulnerable on Mireille's white ceramic floor.

Pity choked me. I shook my head once, twice. "What happened?" I finally managed.

"I'm sorry," he said, and added thickly, stumbling on the words, "You wouldn't believe it."

"Try me," I said, but Tori drifted into the kitchen, passing between us en route to the kitchen counter. "Are you okay, Hope?"

I nodded. "I'm all right."

She poured herself some mineral water and sipped it gravely, her dark eyes passing from me to Alex and back again. I waited for her to leave, but she leaned her elbows against the countertop like she planned to set up camp here. She was delicately built, almost bird-like in her slimness. I'm thin too, but in my mind at least, I'm always battling incipient obesity.

Mireille buzzed in again, like the Energizer Bunny on speed. She stopped when she saw Alex and Tori, but quickly recovered. "Hope. Have you had anything to eat? I made a pesto sauce and a tomato sauce for the pasta, so you can choose. Are you allergic to nuts?" She reached inside a yellow cupboard and forced a plate on me. "Please, help yourself. Don't be shy. We have enough for an army! Tori's garlic bread is excellent. Have some before the men eat it all." She cocked her head, and I heard a faint ringing. "Oh, the phone again. Alex, can you get that? I bet it's Anu. She said she'd come later. Now the gang's all here." She barked a laugh.

I looked at Alex. He shrugged and reached for the phone.

He seemed a bit spineless, not like how I'd first thought of him. Plus he still hadn't explained why he'd abandoned me in a café. I turned up my nose and marched to the food table.

Tori followed me as I loaded up on pasta bows and splatted pesto on them. The pasta glistened like it'd been fried in butter, but I was past caring. I tore off a piece of garlic bread and hesitated at a dish of shredded orange bits.

"It's some sort of Middle Eastern carrot dish," Tori said. "It's good, actually. I think Robin made it."

"Does it have raisins in it?" I asked, poking it suspiciously.

"I think so."

I wrinkled my nose and grabbed some Greek salad and curried potatoes. At least the food was better than Cheerios, and definitely more interesting than at potlucks in London, Ontario.

"Hope!" a guy's voice yelled from the living room, and everyone laughed.

My hands tightened on my dish. I had no idea how my name had come up, but I didn't relish heading in there as the guest of horror. I took a deep breath and squared my shoulders.

Tori's quiet voice stopped me. "They're all right. They're mostly harmless."

I wasn't expecting a Douglas Adams quote from her. My esteem for her rose a notch. "Good to know."

I entered the living room, clutching my plate, glass, and a fake smile. Instead of looking people in the eye, I checked out the décor. Mireille was obviously a big believer in black and white. Her black leather furniture, stereo, and coffee table contrasted against the high gloss, all-white walls. The only accents were a red Persian carpet beside the chesterfield, red dinner plates, and the blue chip bowl. She looked ready for a Canadian House & Home magazine shoot, and I didn't even have a bed to sleep on yet.

Tucker yelled, "Hope!" in the same falling cadence as they used to yell "Norm!" on Cheers. He patted the love seat. I ignored him, heading for a wooden chair near the kitchen.

Anu passed me with a grease-stained cardboard box. "I didn't have time to cook. I hope you like samosas."

"Do I!" The only other time I'd eaten Indian food, I'd devoured those spicy, deep-fried treats.

Alex rose from the sofa. He smiled at Anu, but muttered at me, "I have to talk to you."

My temper flared. "Too bad."

He scowled. He turned and punched a button on the stereo behind the chesterfield. Classical music halted mid-riff.

Code Blues

Techno started to beat out from the speaker behind my chair. I glowered at him while Anu fled into the kitchen.

"All right!" someone called.

Alex stomped away with his beer bottle.

What a loser. Forget his musculation.

Robin winced and turned down the volume. Then he caught my eye and, to my surprise, he crossed over to talk to me. He wasn't wearing a tie today, but more preppy casual-does-blah, i.e. a beige golf shirt and Dockers. "Hello, Hope. Did you have a rough day?"

"Yeah." I speared a forkful of pasta bows so that I wouldn't have to talk. The pesto was pretty good, but not great. My friend Ginger, from med school, did a much better one. A wave of homesickness hit me. I had to close my eyes.

Robin Huxley regarded me steadily. His blue eyes were slightly protuberant. I wondered if he'd ever been checked for hyperthyroidism, but more likely, he was just naturally pop-eyed. "Dr. Radshaw was a good teacher."

"Mmm." For some reason, it depressed me to hear about the goodness of Dr. Radshaw. Like I should have done something to save him. I tried the garlic bread, which had little flecks of green, presumably parsley.

Robin seemed to blink half as much as a normal human being. "He won teacher of the year, a few years back. He was always willing to stay and review cases, no matter how late it got. He wanted us to be evidence-based. He was always bringing articles for us to read." Evidence-based practice meant that you practiced medicine based on solid, current research, instead of tradition and phases of the moon.

Robin sighed and shook his head. "They were good articles. He was the best teacher at St. Joseph's Family Medicine Center. I don't know if you've heard—"

I shook my head. He rolled on as if I hadn't stirred.

"– but a lot of the teachers aren't evidence-based at our center. I wanted to do my residency at the Jewish General Hospital. They do a lot more research there. But I lost the internal match."

His nose was shiny. I also found myself staring at the small, dark hairs that sprung from the pores on its surface. Did Mireille say she left a message with Robin's wife? Someone had married this robot?

"Still, Dr. Radshaw was one of the reasons I ranked St. Joseph's above the CLSC." The CLSC was the community health centre affiliated with the Jewish. "I worked with Dr. Radshaw as a student. He was really good, really concerned."

I ate faster, so I could have a good reason to escape Robin. Fortunately, Anu bore down on us with a platter. "Samosa?"

"Bless you," I said. I took one. It was still warm.

"Were you talking about Kurt?" she asked, losing her smile. "I'll miss him. He was cool. He taught, but he also treated you like a human being."

"What does that mean?" I put the samosa down and wiped my fingers on a napkin.

She shifted her weight from foot to foot, and dropped her eyes. "Well, a lot of doctors don't care who you are, as long as you can answer questions about hypertension. But Kurt asked how you were doing, and he really listened to your answers." She paused for a second. "He and Alex were friends."

"They were?" My annoyance with Alex began to evaporate.

She shrugged. "Alex and I did family medicine together in second year med school, on Dr. Radshaw's team. Alex told me that Dr. Radshaw inspired him to go into family."

At orientation, Alex said he'd wanted to be a family doctor ever since he was a little kid. But both could be true. I could give him the benefit of the doubt. I stood up. "Excuse me."

I dropped my plate back in the kitchen, where Mireille was washing dishes. She grinned at me and stuck a fistful of cutlery in the dish rack. "Back for seconds?"

I rubbed my stomach and laughed. "Maybe in another hour. Have you seen Alex?"

She made a face. "Not recently. How did you like the pasta?"

"Delicious." I glanced through the doorway to the living room, to make sure Alex hadn't reappeared. All I saw was that Anu was now edging away from Robin the robot.

"Are you all right?" Mireille asked, but I waved and said, "Bathroom" and disappeared down the darkened hallway. It was possible that Alex had ditched the place, but I'd give him a chance to plead his case with me. His mentor had died, after all.

There were three closed doors at the end of the hall. I opened the one on the left and found stacks of neatly folded black-and-white striped towels, labeled cardboard boxes, a package of maxi pads, and a bike helmet.

I tried door number two, on the right. It was a fair-sized bedroom that felt about five degrees warmer than the rest of the apartment. It smelled like alcohol and sweat. And there was a man sitting on the bed's blue quilt.

His back was slumped, his head bent in profile to me. A bedside lamp glowed behind him, making a halo out of his hair but leaving his face in darkness. He was so quiet that I could hear his slow, even breaths.

I whispered, "Alex?"

He lifted a hand at me. He clutched a brown beer bottle between his legs.

I leaned against the door frame, pressing the wooden ridge into my triceps to try and make this seem more real. This was not how I'd pictured our grand reunion. He was supposed to come up with a good excuse, beg my forgiveness, and whirl me off to Paris to make it up to me. Not get drunk at Mireille's makeshift wake.

Alex lifted the bottle at me in a mock toast. "Hope. I'm really sorry."

About taking off on me? About drinking? I stayed at the doorway.

"Really, really sorry. Totally sorry. I suck. I'm worthless." He took a swig out of the bottle. I could see his Adam's apple bob as he swallowed. Even in the warm glow of the lamp, he looked strained and exhausted.

I took two steps toward him, stopping short of the bed. "Alex. I don't think you should be in here."

"Is that something else I've done wrong?" He lifted his eyes to the white ceiling. "Help me."

He was wasted. I held out my hand. "You've had enough, Alex. Why don't you give me the bottle?"

He stared at the amber bottle in his hand as if he was seeing it for the first time. "Yeah. Why don't I?" Clumsily, he brought it to his lips and guzzled the last of the beer. "Here." He handed me the empty. The beer was named *Maudite*. Appropriate.

I'd wanted to cut him off. I didn't need his garbage. I stared at him and turned on my heel. "You can do your own recycling."

"Wait!"

The raw pain in his voice stopped me. I stopped, but didn't turn around.

Bang! I whipped around in time to see Mireille's pine, Ikea table wobbling slightly on its spindly legs after Alex had whacked his bottle down on it.

"I'm fucked up," he said. "I know it. I have no right to talk to you, even. But God damn it, someone killed him."

He was in mourning. He didn't know his own head right now. I switched subjects with him and played the devil's advocate. "Well, it could be that, or it could have been suicide, or an accident—"

"Bullshit!" Alex lunged across the bed at me and fell on his stomach. He belched into the quilt.

I backed up. "If you're going to throw up, do it in the bathroom."

He sat up and wiped his mouth and tried to steady his hands. His bloodshot eyes beseeched me. "Someone killed Kurt."

I paused.

He raised his eyes to the ceiling. "You don't believe me."

"Look. It doesn't matter whether I do or not. The police are on it. They interviewed me today. If he was murdered, they'll find him. Don't worry about it."

"The police. Ha. They won't find anything. Kurt was the one who listened. Kurt was the one who cared." He lay down on the bed, his feet dangling off the edge. He was still wearing his leather sandals. Somehow, it made it more poignant, that he was trying not to dirty Mireille's bed. He mumbled something like, "We killed him."

"What?" I said sharply.

He closed his eyes. His whole body seemed to go limp. His lips were still parted, but he didn't speak.

I marched over to the bed and shook his shoulder. "Oh, no you don't. You bring it up, you finish this. What are you talking about? Who killed him?"

His eyes stayed closed, even though I used both hands to shake him so hard that his head jogged up and down, like he was an agreeable rag doll. "Alex. Wake up!"

His lips curved in a smile.

He was like a willful teenager in the emerg. A *drunk*, willful teenager. It pissed me off. "Alex, goddamn it, talk to me, or forget it. I'm not playing games with you anymore." I let go of his shoulders and stood up. His eyes remained closed.

I slammed the door so hard that I felt the apartment walls rattle.

The air smelled fresher in the hall. I'd probably been absorbing Alex's beer-mouth fumes second-hand. Lovely.

I took three righteous steps, before my conscience started to irritate me. What if he was really drunk? What if I left him there, and in ten minutes, he couldn't protect his airway? In the emerg, we try to keep an eye on drunks while they sober up. We don't leave them shut up in a room at the end of the hall.

I swiped my bangs out of my eyes. Fine. I'd send another doctor in here. Or, better yet, they could drag him out into the living room and make fun of him until he woke up. Paint his genitals blue, that sort of thing.

But my conscience wouldn't shut up. What if this wasn't just alcohol? What if he aspirated his own vomit, or started to seize?

The problem with medicine is that you get to know a lot of worst-case scenarios, and they tend to play out in your head, even if they're not very likely. Paranoia with textbooks to back it up.

I heard a toilet flush and water running behind me. I turned around to see Anu emerging from the bathroom. Her brown eyes twinkled. She gestured at Mireille's bedroom. "What's going on in there?"

Had she heard anything? In my limited experience of Montreal apartments, soundproofing was an unnecessary luxury. So far, I'd heard my neighbours' phones ring, their kids scream, even someone playing Mozart on the piano. "Alex had a lot to drink," I whispered, as if I was belatedly trying to maintain patient confidentiality. "Someone should keep an eye on him and his airway."

"Okay." She rapped at the door. "Alex?" She twisted the doorknob.

I left. Maybe when he was drunk, he liked to accuse people of all sorts of crimes. Murder. Police inefficiency. Next stop, infidelity and white shoes after Labour Day.

But I didn't really believe it. Everyone said the pager was practically Dr. Radshaw's third hand. He wouldn't have left home without it. I thought the murderer had taken it. But homicide hadn't contacted me, so they probably weren't going to investigate it.

Well, it wasn't my job to figure it out. Heal the sick, tend the wounded, run the wards, minimize scut—that was my job description. No one said anything about solving murders.

But if Dr. Radshaw *had* been murdered, I'd want to know about it. Especially if the killer was somebody I knew and worked with.

"Just leave him there. Let him sleep it off," Tucker called from the living room.

Anu re-entered the hall and shook her head. "He's drunk. We have to look after his airway. Hope thinks so too, right, Hope?"

I did not want to get involved, but I nodded.

Tucker snorted. "Put him in the recovery position. He won't aspirate."

Anu placed her hands on her hips. "That's not guaranteed and you know it."

"But if we carry him out to the living room and watch him aspirate, it'll be so much better." Tucker snorted and glanced at me.

Mireille darted toward Anu. "What's going on?"

"Alex hit the sauce too hard, and Anu wants me to carry him to the living room, so we can observe him." Tucker gestured at the bedroom door. "I say we just leave the door open and put him in recovery—"

Mireille had already shouldered past him and shoved open the door. "*Ostille*," she swore.

Tucker and Anu ran in, with me right on their heels, but all I saw was that Alex lying diagonally across the bed, on his back, snoring. His left arm was flung outward, his right arm across his chest.

"I did try to put him in the recovery position, but he kept rolling back," said Anu. "That's why I wanted to keep an eye on him."

Mireille lifted steady green eyes to Tucker. "I've seen Alex drunk before, but this is worse. We'd better keep an eye on him, and if he doesn't come out of this, I'm calling an ambulance."

Anu bit her lip, and we exchanged a look. We both thought Mireille was overreacting, but this was her party, and she could call 911 if she wanted to.

Tucker said, "Mireille—"

She climbed on the bed, her knees making divots in the mattress as she slid her hands into Alex's armpits and then hooked her elbows through them. Her cheek was about an inch away from Alex's lips, but he didn't stir. Mireille gave Tucker another long look. "Are you helping me, or are you just going to watch?" And she started dragging Alex off the bed.

Tucker sighed and grabbed Alex's ankles. "On the count of three."

"Can I help?" I asked, but he shook his head.

"One good thing I can say about this bastard is, he's not very heavy," he said, expressionless.

I wished I could master that poker face around Alex. Forget the inscrutable Asian. I'm scrutable.

Mireille must have been strong, because the top part of a body is quite heavy. In the OR, they usually delegate the small women, like me, to carrying the feet when transporting someone from the OR table to the gurney. But Mireille seemed to have no trouble. She gripped Alex's arms, Tucker held the ankles, and they slid him off the bed and down the hall, Alex's butt not quite touching the floor. They trundled him down the front hall and into the living room while Anu and I followed.

Robin Huxley leapt to his feet. "What's going on?" He tried to check Alex's carotid pulse, but it was a moving target, and Mireille said, "Move it or lose it, Robin" and dropped Alex on the ground, in front of the sofa. She rubbed her arms.

Robin knelt by Alex. He bent his head over Alex's nose, surveyed his chest, and announced, "He's breathing." He pressed his index and third finger against his neck. "And he has a pulse."

Mireille clucked her tongue. "Robin, we know that!"

He ignored her. "Alex. Can you hear me?" He rubbed his knuckles against Alex's sternum and was rewarded with a groan and twitch of the right shoulder. "Well, that's reassuring. He squeezed his eyes shut—I'll give him a four, and a groan, that's two..."

Dear God. He was calculating the Glasgow Coma Scale. I said, "Robin, it's over eight, you don't have to tube him, okay?" But I felt guilty. I hadn't calculated the GCS, and I probably should have, even though he'd just been talking to me a few minutes ago.

Robin didn't look up from Alex. He forced Alex's eyelids open, checking the pupils. "Do you have a stethoscope?"

Mireille gave an exasperated sigh and retrieved hers from the hallway. Robin lifted Alex's shirt and listened to his chest and heart. He even lifted his shirt to examine the abdomen. I was embarrassed to see the brown chest hair that ran to below his belly button, and even worse, his small, pink nipples. Then Robin checked his reflexes.

It was very weird to see him do a physical exam on one of our colleagues in the middle of a supposed party. Tucker shook his head, but none of us interfered.

At last, Robin lifted his head. "He seems to be stable. We could probably just observe him. But I'd feel more comfortable if I could check his glucose to make sure it's not an insulin coma."

I hadn't thought of that, even though it was Dr. Radshaw's presumed cause of death. Guilt hit me again, until Tucker said, "For God's sake, Robin, the guy was just drinking! He has enough sugar on board. And he's not diabetic. He's just *drunk*."

"He could have an insulin-secreting tumor," Robin insisted. He turned to Mireille. "Do you have an Accucheck?"

She rolled her eyes. "No. I am not diabetic. Look, Robin. Let's use some common sense. I know Alex, and he's only ever passed out after drinking. He does not have an insulinoma!" Her French accent was more pronounced now.

"I'm just saying that I would feel more comfortable," he said evenly. Hmm. I'd worked with guys like this before—very good at the books, can recite recent studies and guidelines until the consultants nearly faint with pleasure, but not very sensible. Still, they tended to get excellent evaluations. Except from their peers.

Tori and I exchanged a look. She said, "Robin, you did the right thing. We all feel more at ease, after your exam. But like you said, we can probably observe him."

Robin squinted at her. He was still on the floor with Alex, while the rest of us were looking down on him. He rose to his feet and dusted off his knees. "All right."

We all relaxed, marginally.

He said, "I'm going to get some orange juice. We can rub it on the inside of his cheeks. If he wakes up—"

"He's not going to wake up!" Mireille burst out, but she followed him to the kitchen.

Tucker and I looked at each other. He sighed, and we grinned at each other for the first time.

Tori said, "Robin is very...conscientious."

"You can say that again," I said. Medical robots are very good at following algorithms.

Tori glanced back toward the kitchen. "Maybe we should take him to St. Joe's. It's not fair to leave him here for Mireille to follow him."

Tucker grunted assent.

Anu checked my expression. "Hope? Did you want to take turns observing him?"

Not really. I hesitated, she went on, "Because it would be really embarrassing for him, if we brought him to St. Joe's."

"Good," said Tucker. "Maybe that'll teach him to lay off the EtOH."

Fortunately, Alex chose this moment to stir his legs and snort. As if that was his cue, Robin raced in, nearly spilling his glass of orange juice, while Mireille called at his back, "I said I'd do it!"

Robin stuck two fingers in the o.j. Then he bent down to lever Alex's mouth open, streaking juice all over his face before finally sticking his fingers in Alex's mouth.

Alex gargled and jerked his head back. Then he nearly sat up, knocking Robin's arm away.

Anu screamed.

Alex thrashed his arms and legs.

Tucker cursed and yanked Robin out of the way. Robin started to push back, but in that minute, Alex lay back down and seemed to conk out again.

We all froze, watching him. My heart rate slowly settled as Alex remained still. Robin lifted his glass of orange juice again, but Mireille grabbed his arm. I could see her fingers denting his flesh.

Slowly, Robin lowered his arm.

Mireille said, "Don't you dare. You must have choked him. Just leave him the fuck alone."

Robin shook off her grip and clanked the glass on the coffee table. "There's no need to swear."

We all burst out laughing.

Robin looked slightly annoyed, but he didn't pull out the o.j. again.

Mireille said, "I heard you guys. Don't worry about bringing Alex to St. Joe's. He can sleep it off here."

Robin made a face. She turned on him. "Look. Kurt *died* today. Alex is going to be fine in a few hours. If you're so worried, Robin, you can stay with him tonight. But we should be talking about Kurt, not Alex. That's the least we owe him, on the day he died." Her voice broke on the last word, but her green eyes were steely and dry as she stared at each of us in the eye.

Tucker said, "Okay." His voice was calm. "Let's talk about Kurt. Who wants to start?"

Mireille pointed a finger at me. "I want to know what happened."

"No one knows what happened yet. But I'll tell you what I saw." I described finding him in the men's change room, the aborted code, the screaming girlfriend, the police officer. My throat tightened. This wasn't just a guy who had spoken to me at orientation. He was a man, a mentor, a teacher, a doctor. What a loss. But I described the scene as best I could. Some people need to see the body, to believe that the person is dead. My description was the best substitute for tonight.

Mireille pressed her hand to her forehead, but she leaned forward, intent on every word. When I fell silent, she said flatly, "He knew how to use his insulin. He did not overdose on it."

Tucker tried to touch her shoulder, but she twitched away. "I know this, Tucker." She glared at me. Her hands clenched into fists. "No. It was something else. It's bad enough that he's dead. I don't want anyone to blacken his name."

Tori said, "No one is accusing him of anything. We all loved him, Mireille."

"Did you?" Mireille said. "What did you love about him, Tori? I would very much like to hear it."

Tori met her gaze levelly. "I respected him. He was a good teacher. He cared. He had a sense of humor."

Tucker took a step forward. "Remember how he'd swing his briefcase down on the conference table and say, 'What have you got for me today, kids?'"

Anu and Tori laughed, Mireille loosened her arctic look. Tucker grinned, encouraged. "He made me laugh every single time I reviewed a case with him. No one else could do that. Lots of docs want to show off and make you feel stupid."

I silently remembered Dr. Callendar from this morning.

"Kurt was never like that. If I didn't know, he'd say, 'Look it up and tell me about it next time.' He respected us, even though we were just medical students. He encouraged us to go into family medicine. He really was a mentor."

"Evidence-based," murmured Robin.

We all ignored him.

Thinking of Alex, I said, "I heard that Kurt was good at listening to people."

Anu nodded. "I remember, on my first day at the FMC, he said, if you have any problems, talk to me. I'm always here for you."

"So did Bob Clarkson," Tucker noted.

Everyone except me laughed. Bob Clarkson. The putative head of the FMC. I raised an eyebrow at Tucker. "Did anyone talk to Bob?"

Mireille rolled her eyes.

Tucker blew his breath out through his nose. "No one in his right mind would talk to Bob about anything important."

"Why? Is he a dink?"

They laughed again. Tucker said, "You met him, right? At orientation? Nice guy, but not a whole lot upstairs. Very hung up on protocol."

Mireille said, "Once I asked him about improving Internet access at the FMC. He said to call his secretary and make an appointment to talk about it. Then I did, but he spent the whole meeting talking about himself and how good the FMC was already, without the Net!"

"Kurt was kind of the heart of the FMC," said Tori quietly. "We'll all miss him."

Anu sniffed back a tear. She turned toward the stereo, to hide it, but Tori handed her a napkin. She wiped her eyes. The room got very quiet.

"There's something else." I hesitated. I didn't want to make a huge deal out of it, but I thought everyone should know. "I, uh, went through Dr. Radshaw's pockets—the police told me I shouldn't have, but I didn't know—and he wasn't wearing his pager."

Silence. Broken by Mireille's hissed breath. "I knew it!" She threw her head back, eyes squeezed shut. "I knew it, I knew it."

Tori took a step toward her, but when Mireille opened her eyes, they were exultant. "Someone killed him."

My thought exactly, but I hadn't appeared so happy about it.

"Thank you," she said to me.

I glanced around. Everyone looked confused, except Robin, who looked blank. He was probably sorting through his mental file of articles, figuring out which ones applied for evidence-based treatment of bizarre behaviour.

Mireille smiled. "We all know he'd never go anywhere without his pager. It was like his lover. The killer took it away after murdering him." She grabbed my arm, her fingers sinking painfully into my flesh. "What about his cell phone? He always carried it too, so he could call back right away."

I tried to ease my arm out of her grip. "I didn't see any cell phone. Just his glucometer and his wallet."

"Yes!" Spit flew out of her mouth and landed on my cheek. I jerked back. She laughed, said sorry, and handed me a napkin from the pile on the coffee table.

At least she'd stopped gripping my arm.

As I wiped my face, I had to add, "But if he was hypoglycemic, he might've—"

Tucker was nodding thoughtfully, but Mireille's hand shot out as if to snap my words out of the air. "*Non!* I am telling you, I knew him better than anyone in this room, and he never left home without his pager clipped to his belt and his cell phone in his left pocket!"

The ring of agony in her words silenced us.

Tori laid her hand on Mireille's forearm. I could see Mireille's muscles clench in her arm and in her jaw, but she forced herself to take a deep breath. "Okay. Good. I wanted to talk about Kurt. We did. So thank you. Please, let's eat some more. There's plenty of food."

I felt obliged to take a few more sips of water, and Tucker complimented Tori on her garlic bread, but we all started shuffling our feet and taking peeks at our watches.

"Thanks for inviting us," Tori said.

With a relieved sigh, we rose to our feet. Robin shoved Alex into recovery position and propped him up with cushions from the sofa, but Robin was the first to take off without bothering to air-kiss Mireille's cheeks. The last thing I saw, when I waved goodbye, was Mireille's green eyes staring at me from the doorway. She no longer pretended to smile.

CHAPTER 7

It was almost a relief to go to work the next day. I wasn't sure what to think anymore. I'd arranged Henry into so many positions, I'd finally left him sitting with his knobby hands together, roughly approximating prayer position. No more bad luck, please.

In fact, I started off with a stroke of fortune. Dr. Dave Dupuis was on again for my evening shift, while Dr. Callendar was nowhere in sight. Dr. Dupuis looked calm and stork-like again, as he sat in a wheeled black chair at the nursing station, his feet propped on the base. "Hi there," he said. "You all right?"

Close enough. "Yeah. You?"

He nodded. "I've got a good chest pain in B. Go look at her."

Right down to business. I liked that.

In resus room B, I introduced myself to Mme. Cartier, an 82-year-old woman. Behind the white flannel blanket she clutched to her chest, her blue gown sagged so low on her chest that I could see her protruding ribs. Her hands were like the stereotypical witch's claws, the fingers bent and knuckles thickened by arthritis, the nails horn-like and filed to a point.

She was a bit hard to understand, because she'd forgotten her dentures at home and tended to mumble, but I understood that she'd had a burning chest pain for the last two days, radiating to her neck and jaw. She hadn't come in until this afternoon. "I thought it was nothing."

Her daughter, a brunette with careful makeup, picked up the story. "She thought it was her stomach. *Toujours mal au coeur, eh, maman?*" She turned back to me. "She doesn't want to come to the hospital all the time."

"So what was different this time?"

The daughter screwed up her face in thought. "More—intense, eh, *maman*? She called me, but by the time I convinced her to come—" She shrugged as if to say, What can I do?

I wasn't getting much of a story out of the two of them, so I picked up the EKG. My eyes popped. Big ST elevation from V1 to V4

"What do you see?" Dr. Dupuis came up behind me.

I pointed it out, and whispered, mindful of the patient, "Big anterior." A big heart attack. A bad one.

"Uh huh. And did you listen to her chest? And see her chest X-ray?"

I had jumped right from history to the EKG, so I backtracked to the physical exam. I listened to her heart and chest and checked her abdomen. The most remarkable finding was poor air entry and crackles at both lung bases.

I walked out of resus to the hallway between the ambulatory and acute (stretcher) sides, where the light boxes were posted. Mrs. Cartier's X-ray was already up. Instead of nice, black, air-filled lungs, they were quite white from fluid both in and around the small air sacs called alveoli. Congestive heart failure. When the heart doesn't beat hard enough, as in Mrs. Cartier's case, because she had had a heart attack, the fluid backs up into the lungs.

I found Dr. Dupuis in the nursing station, sitting by the monitors. I said, "We have to thrombolyze her."

He tipped his head back to look at me. "Do we? What are the criteria?"

"Well, she has a big ST elevation in four contiguous leads, and she's had chest pain for more than six hours—"

He smiled. "Yes, but she's been having pain for how long?"

I pressed my lips together. Damn. "Two days."

"And how old is she?"

I sighed. "Eighty-two." After more than twelve hours of chest pain, and over age seventy-five, the benefits of thrombolysis— lysing the clot, reducing death and recurrent heart attacks—drops significantly. By now, the risks outweighed the benefit. I could cause this lady's brain to bleed, instead of solving her heart attack.

Dr. Dupuis watched me work it out. Then he said, "You could make an argument for thrombolyzing her, because it's a big anterior. But I'd rather do rescue angioplasty. She's supposed to go over to the Jewish, whenever they can take her. She's hemodynamically stable, but we have to watch her. Read up on thrombolysis and PCI."

"Okay." Pretty cool case. Then I went to see a 90-year-old man. According to his son, the patient had fainted and hit his head on the sink. I was spotting a trend in St. Joe's emerg patients: old and frail. Well, except for Dr. Kurt yesterday, and he'd been beyond our help.

I shook my head steered my mind back to the case at hand. I smiled at the patient. He'd put the hospital gown on over his ribbed white undershirt and tighty-whities. "Had you just urinated or had a bowel movement, sir?"

He looked puzzled, twisting to check with his son. "No."

I wasn't a pervert. Voiding and defecation stimulate the vagal nerve, which could make a patient faint. But otherwise, I was running out of questions to ask. I needed to read up on syncope, too. I fumbled around some more, and when I couldn't think of anything else, I did a physical exam. The guy had a goose egg on his forehead. His right eye was starting to swell shut. No lacerations to sew, though. The rest of his exam was pretty normal.

When I reviewed this case with Dr. Dupuis, a nurse interrupted. "Dave, can 11 go?"

They debated discharging bed number 11 while I thought about how I wanted to call him Dave, too. Like I said, at Western, it wasn't uncommon for residents to called staff physicians by their first names. I wanted that promotion. He probably wouldn't mind. Still, I decided to defer that until I got to know him better. After he finished with the nurse, I said, "So, it's a 90-year-old man with syncope."

Dr. Dupuis replied, "So what do you think?"

Did he not hear my history and physical? I stared at him blankly. "Well, it's syncope."

"But what do you think caused it? How do you want to investigate it?"

He expected me to manage this patient as if I were a real doctor. Man. Here was my real promotion. As a med student, getting the H&P was my main job and managing the case was a bonus, but not expected, unless I was running the floors at night on surgery or medicine. As a resident, I had to pull my weight during the days, too. I started going through the algorithm I'd been taught. Was this neurogenic, meaning brain-based, like a seizure? Cardiac, meaning heart-based, like a heart attack or arrhythmia? Or the combination of neurocardiogenic, like blood pooling in the legs? Dr. Dupuis listened patiently, even as nurses interrupted him: "Dave, bed 14 won't stay in the room. I want sedation." "Dave, number five is still in pain." "Dave, does two still need the monitor? I've got a chest pain in triage."

Somehow, he was able to sort through these and still keep a mind on my story. He asked, "Do you think this guy had a seizure?"

"No. I mean, I could ask again, but he didn't have any seizure-like activity, and he didn't bite his tongue and he wasn't incontinent. He said he was oriented when he came to."

"So what are we left with?"

"Cardiac."

"Anything else?"

"Well." I had to think. "It could be that his electrolytes are off, or that he's orthostatic."

Slowly, our plan came together. Basic blood work, in case it was anything that could be picked up simply. Serial troponins, EKG, and cardiac monitoring for the heart component. He'd still need a Holter monitor as an outpatient.

"Good," said Dr. Dupuis. "Do posturals, and do a rectal exam next time. Make sure he's not bleeding out the back end." But he didn't seem mad, or contemptuous, or superior. More matter-of-fact than anything else. How I imagined Dr. Radshaw would be.

I returned to the bedside to take the posturals, the blood pressure and heart rate lying and standing. The patient hated standing there in his shorts and hospital gown with his skinny white legs sticking out, and I found it awkward to balance the cuff and pump it up while he was standing. But we got through it. There was no significant difference in readings.

Next, the rectal exam. Some people don't mind doing it, but I dread the entire ritual, even just getting them to pull down their shorts and roll over on their sides, with their hairy bums sticking out. The patients hate it, too.

When I did my first few rectals, I worried that I wouldn't be able to find the patient's anus, a secret fear I confessed to no one. Luckily, I always did find it. But sometimes I had to nudge around with a lubricated finger before I managed to squirm it in. This was one of those times.

"You're hurting meeeee—" squeezed out the patient.

"You're hurting him!" accused the son.

I hurt him even more when I dug around a bit, to make sure I got stool and didn't have to go in a second time. "I'm sorry." I checked the gloved finger. Yep, stool. Mission accomplished. "All done, sir," I chirped, and ran off to smear the sample on a little yellow cardboard card that looked kind of like a matchbox. I flipped open one side, revealing two windows for me to smear with stool. Then I closed that side and flipped open the other, to squirt a few drops of developer. A positive sample turned dark blue-green. Negative was no color change. Like right now. No blue-green, just the paper turned translucent, so that I could see the poo on the other side.

I washed my hands thoroughly, documented my negative findings, and picked up the next chart. It was an elderly lady with dizziness.

"Dave, Bed B is desatting," said a nurse with big brown eyes.

Dr. Dupuis and I took one look at each other and tore off to the resus room. Mrs. Cartier was sitting bolt upright in bed. A big oxygen mask covered her nose and mouth, but her eyes were wide open, and she was using the muscles in her neck to help her breathe. With every breath, a large, clear bag attached to her face mask inflated and deflated.

Her sats were at 90, but only just. Even with a non-rebreather mask, she was hovering.

I expected Dr. Dupuis to start barking orders. Instead, he turned to me and asked, "So what do you want to do?"

I blinked fast. "Uh...give her Lasix." That would help her pee out the water in her lungs.

"Okay. How much?"

I was starting to sweat. "Forty?"

He checked the chart. "She already got forty milligrams when she came in, from another resident."

"Okay. Eighty."

"Good. Anything else?"

"Uh..."

"How about this?" He tapped a bottle of nitroglycerine that was already hung up and attached to the IV in her arm.

I smiled with relief. "Yeah. Turn it up."

"Okay. The nurses can take care of that. They titrate to pain, resps, and systolic BP. Anything else?"

I cast my eye around the resus room. The respiratory technician was coming through the ER doors, pushing a large, blocky machine on wheels. "CPAP?"

"Yes! Continuous positive airway pressure, to splint the airways open. I knew you'd get it."

I hadn't been so sure, but I smiled, relieved. Dr. Dupuis was on my side. He waited for me to come up with the answers, instead of running it. He was a good teacher.

The RT, a balding guy in a lab coat, fitted a giant transparent mask over the woman's face and tightened the straps at the back of her head. It gave her an astronaut look. The woman in the bubble.

"I can't breathe!" she said, muffled behind the mask.

"Just wait, *madame*," the RT said, pressing some buttons on his machine. "When you get used to it, you'll feel much better." Mrs. Cartier nodded and he turned to Dr. Dupuis. "I heard about Kurt."

"Yeah."

"I never would have guessed he'd screw up his insulin."

Dr. Dupuis indicated the patient with raised eyebrows.

The RT nodded and lowered his voice. "Sorry."

"Later," said Dr. Dupuis. "Come find me when she's stable. We'll talk." With that, he left the room.

I followed. "So, uh, about Dr. Radshaw—"

His shoulders tensed. For a second, his steps slowed. "Yeah."

"Do you really think it was an accident?"

He stopped just shy of the nursing station to face me. A muscle worked in his jaw. He lowered his voice. "That's for the police to decide."

For the first time since I'd met him, his eyes didn't quite meet mine. Maybe he'd gotten the lecture from the police, too. "Yes, but I wondered what you thought?"

"You know as much as I do."

"Yes, but you knew him much better than I did," I said. "All I knew was that he had a moustache, he was a good doctor, and he answered all his pages."

Dr. Dupuis's mouth twisted into a grin. "Actually, that's a pretty good summary if you add in that we'll all miss the hell out of him."

He was talking to me again. I pressed my advantage. "So you agree about the pager, right? Don't you think it's strange he wasn't wearing it? Or his cell phone?"

He sighed. "Yes, I do. But it's not proof of anything."

"Dave!" called a nurse. "I need you to write a Gravol for twelve!"

"Do it as a verbal," he called back. He glanced at the charts piling up against the far Plexiglas wall of the nursing station and started heading toward them. "Listen. Wait for the autopsy. That'll give us more information."

That was true. They could approximate the time and cause of death and take blood and urine samples. Maybe I could even attend the autopsy. That would be cool, if unlikely in a coroner's case.

Dr. Dupuis was already five steps away, his bony hand stretched out for the first chart. "Here, have an atypical chest pain."

Even as I took the chart, I chewed over his words. Dr. Dupuis was one sharp clinician. I still got the feeling he wasn't telling me the whole story, but when it came right down to it, I knew he was right.

We needed proof Dr. Radshaw had been murdered. The autopsy would probably provide it.

But something in me wasn't content to sit around and wait for the report. The more I found out about Dr. Radshaw, the more I wanted to uncover the truth. I decided to talk to the person who probably knew him the best. His girlfriend.

CHAPTER 8

When I got home, I picked up my phone and checked the message. "Call me. No matter how late you get in."

Alex.

It was almost 1 a.m., but I didn't have to work the next day, so I changed into my raggedy, mauve, Brown University night shirt and called from my sleeping bag. He picked up on the first ring.

I said, "So, you're alive?"

He groaned. "Barely. Listen. I'm so sorry about Friday night. I want to make it up to you."

"What happened?"

He sighed. "Family emergency."

I tried to gauge his tone. It was hard over the phone. I was still torn between anger and "seize the day, life is short" forgiveness. What kind of family emergency crops up at 10 p.m.? But, as a wannabe emerg doc, I knew that anything could crop up at any time. "Really?"

"Yeah. Listen. Can I take you out to lunch tomorrow?"

I sat up cross-legged, propping my back against the wall. A sleeping bag is not enough bum cushion against a hardwood floor. "Maybe."

"If I grovel enough?"

"Yeah."

I heard a tap, like he'd put his phone down on the floor, then some creaks, a lot of swishing, and a few groans. He picked up the phone again. "Was that good?"

I had to smile. "I prefer live groveling."

"Ah. That was a more tasteful. If you let me take you out for lunch, I'll do real, live, up-close-and-personal groveling."

"Hmm." He always made me laugh. On the other hand, desertion and drunkenness were two serious strikes. "Are you going to be sober?"

He groaned. "Believe me, after last night, I'm going to be sober for the rest of my life."

"I find that hard to believe."

"Just find me an AA program, and I'm there!"

There was a time, like a few months ago, when I would have written him off right after the café. Unreliable. Good-bye. But I'd been walking the straight and narrow my whole life, and where had it gotten me? A medical degree. One serious ex-boyfriend, and some forgettable dates. I was twenty-six years old and living alone in a new city. I wanted to take some chances. "Okay."

"Okay, you found me an AA program?"

I laughed. "No. Okay for lunch."

"You're the best."

I stretched out my legs. "Just don't forget that."

At 10 a.m., I rode my bike up St. Joe's semicircular driveway and bumped on to the grass under the poplar trees. Early for lunch, but I wanted to ask Dr. Radshaw's girlfriend some questions.

The receptionist told me that obstetrics was on the fourth floor. I walked through the main entrance, where St. Joe's had spent all its money on a face lift, what with the aquarium and all. As soon as I walked down the main ramp, it was all harsh fluorescent lights, fake tile floor, and yellowing paint.

At least there were windows on each landing as I climbed the four short flights of stairs. I pushed open the door at the top of the stairs and glanced to my left and right. The hall was lined with seemingly identical navy doors, all of them closed. Which way would I find Vicki?

I flipped a mental coin and turned left, following the mustard-yellow, '70s halls until I heard a woman groan. I was walking toward the deliveries. The case room.

I paused. Maybe I should go the other way, toward the ward, instead of invading these people's privacy. On the other hand, I'd be doing OB soon enough. It looked more suspicious to loiter, so I lifted my chin and carried on.

I passed two empty rooms on my right. In the third room, I heard the same woman groan, and another woman saying, "That's it. Keep going. You're doing a great job, Cecelia." I walked faster, head averted.

A man stood in the hall with a Styrofoam cup in his hand, scooping up ice chips from a cooler against the wall, but he paid no attention to me.

I arrived at the nursing desk on my left. It was a long blue counter that paralleled the hallway and separated me from a giant wooden table and some monitors.

"Can I help you?" asked a woman at the desk. She had long, fuchsia, acrylic nails and wore black glasses on the tip of her nose.

I doubted she was an OB nurse. Those nails would really hurt on a vaginal exam. "Hi, my name is Hope Sze. I'm an R1." Now the tricky part. "I'm working in the emergency room. Yesterday, I was called for a code. It was Dr. Kurt Radshaw."

"Oh, yes," whispered the clerk. She leaned forward with wide, avid eyes. "Poor Dr. Radshaw. What happened?"

I was getting to be a pro at this. Briefly, I described finding him, throwing her a gossip bone. I touched my hand to my chest. "It was kind of shocking, to be interviewed by the police. And on my first day!"

The clerk waved me in past the desk. "Sit down, sit down." She pulled out a chair at the table and introduced me to the two nurses sitting there. One had a chart, the other a fetal heart strip, but both items lay spread out on the table, temporarily forgotten.

I said, "After we found Dr. Radshaw, a nurse came in, very upset. I understand that she was Kurt's girlfriend."

The clerk nodded so vigorously that I thought her glasses might slide off her nose. "His fiancée. Vicki. She works here."

Interesting. No one else had said they were engaged. "Is she here? She seemed very upset. I just wanted to make sure that she was okay."

The younger nurse, with the fetal tracing, said, "Well, I think she's all right. I talked to her on the phone yesterday. But she's not here. She's not coming in this week."

The older, white-haired nurse cleared her throat. The younger one glanced at her and fell silent.

The older nurse said, "What is your name, dear?"

"Hope Sze."

"I see." She let that float in the air. "Well, we'll tell Vicki you came by. It was nice of you to ask after her."

Ding, dong, the investigation is dead. I had laid all my cards out at once, inviting confidence. I wouldn't make that mistake again. I tried to salvage what I could, with a sweet smile. "That's too bad. She seemed very shaken. I wanted to give her my condolences."

Silence again. No one except the older nurse would meet my eye.

I scrawled my name, number, and e-mail address on a scrap piece of paper. "If—when—she comes back, could you give her this for me?"

The receptionist took it, folding the paper in half. "I'll make sure she gets it, dear." She avoided the older nurse's eye.

Everywhere I looked, I found politics. Too bad I couldn't make it work for me. I smiled at all three of them. With a little luck, Vicki would get back to me. It was a long shot, but still a shot.

On my way out, the woman in labour was taking deep breaths, while the nurse yelled, "Push! Push! Pushpushpushpush..."

I practically ran down the stairs.

The moving van was supposed to bring my stuff today. It was Monday, July fourth, so they'd avoided the Canada Day crunch and should sail up to my apartment. I imagined good-looking men flexing their muscles as they moved my boxes into the Mimosa Manor. I'd called them this morning and left my pager number, just to be sure.

On cue, my pager went off. I ran to the quiet, green-carpeted library to dial the 1-800 number of my moving company.

A woman asked, "Is this Hope, ah, Zzzz—"

"Sze. Yes."

"This is the Zippy Moving Company."

"Great. When is your van coming?" I hoped I wouldn't have to miss lunch with Alex, but if I did, it would make us even.

"There has been a problem."

My hand tightened on the black plastic receiver. "What's that?"

"All your things were packed in London and scheduled to be driven to Montreal today. However, we had a shortage of trucks over the weekend, so your items are still in storage. In London."

"What?" Visions of my oh-so-comfortable mattress and blanket promptly evaporated. The ache in my lower back ramped up a notch.

"The good news is, we should be able to get you a van tomorrow."

"But I'm sleeping on the ground and I've been wearing the same clothes all weekend!" An exaggeration, but it couldn't hurt. "Do you think that somehow, you might be able to manage—"

"I'm sorry, Ms., ah, Zee, but if you look in your contract, there is a clause about unforeseen circumstances."

Forget the honey. Try vinegar. "This is a *foreseen* circumstance. If you had organized your trucks properly, my stuff would be here today. It's not like a tornado touched down."

"If you look at your contract, you will find the exception for trucks. I'm sorry, Ms. Zee. There's nothing I can do about it. It's one of those things."

"I'll post my feedback on Yelp," I said, in my most haughty voice. "I expect that van to arrive tomorrow. At what time should I expect you?"

"Afternoon."

Of course, I was working a day shift. "I won't be home until after 5 p.m., more like 5:30 or 6—"

"Fine." She hung up on me.

What happened to "the customer is always right"? Ever since I moved here, I'd met so many people who were just plain crazy or rude or both.

My pager went off again. Not the moving company, a hospital extension. I dialed and Alex promptly picked up. "Don't say there's no such thing as a free lunch."

"There's no such thing as a free lunch," I replied.

"Gadzooks! Now you'll have to pay. I hope you brought your wallet. Just kidding. Meet me in the residents' lounge at 11:30."

"Where are we going?"

"It's a surprise. Eleven-thirty."

I wondered if I was dressed right. While awaiting Zippy Moving, I only had three outfits to mix and match, and Montreal was the most fashionable city I'd ever lived in. No one said anything, but just walking down the street, I'd spy a woman in a T-shirt and jeans, somehow looking more chic and fabulous than I'd ever been in my life.

What was the secret? After three days, I was no expert, but at least part of it was their attention to detail, with their hair upswept in careless but flattering 'dos and their understated makeup. Their clothes were more tailored, neutral pieces with the occasional touch of funk. The *pièce de resistance* was impeccable shoes, ranging from designer sandals to retro sneakers.

Which was not to say that you didn't see chubby girls in ripped T-shirts with their bellies hanging over their low-rise jeans. Also, the average man's fashion tended not to be very remarkable. Still, the overriding style was elegance, with a judicious amount of flair.

I could see all this, but I wasn't able to duplicate it. Walking in Montreal was like being in high school again, studying the girls in the hallway, and trying to imitate their style without falling for the millennial equivalent of acid-washed jeans.

Today, I was wearing omni-purpose indigo jeans, a red-ribbed top so fitted that it bordered on tarty, a fitted white cardigan to cover the top at work, and beat-up, hand-me-down brown leather boho sandals from my mother. I thought I fit in okay except for my sandals. Montreal style wasn't built in three days.

I still had almost an hour before lunch, so I hit St. Joe's gym. I'd signed up on the first day. For ten bucks a month, I got a card with 24-hour access. I figured the gym would come in handy between shifts or at lunch time. One of the surgeons once told us during clerkship, "Never stand when you can sit, never sit when you can lie down, and never lie down when you can sleep." So working out was a bonus.

The gym was located in a corner of the second-floor cafeteria, its door tucked at the end of the wall lined with drink machines. I ran my card through the reader. It flashed green, permitting me entry to another world. Four TV's blared CNN, *A Makeover Story*, MuchMusic, and *Musique Plus*, the latter two being the English and French Canadian version of MTV. Two women walked on whirring treadmills. A man rowed in one corner, his jaw set and arms flexing. A well-padded woman stretched her legs in the mirrored corner diagonally across from me. The water cooler beside the door glooped as a man filled his water bottle. No one was using the weight machines. The room smelled like rubber and sweat.

I hadn't brought my running shoes, but no one was paying attention to me, so I did some cursory stretches, pulled off my cardigan, and stepped on the elliptical trainer between the treadmills and the rowing machine. A few strides, and I was up to speed. I like the elliptical machine because it's fun. It feels like I'm bouncing on air. Bikes remind me of biking to work. Running on a treadmill just seems like work, period.

The two women huffing on the treadmills yelled so they could hear each other above the TV's. The one closest to me, a middle-aged lady who was wearing a lot of makeup, called, "Did you hear about Dr. Radshaw?"

"Yeah, I know! Isn't it terrible!" said her hefty friend.

Lipstick Lady shuddered. "I was terrified! I almost didn't come to work today!"

Her friend slowed down her machine. "Why?"

"Well, it was very suspicious how he died. I heard that he may have been strangled, but it was all hushed up. You never know who might have done it!"

Strangled. Where did that come from? I stepped faster.

"Really?" said her friend. "I heard it was drugs. Heroin, actually."

I made a mental note not to die at St. Joe's. Post-mortem gossip was vicious.

The made-up woman widened her eyes. "Honestly, Kathy, that's just ridiculous. I knew Kurt. He was as straight as they come. There is no way he would ever do drugs."

Her friend twitched her shoulders. "I'm just saying what I heard."

"Well, hear this." Ms. Max Factor on the treadmill was a decade or two older than me, wider, and more sure of herself. She smiled at her own image in the full-length mirror, despite the sweat beading her face and dampening her cleavage. "Kurt would never do drugs. There were other things he'd rather do."

Her friend almost stopped walking, but her treadmill forced her to start marching again. "Glenda! I never knew that!"

Glenda shook herself and laughed, running a hand through her spiky hair. "It was a long time ago. When he first came to St. Joseph's. But let me tell you, my dear. He was as *straight* as they come." She gave her friend a large, mascaraed wink.

The other woman pursed her lips.

Glenda laughed again. "Remind me to tell you about it sometime. In private." I felt, more than saw, her glance at me in the mirror. I pretended not to notice.

They fell silent, lifting their heads to watch the VJ on *Musique Plus*.

I checked my watch. It was 11:20. I popped over to the water fountain, gulped some plasticized water, and stretched half-heartedly. My scalp was slightly damp, but I couldn't see any sweat stains. Asian women don't sweat much. It's a genetic thing that's useful in the summer.

I draped the cardigan over my shoulders and ambled down to the residents' lounge. It was just around the corner from the cafeteria and gym, in a hallway full of offices. It was the only door with a combination lock under the doorknob. I pressed the digits for the secret code and twisted the knob open.

The first thing that struck me was the sweet, rotting odor of discarded orange peels and spaghetti in the overflowing blue garbage pail immediately to the left of the door. What a romantic place to meet Alex.

Some other geniuses had left dirty cafeteria plates and plastic glasses on the round table in the corner, near the phone and the computer. Rumpled blankets lay on the two sofas by the TV. Shoes huddled under the mailboxes by the door. Backpacks and shoulder bags were mostly hung on hooks over the garbage can, but had also been abandoned against all four walls and even one on top of the refrigerator.

At least the coffee table was relatively clear, except for a scattered edition of the *Montreal Gazette*. I plopped on a sofa, avoiding the blanket, and clicked on the TV, breathing through my mouth instead of my nose.

Just as I paused at a documentary on whales, the combination on the door went click-click. Pause. Click.

I propped my feet on the coffee table and pretended to be fascinated by the Right Whale. Normally, I would have been. I donate money to the World Wildlife Fund. But this time, I was finely tuned to the man walking through the door.

I saw a flash of red out of the corner of my eye and turned to see a tanned male hand beside mine, pushing down on the sofa arm. Then a chestnut head lowered toward my feet.

I whipped my feet off the table and out of the way. "What are you doing?"

Alex peeked up at me from under his bangs. "Groveling."

I had to laugh.

Alex lunged at my feet again.

I leaped into the corner, behind the intersection of the two sofas. "Stop it!"

"I'm trying to kiss your feet, woman! At least let me do it right!"

I laughed so hard, I practically bent in half. "I've just been exercising. On the elliptical trainer."

"So? You think Jesus's feet were clean and bright before Mary Magdalene washed them?"

I gave him a strange look. "I have no idea. I guess not."

"You bet your sweet ass not." His gray eyes glowed. "So?"

I was embarrassed that he'd commented, even peripherally, on my ass. "So what?"

He laughed. "You should see your face."

I put my hands on my hips. "I think I liked you better groveling."

"Your wish is my command." He stuck his head between the chesterfields and kissed my left foot, between the two straps of my sandals. His lips were soft.

I nearly kicked him in the head as I tried to back away, but I was wedged between the walls, the sofas and Alex.

He grinned up at me. "Aha. You're mine, all mine." Then he kissed my right foot. And gave it a tiny lick.

I bit back a yell.

"Salty," said Alex. He didn't look one bit self-conscious, even though he'd literally kissed my feet and was crouched on the ground, peering up at me from under his bangs. "So. Am I forgiven?"

"Yes," I hissed, angry and humiliated and turned on at the same time.

"Do I still have to take you out to lunch?"

I crossed my arms on my chest. "Do you have to ask?"

He stood up slowly, eyeing my body along the way. When he met my eyes, my face matched both our shirts. He said, "No. But you're so much fun to tease."

I wanted to stamp my foot. I refrained only because it might have highlighted recent lip action, and Alex would have enjoyed it too much.

He extended his hand. I took it and allowed him to assist me out of the corner. His hand was dry and warm.

We smiled at each other. I felt suddenly shy. He opened the door for me and stepped back, without letting go of my hand.

As we walked down the stairs together, he pulled my arm in close to his side. I blushed again. It had been a long time since I walked like this with anyone.

The door at the bottom of the stairs opened. A woman's loud voice declared, "Don't you usually have to fill out a form for that? And he said, 'What form—'"

I stiffened and tried to pull my hand away, to avoid any PDA, but Alex's clasp tightened. His eyes were amused.

Mireille and Sheilagh, the super nice resident coordinator, stared up at us. Mireille's mouth thinned for just an instant. Then it curved upward in a smile, so fast that I wondered if I'd been imagining things. "Hope! Alex! Where are you off to?"

I hesitated. Should we invite them along? It would be polite, especially since she had just hosted a party at her place.

But I wanted Alex to myself. We were holding hands for the first time. That was worth some privacy points.

"Places to go, people to see," Alex cut in, his hand moving to the small of my back. His face was calm, his voice as smooth as Scotch. "See you back in the salt mines." His hand urged me down the hall, toward the emerg doors.

Seeing Alex like this, assured and sexy, I could totally picture him as a doctor, not to mention as a boyfriend. It made me forget the previous, less desirable incarnations. He was a one-man Jeopardy game. *I'll take the Foot-Kissing for $100, Alex.*

I felt like a kid playing hooky when we burst out of the automatic black doors. I'd even been holding my breath. I burst out giggling.

Alex hooked his arm around my shoulders. Our hips were touching. His fingers grazed my bare arm. I took a deep breath and smiled at him.

It was a fine, bright July day. A few people ate, chatted, and smoked at the picnic tables across from us, next to the human resources building. We wound our way up the paved road and curved past the brick Annex building. No orientation today. Then we ambled through the parking lot between the old, steepled church and the metro station tagged by spray paint. Our feet fell out of step a few times, but for the most part, we walked well together.

I cast a longing look at the fruit market, but Alex steered me to the right, along Côte-des-Neiges. A storm of people exited a blue-and-white STCUM bus and cut around us.

He pointed to the store displaying various baguettes and round loaves of bread. The gold leaf sign read Au Pain Doré. When he pushed open the door, a bell jingled, and a woman squeezed by us with a baguette held protectively against her chest.

The store smelled like flour and jam. It was so crowded that people grabbed tickets from a red dispenser. A girl in a forest green apron called, "*Quarante-huit! Quarante-huit, s'il te plaît!*" while one of her comrades grabbed bread out of the window and another used silver tongs to pluck a fruit tart out of the display case. I slowed to admire the *pains au chocolat*, the éclairs, the *crèmes brulées*, the little round cheesecakes, the tiny chocolate cakes, the palm-sized blueberry tarts...

Alex laughed. "Want one?"

I sighed. "All of them. This is wonderful."

He shrugged. "This is Montreal."

I looked around at all the people, lined up for their daily bread and the occasional sweet. He was right. To them, it was perfectly normal to visit a bakery, a fruit market, and a fishmonger instead of a supermarket, even though they had to line up at each store. Food was worth the time and effort. Of course, there was a Metro supermarket right on the corner of Côte-des-Neiges and Queen Mary, but the average person still apparently respected and enjoyed small-scale cuisine. My ex-boyfriend, Ryan, had a roommate from Montreal who hypothesized that the reason French people were thin wasn't so much because of the wine they drank, the olive oil they used. It was because they ate good quality food instead of stuffing themselves on junk. There were no studies to back up his claim, but looking around this bakery, I half-believed it.

I had my first inkling I could make a home here. The city had seemed malignant and alien at first encounter, but maybe Montreal could teach me something, too.

Alex squeezed my hand. I inhaled the yeasty air and felt carefree, like I was falling into the jounce and easy rhythm of summer in the city.

Instead of taking a ticket, Alex led me along the length of the store. In the back, they had a little *boucherie*. No sweets, but refrigerated cases of lunch meat, cheese, and olives. A piece of paper stuck to the brick wall advertised the *midi-express*: your choice of a sandwich, a drink, and the dessert of the day, all for about $6. Alex made a little bow. "Your lunch, *Madame*."

I made a face. I'm still a mademoiselle. I chose the *rosbif*. A guy in a white apron and matching cap swiftly prepared both our paninis.

"And now we have a picnic," said Alex. He insisted on carrying my paper bag lunch as well as his own, and he made a point of opening the door for me.

Alex guided me up a little side street. Immediately, the traffic died down; I could hear our steps on the sidewalk. A few more blocks, and we were beside a little park. Kids screamed with glee as they slid down the slide. It was bright and beautiful but slightly ear-splitting, so on the other side of the fence, we found a grassy mound under the trees, facing the road.

Alex squatted, unpacked his lunch, and smoothed his empty paper bag on the ground. "Your seat, *Madame*."

I imagined the paper bag scrunching under my butt. Very unromantic. "What's with the *madame* business? I'm not married yet."

He grinned up at me. "I don't know. They don't use *mademoiselle* anymore, except with little kids."

"That's too bad." *Madame* reminded me of my many French Immersion teachers, none of them romantic.

Alex squinted into the sun. "Are you going to sit down? Or at least sit on mine if I sit on yours?" He lowered his voice, like he'd said something dirty, and I had to laugh.

Solemnly, I smoothed out my paper bag on the grass for him. Then he said, "One, two, three," and we sat down at the same time, laughing at the crunching noises.

Alex picked up his panini. "Do you want to trade half and half?"

I handed him half my *rosbif* in exchange for his ham.

He popped his Coke and held it in the air for a toast. I raised my can of iced tea back. He tapped it with his own and said, "To truth."

There were a lot sexier things to toast. But I drank to it. The iced tea was deliciously cold.

Alex ground his can into the ground so it wouldn't tip over. "I can tell you're honest. Most people aren't."

I made a face.

He said, "No, really. It's refreshing. You wouldn't believe some of the other residents."

My scalp started to prickle. What was he getting at?

He gazed at the community hall across the street. "Not that they're bad or anything. Or maybe—" He blew out his breath. "I just don't know any more." He bit into his sandwich.

So did I. The roast beef tasted dry and the bread seemed to clog up my throat.

He swallowed and touched the back of my hand for a second. "I've been with them too long. Some of them seven years. I can't tell if they're lying to me or not. You know? That's the problem with McGill. It's too incestuous."

True, a lot of people did premed, med school, residency, and even fellowships at McGill, as if there were no other schools to sample. Incestuous, huh? If it bothered Alex, he should have left Montreal and gone to another city for residency.

As if he read my mind, he said, "I told you. It's something in the water."

I raised my eyebrows.

He shrugged. "I know. Not funny. But I liked it here. A lot. And I wanted to work with Kurt. There was no reason for me to leave. But now..." He clenched his fists. "He's dead, goddammit. I think someone killed him. And I want to know who."

I frowned. I understood where he was coming from, but I didn't know where he was going. "You think it's someone in our program?"

He turned away and chewed off the end of his panini. "It's like this," he said, finally. "I think it might be."

I waited, but he didn't speak. I nibbled at the ham sandwich. It was better than the roast beef because the ham contrasted with a sharp cheese.

Alex stared at his sandals. I was the one who broke our silence. "That's why we're drinking to truth? You're going to investigate?"

He didn't answer right away. Then he looked at me. "Where were you this morning?"

"At the gym." He kept watching me, so I admitted, "I walked up to obstetrics."

He almost smiled. "You talked to Vicki?"

I shook my head. "She's off for the week. I left my number."

"But you tried? And the nurses talked to you?" His eyes were intent, the planes of his face sharper than usual.

"Sort of. One did, the other didn't. I didn't find out much. Why?"

He shook his head. "Why did you do it?"

"I don't know. I guess because I was one of the first people to find him. When I met him, he seemed like a nice guy. And everyone loved him so much. I just wanted to make it up to him somehow. I know that's dumb—"

"That's it! That's it exactly." His gray eyes were vivid, almost feverish. I could smell the Dijon mustard on his breath. "I want to make it up to him."

I drew back a little. "Make what up?"

He grabbed my wrist harder than necessary. "Hope. I know I have no right to ask you this. But could you keep asking around? If you ask, and I ask, maybe we'll find out who did it."

Every time I thought I understood Alex, he mutated before my eyes. I pulled my wrist away, or tried to. With an effort, he relaxed his grip on my metacarpals.

I relaxed a little. "We don't know for sure that someone did it. And why would anyone talk to me? They don't know me from Adam."

"That's the whole point! You're outside all the politics. You're neutral. So they will talk to you, more than me. I know you don't believe me, but it's true."

My wrist didn't ache exactly, but I could feel where each finger had been. As if sensing this, he rubbed my skin with his other hand. "I'm sorry. I'm fucked up."

That was true. I didn't answer, but I let him massage my skin. He covered my wrist with his palm and said, "I think Mireille had something to do with it."

Code Blues

I shook my head as if to clear my ears. "What?"

He checked up and down the street, even glanced behind us to make sure that the mommies and kiddies weren't spying on us from the sandbox. Then he leaned close to murmur, "They were having an affair."

I choked. Mireille was so up-front and bossy, I couldn't imagine her shagging a staff physician. Mind you, if she did, I doubt she'd hide it. She'd probably make a PowerPoint presentation on it.

Then I remembered that heavily made-up woman from the fitness centre. How many women had Dr. Radshaw slept with? Either he was a modern-day Lothario, or his lovers were unmasking themselves after his death.

Of course, I had only Alex's word that Mireille had been involved. I asked, "When?"

Alex sipped his Coke, watching me. He relaxed slightly. "I'm not sure. They were hiding it at first. One of my friends was after Mireille. Finally, she told him to bugger off, she already had a serious boyfriend."

It's not like girls haven't used that line before. "When was that?"

He studied a row of shrubs across the street. "Before Match Day, but after Christmas. I'd say February."

February. And now it was July. Not much time for Kurt to run from one woman to another. "What about Vicki?"

He shrugged. "I guess he and Mireille broke up."

I frowned, remembering Mireille hosting a semi-wake for Dr. Kurt. That didn't suggest a heartbroken murderess to me. "Are you sure she was dating, uh, Kurt?" It was weird to call him by his first name. "It could have been anyone." Or no one.

"Pretty sure. I called his house once, and she answered."

"What were you doing, calling his house?"

"For the group project, he said that if we had any questions, we should call him on his pager. But he didn't answer the page, so the operator called him at home. A woman picked up the phone. It sounded just like Mireille."

I wrinkled my nose. "That's not much, Alex."

"Then I called her house, and she didn't answer. I called her on her cell phone, and she'd turned it off. She never does that."

It wasn't adding up. "Why did you care so much if Mireille was there or not?"

He picked up the ham sandwich and started chewing, avoiding my eyes. "I told you. I had a buddy who was interested. I wanted him to know."

"A buddy—or you?" I balled up the empty sandwich wrapper.

He barked a laugh. "Mireille's not my type at all. Why? Are you jealous?"

"'Course not." I tried to change the subject. "Anyway, if Kurt was that gung ho, maybe she went over to his house for the group project."

He raised his eyebrows. "It would have been quite the project. She was on general surgery at the time."

I didn't have a comeback for that one. But the whole thing smelled rotten. Who calls a consultant at home about a research project? If Alex was telling the truth, why would Mireille reveal their relationship by answering the phone? How did Vicki fit in? I shook my head. "What aren't you telling me, Alex?"

His eyes widened. "What would I get out of lying? I just want to pay Kurt back somehow, you know?"

It felt like shadowboxing. I folded up my ham sandwich in its waxed paper. I didn't have an appetite anymore. "Why don't you wait until after the autopsy? We don't even know he was murdered. Maybe he made a mistake with the insulin. Or maybe it was something else, like drugs."

"No way," Alex snapped. He crushed his Coke can against the ground. "He was very against physicians with addictions. He did an amazing Grand Rounds about it last year." He paused. "He was supposed to do our next Grand Rounds on partner abuse."

"Alex, lots of doctors who do presentations used to be addicts. It's part of their turnaround process. Did he ever say anything about that?"

Alex shook his head stubbornly. "No one thought he was a user. No one. Not for a single second. He was all about St. Joe's, especially the FMC." He shot me a look. "Addicts only care about their next fix. Kurt cared about all the patients, all the students and residents, and the whole FMC." He gestured back toward the hospital. "Just look at the place. It's falling apart. Most of the teachers are just limping along, But Kurt was trying to change all that. He wanted to recruit the best residents, renovate the building or build a new one, really jump-start the place."

It was a mammoth undertaking. I wondered what made Dr. Radshaw care so much.

Alex was still talking. "He was always around. He even came in on weekends. He didn't have time to be a junkie. I'm telling you."

Even dead, Dr. Kurt inspired a lot of emotion. I tried to bring Alex full circle. "Okay. Say I believe you. What does this have to do with Mireille?"

His shoulders sagged. "I don't *know*. But she's part of it. I'm sure of it." He smiled a little. "Man's intuition."

I smiled back, but Dr. Radshaw could still have been a user. Some buzz from speed or crystal meth, and he could do the FMC and Mireille and Vicki and the treadmill woman and still have energy to burn.

During med school, at a doctors and addiction presentation, they told us about an anaesthetist at Western. He was shooting up in a closet between OR cases. He meant to inject Fentanyl, a narcotic, but by accident, he'd grabbed succinylcholine. He ended up paralyzing himself. He couldn't scream for help. He couldn't even breathe. No one knew where he was. The last thing he remembered was falling like a cut tree and knowing he had inadvertently committed suicide.

His colleagues heard the crash. They secured his airway, saving his life. After that, his addiction was literally out of the closet. He got help.

Before I could tell Alex, he brushed the hair out of his eyes and said, "I know for sure about him and Mireille. We followed her the next day, okay? Me and my friend. On the metro. She went right from her hospital to Kurt's house and spent the night."

I imagined Alex skulking outside Dr. Radshaw's place until dawn. It wasn't pretty.

Alex shrugged. "I know. It was lame. Anyway, my friend got over her after that. The point is, Kurt and Mireille were serious. When he broke up with her and went out with Vicki, Mireille was upset. Had to take some time off." He lowered his voice. "I heard she was maybe even suicidal."

I felt a pang for her. She acted so tough at the orientation.

"I've been in school with her for the past four years. She was a competitive swimmer. She doesn't give up. When she gets mad, she gets even."

Okay. I could see that. There was something hard about her. A lot of women cover it up with smiles and honey, but Mireille let it ride closer to the surface. Still, that was true of a lot of doctors. Med school trenches strip off sweetness really fast. I used to think I could save the world. I lost that sometime during clerkship.

Overall, I didn't trust Alex, but I was willing to play ball. "All right, let's say Kurt was murdered, and that Mireille had something to do with it."

He nodded and ripped up a handful of grass. "Yeah."

"How would she have killed him? Alex, I saw him. There weren't any signs of struggle. Do you really think he would have just let her stick him with a needle? He would have kept his distance, and he would have been stronger than her."

He tossed the grass away and rubbed his forehead. "I know. I've been thinking about it, too." His grey eyes met mine again. "But I do know he was murdered, Hope. And I want to find whoever did it. We can't let them get away with it." He held out his hand, palm up. "Will you help me?

I looked from his hand to his face. "Where did you go on Friday night?"

He sighed. His hand curled, but he didn't withdraw it. "I told you. I'm sorry."

"Yeah, but what happened?"

He dropped his hand to the grass and curled his fist around another tuft. "You know already. Family emergency. I called you."

Not until I got home. Although, to be fair, he probably didn't know I hadn't been wearing my pager. "What kind of emergency?"

"I can't say," he said to the grass. "I just can't. It's not my story to tell." He brought his gray eyes up to meet mine, steady now.

It wasn't like I needed details. If he'd just say, My dad had an MI (heart attack), I wouldn't press for more. The one-liner told me enough info. But a total information blackout, after ditching me? I wanted more.

I tried to make a joke out of it. "You can't even say if it was a Code Red, or a Code Blue, or Black?" Red is fire. Blue is a cardiorespiratory arrest. Black means bomb threat.

His lips twitched. "I guess kind of Black. Seriously, Hope, I can't say any more. Do you trust me?"

Kind of. Black could mean mourning. Maybe someone died in his family. "I guess."

He smiled. "Thanks for the vote of confidence. Are you in?"

If there was a murderer among us, I wanted to know it. There wasn't much risk in asking questions. And I liked Alex. So I nodded. "I'm in."

He wrapped his arm around me and kissed the top of my head. "Good. I don't know how we got onto something so heavy."

I looked up at him. The wind blew my bangs into my eyes. I pushed them out of the way and he smiled. "So. Let's talk about you."

"What about me?" He smelled good. Warm. Masculine.

"What do you like to do?"

You, I thought, and quelled it. "Uh. I like to Rollerblade. In London, I used to go up and down these great footpaths by the Thames River."

"Yeah?" He rested his cheek against my head. "I heard about those paths. Don't they get flooded sometimes?"

"Yeah. In the spring. Once, I was trying to bike, but it was so deep, a family of ducks came swimming along." I pulled back to look at him. "How did you know about that?"

He shrugged. "A friend."

He had a lot of friends. But he was from Kitchener, only about an hour away from London. It wasn't so surprising. "Do you like to blade?"

He shook his head. "I'm a klutz on wheels. You can teach me."

I smiled at the thought. He pulled me close again. "I like soccer. You?"

I made a face. "Lots of running. And why would I want to hit a ball with my head?"

He rolled his eyes. "Boy. Have I got a lot to teach *you*. Did you want your dessert?"

I groped beside me for my *millefeuille*. "Just try and stop me."

He snatched it away and held it up above my head.

I stood up to grab it. He stood, too, and held it out of range. His half-foot on me made all the difference.

I twisted and dove for his rum ball. He bellowed with rage, but I was too fast. I snatched it up and held it behind my back. Then I stuck my tongue out at him.

He sidled closer. I moved away just enough to keep the same distance between us.

"You don't even like rum balls," he said.

"Well, you promised to be sober for the rest of your life. It would be my moral duty to keep the demon rum away from you." I held it up in front of my nose. "Smells pretty good, actually."

"Not as good as your *millefeuille*." He closed his eyes and took a deep sniff. "Mmm. Real whipped cream."

"You can't *smell* that," I protested, but he opened his mouth wide and took a bite. Cream squished out between layers of pastry.

"You bastard!" I yelled, swiping my pastry back. He laughed with his mouth full. I examined his teeth marks gloomily. "Now it's got your cooties."

"Oh, yeah?" He grabbed my chin and kissed me. I was so surprised that it took me a second to respond. His lips were softer than I'd expected. He ran his tongue along my lower lip, a quick flick, and drew away. "Now *you've* got my cooties."

I swallowed hard. He was smiling, so I smiled back, a little tremulously, and showed him his rum ball. I'd squashed it in surprise. Cocoa and chocolate stained my fingers. "Sorry."

"It was worth it," he said. He took the rum ball, but looked at my fingers. "I can clean those for you." He licked his lips.

"Uh..." I remembered those lips on my feet. I swayed toward him before I checked the park. Three mothers were watching us. One turned away with a sniff, but two others continued to glower. The kids were mostly oblivious, except for a little boy whose mouth hung open.

I knew I was blushing furiously. "Better not."

Alex grabbed a napkin and took my empty hand in his. "Better luck next time."

He patiently wiped away the chocolate while my body hummed with promise.

Under his breath, he said, "I still can't believe Kurt's gone. I know he's dead, but whenever I go to the FMC, or get ready for work, or think of something I have to tell him..."

I nodded. Our picnic had taken another melancholy turn. I wondered if it would always be this way between me and Alex, if we could never just talk and have fun without Dr. Radshaw's shadow over us. Maybe if we looked into his death, it would help free Alex.

My hand was still sticky, but reasonably clean. Alex offered me a bite of his rum ball. I took a nip. It tasted like chocolate, made darker and more complex by the liquor.

Alex kissed the tip of my nose. My eyes flew open, startled, and he laughed.

I walked him back to the hospital, hand in hand. At the main entrance, he squeezed my hand. "I'll call you."

That was it. No kiss. I walked away, happy but curiously disappointed. I never knew what to expect from Alex. In some ways, he was the complete opposite of my ex.

Ryan and I had basically been set up by our grandmothers. He was a smart, hard-working, good-looking Chinese boy. In other words, Grandma's idea of manna from heaven, and not far from mine, either. We were friends before we started dating in university. He was going to Ottawa U for engineering and I was at McMaster, at the other end of the province. He tolerated the six hours' drive for two years, but he wanted me to come back to Ottawa for med school. So did I. The only hitch was, they put me on the waiting list and never took me off of it, while Western accepted me outright.

"So come back. Do your Master's at Ottawa. They'll take you next year," said Ryan.

I ground my teeth. "Ryan, it doesn't work like that. It's a crap shoot. I could get a crazy interviewing team, or they could raise the MCAT score I need. You know how many good people don't get into med school? There was a woman at McMaster who applied for *eight years* in a row! I have to take this."

He just looked at me with flat, brown eyes. "You could defer for a year. You mean you don't want to wait."

"I can't."

"You don't want to." He didn't add, You won't wait for me. He wasn't into drama. But that was the turning point. We tried for another two years, on and off, but it only got worse in clerkship, when I worked in the hospitals for up to 36 hours straight. We finally cut each other loose. Last I heard, he was dating a girl named Lisa. "Very serious," said my grandmother accusingly. "They might get married." Like Ryan and I might have. If I hadn't been stubborn. If I hadn't put my career first. But if I wasn't true to myself, who would I be?

One thing about Ryan, he was dependable. If he said he'd call at 8 p.m., he'd call. I never thought he'd cheat on me. He was thoughtful, brought me flowers on our anniversary, daisies the first year, roses the next, then lilies, and finally carnations. The last one was the death knell for me. Carnations are about the cheapest flower you can find.

Ryan said, "The lady in the shop told me they'd last a long time."

I raged. "What? You bought me flowers to be practical? Flowers aren't practical! That's the whole point!"

Alex was the reverse of Ryan. He understood romance. He understood women. But *I* didn't understand *him*.

OTOH, Alex was obsessed with Kurt's death. Once we unraveled that mystery, he'd be back on track.

I coasted home along Péloquin. Around Côte-des-Neiges, I noticed a Mediterranean restaurant with a *térasse* alongside more modest Lebanese and pizza joints. A travel agency. A fruit and vegetable store with paper signs in its window advertising everything from pears to beer to toilet paper. Cars lined up at the parking meters, except on the corner where a truck unloaded its wares.

I was more used to cars and malls, but I liked this better. I smiled at the people on the *térasse*. They sat at white plastic tables, shaded by green umbrellas, drinking beer and laughing.

Farther along, Péloquin became quieter, more residential. Brick or stone-faced duplexes lined the street. From my apartment hunting, I'd figured out that a duplex held two separate apartments in one building, so one family could live on the ground floor and another on the upper level. The wrought-iron stairs stretching to the second floor meant that both groups had a private entrance. Although the duplexes pressed against one another, and each only had a small front yard, they generally boasted neat lawns and petite gardens. A few guys in shorts and no shirts balanced their bare feet on their balcony railings. I dodged a sprinkler and smiled some more. This wasn't Orleans, the suburb where I'd grown up, but it wasn't such a distant relation, either.

When I got home, I read about two pages of Guy Gavriel Kay's *Sailing to Sarantium* before I crashed.

I awoke to a harsh buzz ripping throughout my apartment like a giant mechanical wasp. It took me a minute to recognize it as my buzzer. Someone was here to see me.

I groaned. My teeth felt fuzzy and wrong. My breath was probably enough to make a dog's hair stand on end. But I dragged myself out of bed for Alex. I brushed the sleep out of my eyes, finger-combed my hair, and rinsed with mouthwash. Then I threw open my front door.

No one was there.

I squinted down the stairs, toward the main entrance.

I glimpsed a stocky pair of women's legs. The rest of her body was cut off from view by the sloped ceiling of the stairs. The visitor turned toward the inner apartment door and jostled the handle. Then she began jabbing my buzzer again. I still couldn't see her face, but I figured it out. Unless Alex had gone for gender reassignment surgery this afternoon, it was Mireille.

What was she doing here? I was too tired to think it through. She'd tell me soon enough. I buzzed her in.

Mireille burst through the apartment door and bounced up the stairs, two at a time. Her brown curls sprang with each step. "I hope I'm not disturbing—oh! Were you sleeping?"

No point in lying. "Yes. But it's okay. I should have been up."

She air-kissed my cheeks. "I feel terrible! I thought I would drop by, see how you were doing."

"I'm fine." From the way she leaned forward expectantly, I'd have to let her in. I stepped aside.

She was wearing a baby blue tank top that emphasized the breadth of her shoulders and the muscles in her arms. Was she really strong enough to hold down a grown man?

"Shall I take off my shoes?" She stepped out of her sandals before I completed my nod. "What a nice apartment! I like the floors. And it's bigger than mine!"

"Not really." I should offer her something to eat or drink. My fridge was still pretty paltry. "Would you like some water?"

She waved me away. "No, no, don't go to any trouble." She strolled into the living room. "It's good that you have a balcony." She surveyed my boxes and bare white walls. "You keep your room quite bare. Is that your look? Very Zen!"

I was annoyed. If I were white, she would have called it moving in, not Zen. "I had a problem with the moving company. The furniture's coming."

"Oh." She turned to me with round, innocent eyes. "I thought it was *feng shui*."

I reigned in my temper. She saw my face and assumed I was all-things-Asian. It's not uncommon, especially with older people, but I wish they would grow up and smell the multiculturalism. Some people meet you and immediately think they know you through the o-so-true stereotypes: hard-working Asian square who likes Hello Kitty. Others take it as an opportunity to tell you all about their trip to China thirty years ago. "Zen is a certain style. It doesn't mean an empty room."

"Oh." Again, the wide eyes. "Well, I imagine you know all about it."

"Not really. Just a few things I've read." Irritation was waking me up fast. "Can I help you with something?"

"I hope you will." She strode to the opposite wall of the living room and leaned against the windowsill, one leg bent so her bare foot pressed against my non-functioning radiator. "It's Alex."

I tensed before consciously relaxing my shoulders and voice. "What about him?"

"He's torn up about Kurt's death."

She stated Kurt's name calmly, with no hesitation. I eyed her. "Are you?"

She shrugged. "Yes, but I can handle it. Alex cannot." She turned to look at the bean tree shadowing my balcony. "He has never been able to handle stress."

"So why are you talking to me about it?"

She laughed lightly. "Well, he seems to have found a new confidante in you. I wanted you to be aware."

I waited. We were taught that silence is a good tool for interviewing. But maybe Mireille got the same lesson at McGill, because she just stood there with a little smile on her face.

She was a cat person. She liked to toy with people. She could have told me this on the phone. What was she looking for? I scanned the living room, but the only remarkable thing was my doll Henry, still praying for good luck. She followed my gaze to Henry. I leaned on the desk to block her view. "Okay. I'm aware. I'll be nice to him."

She nodded. "I know you will." She stepped over to the desk and peered over my shoulder at Henry.

I pulled myself up to my full height to block her again. "Was that all?"

We stared at each other. The amusement extinguished from her eyes. We were so close that I could see the small brown freckles on her nose, cheeks, and forehead. Her breath ruffled my bangs.

At last, she said, "That's all." She gave me a wide, enigmatic smile and turned to leave.

I remembered Alex stalking her, supposedly on behalf of his friend. Before she'd taken five steps, I called, "Do you and Alex have some sort of...understanding?"

She spun on her heel and laughed, showing large white teeth. "Heavens, no! Alex and I don't have *any* kind of understanding."

Just friends, then? But their friendship had a peculiar intensity.

She flapped her hand. "You're welcome to him. I just wanted to tell you to handle him with care." She gave me a nod. The queen permitting me leave.

"How kind of you. Do you have experience in handling men?" This was mean, kicking her when she was down about Kurt, but I wanted to provoke her. She had come to my house uninvited, dropped insulting hints about Alex and my non-existent décor. She needed a little back.

Her eyes narrowed for a moment. "Who told you that?" She brushed non-existent lint off her pants. "Alex is prone to exaggeration."

My truth-telling gene took control of my mouth. "So you deny you were having an affair with Kurt?"

Her eyes blazed for a moment. "That is none of your business."

She'd just confirmed it. That was one up for Alex. "But Alex is your business?"

She lifted her chin. "I look out for the well-being of my colleagues. And my friends."

I said, "Okay, you and I are colleagues. So tell me. How are *you* doing?"

More non-existent lint. "I told you. I am fine." Her laugh was a hard tinkle. "Why wouldn't I be?"

"Because one of your friends and colleagues is dead." I felt somewhat sorry for her now. "You said you're here for Alex, but we both know you were closer to Kurt. It's okay to mourn. Especially if you had unfinished business."

She ducked her head and stormed back into my front hall. "I cannot believe that you are saying this! You are prying into my business!" She stuffed her feet back into her shoes. "Clearly, I was wrong to come here!"

I blocked the door. "Look, Mireille. It's okay that you came. Did you want to talk to me? About something besides Alex, I mean?" Maybe he was right, she wanted to talk to a relative outsider.

Her eyes glittered. Up close, they were hazel, green with brown webs in her irises. "Not at all."

I felt a little hurt, even though I'd never liked her. "Okay. Fine. If you want to, though, you can. I'm the only one who didn't really know Kurt, and I'm not big into judging people."

"Aren't you?" She came close enough that I could smell her breath. It was strong and a bit sour, as if she'd eaten Gorgonzola cheese.

I was suddenly conscious of our relative size. I'm thin, with matchstick arms, so I hit the gym or do push-ups with variable dedication. I still occasionally have trouble opening doors in public. I do have strong legs, but I wasn't eager to test them on her.

Mireille had a few inches on me and big, swimmer's shoulders. She wasn't fat, just muscular and compact. She would have no trouble opening doors.

I also lived alone and hadn't met my neighbours yet, in what Alex described as a bad neighbourhood.

Do not be afraid. I swallowed and lifted my own chin. "No."

She made a dry, spitting sound.

I jerked back involuntarily.

Her lips thinned and jerked upward in a slight smile. "Alex is very paranoid. He sees conspiracies everywhere. He probably thinks Kurt was murdered. Am I right?"

I stayed silent. My heart was beating so hard I could feel it in my throat.

She pushed her face in mine. "Maybe he even thinks *I* killed him! Ha!" She sprayed a drop of saliva.

I flinched backward. It still hit me in the chin.

Her eyes were wide, exultant. "That's it, isn't it! He thinks I'm the killer! Oh, that's rich." She pressed so close that our noses almost touched. "That's hilarious. If you are so interested, I suggest you dig more into Alex's past—and less into mine." Her hand rose into the air. I raised my arm protectively, but she was only unlocking the door. She gave a sharp laugh and sauntered out.

My only reply was to slam the door and throw the bolt. I could still hear her laughing as she descended the stairs.

CHAPTER 9

Tuesday morning was my first family medicine clinic. Even though I was doing emerg, I still came back to family med twice a week, including biweekly teaching. The entire department attended the monthly Wednesday Grand Rounds, if only for the free food.

I wasn't sure what to expect as I sprinted up to the fourth floor. As I'd learned on orientation, the family medicine department was split on to two floors, the second and fourth. It figured that I'd be on the top one. I didn't know why they didn't make it consecutive floors, at least, except that administration took up the third floor. Make the doctors and elderly patients walk up the stairs, as long as the bureaucrats don't have to stir far from their plush chairs.

My watch showed 8:30. I was already supposed to be at the clinic. I usually set my watch two minutes early, just to get my butt in gear, but I was cutting it pretty fine for my first day.

I pushed open the dead white door at the top of the stairs. The clinic was laid out in a U-shape. I just had to rush from the bottom of the U up to the top at one end.

I turned left and dashed past the secretary's office and a waiting room with a TV continuously playing static. Left again at the end of the hall, past the nurse's office. At the end of the hall, I found my target conference room on the right.

I ran through the propped-open door. To my horror, the first face I saw was Dr. Callendar's. Dr. Evil from the ER, come back to haunt me.

Dr. Callendar scowled at me. "Good afternoon."

The feeling was clearly mutual. I wasn't *that* late. However, I wasn't about to give him the satisfaction of checking my watch. "Hi. I think I'm in the wrong room. I'm supposed to be in Dr. Levine's group." I started to back out. I'd have to run to the other end of the U.

Dr. Callendar waved his hand. "Dr. Levine was supposed to be the primary team leader, but because of...other commitments, he is now going to take the Friday clinics every other week. I will be your primary team leader." His eyes glittered. "I will see you every Tuesday morning. Punctuality is the pride of princes and *princesses*, Dr. Sze." He gave the "doctor" a sarcastic flick.

I tried not to wince. Maybe I should have taken the elevator, but Alex had warned me not to. "It didn't move for three minutes," he'd told me. "I timed it. Then it sank down to the basement and back up to the ground floor to pick up a hundred-year-old couple. It stalled out on the second floor, where no one got on. It creaked up to the third before it sank back down to second. By the time it got to the fourth floor, I could've run up ten times."

"Please. Have a seat." Dr. Callendar smirked at me now. "Join us." He sat at the head of the table closest to the door. The three other residents had left a few chairs between him and them.

Like the rest of the FMC, the room was ancient and run-down, but at least it had linoleum flooring instead of the battered grey carpet, mended with duct tape, that lined the hallways. A bookcase filled with forms squatted in the far left corner. A few old textbooks, a Harrison's and a Nelson's, leaned on its uppermost shelf. Someone had opened the four windows along wall opposite the door, but the room already felt hot and stuffy without A/C or a fan. Or maybe that was just Dr. Callendar's presence.

Tori caught my eye and lowered her eyes at the seat next to her. I circled halfway around the table and pulled out the chair, happy that she was the other R1 in my group.

The other two residents, the R2s, were both guys and looked nice enough. I smiled at them.

Dr. Callendar glowered down the table at me. "Now that everyone has finally arrived—" He glanced at the wall clock, which read all of 8:36 and was actually three minutes fast—"we can begin our introductions. Do you all know each other?"

I shook my head. Dr. Callendar raised his eyebrows like it was a personal failing. "Introduce yourselves," he said, gesturing at the residents I didn't know.

The first resident had rosy cheeks, a big smile, and a sea green *yarmulke* on his head, so he was obviously Jewish. "Hi, my name is Stan Biedelman. I'm from Montreal. I was going to be a lawyer, but then I saw a way of making less money for longer hours and decided to go into medicine."

Great. I liked him right away.

The other guy, who was thin, neatly-dressed, and Arabic-looking, said, with a moderate accent, "My name is Omar Hassan. I am from Oman."

It was kind of like a poem. Omar Hassan from Oman. He and I exchanged small grins.

Dr. Callendar stated, "Jenny Caldwell, also an R2, is on maternity leave."

Cool. Tori gestured for me to go next. I said, "I'm Hope Sze. I'm from Ottawa. I did my undergrad at McMaster, med school at Western, and now I'm here, so I've been all over the place." I wanted to make a joke, like Stan, but couldn't think of anything clever.

A flicker of distaste passed over Dr. Callendar's face. Perhaps one of my schools offended him. He turned to Tori with his biggest smile to date. "Dr. Yamamoto?"

Her low voice to was a bit difficult to hear. I bent toward her as she said, "My name is Tori Yamamoto. I studied biology at the University of Alberta, and went to McGill for medical school."

Dr. Callendar nodded approvingly. At what? Her quiet voice? Her Alberta-ness? Her sojourn at McGill? Her simple white T-shirt and khaki cargo pants?

If I kept trying to second-guess Dr. Evil, I would go mad. I took some deep breaths. Happy thoughts. My mind turned to Alex, who'd said he was a soccer player. I'd never been into jocks, but it was a mild turn-on. Instead of a bulky football player, I'd found a lean guy with good legs and stamina to burn. Intriguing.

Dr. Callendar launched into an orientation speech. It was really an excuse to lecture us about patient care, confidentiality, home care, following obstetrics patients even during our other rotations, blah blah blah. He seemed to scan me for a slip-ups (spinach in my teeth, less-than-alert expression), and it bothered me until I noticed he looked at the guys the same way. Maybe with a shade less animosity. The big compare-and-contrast was when he turned to Tori. His thin lips always stretched into a smile.

Clearly, he made a pet out of every group in order to divide and conquer. I'd met people like that before. I was more interested in how Tori was taking it. I can't stand pets who preen and strive ever-harder to please the massa.

Tori watched him, expressionless. A good omen.

Dr. Callendar managed to drone through the entire introduction hour. "Normally, this time would be reserved for teaching and reviewing home care and obstetric patients. You will be expected to prepare presentations regularly." Another poisonous glance at me. "If you have any questions, you can page me through locating. Of course, I will see you every Tuesday morning. Now go see your patients."

What a difference from Dr. "I'm your man, 24/7" Radshaw. Maybe it showed in my face, because Dr. Callendar shoved a piece of paper at me in dismissal. "Your schedule, Dr. Sze."

I felt like sticking my tongue out at him. Like Red Green said, you can't stay young, but you can stay immature. Instead, I peered at my schedule. I'd already done two emerg shifts as a resident, but I was worried I'd enter the room and have no idea what to do. Luckily, I had only two patients in the next two hours. That should give me enough time to figure out each one.

My first was an elderly woman who took a lot of medications and needed prescription renewals. Straightforward, right? Except I'd never met her before and I had little idea what half her medications were. At Western, we were encouraged to learn the generic names of medications instead of the catchy pharmaceutical brand name, which was probably a good idea to minimize branding in our head, but it meant that I was frantically flipping through my pharmacopoeia, trying to figure out what was what. After all, my signature was going on the prescription.

In the ER, I'd rarely made new decisions on my own. If the patient was admitted, I continued whatever they were on before, adding or subtracting as needed and as directed. I added antibiotics for a pneumonia, or a raft of heart medications for a new cardiac patient, plus Tylenol, Gravol, and Ativan so we wouldn't get called for the average headache, nausea, or insomnia. For one dehydrated patient, I forgot to stop her diuretic, but the nurse caught it, and Dr. Dupuis just laughed. I could also handle the walk-in patient who came in for a single, relatively straightforward problem, like my woman with the UTI.

This patient was different. She was supposed to be mine for the next two years. Plus she'd be using these meds until her next appointment with me. I wanted to get it right.

Not to mention that if I could avoid another Dr. Callendar roast-me moment, it would be a big bonus. Luckily, a patient summary was the first page of the chart. Phew. Then I took a closer look. Her problem list hadn't been updated since 2005. On the next few pages, some of the handwriting was execrable. Eventually, I excused myself. It looked unprofessional to squint and frown at the chart and my pharmacopoeia when I was supposed to know what I was doing.

I was in the conference room, trying to decipher the family history, when Dr. Callendar bore down on me. "Well?"

I launched right in, more comfortable presenting patients after two emerg shifts under my belt. "I have a 77-year-old woman with diabetes, asthma, COPD, gout, osteoarthritis, peptic ulcer disease, and an MI in '02. She says she's here for a prescription renewal."

"Let me see that." He grabbed the chart and read it, then threw it back at me. It flopped shut on impact. "So? No complaints?"

"No."

He bared his teeth in a grin. "Did you ask her about chest pain? Shortness of breath? Orthopnea and PND? Peripheral vascular symptoms? Abdominal pain? Pain in her joints? Tophi?"

I shook my head. "I asked her if she had any complaints."

"And you took her at face value? You did not do a complete review of systems?"

I shook my head.

"You know, Hope"—a faint, scornful emphasis on my name— "you may want to be the kind of family doctor who just pushes prescriptions, but that's not what we're training you for here. How can you figure out what medications she needs, and how you need to adjust her prescriptions, if you don't even ask her?"

My skin did toughen up during medical school. But all the same, I felt a burning at the back of my eyes. I had to figure out what all the drugs did before I could decide if she needed them or not.

"Family medicine is patient-centred. That means we focus on the patient." He jabbed a hand toward my clinic room. "Not on the chart, or on drugs, or your own ego."

My ego. What did that have to do with anything? It was about the size of a dust mote right now.

He had a point. I had an hour with this patient. I could have talked to her more. But he didn't have to be such a dick about it. I took a few deep breaths, willing the tears away. Dr. Dave Dupuis had taught me without relying on mortification.

"Dr. Callendar?" Tori called from across the room. She had silently pulled up a chair at the opposite end of the table. "I wonder if you could help me with Mrs. Abramovitch. She has a lot of questions this time."

"Just a minute, Tori." Dr. Callendar slapped my patient's chart, avoiding my eyes. "Think about it." He hastened over to Tori's side. "I know Mrs. Abramovitch very well. Has she been on the Internet again?" He chuckled and shook his head.

In the hall, I took a few breaths while I was still out of earshot and eyesight of my patient. I didn't want to cry all over her. Maybe I should hit the bathroom for a few minutes of privacy. I looked around, but all I saw was the men's. Then I remembered that women's was in opposite wing, on the other side of the U. Another reason to curse the FMC.

A fake wood door opened in front of me. I reared back, clutching the chart to my chest.

It was only Stan. He shut the door behind him at the sight of my face. "Hope. What's up?" His loud voice echoed down the hall.

I turned away. "Nothing."

"Bullshit." Stan gestured for me to come with him. I hesitated before following him down the hall, past the conference room, into an unmarked room on the left.

It was someone's office. Charts spilled over the desk, photos were propped by the phone, and textbooks lined the wall. The last thing I needed was to get busted for trespassing, but before the door closed behind us, Stan asked, "Dr. Callendar raking you over the coals?"

I nodded without meeting his eyes.

"Look. Don't worry about it. He did the exact same thing to me when I was an R1. He's just happy to have someone new to yell at. He probably has a small penis. His problem. Okay?"

I half-snorted a laugh. Stan's brown eyes were bright and interested. His features were too coarse to be good-looking, but his energy and confidence were appealing. I started to cheer up. "Doesn't he get to you?"

Stan laughed. "He used to. When I was a medical student. When I found out I was going to be on his team this year, I said, 'God, no, not the demon doctor!' But I have him figured him out. He likes having someone to pick on. You should see him making fun of Omar's accent."

"What?" My blood began to boil. It felt better than weepiness. "That's just wrong."

"Yeah, he's a dickhead. But if you can handle the attitude, he can teach you a few things. He's worse than usual today, probably mad that he had to be a team leader. They brought him in because of Kurt." Stan's face dimmed. "They had to switch all the teams around."

Kurt had left so many holes to fill. We found his body on Saturday morning. In the past few days, not only were people mourning, but they must have scrambled to find a new team leader and someone to take his patients.

Dr. Callendar had stepped in. I still didn't like him, but at least he did that much.

Stan cast a quick glance at the desk. "It's hard to believe Kurt's gone."

I gulped. "Is this his office?"

"It was. I guess it'll be Dr. Callendar's now. But he hasn't changed anything yet." He cheered up a little. "St. Joe's probably can't afford a cleaning crew. It'll stay like this a while. Man, I don't envy whoever has to go through all the papers. Kurt was always beavering away on something. Last I heard, it was spousal abuse. He wanted to set up a resource centre at St. Joe's. Even a hotline! I told him, who wants to run that?"

I was still a few thoughts back. A cleaning crew would clean away any evidence. I stepped toward the desk.

Stan sounded alarmed. "What are you doing?"

"I'm just curious about his pictures. Everyone talks about him, but I never really knew him." I peeked at the framed photos on his desk. One of them was a picture of Dr. Radshaw, sans moustache, wearing a ragged red-and-white football jersey. He was hugging a girl with a dark bob. She pressed to her face to his chest, but I could tell it was the woman in purple scrubs, Vicki.

I scanned the other photos: a black-and-white picture of a family, probably historical, and one of a mutt pressing its muzzle toward the lens. My heart twisted. I wondered who was taking care of the dog. I glanced at the wall, under the bookshelf, he'd hung his McGill medical degrees, which were written in Latin.

"Uh, Hope. We should get back."

"I know." I smiled at him. "Thanks."

He was already turning the doorknob when I noticed McGill class photos hung alongside and over the doorway. The one by the light switch was for the class of 2010.

I hesitated and pointed.

"Yeah. He likes—liked—to keep the class photos from when he started teaching. Come on. Callendar's going to lynch us."

"I'll cover for you."

He didn't look reassured. We crept into the hallway. All the doors were still closed. No one had noticed our absence. Stan whispered, "Just think about how small his dick must be. Miniature. Okay?"

"Okay."

He pushed open the door to the conference room. I headed down the hall to my patient, but with every step, I recalled the class photo. Right by the light switch, where Dr. Radshaw would have seen it every day, Mireille's face smiled out from the middle of the pack.

Chapter 10

If Dr. Radshaw had hung up class pictures for years, it would have been strange for him to stop just because his ex-girlfriend was in one. In fact, they might have still been dating while he displayed it. I kind of liked that Dr. Radshaw had kept her around post-breakup.

Still, he must have looked at it every day.

When Ryan and I broke up, I didn't destroy our stuff, but I put it in a locked box in my parents' cold storage. I burned a playlist of "our" songs on to a DVD and deleted them from my computer and iPod. Slowly, painfully, I got over Ryan. Still, when I found dried rose petals I'd forgotten, pressed between the pages of my dictionary, I cried.

Maybe Dr. Radshaw was less sentimental than I was. Heck, Mireille was a resident at his hospital. He'd see her in person all the time, never mind her picture.

But the more I got to know about Dr. Radshaw, the more curious I got. I'd agreed to ask questions, partly for Alex, but now I wanted to know the answers, too.

After I saw my second patient, I had to wait to review her with Dr. Callendar because he was too busy lashing Omar. "You don't understand. In Canada, we do things differently." He even exaggerated his pronunciation, as if Omar was retarded or hearing-impaired.

Omar nodded. "Yes. Of course. Yes!"

Dr. Callendar might have stepped into the breach, but he was still an asshole, same as Saturday morning.

My eyes narrowed. Saturday morning. He worked the night shift on Friday—the same night Dr. Radshaw died in the men's change room. I'm not saying it was Callendar's fault, but maybe he accepted the team leader position out of guilt.

Dr. Callendar stabbed a knobby finger toward Omar's note. "I can't read your handwriting. Medico-legally, your writing has to be legible. It doesn't matter what you say it says, someone independent has to be able to read it if you go to court. You'd better practice. Do you understand me?"

I snorted under my breath. This from a guy who squiggles so bad that he uses a stamp on his ER notes, and you still can't read them. He was born to belittle.

Could he love it so much, he'd have killed Kurt to have free reign in humiliating residents?

I watched him. The way his black hair stayed still as he shook his head, meaning he was vain enough to use spray or gel. The brackets around his mouth and across his forehead from frowning. The way the end of his nose turned up slightly, like a pig snout. He wasn't a big guy, but he had square shoulders and thick limbs. He probably packed some muscle under his lab coat. He might have been able to take Dr. Radshaw on.

Nah. Team leader wasn't worth killing for.

Still, if I did happen to find info that nailed Dr. Callendar, it couldn't happen to a nicer guy.

Dr. Callendar's head jerked up. He snapped at me, "Do you have someone to see?"

I held up my chart. "I'm just waiting to discuss my last patient of the day. Sir."

He squinted suspiciously.

I smiled back, partly because of a new brainwave.

I had to search Dr. Radshaw's office before it became Dr. Callendar's. And before the police decided to seal it off.

At the end of clinic, I had to stay late to write up my charts and fill out paperwork. Stan took off with a "See ya!" tossed over his shoulder. He was the only one. Tori and Omar's pens scratched alongside mine.

Dr. Callendar cleared his throat. "Just leave the charts here. I'll sign them off afterward." He grabbed his briefcase and disappeared. Maybe he'd got stuck in the elevator.

Omar was printing in his charts, his eyes wide with concentration. Even so, he finished before me. He closed the last one with a sigh of relief. "Good-bye. It was nice meeting you."

And then there were two. After a few minutes of scribbling in silence, Tori asked, "Are you almost done?"

"Almost." One patient per hour should be yawningly easy, but after interviewing and examining the patient, enduring Dr. Callendar's whip once, returning to the patient to ask reams of questions, conferring a second time with Dr. Callendar (hit me again, sir!), and then writing out prescriptions and forms, I was running late. Again.

At least Stan had showed me Dr. Radshaw's office. Lunch hour was a perfect time to spy.

I considered shoving my forms aside and saying I'd come back to them, but I didn't want to attract Tori's attention.

My second patient needed some physiotherapy for her shoulder. Dr. Callendar had informed me the waiting list was about six months long, so if I wanted to bump my patient up, I had to call the physio and personally plead my case. I dialed the number and left a message, but it was almost 12:15. No doubt she was at lunch.

I was astonished by the mountain of paperwork I'd piled up on just two patients. For anything I wanted—blood tests, ultrasounds, CT scans, physiotherapy, consultation of specialists, *quoi que ce soit*, I had to fill out who I was, what I wanted, who I wanted and when, Dr. Callendar's name and billing number. Then, in the upper right hand corner, I was expected to write the patient's name, birth date, FMC chart number, and hospital number. On each sheet!

That's a clerical job. Sure, I'm still learning, which is the excuse for paying me a pittance as a resident and charging me tuition on top of it, but why should I spend my ninth year of post-secondary education filling out forms?

As a final insult, each chart had a patient card we could have stamped on to each form and saved ourselves half the time. "Why don't we have an addressograph?" I asked Tori.

She laughed. "You should ask Stan about it. He tried to get one last year. They said it cost $1000. It's more cost-effective to have us fill out the form."

Unbelievable. The entire FMC was an exercise in mortification. It boggled my mind that they'd rather have a dozen residents filling out paperwork instead of seeing patients. There's a shortage of doctors in Montreal. Subtract the paperwork, and even I, a fledgling doctor, could probably have squeezed in one more patient in this morning.

No wonder half our orientation had been devoted to filling out paperwork. Forms, stabbing ourselves to test our glucose, and a tutorial on how to do pelvic exams in a room with no running water. I steamed as I filled out the physiotherapy form. This one had extra sections for medical problems, medications, allergies, and all that fun stuff.

Tori broke the silence. "Want to go to lunch?"

"Sure." Maybe I was doing some Asian stereotyping myself, but she seemed so much quieter and self-contained than me. Then I realized that if we did lunch, I wouldn't get a chance at Dr. Radshaw's office.

"Good," she said. "I'm almost done. Are you?"

"Uh, nah. I have a lot to do. Maybe you should go to the cafeteria and I'll meet you there." I checked my watch. It was 12:21. I started in the emerg on the hour. "On second thought, I might not make it at all. You have fun."

She gave me a level look. "You have to eat."

"Yeah. I brought my lunch." I pointed at my backpack. I should have stuck my lunch in the fridge, but there was only one food-worthy refrigerator for the entire FMC building. On the second floor, naturally. "It's cool. I can fill out forms with one hand and eat with the other."

She shook her head. "I'll keep you company." She pushed her charts to one side and lifted her black shoulder bag on to the table.

"I brought my lunch, too." She ripped open the Velcro of her purple cloth lunch bag. "Don't mind me."

I couldn't exactly ask for privacy because I had a room to search. "You know what? It's too hot in here." I waved at the windows. "You don't have to suffer with me. Seriously. I feel bad."

She smiled. "I'm fine. Finish your forms. We'll go outside to eat." She began unwrapping a pita.

My stomach rumbled.

She quirked her eyebrows at me. Now I couldn't even pretend not to be hungry. "I might be trapped here waiting for the physio."

She shook her head. "Leave another message with your pager number. She probably won't get back to you until you're back in the emerg."

"How did you know I was doing emerg?"

A smile danced around the corners of her mouth. "I saw it on the master schedule. Dr. Callendar also mentioned working with you there."

Goody.

She paused. "You'll get used to Dr. Callendar."

I glanced at her sidelong. "I heard he has a small penis."

She smiled. "Maybe. Stan would know better than the rest of us."

I laughed. She was sharp. She'd figured out how Stan had cheered me up. There was no way I could escape to search Dr. Radshaw's office in the next twenty minute anyway. I left a message for the physio, scribbled the last of the paperwork, and stood up. "Shall we go?"

As we descended the stairs, I wondered how to bring up Dr. Radshaw and Mireille.

Doctors are not supposed to fraternize with patients. When I was at Western, we sometimes giggled over the inappropriate behavior in *Dialogue*, the journal of the regulatory College. One woman testified that her doctor did a pelvic exam and spent a long time rubbing her clitoris. "I asked him if he was digging for gold," she was quoted as saying. Then there was a psychiatrist who was supposed to treat eating disorders, but spent more time rubbing his patients' breasts. The cases weren't really funny, of course. One case, about a doctor who abused a mute man in a wheelchair, was just horrendous. I guess we were laughing over how inappropriate the doctors were. In med school, some people argued that you shouldn't even hug a patient. "If he or she comes at you with open arms, step back. Tell them you don't hug. Offer a tap on the arm at the most."

Someone made up guidelines about dating patients. If you're an emergency room doctor, seeing a patient as a one-off encounter, wait six months before asking him or her out. If you're a psychiatrist, never. Other doctors fell somewhere in between.

We never talked about relationships between staff physicians and residents or medical students. It's unofficially frowned upon, but you can do it.

Tori paused outside the main doors of the FMC. A blue Beetle honked at us before it zipped around the corner to park. She pointed to the small deck across the road, between the Annex and the Human Resources building. "Would you like to eat outside?"

Yes, but not with so many people around. I pointed at the two smokers on the deck. "Maybe somewhere less toxic?"

She chuckled. "That's a tall order. Everyone smokes in Montreal."

"Do you?"

"Never." She pointed to a strip of grass in the sun, beside the human resources building and across from the emerg entrance. "Is that okay?"

The grass patch was empty. A second picnic table, next to the human resources entrance, had a group of people chatting and one lighting up, but if we kept our voices low, no one had to hear. "Sure."

She sat right down on the curb without fussing about dirtying her light khaki pants. I sat on the grass and stretched my feet out, kicking my sandals off. I enjoy lying barefoot in summer grass. One of the things I missed most in medicine was not having a proper summer. We did for the first two years, but clerkship meant that we'd often rise before the sun and come home after it had set. While my other friends spent their glamorous twenties making money or setting their own schedules in graduate school, I was doing surgery and OB/gyn.

Don't get me wrong, I felt lucky to be there. But I was conscious of the sacrifice. I was a SSINK. Actually, a SSINK-NB: Shitty Single Income, No Kids, No Boyfriend. But the last part might change. And I found joy in smaller pleasures, like eating barefoot in the sun with Tori.

Some smoke drifted by from the picnic table. I waved it away and took a bite of my dry peanut butter sandwich.

I needed a subtle way to bring up Kurt and Mireille. Tact wasn't one of my strengths. I decided to start off bland. "So how long have you been in Montreal?"

She held up four fingers and swallowed her pita.

"Why did you stay here instead of going back to Alberta?"

She shrugged. "I liked it here. How about you?"

"Well..." I didn't really want to get into my messy love life. On the other hand, if I played True Confessions, maybe she would, too. "I got into med school at Western. My boyfriend at the time—" I swallowed hard. Ryan's face flashed into my mind, with its pointed chin and the darkest brown eyes I'd ever seen up close. I remembered how we used to play tennis together. He'd beat me but never gloat as I vowed to do better next time. "—couldn't handle the long-distance thing. I liked London, but I didn't plan to stay seven hours away from my family. Ottawa—well. I wanted to try something different. Montreal's only two hours away. My mother can live with that. So here I am."

"I see." Her quiet voice and sympathetic eyes made me feel like she understood.

"So." I tried to lighten up. "How are the men here?"

She smiled. "Not bad. Not bad at all."

"Oh?" I would have nudged her if she'd been one of my Western friends. "You've got one?"

She laughed. It was the first time I'd heard her laugh out loud, a low-pitched rumble. "No. But I've dated."

"How do you meet them?"

She shrugged. "It's hard, you know, with our schedules. But I went out with an RT I met when I was on surgery." I nodded. I've met some fine-looking respiratory therapists. Too bad half of them are female. "And sometimes I meet someone when I go out. But it's not a priority for me."

"Do you go out with other doctors?"

"Like Alex?" She looked straight at me.

I found myself blushing. So not cool. "Well, sure."

She shook her head. "I did date a few guys from our class, or other years, when I first came to Montreal. But it was too incestuous."

That word again. "What do you mean?"

She brushed a crumb from the corner of her mouth and stared at the brick wall of the hospital across from us. "For example, if I were to go out with Alex, it would be awkward because I know Mireille."

Slam. Bang. "They used to be together?"

She eyed me. "He didn't tell you?"

"No. Well, not straight out." Inside, I was seething. What exactly had he said? *Not my type.* And she said they didn't have an "understanding." Not exactly lying, if they'd broken up, but certainly not wholly accurate and aboveboard. Why hide it?

A toast to truth. Yeah, right.

Tori touched my wrist. "I'm sorry. I've upset you."

I looked down and noticed that I'd pinched the end of my sandwich so hard that my fingers were nearly meeting through a thin layer of bread. I took a deep breath. "It's okay." But it wasn't. Why would Alex want me to play detective and then hide things from me? Why did Mireille come over and warn me off Alex, only to sic me on him? Was any of this a clue to Dr. Kurt's death?

Tori said, "I am sorry. But you would have found out, sooner or later."

"Yeah." I took another deep breath. "It's fine. I'd rather have it out in the open."

She pushed the last piece of pita in her mouth. The sun passed behind a cloud, as if it was depressed, too.

I hated Alex lying to me. After Ryan, I never wanted another guy to hurt me. So I went on a few dates, but I kept it light, never got involved. But after two years, the clamshell act was getting old. A new city, a fresh start, time to take some chances. I felt a real spark with

Alex. I didn't have to fake interest in his pet wombat or try to ignore his abnormally prominent gums. I liked him right away.

Which just went to show what a sucker I was. A little zing and I was ready to commit break and entry for him.

Well, screw that.

I'd still consider B&E into Dr. Kurt's office, but not for Alex.

Even though I never really knew Dr. Kurt alive, I still respected him and wanted him to be at peace. This sounds gross, but I remember when my dissection partner said he wouldn't be donating his body to medical school. "Look at them," he said, pointing at the cadavers around the room. "They're not at peace."

Dr. Kurt's mottled face and glassy eyes popped into my head. He wasn't at peace, either. I hadn't been able to bring him back to life. But maybe I could make sure he hadn't died in vain.

Chapter 11

When I hit the ER, my mind was not on work, but on escaping the walk-in side ASAP.

It was almost like a clinic. I picked up the chart for a middle-aged guy who said his knee hurt. I did a full exam, stressing all his knee ligaments. Then I reported to Dr. Trigiani, a female physician who bustled around the ER in real clothes. Not greens. A full-length, stretchy black skirt, a white cotton shirt, even a chunky bead necklace.

I always wore scrubs. The emerg is a messy place. Blood, vomit, plaster casts. Of course, most of the time, the grossest thing you had to worry about was a stray sneeze, but I wasn't willing to risk that ten percent spew factor while nearly all my wardrobe remained in another province.

Dr. Trigiani listened to my presentation, her head cocked to one side. "Okay. Did you check his hip and ankle?"

Oops. I turned red.

She laughed. "It's a good rule of thumb. Always check the joint above and the joint below. Are you sure there's no history of trauma?"

"He says no."

She checked the triage nurse's note. "'Knee pain x 1 month. O trauma.' Okay. We'll X-ray him, and it'll probably be negative."

By 4:30, I'd seen a few other patients, but I kept checking. No films for my knee man.

"Yeah. X-ray's really backed up," said Dr. Trigiani. "It's been like that all day."

I might end up here past five, just to babysit this guy's knee. I didn't want to enter the FMC too late. It might look suspicious if I pretended to need a chart at 7 p.m. I darted around the corner to check the film counter again.

Dr. Trigiani laughed at me. "It's okay. Go see another patient."

I smiled weakly. It took me thirty to sixty minutes with each patient. At this rate, I was going to stay past five anyway.

Luckily, it was a 26-year-old guy with ear pain. I'd seen some kids before with middle ear infections, called otitis media. The trick was to pull on the pinna, the outer ear, to straighten the external ear canal and have a good look at the ear drum. Like I'd been trained, I checked his good ear first. No problem. I pulled on his tender ear.

"Ow!" He yanked his head away and glared at me.

"Sorry." I hadn't even managed to insert the otoscope. "I have to take a good look."

"Well, be careful."

I don't think anyone is more gentle than I am, but I tried even more gingerly.

"OW!"

This time, I got a glimpse inside. His external ear canal, which normally looks like a tunnel of skin, looked like it was covered in weeping wax. I could hardly make out the ear drum.

I went on to check his mouth, feel the few lymph nodes in his neck, and listen to his chest and heart. Then I wrote up his chart, my ear cocked for Dr. Trigiani. It was 4:48

She came around the corner, holding a large brown envelope. "Guess what I found!"

She popped the films on to the light box. "What do you see?"

I surveyed them. "It looks normal."

"Name the bones."

"Femur." I pointed to the big thigh bone, tracing its lines. "Tibia. Fibula. And of course, patella."

"You wouldn't believe it, but some students don't remember."
I let the student reference pass, although I hoped she knew I was a
resident. I'd introduced myself as an R1. She went on, "What would
you look for in osteoarthritis?"

"Narrowing of the joint space. Sclerosis. Bony spurs." I tried to
remember the last one and couldn't.

"That's pretty good." She pulled the films down and wrote
"0" and signed her name on the front of the envelope. "How's your
guy's ear?"

"I think he has otitis externa."

"Has he been swimming?"

"Yeah, but it was last week. I think that's what it is, though." I
described my findings. She waved her hands, her brown eyes snapping.
"Sounds good to me. Let's write him a script. Then you're outta here.
You're off at five, right?"

"Right." Wow. A doctor who didn't want me to stay late to prove
myself. I liked her more and more. But I was still glad to clock out
of there.

It was twenty past when I crept up the stairs of the FMC. I felt
like a burglar. I avoided touching the wooden banister, as if they
could date my fingerprints. I noticed the door on each landing had a
large pane of glass and windows on either side. Anyone could see me
passing. I ducked my head and tiptoed even more quietly.

Just past the third floor, I heard a door open on the fourth. "Yeah,
it's hard to say," said a guy's voice.

Someone was entering the stairwell! I hurried back down to the
third floor and pushed open the door, turning left, down one corner
of the U. I had to get away from the windows on the landing.

I was almost at the end of the hall before I realized I had even
less excuse to be on the administrative floor.

Fortunately, all the room doors were closed and presumably
locked. No good bureaucrat would stay past 4 p.m. I took deep
breaths. I was not doing anything wrong. I was a resident here. *Just
lost, sir. Just needed to pee, ma'am. Sorry to bother you.*

I heard footsteps clatter down the stairs and fade to a
distant echo.

My heart thrummed like a rabbit's, but I forced myself to count to twenty before I inched back to the stairwell.

It looked and sounded deserted. Fine. I took a deep breath. One more floor. I could do this.

On the fourth floor, the secretary's door was closed and locked.

I tried to glide past the conference room, which was free and clear except for some charts on the table. The wind picked up and blew the blinds. They banged back against the window.

I flinched, caught myself, and carried on down the hallway. *Nothing to see, Dr. Callendar. I just took a wrong turn on the way out of the conference room...*

I pulled on a pair of non-latex gloves I'd swiped from the emerg and reached for the doorknob of Dr. Kurt's office. It turned easily in my hand.

I pulled the door closed behind me and scouted the tiny office. If I'd laid down on the worn grey carpet and stretched my arms above my head, I probably could have touched a wall with my fingers and the opposite wall with my toes.

Bookshelves stuffed with books, journals, and manila folders lined the walls on either side of his desk, He'd sat with his back to the window, facing the door.

His chair was an adjustable secretarial model, in ultramarine-blue fabric lining. The seat was slightly compressed, but otherwise it looked quite new. The man cared about his back and his posterior.

I needed more clues. Where to start?

The desk was most obvious. There was a square of space along the edge I hadn't noticed before. I tried to recall what had been in it when Stan and I came in, since every surface had been covered in paper.

Patient charts. All the patient charts were gone.

Was it possible a patient had killed him and tried to hide the evidence?

It sounded ridiculous, but I had to keep an open mind. The charts were the only obvious things missing.

Maybe the police took them. But they should have sealed off the room if they'd searched it. They must still be treating it like a suspicious death, not homicide.

I sifted through the remaining papers, trying to touch as little as possible. I saw numerous journals like the CMAJ and the Parkhurst Review. Some photocopied articles on renal colic, child vaccinations, and the new hypertensive guidelines. A printed e-mail from <u>bob. clarkson@sjhc.qc.ca</u> to dr-kurt, dated June 27th.

Hi Kurt,

I appreciate your suggestions. We all want to make the FMC a better place. Why don't you make an appointment with my secretary to talk about them?

Bob

I almost smiled. It sounded like Bob Clarkson. But why had Kurt bothered to print the message out? It sounded pretty innocuous.

I found a bunch of articles on crystal meth, GHB, heroin and physician addiction in a stack labeled "Grand Rounds." Alex had mentioned Kurt's presentation. Not too useful for me right now, but I kept searching the piles, hoping for something more incriminating.

Kurt had one of those desk file organizers where you stick file folders in between black metal loops that keep the folders upright. The one labeled Future Grand Rounds was empty. Hadn't Stan said something about spousal abuse? Oh, well, maybe Kurt took his stuff home to work on it.

What I really wanted was to break into his desktop computer. I took a deep breath and pushed the power button with the knuckle of my index finger. The computer hummed obediently, but instead of loading up the usual Windows crap, it jumped to a screen with the message "Command File Not Found."

I took a programming course in high school, but this was really beyond my ken. I tried pressing Return and Escape, to no avail.

Was it possible that Kurt used a laptop and never touched this ancient technology? Sure. But even though the bulky old-school monitor had collected brown balls of dust in its furrows, the tops of the keyboard keys and the tower's power button weren't dusty, suggesting that he did use it. Strange.

126   *Code Blues*

I turned off the computer and tried more low-tech solutions, i.e. I opened his desk drawer. It got stuck a third of the way through. I jiggled it loose, peering at the blue ballpoint pens and Post-It notes.

The phone rang.

I jumped, banging the drawer. It got stuck again. I rattled it loose and shoved it closed.

The phone rang three times before it got cut off mid-ring.

My stomach slowly unrolled, and I started breathing again. Thank God for voice mail.

Speaking of which...I stared at the phone. What if I could get into his voice messages?

I studied the phone. Considering how primitive they kept the rest of the FMC, the sleek black Bell phones stood out with their buttons for hold and speed dial and messages.

I reached for the receiver. It was risky, so soon after someone called. Still, my fingers circled the black plastic.

The office's closed door rattled. The doorknob turned.

I dropped the phone back into the cradle. My first thought was to jump out the window. But four stories later, they'd have to scrape me off the pavement.

I dove under the desk and curled into as small a ball as possible.

I lay on my right side, hugging my knees. My head was pressed against the back of the desk. My left arm was wedged under a fake wood drawer. I stared at the wall under the window as footsteps approached. Never had I been so conscious of my own breathing.

The door closed. Heavy, male-sounding footsteps grew closer. I was facing the window and didn't dare turn to check the shoes. If I made a sound, I'd find out soon enough who was wearing them.

My neck started to cramp up. My teeth clenched.

I heard a bang and felt a whack on the desk. My eyes widened, but I made no noise.

If this guy pulled the chair up to the desk, he'd run into me with his knees or his feet. Game over.

A BEEP, BEEP, BEEP shrilled through the air.

My hand flew to the pager on my waist. I was dead meat. Dead, roasted, smoked, and sliced meat.

The man grunted. His hand moved up and I heard him clicking the buttons on his pager.

His pager. Not mine. I couldn't even breathe a sigh of relief, but my shoulders relaxed marginally.

He propped his butt on the desk and leaned across the desk to punch in the number. "Yeah. Callendar."

My worst fears made flesh. I tried to scrunch into an even tighter ball.

He heaved a long sigh. "Can this wait? I've got to—" He fell silent. "The preliminary PM? I don't—all right. Fine. Twenty minutes."

He banged the receiver back into its cradle. He snorted under his breath. He grabbed the handle of his briefcase, muttered, "Suspicious death, my ass, Bob," and stormed out of the room.

Chapter 12

I didn't dare search the office any more. It sounded like Dr. Callendar had offered to meet for twenty minutes, but he could easily return in twenty seconds. I waited a few breaths, uncurled from under the desk, and beat it to the conference room, where I could legitimately sit and gather my breath and scattered wits for a moment. Then I dashed to the staircase on the opposite end of the FMC and strode down the stairs, struggling not to run any more.

The July afternoon sun glowed in the west. The air was warm, but not oppressive. I took a deep breath. I was free. I'd made it.

And I'd never do that again. A little risk was a fine thing after playing the good girl my whole life. But I had no taste for outright danger. I could have been arrested. I could have been expelled. I could have been strung up by Dr. Callendar if he hadn't been called away by a suspicious death.

Suspicious death. He had to be talking about Kurt. Unless St. Joe's turned out to be a hotbed of killings as well as incest, we'd only suffered once suspicious death recently.

I wasn't sure what Dr. Callendar meant by a PM, but Bob had to be Bob Clarkson, the FMC director. Why were he and Dr. Callendar having an after-hours rendezvous about this suspicious death? Like I said, no bureaucrat voluntarily stays late. Bob Clarkson was originally a family doctor, but he'd cut his patients loose after he'd gone into administration. I heard that he'd added his patients to the FMC pot, telling them he'd supervise them once in a while, but really dumping them on the residents.

Could that lazy administrator really have killed anyone, even with Dr. Callendar's help?

Now I was the one seeing conspiracies everywhere.

I unclenched my fists. They ached. My fingernails had bitten into my palms. I rolled my shoulders out and headed for home.

I was halfway down the block before I realized I'd left my backpack in the emerg residents' room, which meant I had no keys to unlock my apartment door.

I was losing my mind.

I ran back into emerg, trying not to meet anyone's eye as I swiped the giant yellow key stick from the unit coordinator's desk. Some stretcher patients goggled at me. I pretended not to notice, striding to the residents' room in the back hallway. As I shouldered my backpack and pulled the residents' door closed, I overheard a woman's voice from the staff kitchen across the hall. "Did you hear about Kurt's autopsy report?"

I slipped back into the residents' room, leaving the door slightly ajar. I could still hear them.

"No. Did you?"

"Yes. The preliminary one." The woman lowered her voice. "They think he died from airway obstruction."

"Well, I guess! Dave said they found him face-down."

I had to strain to hear the first woman now. "But his blood tested positive for succinylcholine."

"Succ? No way!"

I caught my breath. Succinylcholine was what we most often used to paralyze a patient before passing a tube between his or her vocal cords. Kurt had been paralyzed.

He'd been *murdered*.

"Sylvie!" a man bellowed from the belly of the ER. I recognized the voice. It was the big male nurse who'd been working the acute side. "I need you!"

"You'd better go," said one woman, and the other one, presumably, Sylvie called back, "I'm coming!" Her footsteps trotted away.

I waited a decent interval before leaving the room and returning the room key. I seemed to be doing a lot sneaking around today.

Someone had murdered St. Joseph's most popular doctor. The police would be right on it. Dr. Kurt's desk would be sealed and searched. It was a good thing I'd made it in before they came.

I was halfway home, cutting on to Edouard Montpetit avenue, before I considered that Dr. Kurt may have committed suicide. If you want to off yourself, succ (pronounced sucks) would make darn sure of it. A doctor would know how to do it right.

But no one thought he'd been depressed. Days before his death, Dr. Kurt was e-mailing Bob Clarkson about the FMC. The day of, he was telling us we could page him 24/7 and winking at me across the orientation room. Plus the whole Mireille-Vicki thing. He'd seemed anything but depressed.

Also, if he offed himself, he wouldn't do it at St. Joe's. The publicity could bring the ship down.

It could still be an accident, like the anaesthetist at Western, but the druggie anaesthetist grabbed the wrong medication in his hurry between cases. He didn't say, Geez, I wonder if I can paralyze myself, because that would be such a blast. I mean, what's the first thing you learn in first aid? ABC's. Airway, airway, airway. No one wants to choke on their own tongue.

I looked up at the University of Montreal's most impressive piece of architecture, a sandstone-colored tower balanced on the mountain. Its round roof had oxidized to green and windows poked in the front, like eyes.

My eyes fell on the women milling in front of the university. Because of the heat, many of them had twisted their hair up. I've always wanted to do my own hair but never mastered anything more than a hair clip, a ponytail, or a basic braid. So I cut my hair off.

Only one woman had tamed her curly brown hair in a ponytail with a simple black elastic. My kind of woman.

Then she turned her head to talk to the guy next to her, and I saw it wasn't my kind of woman at all. It was Mireille.

I walked up on her other side. "Hi there."

Her half-smile dissolved as soon as she recognized me. "Oh. Hello." She glanced at her friend, a guy with sandy-colored hair and freckles.

"Hi. I'm Scott. I'm in general surgery at the Jewish."

He still looked fresh, no dark circles under the eyes. Of course, we were only a few days in. "What year are you?"

"First. Are you in medicine, too?"

"Yeah, first year family med at St. Joe's. My name's Hope."

He smiled at me. His front teeth just crooked enough to be charming. "Pleased to meet you."

"Likewise."

Mireille took his arm. "Well, we're on our way. Nice to see you again."

Scott turned to me. "You want to join us? We were thinking of going to a café."

I loved how Mireille's face turned puce, so I said, "Really? You have time for a café on gen surg?"

He laughed. "I'm post call. Mireille was going to fill me in on all the gossip from St. Joe's."

"Like that she and Alex used to be together?"

Mireille's lips parted as she gave me a measured look, but Scott laughed. "Old news. I went to med school with them."

Still, I'd gotten a double dig at Mireille. Now she knew I knew, plus I'd reminded Scott of her past if she was planning to get jiggy with it. I gave him a lingering look. "Maybe you're the one who should fill me in."

He laughed, glanced at Mireille, and sobered. "Nah. I guess there's more serious stuff going on."

Regret sobered me, too. I shouldn't act so bitchy with her ex-lover dead. "Yeah. I heard the preliminary autopsy report came out. I'm sorry."

Scott raised his eyebrows. "Autopsy report." Mireille gave him a fierce look, and he backtracked. "I guess that's one of the things I'll hear about."

I glanced at Mireille, wondering if she knew the report, too. Probably. I waved them off, and turned down Louis Colin, a small street leading to the Haute École Commerciale, a steel-pillared monstrosity that dominated the other university buildings. Today I hurried by HEC, focusing on the ultramarine-blue day care instead. The railing on one side was made out of sheet metal embossed with a skateboarder. The kids' paper suns grinned down at me with crooked smiles.

I came home to two messages on my call answer. The so-called Zippy Moving Company's truck had broken down just outside of Montreal. There was nothing that they could or would do about it. "We are very sorry, but of course, mechanical problems are not our responsibility."

Then whose responsibility was it?

"Your truck will arrive tomorrow. Please call us if you have any questions."

Yeah. Like they'd be waiting to hear an earful from me after 6 p.m. Worse and worser. I sat on my sleeping bag and massaged my aching insteps.

The second message was a woman's muffled voice. "Hi, uh, Hope? I heard that you, um, want to talk to me? So I'm calling you back." She left a number and said, "My name is Vicki." And then she hung up.

Victory at last! I dialed the number. It rang four times and clicked over to "The AT&T wireless customer you have dialed is not available. Please leave a message."

Were these people allergic to turning on their cell phones?

I left a quick message asking her to call me. Then I double-checked the time when Vicki called. Less than an hour ago. Too bad.

Thirty minutes later, the phone rang. I grabbed it. "Hello?"

"Hope." Alex pitched his voice seductively.

My back jerked up, rigid. "Hello."

He paused. "Is something wrong?"

"Should something be wrong?" I countered.

"Are you mad at me?"

"I'm not mad." Pissed, betrayed, seething—okay, mad. "Is there something you wanted to tell me?"

"Well, yeah."

If he confessed his hot and heavy past with Mireille, maybe I'd cut him some microscopic slack.

"Did you hear about the autopsy report?" he asked. "I was right! He was murdered!"

"I heard that they found succ in his blood," I said coolly. "He could still have injected himself."

"Kurt? No way! Weren't you listening to me?"

"Too well," I answered, and my line beeped. "Sorry Alex, must go. Ta ta." I hung up. "Hello?"

"Hope?" It was Vicki's high-pitched voice.

Finally, things were going right. "Vicki! I'm so glad to hear from you. How are you?"

"Terrible." She blew her nose.

"Oh." How could I cheer her up? "I know this is a very hard time for you. Kurt was your fiancée?"

"Yes." Rather squashed-sounding. She blew her nose again. "You wanted to talk to me?"

"Yes." I tried to inject warmth and sympathy into my voice. "Thanks for calling me on such a difficult day. My name is Hope Sze. I'm a resident. You may not remember me, but I was in the locker room, when we, ah, found Kurt. You seemed very upset. I wanted to make sure that you were all right."

"Well, I'm not." She sounded plugged. I wondered if she was holding a tissue to her nose as we talked. "I want you to leave me alone."

"Excuse me?" It was the last thing I expected. She was the one who had called me. Twice!

"Leave me alone." Click. She hung up on me!

I banged my own phone down. I knew she was in mourning, but it wasn't like I was harassing her. I left my number with the clerk, and then she called me. If she wanted to be left alone, she should have just let it die. I winced. Bad choice of words.

The phone rang. I picked it up. "What! I mean, hello."

"It's Alex."

I'd forgotten about him. I'd thought that he'd hung up after I had. "What's up?"

"That's what I wanted to know. You brushed me off like I was a case of food poisoning."

I laughed reluctantly. "You can't brush off food poisoning. It makes you puke."

"I hope I'm not that bad. Did I piss you off somehow?"

I paused. He'd lied to me. Bad news. The end. On the other hand, there was still that darn spark. No. After the desk-hiding episode, caution won. "Forget it."

"Come on, Hope. I want to know."

"Too bad, then." It sounded harsh, so I added cheerfully. "I'll talk to you later, okay?"

Long pause. "Okay." Before he'd finished the word, I hung up. I had to laugh. I got the feeling Alex appreciated me more if he had to work for me. It wouldn't hurt him.

Now I was all keyed up. I didn't want to sit around my apartment alone, brooding. Alex should be left alone to repent his sins, not me.

I rummaged through the orientation package on my desk for the list of residents' names and numbers.

Tori picked up on the second ring just as I pulled Henry into a marching position. Time to party, girl style.

"Hi. It's Hope. Wanna do something?"

She paused. "Like what?"

"I don't know. You've got four years here on me. Any suggestions?"

She laughed and thought a minute. "Have you been to the Jazz Festival?"

"That sounds awesome." Then I remembered my line of credit. "Is it expensive?"

"No, they have a lot of free shows outside."

"Perfect."

"Tucker and Anu and I were talking about going on the weekend. I could call and see if they want to go tonight instead."

Tucker was way too loud. "Uh, I'm feeling low key tonight, you know?"

She laughed. "Maybe we'd better not go to the Jazz Festival, then."

"I'd kind of like to go. I've never been. I just don't feel like screaming over the music, in a big group. But if you want to, that's cool."

"No, that's all right. We can always go out with them on the weekend."

We arranged to meet at the Snowdon metro station. Tori said she'd be wearing a tangerine shirt and a glow stick around her neck.

"I love glow sticks! Don't you?"

She laughed. "I keep a couple. It makes it easier to meet people."

The Monday night metro was packed, the working-late crowd mixed with the dinner dates. The black guy beside me zoned out with his headphones, his knees pointed into the aisle. I tried to relax in my orange and white plastic seat, listening to my neighbor's bass beat and the screech of the subway. I was going to see the city and have a good time without Alex.

Two short stops later, I stepped off and met Tori on the platform. She was sitting on a bench, a blue glow stick wrapped around her neck, her legs tanned against her white jean shorts.

"You made it." She handed me an inert green glow stick. "Here's your prize."

I hesitated. "Do you want to save it? You know, in case you need to meet someone else?"

She laughed. "Don't worry about it. I get them at the dollar store."

I bent mine in half until it snapped and glowed fluorescent lime green. She helped me tie the string on the end to my left wrist. As we stepped on the next train, she said, "Why don't we get off at Place-d'Armes and walk? If we switch to the green line for Place-des-Arts, it'll take longer."

I held up my hands. "You're the expert. I'm just happy I got the glow stick!"

She laughed and shook her head. "Have you ever been to the Chinatown here? It's right around Place-d'Armes."

"No way. I've been held prisoner at St. Joe's."

Code Blues

"Yeah." She paused and added, "I know the feeling. I'm at the Children's for peds."

"How's that?" I hadn't visited the Children's Hospital yet.

"Good. The clinics are easy, but we do a lot of emerg. When you do the noon to ten p.m. shift on the weekend, it doesn't leave much time to do anything else."

"I'll say!" I noticed a book peeking out of her straw tote bag. "What are you reading?"

She showed me. "It's on the history of Japanese art."

"Are you an artist?" I've always wanted to draw, but never managed more than crude cartoons. Henry is my only significant legacy.

She shook her head. "I like to paint. I wouldn't call myself an artist."

She was pretty modest. "Are you more interested in the cultural history?"

She nodded. "My parents brought me to Canada when I was five years old. I don't remember Japan very well, but I've visited three times."

"You speak the language?"

She nodded.

"Well, I don't speak Chinese. My parents thought it was more important for me to learn French."

She wrinkled her nose. "That's too bad."

"I guess. But if I really wanted to, I could learn. I just haven't bothered yet." My mind flitted to Dr. Kurt. I wanted to bring up the autopsy report, but couldn't think of a good segue. "I'm glad that we're going out tonight. It'll be fun."

She smiled and touched her glow stick.

"Maybe we'll run into other residents." I glanced around the subway car. I could see my own reflection in the windows, but no St. Joe's people.

She nodded. "I'm always running into people I know downtown."

Time to ease delicately into investigation mode. "That's cool. Our class seems pretty tight."

She shrugged, a lift of her slim shoulders. I've always been small-boned, but Tori made me feel almost oafish.

I flashed her a smile. "Like you said, at lunch, there's a lot of history I don't know about. Life in the big city." This was her cue to start gossiping.

She studied me from under slightly raised eyebrows. "Be careful, Hope."

Guilt stabbed my stomach. "What do you mean?"

Her dark eyes didn't waver. "Alex."

I countered, "What about him?"

She shrugged.

The subway screeched to a stop and jerked open its doors. Tori stayed mute until we started up again and the recorded voice announced the next stop. Then she shook her head. "I don't know either of you very well."

So? But I bit my tongue.

She said, "It's none of my business. Let's talk about something else."

I shook my head. "Let's finish this. What do I have to be careful about?"

Her eyes creased in thought. "You seem like someone who is very...passionate."

Blood rose into my cheeks. "And Alex isn't?"

"I don't know him very well. Really." She glanced around the subway car.

I was making her uncomfortable. I'd never get another word out of her. "Okay. Forget it. What bands are we going to see tonight?"

Her shoulders relaxed. "I haven't seen the program, but it's usually a Latin American band at the main stage. You know, like the Buena Vista Social Club?"

"Sweet. I like them."

We got off at Place-d'Armes, along with a third of our subway car. In Montreal, the people waiting for the metro didn't stand aside to let you off as polite Torontonians did. Montrealers just stood there, blocking you, and tried to shove on as soon as possible, jamming the doors. Kind of a barometer of the city.

Otherwise, the July night felt just about perfect. After the heat of the day, the evening bathed us in breezes and the last of the sun's warmth. We walked past the Holiday Inn, which was topped by an ornate, Chinese pagoda-style roof. Otherwise, Chinatown seemed to consist of restaurants and some stores selling teapots and Hello Kitty.

The Jazz Festival was set in the heart of downtown, along Ste-Catherine. It took us only minutes to walk to Place des Arts. The road had been closed to traffic. White tents lined Ste-Catherine, and fellow pedestrians streamed alongside us. We could hear the music already, a trumpet punctuating the air.

Tori darted to one of the first tents and grabbed us a program. "Want to go to the main stage?"

"Wherever the action is." I grinned at her. She smiled back.

People emerged from the beer tents with armfuls of plastic tumblers. One lucky café was only about a block away from the action. Its *térrasse* bulged into the street, allowing people to eat and listen to music.

As we swam upstream through an increasingly thick crowd, Tori grabbed my hand. Even with the glow sticks, she wasn't risking separation. I had to turn sideways and twist through the mob. One guy, who held four tumblers of beer above his head, two in each fist, accidentally dripped brew on my hair. I squealed.

The guy yelled, "*Pardon!*" and escaped.

Tori squeezed my hand, threw me a sympathetic look, and tried to pull me ahead.

I brushed my hair off as best I could one-handed. My hand, hair, and neck felt stickier by the second. I now smelled like Labatt's Blue.

I don't even *like* beer.

As far as I could see, not one drop had fallen on Tori. When we were out of range, she called, "Are you okay?"

I nodded. There are naturally neat girls, the ones whose hair always looks freshly combed, the ones who eat spaghetti while wearing white linen dresses without any fear of spillage. That was Tori. And then there were girls like me. We're not slobs, but we have to work at looking polished. We're more likely to attract beauty disasters, like smudged mascara when it's not '80s night. Or beer in the hair.

A wasp dive-bombed my head. I ducked and hollered.

Tori tugged me through the horde. I think I helped part the crowd because I waved madly at the hornet, my glow stick jerking through the air.

At any rate, we got reasonably close to the stage and far away from the wasp. I relaxed into the music. A dozen band members dominated the black-draped stage. The drummer played a steady rhythm. The saxophonist wailed. Three trumpeters tooted an answer. Then a man playing the pan flute dropped to his knees, piping his heart out.

I cheered. Tori gave a sharp whistle and we grinned at each other.

A grandmotherly woman in front of us, complete with white curls, raised her hands above her head like she was praying to Jesus.

By the time the drummer rattled out his five-minute solo, I had forgotten the smell and press of the crowd and the beer in my hair. I started to sway and air drum. Before the solo broke, I was out and out dancing.

I was outdoing the Jesus lady. This was what I wanted from Montreal. A party in the street.

A black guy grabbed my hand. I hesitated, startled, but he smiled and lifted our hands above our heads, gesturing for me to twirl. So I did, laughing. He took both my hands in his and hummed under his breath, leading me through a few more turns. The crowd moved aside a little, giving us room to move.

I hesitated, but he loved it. He tried to count me through some swing moves, including kicks. I wasn't half as good as he was, but for once, I didn't care if I made a fool of myself.

My dance partner had a round, fine-boned ebony face and long, lean limbs. Out of the corner of my eyes, I saw his friends alternating between laughing at us and breaking into dance themselves.

The guy spun me into an embrace. I could smell him, dusky, in a pleasant, mysterious way, my face close to his neck, and then he spun me away and bowed. His friends clapped him on the back and pulled him off. Within a minute, he'd completely disappeared in the throng.

I wiped my forehead. The crowd turned back to the band, swaying to the beat. A black man in sunglasses was now singing in rapid-fire Spanish, one hand on the mike, the other raised in the air. The Jesus woman closed her eyes and hummed along.

If I hadn't been still been breathing hard, my dance with a stranger might have been a dream. I searched for Tori and found her off to the right. She was chatting with a petite woman with short, tousled brown hair. I said, "Hey there."

The woman turned. She looked strangely familiar. I couldn't quite place her, though. She had a tiny nose, like a bump with nostrils, and hollow cheeks. Her eyes didn't quite meet mine.

Tori stepped in. "Oh, Vicki. I don't think you've met Hope Sze. She's one of the new R1's. Hope, Vicki."

"Pleased to meet you?" said Vicki. She had a wispy voice that curled up on the end.

I stared at her. Vicki. Could it be Kurt's fiancée? She was wearing black, head-to-toe, but that wasn't so unusual in Montreal. "Hi, Vicki. Did I just talk to you on the phone?"

The woman glanced around uneasily. "I don't think so?"

Her voice didn't match my caller's. This woman's was wispy, more child-like. Tori cut in. "Vicki's been in mourning after...the incident at our hospital." She turned back to Vicki. "We're so sorry. I'll call you."

Vicki gave me a wide-eyed look before she allowed a middle-aged woman to draw her away.

Tori cocked an eyebrow at me as a sax solo speared the night. I had to yell above it. "Someone called me this afternoon. She said she was Vicki."

Tori shook her head. "Why would she call you?"

"I left my number on the OB/gyn ward." That sounded pretty nuts, so I added, "I wanted to give her my condolences. You know. After Kurt died. She was, uh, screaming."

Tori's eyebrows knit. She stared at me and shook her head again before turning back to the music.

"What?" I yelled.

She gestured at the stage, but I'd lost my taste for the music. I kept trying to read her face, and finally she got sick of it and hiked her thumb. "Let's get a drink."

I nodded. She didn't take my hand this time as we burrowed our way back out. After about a block, the music dimmed and flattened, but we could walk side by side and talk at low volume. She said, "There's a lot you don't know about the people here. Everyone is very friendly, but—"

"Hope!" a guy bellowed.

I turned automatically. One advantage of an uncommon name, when you hear someone calling, it's for you.

Tori sighed, but I soon spotted the cause of the commotion. Alex was almost pushing people aside as he tunneled his way out of the mob. "Hooooooope!"

Tori stood there, silent and expressionless. I said, "We'll talk after, okay?" But she gave a little shrug and watched Alex approach. He was wearing a faded red T-shirt and beaten-up cords.

I was in a silly mood after dancing with a stranger. Less likely to probe into the past, more "Girls Just Wanna Have Fun." Spotting Alex's shaggy, chestnut head still gave me that zing. I put my hands on my hips and called, "What about Tori?"

"Toriiiiii," he yelled, but turned down the volume as he neared us. Still, a few passers-by shook their heads.

His eyes were on me. "Fancy meeting you here." He leaned forward. Now wise to Montreal ways, I pursed my lips for the greeting kiss, but he pressed his cheek against mine and started to hum, one hand settling on my waist, the other clasping my hand in the air.

Wow. I was doing impromptu dancing for the second time in fifteen minutes. I felt like Sleeping Beauty in a very crowded, urban forest. Alex wasn't as skilled a dancer as the previous guy, but I felt more nervous in his arms. I nearly tripped over a tent peg. He caught me, embracing me so tightly that I had to hold my breath, feeling dizzy.

At last, he loosened his hold. Secretly disappointed, I started to back away. Then his arms tightened again and he stepped forward, tipping me backward. I gasped but kept my balance. At the last second, I even kicked my leg in the air, Hollywood-style.

He brought me slowly back to earth, his face filling my vision. His grey eyes were suddenly serious. I bit my lip. When I was back on my feet, he pressed his face toward me, nearly nose-to-nose, until I went cross-eyed. "Stop it," I breathed.

He pressed a long kiss on both my cheeks and released me. I crossed my arms so I wouldn't look like I wanted his touch.

More formally, he turned to Tori. "Hi."

"Hello." She just stared at him. He leaned forward from his waist and pecked her on each cheek. She accepted it, but made no move toward him.

She didn't have to say it out loud. She didn't trust him.

I was beyond caring. I always wanted a guy who could dance. Ryan never did more than a reluctant, slow-dance shuffle.

"What are you girls doing here?" he asked, his eyes moving to me.

Tori waved at the main stage. "The usual."

"We're getting drinks," I piped up.

"Well, then, allow me." He made a bow toward the nearest beer tent. "My treat."

Tori shook her head. Her face was so blank that I told him, "The dance was enough."

Alex said grandly, "Not nearly enough." He turned his gaze on Tori. "Come on. One drink. I insist." He offered us each an arm, making crooks at his waist.

I'd never liked those pictures where a tuxedoed man escorting two women, one on each arm. Plus Tori's reserve was starting to trickle through. I was mad at Alex. I was supposed to be making him pay for lying about Mireille.

I said, with dignity, "Tori and I are having a girls' night out."

Alex's face fell so comically that I wanted to giggle, but I suppressed it. He was a liar, I reminded myself. Ixnay.

Tori added, "Who are you with, Alex?"

Alex spread his arms out, embracing the night, nearly hitting a bald man. "Uh, sorry, man." To us: "The night is my companion!"

A breeze made me shiver. I said, "Good. Then you won't miss us. Let's go, Tori."

Now that I was playing hardball, Tori cocked her head to one side and gave him a look. "You can come, Alex. But we'll pay for our own drinks."

And so we did. As a feminist, I approved. As a poor student, I wished he'd paid for Tori's beer and my bottled water as well as his own Blue. I pointed to Alex's plastic tumbler as we backed away from the tent. "If you want more, you can inhale the fumes off my hair. Some guy dripped it on me." I touched the top of my head, fingering the sticky mess there and the tangled ropes of hair running down the back of my head. Yuck.

Alex surveyed my hair. Then he turned back to the beer tent. "I'll be back in a minute. Hold my beer?"

Tori took it. We exchanged puzzled glances. Alex definitely had a mercurial temperament. Maybe I'd triggered his need for seconds, because he was leaning over the plywood counter of the makeshift bar, holding out some coins and talking to the server.

I said, "I guess he really wanted to pay. Or do some two-fisted drinking."

Tori shook her head. "You can never tell, with him." She raised her glass and sipped her beer, while balancing Alex's in the other hand. Even doing that, she looked like a lady.

Alex returned with a second bottle of water. "Come here."

I gave him a weird look. "Thanks, but I haven't finished the first one."

"Come on." He beckoned me toward a garbage can.

I'd had my fill of close encounters with hornets. "No, thanks."

Tori held out his beer. "Do you want this, Alex?"

"In a minute." He turned back to me. "Come on, Hope. I'm not going to hurt you."

Tori said nothing. Her eyes moved between us.

He broke the cap off the water bottle and tossed it in the garbage. "Please?" He lost his smile, and his eyes gave a quick flash of vulnerability.

He wasn't about to harm me in front of Tori and a few hundred other witnesses. Avoiding Tori's eyes, I made my way over the garbage can. Alex sniffed the mouth of the water bottle. "A fine vintage."

I started to back away. He grasped my wrist and tugged me to his side. "It's okay. Lean over the can. I'm going to wash your hair."

Since I reached adulthood, no one has ever offered to wash my hair except a hairdresser. It would never have occurred to Ryan. To be fair, I'd never thought of it either. But it was, abruptly, the most romantic gesture I'd ever conceived. Except for the garbage can.

I bent over, holding my breath at first. But it actually didn't smell too bad, mostly fermenting beer, the mustard from half-finished hot dogs, and the occasional buzz to remind me this wasn't the smartest idea in my life. But Alex's hands were gentle on my hair, lifting the stickiest locks away from the rest. He poured water, splashing down my neck and cheek. I bit back a cry. The water felt icy.

"Sorry," Alex whispered, his lips close to my ear. He tipped the bottle so it spouted into his cupped palm, then dribbled the warmed water over my head.

I laughed shakily. "That won't work."

"It will, but we'd be here all night. Are you ready for the second course?"

"Yes." The trash can caught my whisper and magnified it.

Alex pressed the bottle opening against my head and tipped a few more spoonfuls as he finger-combed the water through my hair, diluting the beer and smoothing out tangles. On stage, two men sang in harmony together. The throng howled encouragement. It felt like it was for us. My heart drummed. I could hear Alex's breath in my ear. This was as intimate as anything Ryan and I had done.

A few people strolled by and laughed. One guy yelled, "All right!"

Alex didn't pause in his work. I could feel the force of his concentration, like washing my hair was his most important task on earth.

His fingers slowed and stopped. He tipped the bottle and gave me a careful rinse. "It's a good thing you have short hair."

"Yeah," I lied. I could have stayed here with him all night. His touch was an apology and a benediction and a seduction rolled into one. I wanted to lean into his hand like a cat. I wanted to lick his cheek. I wanted to bury my face in the crook of his shoulder and grind my pelvis over his. I could feel my nails digging into my left palm and the ridges of my water bottle cap imprinting on my right. Alex's breathing had slowed down and his touch pressed deeper, more surely.

His fingers ran along the back of my neck. I had to close my eyes. I wanted to arch into his hand. I wanted to climb into his bed.

He backed away. I heard water sloshing in the bottle as he righted it. "Uh, I guess I'm done now."

"I guess." I straightened.

His eyes were narrowed, his lips pressed together. I could smell his sweat, see desire in the way he held his rigid posture. And I was glad. More than glad. I wanted him to shred his control and—

Tori cleared her throat. "You didn't even use the whole water bottle."

We both started, and looked at the bottle in his hand. It was still about a quarter-full. He held it out to me. "You can have the rest."

Yeah. Give me the rest. I ran my fingers along his knuckles.

He gripped the bottle hard enough to dent the plastic. I chuckled and drew the bottle from his hand. "Thanks."

I waited for him to say I was welcome. Instead, he took a breath and surveyed my hair. "It's better. But it's all wet now."

Well, duh. He'd just poured two cups of water over my hair. I smoothed my bangs back from my face. "It'll dry."

He whipped off his T-shirt. I got a glimpse of his bare chest and abs before he threw the shirt over my head and started scrubbing my hair dry.

"Alex!" I yelled, muffled under the cloth.

"I don't want you to catch pneumonia," he said cheerfully, rubbing my head with extra vigor as I tried to push him away.

"I won't catch pneumonia, you kook! That's an old wives' tale, and anyway, it's July!"

"Atypical pneumonia," he said, a medical joke that made both me and Tori laugh, even as I ripped the T-shirt out of his hand and tossed it back to him, looking his lean shape up and down as I did so. He had a little chest hair, including a line running down to his belly button and below. "That's enough," I said.

He caught the shirt in one hand and let me look for another long beat. "If you say so." Then he slipped the shirt back on and grinned at me as his head popped through the collar.

A guy wolf-whistled, and a girl yelled, "Take it off!"

Alex watched me with a half-smile.

"Show-off," I said.

His smile widened. "So are you."

I guessed he meant the dancing earlier. I laughed. "A little. But you take the cake."

His eyes gleamed. "Tastes better that way."

It sounded like a come-on. I found myself blushing again. I wished Tori would say something. She just threw her empty cup in the trash can, making us back away from it.

It was a lot easier to be mad at Alex in the abstract than in the flesh. I'd been pissed because he lied to me, but I'd also been jealous Mireille had had him first. Not to mention gun shy after Ryan. Ryan and I had never had any significant ties before each other, but now that I was in my mid-20's, a virgin with a clean record was going to be pretty hard to come by, unless I started cruising the high schools. Maybe even middle schools.

As long as Alex didn't lie to me any more, I could handle his history. I smiled at him as I finger-combed my hair into place.

"You look beautiful," Alex said softly.

Tori walked up to him and held out his Labatt's. "Here's your beer."

I eyed her carefully, but she was more focused on me than him. In the depths of her gaze, I saw concern. She shook the beer cup at Alex.

"Thanks," he said, his eyes still on me.

If it had been just Alex and me on Ste-Catherine Street, I might have followed him home and taken off his T-shirt again.

He watched me over the rim of his cup, his eyes flicking up and down. He was thinking the same thing.

But we hadn't talked about Mireille yet. More importantly, Tori was here, and I wouldn't abandon her or slag her off. She deserved better. So I tried to break the mood with a joke. "Free hair washing. Almost worth getting beer in my hair."

"Maybe it was good for your hair," said Tori. "Some women use beer like shampoo."

"Oh, yeah, I heard that," I said, finally taking my eyes off Alex. But when I glanced back at him, his eyes were still fastened on me. I gulped water, finishing the bottle Alex had used on my hair.

Tori said, "We just ran into Vicki. Kurt's fiancée."

Alex's eyes flickered.

"Yeah." I roused myself. "That was weird. I got a call this afternoon from a woman who said she was Vicki. She wanted me to leave her alone. But we just ran into the real Vicki, and she didn't know what I was talking about."

Alex said, "Huh. That's weird. You think someone was impersonating Vicki?"

"Either that, or she's got multiple personality disorder," I said.

Alex and Tori exchanged a glance.

"I'm joking," I said. Then I looked at them. "You think that's possible?"

Tori laughed. "I don't think so. I did obstetrics at St. Joseph's as a med student, and she was pretty reasonable. But you do hear stories."

"What stories?" I asked.

She shrugged. "Gossip."

Man. She was tight-lipped. Alex stepped in. "You get some weird personalities on OB. When we started, the residents told us to avoid certain people." He lowered his voice. "One of them was Vicki. She came off as sweetness and light ninety percent of the time, but the other ten percent, watch out. She'd tear your arm off if she thought you weren't delivering the baby right."

I frowned. "But you guys were always supervised during deliveries, right?"

Alex quaffed some more beer. "Pretty much. Either a resident or staff would be there. But once in a while, in the middle of the night, the student would be the first one on the scene. If it was Vicki's patient, watch out. She didn't trust us."

Tori made a face. "That's normal on OB."

I nodded. "And peds." Those are two the specialties where the nurses are notoriously protective of their patients and think that med students are rabid creatures to be kept at bay. It's understandable. You don't want some dopehead med student bludgeoning a sick kid or difficult delivery. Some of the nurses there have been working longer than we've been alive. On the other hand, these are teaching hospitals, and if the nurses won't let us learn, future doctors won't be properly trained. Since I'd just started here, I had no evidence if Vicki was really off-kilter or if the residents didn't like her because she was overprotective. "I wonder how she hooked up with Kurt. He seemed like the original champion of medical education. I don't know why he'd pick a girlfriend who dismembered med students." I smiled. They didn't smile back. I decided to put the screws to Alex, at least lightly. "Plus the whole Mireille thing."

Alex exhaled and studied the pavement. Tori glanced at him, waiting for him to answer, but when he remained silent, she finally stepped in. "Kurt was—" She stopped, choosing her words carefully. "—very popular. Easy to like."

"He, ah, dated around?" I would have said screwed around, but Tori was a lady.

She eyed Alex again. "Well. Mireille was the only student he was ever involved with, as far as I know."

He lifted his head and swigged the last of the beer before he said, "She broke up with me and hooked up with Kurt." He threw his empty cup in the garbage.

I raised my eyebrows. It was one thing for Alex and Mireille to go mini-golfing together a few times in first year. It was quite another for her to dump him right before taking up with a teacher. Could Alex have been upset enough to kill Kurt?

But then why would he ask me to investigate? This was so screwed up.

Alex's mouth twisted wryly. "I didn't kill him, if that's what you're thinking."

I shrugged. "Well, you're the one who'd know." I left a questioning note on the last word.

He snorted. "Great. Now I'm a killer. No, seriously. No one likes to be dumped, right?" He pulled at the collar of his T-shirt. "But that's, like, WTLY." He pronounced it like "wit-ley," saw my confused face and explained, "Welcome To Last Year. I'm over it. Mireille was the one who botched it; Kurt didn't even know we were still going out. He called me at home, asked me if I was okay with it, offered to break it off with M." Alex's voice softened. "He was really a decent guy."

I checked Tori's face, but she was doing the poker face again.

The crowd cheered the end of the song, with one guy yelling, *"Ay caramba!"* I laughed a little, and Alex shifted his weight, more relaxed now.

I said, "First of all, you should have told me you and Mireille were going out instead of this junk about a 'friend.'"

"I didn't want you to get—"

I held my palm to his face. "Hand." Since it was his turn to look confused, I added, "Talk to it." He wasn't the only one who knew slang, even if mine was a little out-of-date.

He stopped. "Okay. I guess I deserve that."

"You deserve more than that. Don't lie to me." He started toward me, but I backed away. "Don't lie to me, don't ditch me, don't do anything you wouldn't want me to do to you."

He exhaled, extending his head and surveying the night sky. "The golden rule."

"Not just for Christians anymore."

"Sounds good to me," Tori said in a low voice.

I flashed her a smile and waited for Alex.

His shoulders sagged. "Yeah. You're right." He looked at me levelly, no flirting now, straight up. "Sorry."

I nodded.

"I'm an asshole. *Odey-oh,*" he added.

Hey. That was an obscure song reference. I liked it. "Okay. Just go forth and asshole no more."

He choked on a laugh. "I'll do my best. Seriously."

I'd had enough *mea culpa*. I turned to include Tori in the conversation. Her eyes gleamed with approval. I gave her a small smile. "Now that we've solved that mystery—" I tilted my head. "Well, actually, I still don't know why Mireille ended up with Kurt. But the bigger question is, why did Kurt end up engaged to Vicki?"

Alex shrugged and grinned a little. "I think Kurt didn't trust Mireille completely after she lied about me. Too bad, so sad."

In the distance, the band started up again, the brass wailing another tune. The crowd cheered and clapped.

Tori waited for the noise to subside a little before she put in, "It's not against the law for a staff member to date a student. But it's not approved of, either. It probably would have been all right if Mireille had gone into surgery, as she'd planned. But at the last minute, she ranked family medicine first and asked to be at St. Joe's."

Alex snorted. "Yeah. She had to get greedy."

I remembered running into her on the street with the surgery guy from the Jewish. I looked from Alex to Tori. "Mireille wanted to be a surgeon?"

Alex raised his eyebrows. "General surgery, no less."

Arguably the most draining kind of surgery. Gen surg used to cover everything from thyroid to basic ortho, C-sections, and bowel CA, but now, with subspecialization and turf wars, they've largely been confined to "breast and bowel," as I'd heard one resident sum it up.

Bowel includes the appendix, and when I was on call for gen surg, almost every single night, we'd go to the OR for at least one appy, plus they'd have to cover any trauma. No other surgical consultants had to come in every night. Generalists also tend not to get paid as well as specialists. Of course surgeons usually do well, but everyone envies the ophthalmologists who tend to work from 8 a.m. to 4 p.m. and make a killing on cataract or laser surgery. To be a general surgeon, you have to love the work.

Mireille must have loved the work. Instead, she chose her boyfriend, only to have him toss her away.

If what they were saying was true, Mireille hadn't just lost a boyfriend. She'd lost her career. And at this stage in our lives, that's everything. If it were me, I'd be questioning my choices, seething at Kurt and Vicki, and most of all, flagellating myself while trying to put on a happy face for family medicine. I asked, "Can she switch to gen surg?"

Alex half-laughed. Tori said, "I think she may try to. But she could lose the year."

Losing a year was bad. Doing family medicine against her will was arguably worse. It didn't excuse her rudeness to me, but it helped explain why she was already pissed before I started poking around.

And yet, when I pictured her in my mind, I couldn't forget her powerful shoulders and arms. She could have dragged Kurt in the locker room. She had good reason to hate Kurt, the best motive I'd uncovered so far. Mireille was definitely a candidate.

Too bad. I wanted it to be Dr. Callendar. The whole two birds, one stone thing.

I tried to work out the timing. We applied to residency last fall. Alex implied he and Mireille had broken up before the New Year. I think we submitted our rank lists—the list of programs we'd accept, in descending order of preference—in February, a month before the match. We got our match results on March 15th, telling us which residency program and which city we'd been matched to.

So her romance with Kurt must have lasted until at least Valentine's Day, or else she would have changed her rank list. Sometime between February and July first, he had broken up with her and proposed to Vicki. Five months. Fast work. I found myself not liking him as much.

I had to verify my calculations. "When were Mireille and Kurt dating?"

Alex snorted. "October to April. As far as I know." He looked at my half-empty water bottle. "Are you going to finish that?"

I handed it to him. "And when were you and Mireille together?"

He took a long swig. "On and off, until December. For a year."

A year. That was pretty serious. It also didn't seem to go with his previous timeline.

Alex waved his hand. "More off than on. We hardly saw each other. We were finishing clerkship and applying for residency."

Tori's eyebrows quirked, but she said nothing.

I tried to shove aside my own disappointment. "If you guys were together for that long, and you both did family medicine at St. Joseph's, Kurt must have known that you were together, just the way you acted around each other."

Alex recapped the water bottle and handed it back to me. "Uh uh. At McGill, we rotate through the hospitals starting in second year, as an introduction, and then again in clerkship. Mireille and I were both here in second year, but in different groups. Then she came back in clerkship, but I was at the Jewish. Kurt never saw us together."

Tori said, "So how did he find out you'd been dating?"

Alex suppressed a burp. "ESP."

We both wrinkled our noses. He said, "Sorry."

Tori repeated, "If he never saw you together, how did he find out you'd been dating?"

"Maybe Mireille told him."

Not likely. It wasn't in her own best interest. She wasn't about to say, "Guess who I used to do, right before you?" Or, even worse, at the same time as I was doing you?

Alex grimaced. "Oh, all right. I told him off for dating a student. He figured out the rest." He spread his arms. "But that goes way back. When Mireille told me they were getting engaged, I said *Mazel tov*. What's it to me?"

Was he Jewish? No, I thought he was, if anything, a Mennonite. Maybe Mireille was Jewish. Oh, who cared. I was getting distracted from the important stuff.

Tori stepped in. "I never heard they were engaged."

Alex smiled wolfishly. A lot of teeth. "No, you wouldn't have. Because soon after she told me that, he dumped her and took up with Vicki. Tit for tat." He cackled.

Despite how much he protested, Alex didn't seem over Mireille. Even wanting to nail her as a killer meant he wanted to nail her in one form or other.

Tori said, "She must have been hurt."

Alex bobbed his head up and down in cheerful agreement. "That's why she may have killed him."

"No, Alex," Tori said. "That's a terrible thing to say."

Alex held his hands, palm up. "The truth hurts."

His definition of truth was pretty lax. Not attractive. Also, if he expected me to root the dirt out on Mireille just so he wouldn't look petty while she took the fall, he'd have to try a lot harder than hairwashing. I took a step back. "I have to go."

Alex stepped forward, his arm raised and ready to loop around my shoulders. "Aw, no. Not yet. The night's still young, Hope."

I made a show of checking my watch. "Not young enough. Thanks for the hairdressing. See you. Coming, Tori?"

She said, "Yes. It's been a long day. 'Bye, Alex."

I felt a sour triumph. I wouldn't play his fool.

On the other hand, I probably wouldn't get to play with him at all. I should have felt liberated.

Alex said, "All right. I'll go listen to some jazz. 'Bye, ladies." He kissed Tori's cheeks fast, and then drew me close. His breath was heavily sautéed in alcohol, but his twin kisses were warm and tender against my skin. He stared deep into my eyes. "*Auf wiedersehen.*"

My heart thumped twice. It sounded so poignant when he said it. I knew enough German to translate it as "until we see each other again." It meant the same as the more predictable French "*au revoir*," but on his lips, the German somehow carried more intimacy.

Or maybe I was reading too much into it, as usual. Didn't Mennonites speak German?

I spread disinterest over my face and turned to Tori. "Subway calling?"

She nodded.

I glanced over my shoulder, at Alex. He waved and began weaving back through the crowd, but he turned once to give me a regretful grin before his lanky figure cut into the night crowd.

My stomach squiggled again.

Tori shook her head.

"What?" I said.

She quirked her eyebrows until I rubbed the pavement with my sandal, pretending to polish a piece of gum off the sole. I said to the asphalt, "I know what I'm doing."

I felt, more than saw, her shake her head, but she dropped it. "You still have time to catch the blue line. The last train is around 11:15."

My jaw dropped.

She laughed. "Did you not see the signs in the station?"

I shook my head. I'm usually people-watching, or staring at the map, making sure I'm heading the right way. "Well, that sucks! How am I supposed to go out at night then?"

"Taxi. Or, depending exactly where you are, you could walk from the orange line. You have a lot to learn about—Montreal." The slight pause made it clear the city wasn't all that she had in mind, but I wasn't ready to talk about Alex. I was embarrassed by my strong reaction to him. Zing is good, but he was someone who could carve his way into my heart, leave footprints on my brain, and inscribe his initials in my small intestines. If I let him.

Part of me wanted to jump into free fall. The other part, the careful part, the doctor part, the Tori part, whispered, *he is dangerous. Run away and stock up on garlic and crucifixes.*

But whenever I was with Alex in the flesh, the first part won.

I honestly think I'm somewhat screwed up from being good so long. The most hazardous thing I've ever done was to get drunk and kiss a stranger when I was sixteen. But it was never perilous. I was tipsy, but I knew exactly what I was doing and how far I was willing to go. The guy was toasted enough to be harmless. When I decided I'd had enough, I took a cab home. Granted, it was 4 a.m. and he was a decade older than me, but it's the wildest thing I've ever done in my life. And that was ten years ago.

So it wasn't just Alex. The tiger in me was sick of being caged in white coats and the Dean's Honour List. It wanted blood. It wanted sweat. It wanted sex. It wanted *life.*

So Alex seemed like a good start.

We walked to the metro in silence. How could I explain all this to Tori? She seemed grounded, which was good, and not a gossip, which was also good, but she was very, very controlled. She looked before she leaped. She was quiet. Reflective. Self-contained. Plus, I just met her. How do you say, "You know, I really want to fuck that guy. You should admire my self-restraint" to the ultimate good girl?

Maybe it had something to do with her background. She was my first friend who'd been born in Japan. Their culture is all about honor and respect.

I'm not sure what you'd say about Chinese culture nowadays. Respect is a big part of it, but so is food. To distract myself, I asked, "How come your name's Tori, anyway? Is it like Tori Amos?"

She said, "Tori is a Japanese name. It means 'bird.'"

I wondered if Tori Amos knew that. Probably not.

By the time we were riding the escalator down to the bowels of the metro, I couldn't stand it any more. I'd lasted about five minutes. "So. You knew Alex and Mireille when they were going out?"

"Yes." Her eyes fixed on the brick wall, like she was reading the ads. As if.

"Were they really serious?"

"They were discreet at the hospital."

I chewed my lower lip. "What does that mean?"

She sighed. Her eyes were almost black in the flickering fluorescent light. "He's not over her."

It stung twice as hard because I'd gotten the same feeling. I concentrated on stepping off the grooved escalator step on to the metal mat at the bottom. "How do you know?"

She just looked at me.

I sighed. "Okay, dumb question." Not as dumb as me, though. I'd been broadcasting my interest, and Tori could read me like a billboard. I dug through my change purse for my metro ticket, avoiding her eyes. The metal gate beeped, and I pushed the turnstile extra hard. She ran her metro pass through and followed me without a word.

While she pressed the button for a transfer, I said to her back, "Okay, you warned me."

She turned around and handed me the transfer, a flimsy strip of newsprint stamped with the station name. "In case you get lost and need to take the bus."

I shook my head in irritation. "I'm not that much of an idiot."

"Please," she said quietly. "Just in case."

I took it with bad grace. She obviously thought I was a doughhead.

"We all get lost sometimes," she said evenly. "It's understandable." Then she turned toward the *Côte-Vertu* orange line.

I ran up to her. "You mean, you and Alex—"

She broke up laughing. "No. Absolutely not."

Of course, no one seemed willing to admit to past bed partners. She read my expression. "I'm not a liar, Hope."

My gut believed her. Montreal felt kind of like the riddle where there are three daughters. One only tells the truth, one always lies, and the third only lies about family matters. I'd finally found the one who told the truth.

The only problem was, she didn't speak a whole lot. But I could live with that. Better an occasional prophet than a non-stop fibber. Especially if she was going to dog on me about Alex.

She laid a finger just below my elbow for a second. I could already tell Tori didn't touch people much, so this was a big deal. "I'm worried about you. You don't know people here."

"I'm a big girl. I'll be okay."

She nodded once. Her face was unconvinced.

Time to change the subject. I headed down the stairs, throwing over my shoulder, "Interesting about Kurt, huh? He must have liked weird women."

Silence from Tori. I peeked and got her expressionless face. I was starting to translate it as her version of disapproval.

I added, "Sorry, but you know what I mean. Mireille was a student, and—" Should I tell her that Mireille had come to my house to semi-threaten me? No. Maybe they were friends. "—changed her career for him." That was means and motive right there. All we needed was opportunity. I'd look into that later. I took a deep breath and moved on to the next suspect. "You guys were saying that Vicki—"

"Shh!" She glanced around the station uneasily, even though there was only a handful of people on either side of the tracks. The giant ads on the walls outnumbered the humans.

I lowered my voice anyway. "I know Vicki's your friend, but Alex said she had a questionable rep. Unstable, right?"

She kept her face turned away, even craned her neck like she was watching for the train's lights in the depths of the tunnel's shadow.

I kept talking. Even if it was only for myself, it helped to work out my thoughts. "That's two for two. Plus he got engaged to Vicki within months. That was pretty sudden."

At last, her lips barely moving, she said, "He dated Vicki before Mireille."

"No shit." I don't swear that much, but I was surprised. McGill's medical soap opera was like a complicated bridge game. Every time I thought I'd figured out the hand I'd been dealt, someone turned over a new card. "Were they serious?"

Tori gave a slight nod.

"Interesting." Now I had a lot more combinations to play with. Vicki had Kurt, didn't have Kurt, won him back, and now he's dead. Mireille, the student, maybe stealing him away, only to lose him again. Alex, the jealous, spurned lover.

Who had lost the most?

Kurt, obviously. But for second place, I'd pick Mireille. Or Alex.

I really had to figure out what she'd been up to that Friday night.

I licked my lips. I didn't relish confronting her again. She was bigger, stronger, and angrier than me. This was her city, not mine.

Maybe I should drop all of this. The police had to be involved, now that they'd found succ in his blood. I should concentrate on getting into the third-year emerg program and leave Kurt's death to the pros.

But something kept pulling me back. For one, I'd found his body. For another, it wasn't like we could all comfort each other and say it was his time, or it was a blessing, or at least his suffering was over. No. He hadn't been sick. He'd been in the prime of his life, trying to revitalize St. Joe's and marry his woman of choice. His death wasn't right. I wanted to fix it.

Just as important, I am incurably nosy. Give me a mystery and I'll try and unravel it.

If Mireille was the killer, I didn't want to work with her. I wanted her safely behind bars.

And then there was Alex. But I refused to think of him any more. It was too confusing.

I said, "I guess you and Mireille are pretty close."

Tori lifted her shoulders slightly. "I've known her for four years."

Answering without answering. The train rumbled in the distance. I leaned forward to see its headlights spiking the dark tunnel. As the tracks rattled, I leaned closer and raised my volume. "Do you know where she was on Friday night?"

Tori pressed her lips together. The blue and white train screeched to a halt, saving her from having to answer.

I stepped on to the metro and sank in a two-person bench, but instead of sitting beside me, Tori chose the one-person chair next to the door and diagonally across from me. Hmm. Tread carefully.

I studied the crescents of dirt under my nails while the subway dinged its warning and shoved off. Maybe I should give up the detective beat. I was too forthright. I'd alienated Tori by treating her as a witness instead of a new friend. I sent her an apologetic smile.

Tori leaned toward me and whispered, "If you're asking me, do I think she would have killed Kurt, the answer is no. I don't believe she would risk her medical career to kill him. None of us would. If there was any crime, it's the police's job to figure it out." Her lips pressed into a thin line. Then she arranged her knees to face forward and looked straight ahead.

Yep. I was in the dog house. "Sorry," I said, but she pretended not to hear me.

She had a point. It probably didn't matter what Alex or I did. The police were on it. It was their job. I didn't ask them to handle anaphylaxis or child immunizations. They didn't ask me to butt in on their investigations. Well, except the cop had given me his card. But it was more like if I heard anything, pass it along to them.

Still, I'd ask someone else what Mireille had been up to on Friday night.

In the meantime, I had to rethink my hypothesis. I'd been concentrating on doctors, but anyone could have killed Kurt. Anyone with medical knowledge and access to a paralytic agent. That would include nurses, respiratory technicians, and even a patient with light fingers.

I knew that the narcotics in the emergency room were locked up—the nurses were forever asking each other for the keys—but I wasn't sure if they bothered locking up the paralytics. Even if they did, the killer could make a duplicate of the keys, pick the lock, or happen upon an unlocked cabinet. The OR was also a good source. They were always intubating and anaesthetizing people. On obstetrics, the patients were usually awake for C-sections, but if they needed to move to general anaesthetic, the anaesthetist would have the succ on hand. Vicki was still a possibility.

I sighed. No wonder we needed the cops. The net was just too huge.

Still, it wouldn't hurt for me to ask around. I had a brief fantasy: YOUNG DOCTOR SOLVES MD MURDER CASE. My picture in the papers, broadcast on TV, lighting up the Net. Alex would have to kiss more than my feet.

No. This had nothing to do with Alex. Really.

Tori said abruptly, "I worry about you."

I turned to her. "Why?"

"You're too innocent."

I laughed. I haven't felt innocent since I was, oh, a preteen. "I'm fine."

She shook her head and went back to staring across the aisle.

"Really," I insisted. "I know the facts of life."

She shook her head again without meeting my gaze.

The train pulled up to a stop and a crew of guys spilled on, talking in French and punching each other on the shoulder, followed by a silent couple that brushed by us. They looked like they were in their 20's, but the guy was wearing khakis with a knife-like crease down the front.

He jerked his chin downward at me in greeting.

I blinked. Did I know him?

His blue, pop-eyes met mine and clued me in. It was the tie guy. Robin Huxley. You know how some people, you feel like saying their whole name instead of just their first name, like Charlie Brown?

That was Robin Huxley.

I don't know why he bothered me so much—I'd met other geeks and keeners before; medicine was littered with their bodies clutching journal articles and flashing the latest studies on their iPhones—but he did.

The pale woman now sitting beside him glanced at me, a quick, startled glance before her gaze returned to the subway floor.

I checked out her way her shoulders seemed to huddle against him. She was wearing a non-descript, black shirt and white, knee-length shorts that made her look hippy. He glanced down at her, a swift frown before he put his arm around her. He glanced at Tori, who'd plugged earphones in her ears and closed her eyes, and pulled out his iPhone and started clicking with his thumb.

I nudged Tori with my foot. "It's like a McGill reunion in here."

She glanced up at me and turned down her music. "Sorry?"

"Check it out. Robin Huxley."

She turned to look at them. She waved at him and nodded at the woman.

"I didn't know he had a girlfriend." I'd never really pondered Robin, but I would have pegged him as asexual, or maybe gay. I realized I was always dissing the guy, and tried to think nice-girl thoughts instead. He was pale. That meant he avoided the sun. That was a wise thing to do. In general, he was probably two hundred times as smart as me. He could probably power cities with his cerebellum alone.

"It's his wife," said Tori.

I blinked. "Really? He doesn't wear a ring." I glanced at them, double-checking his naked left hand to be sure. Then I remembered Mireille mentioning he was married. I guess I'd forgotten because it didn't fit my "Ee er I am robot" stereotype of him.

Tori shrugged. I noticed the wife—I didn't even know her name—was wearing a teeny diamond. That reminded me of my mother, who always complained that she and my dad got married too young and all she got was a microscopic diamond. Of course he worked his ass off and bought her a full carat later, but ohhhhh, we always hear about the sacrifices she made.

The train speaker blathered the next stop name almost incomprehensibly. Robin stood up, allowing his wife to go first. Normally, I liked the courtliness of the gesture, but he held himself so rigidly, like it was his duty and he had to carry it out despite the stick rammed up his bum.

I shook myself. Give the guy a break.

He put his hand on her shoulder and nodded coolly at Tori.

She waved and murmured, "See you tomorrow." They must rotate at the Children's together.

His blue bug eyes rested on me next. I tried to smile at him, but it felt fake, so I looked at his wife. She ducked her head and nodded back, but had to grab the pole to balance as the subway screeched a halt. Then the door opened and she kind of had to bob and weave as the people on the platform tried to get on without letting the train people off first.

For the second time, I remembered Toronto's subway, where the people on the platform wait for the train people to disembark.

But, like Alex said, I wasn't in Kansas anymore. Or London, for that matter.

Alex.

The doors whooshed closed behind the odd couple and I thought, Maybe I'm just jealous. Of Mireille. Even of Robin because, antisocial nerd that he is, he found someone to love him, or at least love his future income.

Tori pulled the earphones out of her ears and wound the cord neatly around her MP3 player, so I tried to chat, but not about alibis. "How do you like the Children's?"

"It's good. I'm doing the outpatient clinics, the PCC. Stan calls it the Pediatric Constipation Clinic." She smiled.

I didn't. I don't like poo. "Is it the constipation clinic?"

"Kind of. But the kids are cute. Like I said, the only downside is that you have to do a lot of emerg call where you work all weekend. Next weekend, I do all day Saturday, all day Sunday, and then back again for Monday to Friday."

"What a drag." If you work seven days in a row, and then work another five days in a row, plus evening call, the days turn into a blur.

"Yeah. But I like kids." Her face lit up just thinking about them.

I'm not crazy about peds. The kids are sometimes cute, but often they're screaming or have snot smeared over their faces. And I like the kids better than the parents, who are all like, "Little Aidan has a cough, and I'm sooooo worried about him!" and won't believe you when you tell them he has a cold. Still, after the geriatric clinic at St. Joseph's, I missed the kids more than I thought I would.

At Snowdon, we jumped on to the platform. The train pulled away, stirring our hair and echoing throughout the station. Tori waited until the noise died down before she spoke. "This is my stop. Do you feel safe walking home from your stop?"

"Yeah." I frowned. "Shouldn't I?" I didn't want another lecture about how unsafe my neighbourhood was. I made it the last time.

Tori nodded. "I feel safe walking almost anywhere in Montreal. But there's always a taxi at the metro, if you're worried."

I shook my head. She accompanied me partway to the St-Michel platform. "Thanks for coming out with me."

She looked at me, unsmiling. "Yeah." Then she turned away. No farewell Montreal kiss.

I sighed. I felt like I was doing everything wrong here. Mireille seemed ready to squish me. Alex couldn't make up his mind if he wanted to seduce me or set me up as his fellow detective. And Tori said very little but seemed to see everything.

There's a joke in medicine, something like, "Internists know everything but do nothing. Surgeons know nothing but do everything. Pathologists know everything and do something, but it's always too late." Tori was an internist. Alex, sad to say, was probably a surgeon. I was...NYD.

But who cared. A blue train lurked at the station. I dashed into the end car. It was practically empty, except for a rotund black woman who leaned her head against the glass.

Now that Tori had left, withdrawing her not-so-silent disapproval, I hugged the memory of Alex to myself, starting with his surprisingly gentle touch. The way he washed and dried my hair. How well we fit together when we danced. The way he looked at me, like I was the only woman in the universe. His smell. His lean chest. The light in his eyes when he let me look at him shirtless.

The memories made me clench my teeth. I wanted him bad.

Now my brain kicked in. Rebound guys are bad news. Hell, even without Mireille, Alex was bad news. Caution. Do not enter. I didn't need Tori or my mother to tell me that.

But Alex and Mireille broke up in December. Half a year ago! He had to be mostly over her. I could be the final step, the shot in the arm.

I pressed my knee against the cool, corrugated metal side of the train wall like I was trying to tattoo its irregular pattern on to my skin. But really, I was trying to forget about Alex.

I couldn't.

CHAPTER 13

In the emerg the next day, I was too busy to brood about the boy. Anu showed up in her white coat. She rolled her eyes and fanned her three geriatrics consults at me. "That's the problem with geri at St. Joe's. There are too many patients!"

"Yeah, sorry," I said, since two of them were ones I'd referred to her. But Dr. Wiedermeyer had pointed out, "If they can't walk, they can't go home. Any elderly patient with no pressing medical issues, or with multidisciplinary problems, goes to geri."

I tugged at the sleeve of my white coat that I didn't normally wear. I whispered to Anu, "This is so I'll get more respect from patients."

She laughed and held out her hands toward me in a grand gesture that showed off her own white coat. Mine had a worn iron-on transfer for St. Joe's above the front pocket, but hers had McGill embroidered in black and red thread. Hers looked more expensive. Anu said, "I think it helps. But they still ask me how old I am!"

One of the R2's had told me she now wore pantyhose on internal medicine and the patients had stopped asking her age. So, in addition to my white coat, I had abandoned my greens and was wearing a fitted, ultramarine blouse and white, pleated skirt which fell about mid-thigh. I drew the line at the pantyhose, since it was July, and St. Joseph's didn't seem to have any functional air conditioning. I usually saved this skirt for going out, but the female doctors in Montreal wore sexier clothes than I was used to. I figured the skirt was legit, especially under my white coat, but kept the coat partially buttoned, just in case.

Anu grabbed the chart for bed number 11, and said hello to Tucker, who was further down the counter, in the psych corner. He grinned at us. "Hello, ladies." He stood up and moved closer to me. He'd cut his hair into a flat top, with the gelled ends sticking up.

"Hi," I said, trying not to stare at the tips of his blond hair. They reminded me of a stiff field of wheat. Maybe wheat after it had been attacked by freezing rain.

"You like my hair?" His hand rose up toward the back of his head.

I recognized the self-consciousness of the gesture. "Kickin'."

He smiled. "Yeah?"

I had to smile back. "Yeah." I'd seen him around a fair amount, working on the psych patients, but we hadn't really talked.

He rested his elbows on the white block in the middle of the nursing station. It was like a rotating shelf for forms, a paperwork lazy-Susan. "Can you tell me anything about the guy in 14?"

I shook my head. "Not my patient. Sorry." He seemed to want more, so I added, "The psych nurse probably knows all about him, though."

"Yeah." He didn't take his elbows off the shelf-thing.

I glanced around. I didn't see Dr. Wiedermeyer, but I didn't want him to think I spent all my time chatting with my friends instead of working. Competition was pretty fierce for the emerg year. I pointed to the clipboard in my hand. "Well, I guess I'd better go see this patient."

"Yeah." His hand strayed to his hair. Then he remembered that he didn't have much to flip any more, and his hand crept back down to the shelf thing. "You want to go to lunch?"

Sometimes residents eat together in our lounge, or, more rarely, in the cafeteria, but Tucker was frowning at me now, and pressing his palms against the shelf.

It percolated through. The dude was uncomfortable. He was asking me out.

Maybe I should lay off the miniskirts. "Sorry. It's a zoo in here." I gestured at the charts of waiting patients. On the acute side, the nurses lined the charts on one counter, against the Plexiglas. The red plastic cards jammed under the clip on the clipboard denoted the order they were to be seen. There were two charts. Not exactly a zoo, but a good enough excuse. "I probably won't be going for a while."

"It's okay." He coughed into his hand. "I'm on psych. I can go any time." He glanced around. A blush crept up under his collar. The unit coordinator, a middle-aged woman with a spiky 'do and an eyebrow piercing, was giving him the evil eye.

The guy needed a break. Alex who? "Okay," I said, and smiled at Tucker.

He smiled back. He wasn't bad-looking. Just a player, and not my type. "Here's my pager number." He grabbed a progress note sheet to scribble on.

"Wait!" I grabbed my navy notebook and flipped it open in front of him.

He gave a low whistle. "Am I in your little black book now?"

The unit coordinator was giving me the evil eye now. I glowered at him. "That's my medical notes book. I'm just trying to save paper. Those progress notes—oh, forget it." The progress notes he'd reached for were printed on carbon paper, so he'd be wasting two sheets instead of one. But I should have let him kill a tree and save me the embarrassment.

"Whatever you say," he sang out, and scratched his numbers down with his left hand. Ink smeared along the side of his hand. "Here's my home one, too. What's yours?"

I flipped to the back of my notebook and ripped a page out, writing as fast as possible. "I can't promise anything. Maybe I can go in an hour."

His brown eyes were laughing at me. "Dr. Wie is cool. Just tell him you're going to lunch, and he'll run the show."

Actually, what happened was that ten minutes later, Dr. Wie, a portly, balding man, emerged from room 3, stripped off his yellow isolation gown and gloves, and said, "I'm going to grab a sandwich. Do you want anything?"

"I'm all right, thanks. I'll keep seeing patients, and then I'll go to lunch after."

"Great. I'll be just a minute." He bustled off.

I walked to stretcher number 5, a thin, 26 year-old brunette, with chest pain. She watched me approach. I held the chart up like a shield. "Ms. Gravelle? Hi, I'm Dr. Sze. I'm the res—"

She waved off my intro, clutching at her chest through the gown. "I was working at the computer, and I got this sharp pain, so sharp, I was almost crying. My friend called 911."

A sharp pain. Atypical. Plus she was 26. I opened my mouth to ask more details about the pain, when, from behind me, a man called, "Carla? Carla?" The patient looked over my shoulder and her face crumpled. "Eric! I was so scared!"

A middle-aged guy came around the other side of the stretcher and grabbed her hand. "I'm here, baby. It's okay. Everything's going to be okay."

She started to weep into the shoulder of his dress shirt. Her free hand still clenched the front of her gown.

"Are you having pain now, ma'am?" I asked.

Her significant other gave me an odd look. "Are you a nurse?"

"No." The white coat and grown-up clothes weren't working. "I'm Dr. Sze." I pointed to my badge. The guy read it with critical frown, as if he was trying to detect a forgery.

The woman wiped her eyes. "I thought you were a nurse."

"No. I'm a resident doctor. I started to introduce myself—"

"I didn't hear you." She started crying some more, clinging to her man.

Obviously, this was going to take a while. I wanted to tell Tucker I had business for him after all.

Eventually, I got a history and did a physical exam. When I pressed on her chest to see if the pain was reproducible, as Dr. Dupuis had shown me to do, she screamed, "Eric, she's hurting me!"

The man whirled on me. "What are you doing to my wife?"

I backed right off. "Nothing. I'm finished." In more ways than one. Dr. Wiedermeyer could deal with the two of them. They'd be happier with a staff physician, and he probably knew how to handle them. Win-win. I carried the chart back to the nursing station and checked my watch. With all the drama, my H&P had taken forty minutes.

Dr. Wie was already writing up a new patient while ignoring the half-eaten egg sandwich and cup of coffee resting beside his left hand. I felt embarrassed. He'd gone to the cafeteria, started eating, seen a patient, and was writing him or her up, while all I'd managed to do was antagonize Tweedledum and Tweedledee in 5. I couldn't wait to get to be like him when I grew up.

Dr. Wie smiled at me. "I'm glad you're here. Maybe now I can eat!" He pulled the cellophane further down his sandwich and took a hearty bite.

While I presented the case, my pager went off. I glanced at the number and silenced the pager. Tucker could wait.

"Oh, answer it," said Dr. Wie, bolting down some coffee.

"No, it's okay."

Dr. Wie laughed. "I'm not going anywhere."

Reluctantly, I dialed, hunching over the black receiver. It seemed so unprofessional to talk about lunch while I was in the emergency room. As soon as he picked up and said hello, I hissed, "Tucker, I'll call you in a bit."

There was a silence. "Tucker? Why are you calling him?"

It took me a second to figure it out. The voice had been slightly more of a tenor than a baritone. "Alex?" My eyes slid to Dr. Wiedermeyer, who was now talking to a nurse. "Can I talk to you later?"

"I guess," Alex said. "After you call Tucker, right?"

Gah. "Goodbye, Alex." I hung up, rubbed my forehead, and smiled at Dr. Wie to cover my embarrassment.

He grinned back at me. "Man trouble?"

I wished ten more nurses had come up to talk to him during my phone call. I shook my head. "Oh, no." I pointed to the #5 clipboard. "Patient trouble."

"She does sound like a difficult personality. The husband too. Start with the physical exam."

It was so nice to have a doctor treat me like a person instead of a cyborg in training. Dr. W. must have been in his forties, plump, and with only a fringe of hair at the back of his head, and while I've never been one to go for older men, it was very pleasant to have him listen to me as if I had something intelligent to say. That must have been part of Kurt's attraction.

In the end, we agreed the patient was probably non-cardiac, but that we'd do two sets of trops on her, just in case.

"Now," Dr. Wie, said, eyes twinkling, "It's your turn for lunch. Take your time."

"If we're busy, I don't mind—"

He waved me away. "I'll handle it. Take your time."

He meant it. Truly a nice man. Still, if the staff's a jerk, you can't leave them alone too long for fear of reprisal. If the staff's nice, like Dr. Wie, you won't leave 'em alone too long because you want to help them. Plus I was having second thoughts about Tucker. I didn't want to string him along if I had a chance with Alex.

To avoid any other curious ears, I went up to the residents' lounge to phone Tucker. As soon as I opened the door, I saw his blond hair bent over the computer. He twisted around and smiled at me. His teeth were perfectly straight. Must have had braces as a kid, same as me. "Hey! Ready to go?"

"Just a sec. I have to answer a page." I debated popping down the hall to the library to call Alex, but figured I was being silly. It wasn't like these guys would fight a duel over me or anything. I eased around Tucker to grab the phone mounted on the wall in the corner behind him.

He leaned out of the way, grinning.

I cupped my hand around the receiver in an attempt to muffle my voice. Tucker raised his eyebrows but still wouldn't move his chair.

A mature woman answered. I asked if I could speak to Dr. Dyck and promptly blushed. Alex got the worst name prize on that one.

"The resident? He's gone now. You want to page him?"

"No, thanks." At least this way, I'd tried. "When he comes back, can you tell him that Dr. Hope Sze called?"

"Of course, dear."

I hung up and I smiled at Tucker. "Ready."

He turned his back on me. "Let me log out."

I took two giant steps out of the corner. I didn't feel comfortable standing so close to him in a short skirt, even before his vibe changed. I checked my watch. It was 12:10.

Tucker closed his browser and stood up, frowning at me. "Why do you bother with him?"

"Who, Alex?"

"Yeah." He shook his head.

I shrugged. It was so none of his business. And even I didn't know why I bothered with him.

He exhaled. "Fine. Where do you want to go?"

I liked a guy who knew when to fold 'em. I smiled at him. "You know Montreal better than me. But I can't be away too long. Emerg and all. It's not like psych."

He smiled, stretched his arms out, and sighed like he was ready for a piña colada on the beach. "Hey, this is the life. When are you doing psych?"

"Next." I made a face.

He rolled his eyes. "You're hard core! What, you'd rather do ICU next?"

"Well..."

Tucker laughed.

"Well, almost," I admitted. I hung my white coat up on a hook.

When I turned back, his eyes flickered from my legs back up to my face, but mostly he was still laughing. "I'm going to call you hard core from now on."

"Thanks a lot!"

"Nah. You can say thanks after lunch. You're going to love it." He took a few long strides to the door and opened it for me. "Are you vegetarian?"

I shook my head. "I'd like to be."

"Put it off for one more day." He waved me through the door. "Do you like sausages?"

That must be the funniest question anyone's ever asked me on a quasi-date. I laughed, he joined in, and I said, "Sure. Let's try it."

We walked along Péloquin until we reached the corner of Côte-des-Neiges and crossed the road to a little restaurant called Chez Better. I raised my eyebrows, but Tucker said, "No scoffing until you taste the food."

He pulled the chair out for me on the little *térrasse* made of red paving stone. I sat and made sure my skirt fanned out to cover everything.

Tucker pulled up his own white plastic chair, while I belatedly remembered I hadn't applied sunscreen this morning. I like sun, but not wrinkles or skin cancer. I tilted my head under the shadow of the forest green table umbrella.

A white guy in a white shirt and apron, with pinchably rosy cheeks, turned up our glasses and poured us some water. He left the pitcher on the table along with some menus. Tucker moved his chair closer to mine to recommend a tasting platter of three sausages.

I didn't move away. I liked the crisp lines of his white shirt and the angle of his cheek. Coincidentally, both of us had dressed up that morning. I also could smell earth and the pansies in the window boxes, traces of beer, and a tangy, masculine smell from Tucker. It was not unpleasant.

Tucker greeted the server in German, causing him to light up and chat back.

Tucker spoke slowly, with what sounded like a rudimentary vocabulary, but at least ten times what I could say. Also better than Alex's *auf wiedersehen*. The waiter ended up calling out to the chef as he walked in the restaurant to place our order. Maybe we'd get free dessert out of it, or at least sausages cooked with extra TLC.

I smiled at him. "I didn't know you spoke German. Is that your background?"

"Nah." He was blushing. "I took it in high school. But I try to practice if I come here, or if I see any German patients, and they appreciate it."

Interesting. I gave him a second look. Why had he annoyed me so at first? I didn't like his pick-up lines. But maybe he just wasn't good at delivering them. He was probably a decent guy. And not bad-looking, with a long, straight nose, enviably long eyelashes, and a sexy bow to his upper lip. We were sitting close enough that I could see the stubble on his cheek. It was yellow blond, darker than the hair on his head, but it still made him a natural towhead.

He said, "I learned a little Japanese in high school, too. I went on a student exchange."

"Really." I was impressed. "How was that?"

"Great. But I don't remember any Japanese except 'Where is the bathroom?'"

I laughed. "Well, that's important!"

"I must have thought so." He grinned back. "In an ideal world, I'd like to be able to order in the native language whenever I go to a restaurant."

"Yeah." I leaned back in my chair. The plastic rebounded gently against my weight. "I never thought of that. You should do it."

He pursed his lips. "Well, it's a lot of work. We should tag team. I could take German, you could take Lebanese—"

"Are you going to stick me with all the hard ones? Finnish, Urdu..."

He waggled his eyebrows. "You've caught on to my cunning plan."

I laughed. "We could make Tori do Finnish."

"Yeah." He frowned a little, probably because I'd brought in an extra wheel.

I pretended not to notice. I didn't want Tucker to make plans with me, even as a joke. He was a nice guy, but I already had Alex, unless he'd changed his mind after I called him Tucker. I sighed inwardly. Be careful what you wish for, especially if you wish it would rain men. I decided to change the subject. "So what do you think about Kurt?"

He took a sip of water. "It sucks."

I blinked. Hello, nutshell.

He half-laughed at my expression. "Sorry. But that's what it all boils down to. He was a great guy, a great teacher, way too young. And he would have hated what the tabloids are doing with it."

I shook my head. "What are you talking about?"

"Did you see the Gazette this morning?"

"No." I barely got my butt out of bed this morning.

"You should take a look at it. The lead is about how he was murdered. But they made insinuations about our poor security, how dangerous the city has become if you can't even be safe in a hospital, the police aren't doing enough, blah, blah, blah. But it's a huge slap in the face for St. Joe's." He ran his hand over his gelled hair. "It just roasts me, because it's the last thing Kurt would have wanted, you know?"

"I know." If I'd learned nothing else about the guy, I knew he loved this hospital. I glanced back along Péloquin, but the building was too far away and shrouded in trees.

His hands laced around his small glass of water. "Now that the Gazette has started, *La Presse* will, too. You'll see. You'd think his death would be enough, but no. They have to jack it up."

"That does suck," was all I could think to say.

"Yeah." He gave me a small smile.

I unfolded the paper napkin and laid my knife and fork on it. Tucker watched my hands. At last, I cleared my throat. "So who do you think did it?"

He caught my eye and burst out laughing. "That's what I like about you. You don't mess around."

I laughed, too. It was true.

He leaned closer and lowered his voice. He had lovely brown eyes with black specks in the irises, an unusual combination with his blond hair. "We've all been thinking about it. It could have been anyone, but my money's on Bob Clarkson."

Abruptly, I remembered hiding under Dr. Callendar's desk. If the FMC head honcho hadn't called, Dr. Callendar would've had me for dinner. But come on. Bob Clarkson? "Why?"

He was watching me, his head tilted slightly to one side. "Jealousy. Bob always wants to be top dog, and he was in theory, but Kurt ran the show. We all knew it."

I tried to play the devil's advocate. "It makes no sense, politically. If Bob ever got caught, his career would be over. You can't run St. Joe's from jail."

"Or from heaven," Tucker muttered. He poured some more water for himself. "You want some?"

I bolted down my glass and held it out.

He poured some for me before he refilled his own. "It wouldn't be for politics. It would be out of jealousy. He'd never expect to get caught. No one ever does."

I shook my head. "I just don't see it. It's against everything we stand for. *'First, do no harm.'*"

He just looked at me. "Yeah. And how many doctors live up to that? You know the doctors who're addicted to prescription drugs, or the docs who abuse their patients."

"That's not murder," I insisted. "I've never read about a murder in *Dialogue*. That's the Ontario disciplinary journal," I explained, since he looked confused. "I don't know what the Quebec one is called. But have you read about any murders in it?"

He shook his head. "Still."

"No. It's a whole other boundary. I mean, yes, we stop treatment all the time." I remembered this one poor kid with leukemia, and had to shake my head before I continued. "But you don't see doctors running around with machetes. I know we're not perfect, Tucker, but most of us do believe in the sanctity of human life. That's how we got into the game."

Before Tucker could reply, out of the corner of my eye, I saw a ceramic plate bearing over my shoulder. "Thank you," I said to the server. It smelled delicious.

Tucker said, "*Danke schön*," and I mentally kicked myself. I could have figured that one out.

Tucker's eyes crinkled like he knew what I was thinking. "*Bon appétit.*"

"*Bon appétit.*" I like how Montrealers often say this before eating. It's not a prayer, but still a sort of benediction.

I cut into the Balkan sausage first, trying not to wince at the grease squeezing on to my plate. "Hey, this is good!" It actually wasn't as greasy as I'd expected, and had a strong, meaty flavor which went well with the slightly bitter sauerkraut.

Tucker pumped his hand in the air. "Yes! I knew you'd like it."

I laughed, but part of me thought it was strange. I'd hardly spoken two words to the guy. How would he know if I liked sausages or not?

Why had he asked me out, anyway? It was flattering, but I wasn't such a prize that men had bowled each other over for my number in London.

Could his interest have something to do with Kurt's murder?

No. That was paranoid. Tucker had respected Kurt and had no apparent motive. On the other hand, no one had a motive except Mireille.

Okay. Forget the motive. I had to think about the means. I tasted some rice. Not as much flavor, but it helped dampen the *diable*, the hot Italian sausage. "So what were you up to, over the weekend?"

He smiled wryly. "You mean, what was I doing on Friday night?"

Darn. This was me at my most subtle. "Well, sure."

He shook his head. "You don't remember? I ran into you downtown. Tori and Anu will vouch for me."

"That's right!" I'd been so distracted by Alex, I'd forgotten all about it.

His gaze was knowing. "What were *you* doing Friday night?

"Uh, well, I was downtown. I had some sushi."

"Alone?"

I didn't meet his eyes. I knew what he was driving at. It was the same thing that had been nagging at the back of my head since Alex's disappearance and Dr. Kurt's reappearance in the change room. I said, to my barely-sampled sausages, "It doesn't mean anything. When we found Kurt, he'd been dead for hours. It could have happened at 2 a.m. I bet Tori and Anu can't vouch for you then, right?"

"A lot better than anyone can for Alex, though. Am I right?"

Silence. I nodded with my eyes on the sausages.

"Look. Hope." His hand reached for mine, but I shifted them into my lap. "Fine," he said. "I'm not trying to tear Alex down because he's the competition. I don't think he killed anyone."

My eyes flew up to his. "You don't?"

He chuckled and shook his head. "Nah. I've known the guy for four years. He's not my favourite, but he's okay." He looked straight into my eyes. "It doesn't mean I like how he treats women."

I flicked my wrist. "Except for that time on Friday, he's been pretty good."

His brown eyes never wavered. "You deserve better."

Okay. I knew what he was saying. "I'm flattered."

"But?" He raised an eyebrow.

"I hear you. You may well be right. But it's just where I am right now. I'm willing to give Alex a chance."

"Even though he disappeared on you the night Kurt got murdered?"

I pleated my napkin against the table, sharpening the crease with my fingernail. "You said yourself you don't think he did it."

"He still ditched you."

I winced. I'd said the same thing to myself, but it sounded worse aloud. "Yeah. You're right."

The corner of his mouth twisted. "You're still going with the bastard?"

I couldn't explain it beyond *le coeur a ses raisons que la raison ne connait point*. But that was so pathetic. Not rational, not practical, not survival-oriented. I gave him a sad smile. "I'll ask him more about Friday. I was going to, anyway."

He gave me a long look. "I could say a lot more."

My shoulders tightened. "I know."

"Like, why do women do this to themselves? Why do *you* do this to yourself?" He set his fork down hard on the table.

I pointed the tines of my fork at him. "Hey. I am not a type."

"Women and bad boys. They beat you and you beg for more."

I glared at him. "I am not a masochist! I've only ever been with one guy, and he treated me fine."

Tucker raised his eyebrows. "Why did you break up?"

I waved my fork in the air. "Long story. Basically, long distance. But we loved each other. We did not cheat. He did not beat me. We were together for four years. I bet you haven't seen anyone for half as long."

He made a face. "Okay. Sorry. You're right about that. The longest I've gone is a year and a half. I'm no one to point a finger—or a fork."

We both stared at my fork jabbing toward his forehead. I laid it on the table. "Sorry."

He laughed. "I'm sorry, too. Not for the fork."

I gave him a crooked smile. "So are we okay?"

He picked up the fork and handed it back to me, handle first. "Eat your sausages. You're going to need your strength."

I pretended he meant for emerg. I checked my watch. The past half hour had galloped by. I positively attacked my sausages and polished them off, along with most of the sauerkraut and the rice. When I wiped my mouth, Tucker was shaking his head. "Eat and run, huh?"

I shrugged. "I'm on emerg. Sorry."

"Dr. Wie doesn't mind. He always gives us a lunch break."

"Yeah, but I don't want to leave him alone too long." I threw my napkin on the table.

Tucker started cutting his sausage. He'd already polished off his chicken schnitzel. "Do you have time for coffee?"

"Maybe some iced tea," I conceded. I glanced across the street. A pedestrian had stopped dead on Péloquin, scowling at us from under his shaggy brown hair, his body curved in a question mark.

Alex. Jumping to all the wrong conclusions, after I had so carefully told Tucker thanks but no thanks.

Tucker had his mouth full, but he twisted in his seat to follow my gaze.

Alex bared his teeth at him, shot double daggers at me, and turned on his heel, stalking back to St. Joe's. He barely detoured around a little old lady with her walker. His head was bent low. He hardly seemed to see where he was going.

I didn't call out to him. He still owed me an explanation for Friday night. So I picked up my napkin and smoothed it in my lap, forcing a smile at Tucker. "So. Iced tea."

In the shade of the umbrella, Tucker's eyes were unreadable. He repeated obliquely, "You're going to need it" and signaled the waiter.

Chapter 14

I paged Alex twice more that afternoon. He never answered, and don't tell me it was because palliative care was so pressing. Well, screw it. I'd come here man-free, and less than a week later, I'd blown it with two of them. Fine. There were still many more guys in the city, although at this rate, I'd run through all of them during my two years of residency.

When I asked Dr. Wiedermeyer to fill out my evaluation form, he said, "With pleasure. I hope we work together again."

Great. Especially after I'd dared go out for lunch instead of bolting down some leftovers in the fridge. I smiled with relief as I sailed out of the emerg. Career 1, boys 0. I could live with that a little longer.

Alex's radio silence made me less likely to blast him about Friday. Maybe that was the point. I shook my head. He was an enigma-and-a-half.

At any rate, I was glad I'd carted my bike up from London. I felt like pedaling away the stress. I'd pumped up the tires last night and ridden it in this morning, shaving ten minutes off my commute. If I broke it out again, I might even make it on time to my next family medicine clinic.

The wind fluttered the poplar branches hanging over the bike racks near the ER. I took a deep breath, relaxing to the rustling leaves. It was one of the classic sounds of summer, along with the burr of the lawn mower and the sounds of kids splashing in a pool. My keys jangled as I bent over to unlock my bike, my back to the hospital.

I caught a whiff of smoke. Patients are supposed to smoke a certain number of feet away from the entrance, but it just moves them closer to my bike rack. Irritated, my keys missed the lock and jangled on to the ground. As I bent over to pick them up, a low voice behind me said, "So."

I whirled around. Alex was leaning against the trunk of a poplar tree, half-shrouded by the canopy of leaves. He tilted his head to meet my eyes and took a drag off his cigarette.

"You scared me," I said, my hand pressed against my chest hard enough to feel my heart thumping.

Alex flicked some ash. "Yeah."

My annoyance mounted. I wanted to jostle him out of his Camel ad complacency. I scooped up my keys and faced him with my hands on my hips. "You were waiting for me?"

He shrugged.

"Or is this just a good place to smoke, where you might light the tree on fire?"

That drew a laugh out of him. "I'm not going to set your tree on fire."

"Good. Then maybe you're here to explain where you went on Friday."

He faded back against the trunk with a mutinous expression. "I told you."

"You didn't tell me a hell of a lot."

"What, I have to confess my life story before I can say hello?"

"Yeah. That and answering my pages might be nice."

His grey eyes blazed. "After your nice, long lunch? Which one of us are you going to string along, Hope? Or are you just going to hop from me to Tucker and back again?"

I wanted to slap him, but refused to let him see how much he'd gotten to me. I picked out my bike key and opened the U-lock, reassembling it on my bike. Then I looked him straight in the eye. "You know what, Alex? If you're not going to explain yourself, neither am I. Have a nice life." I tossed my head and started backing my bike out of the rack.

He walked over to my right, cutting me off. "Hope."

I started to wheel the bike around him. He blocked it again. "Hope. I'm sorry."

I stared at him. "Alex, it's getting tired. You can't just screw me around and apologize afterward."

His expression darkened. "Look. I know I'm not perfect, but I'm not the one screwing around."

If he expected me to faint over that, he was sadly mistaken. "Yeah. It's a real crime of passion to eat sausages with one of our classmates in broad daylight. So sue me. And get out of my *way*." I aimed my front tire at his shins.

He didn't move. I stopped short. "What do you want from me, Alex? You want me to be your pet because we shared a rum ball? It doesn't work that way. You have to earn me. Insulting me, not answering my pages, accusing me of running around when I was just having lunch—" I bit my tongue. I wanted to say, no wonder Mireille left you, but that was low. I shook my head. "I'm starting to think you're not worth the trouble."

He studied me for a long moment. "Earn you, huh?"

I nodded firmly, even though I was trembling inside. The grass rustled as he planted his feet on either side of my front wheel and placed his hands on my handlebars. I avoided his eyes, staring at the muscles in his arms, his tanned hands on either side of my own, so close that I could feel the heat from his skin.

He bent forward and whispered, his lips grazing my ear, "Leave the bike. You're coming with me."

My hands tightened on the plastic handles. He still hadn't answered me about Friday night. But he was so sexy, he made me want to straddle my bike and promise him whatever he wanted. I closed my eyes.

He flicked my earlobe with his tongue. "Come on, Hope. Let me"—he explored the tender skin behind my ear—"earn you."

My fingers tightened on the handles and relaxed again. He tugged my key chain off my index finger. The keys rattled as I let them go.

My eyes flew open. "Alex—"

He ran his fingers lightly up my arm, making the hairs stand on end. I shivered. He glanced at my chest and grinned. I crossed my arms over my nipples. He grinned some more and tugged the bike away to lock it up again.

I watched him lean over. His baggy cargo pants did not do justice to his butt.

When he straightened, he gave me a crooked grin like he'd read my thoughts. He came closer and ran his fingers along the inside of my arm. I swallowed hard.

I cast a nervous glance toward my bike. Even with his magnetic pull, I'd heard that there was a lot of bike theft in Montreal.

"It's all locked up," he whispered. His breath was hot and damp on my neck. "Want to check?"

Everything was sexual with him. I leaned over and gave the lock a quick tug. "Good job."

He grinned at me. "I like that skirt."

Blood rushed to my face as I surreptitiously made sure my white miniskirt was in place.

We should not be doing this. Over his shoulder, I spotted the faces of two middle-aged women on a bench under some neighboring trees. Their bench faced the parking circle, but they had turned around to gape at us. Alex hadn't even kissed me on the lips, but he'd broadcasted his intentions load and clear. All we needed was for Dr. Callendar to run up at us, brandishing a crucifix and a Bible. I took a step back from Alex.

Unexpectedly, he reached up to my shoulder. "Give me your backpack."

I backed away some more. "But I need—"

"Relax. I just want to carry it for you. And look at you." He grinned, his eyes crinkling.

"Then you'll have two." His own army surplus bag was slung over his left shoulder.

He shrugged and slipped mine on his right shoulder. "No problem."

I did feel liberated without my backpack, but also more naked. Alex urged me on to the subway station, occasionally dropping behind me to squeeze through the sidewalk crowds, but when I glanced at him, he was checking me out. He raised his grey eyes to meet mine, unashamed.

Urban foreplay. Somehow, he knew exactly how to make me hot.

We headed into the damp coolness of the metro, down the escalator, past the woman selling day-old flowers and the *dépanneur* stand. I started to reach for my backpack, to grab my tickets, but Alex waved me off. "I'll take care of it."

He dug out his wallet and dropped two tickets in the fare box. He said, "Go on." As I pushed through the turnstile, he grabbed my ass in a quick squeeze.

I whirled on him. Ryan had never grabbed me in public. My white miniskirt inspired a lot of illegal moves. "Don't do that."

"Hey, I paid your fare." He waggled his eyebrows at me.

I scowled. What, he thought he could buy me with a two-dollar ticket? There was a line-up behind him, so I stormed toward the stairs. Alex reappeared at my shoulder. I snapped at him, "Ryan, that was—"

He went very still. "Who's Ryan?"

Ersh. I was a bucket of surprises today. "No one. Sorry. Must have been a patient."

He went very still. "Don't lie to me."

That was the last straw. I snapped, "Why don't *you* stop lying to *me?*"

"*Excusez, Madame,*" a middle-aged guy, reaching somewhere beyond my midsection for the transfer machine.

Alex pulled me back toward the wall, out of the way of rampaging commuters. He ran his hand through his already- disheveled hair. He said, low and fast, "Look. I fucked up. You fucked up. Can we start over?"

"I did not fuck up!"

He sighed. "Okay. I'm the fuck-up. I left you in the café. I didn't tell you about Mireille."

"Yeah!" I got mad just thinking about it.

"My bad. But—" He leaned closer. His grey eyes filled my vision. I could hear him breathing, even feel his exhalation against my upper lip. We were close enough to kiss. "*You* are fantastic."

"Yeah?" My mouth felt dry.

He pressed so close, our noses nearly bumped. "I could take you right here."

"You could not." But my heart skipped a beat. I glanced at the waves of people rolling by. The black-stained red brick walls. The fluorescent pot lights. The station attendant in his Plexiglas-and-stainless-steel booth. The screech of the trains below us. It would be a very messy and public place,

He bent forward and kissed me, hard and fast, with a possessive thrust of his tongue. I still had my eyes closed when he drew away and said, "But I'll try and wait until we get to my place. If that's how you want it."

I looked into his grey eyes and thought, I want it.

No! I blinked again, rubbing my forehead. Ryan and I waited over two months before we stripped. I hadn't known Alex two weeks.

On the other hand, Alex was very tempting and seemed a lot more experienced. Do not think about Mireille. I pushed her image out of my head, concentrating on Alex, his smell, the line of his cheek, the warmth of his hand lingering on my hip.

Alex smiled, a slow curve of his lips. But all he did was gesture me down the stairs. "After you."

He moved his hand to my shoulder as we descended. Neither of us wanted to break contact now. When we reached the platform, I looked for non-existent space on the few benches along the wall, but Alex kept me moving down the line until the crowd had thinned. Then he stood behind me, wrapping his arms around my waist. The entire length of his body pressed against me, somehow managing to press his hardness against my ass. I shifted, but he moved with me, his hands tightening on my hips.

Code Blues

I glanced around. For once, no one was looking. I relaxed slightly.

He rested his chin on top of my head. I could hear the smile in his voice. "Why did you wear this skirt to work?"

I bypassed the whole looking-older-for-patients conversation. "To drive you crazy."

"It's working." His voice lowered further. "How could you ride a bike in it?"

A pleated skirt falls into place and looks quite maidenly on a bike. It's not like a tight skirt that flips up to show the world your panties. But I just smiled and shrugged. He squeezed me against him, his fingers splaying against my hip bones. His chest rose and fell against my back with his breath. I felt sexy and excited and scared. Like Ralph Waldo Emerson wrote, "Do what you're afraid to do."

Ralph had never met Alex. But right now, the anticipation alone seemed worth the price of admission. I was both sorry and relieved when I spotted the oncoming train's headlights. Most of me wanted to ride the wave and relish every second as he tried to win me. The other part of me was ringing alarm bells and calling 911. But I was tired of sensible Hope. I wanted to get crazy. I wanted to taste danger and lust.

When the train's doors whooshed open, commuters poured out while the rest of us tried to jostle on. Alex snagged a chair for me and stood at my side, his hand resting on my shoulder near where it joined my neck. A few times, he ran a finger under my hair to trace a circle on my nape. I shivered.

We switched to the orange line at Snowdon. This train was even more crowded. We ended up squeezed just inside the door. Alex kept one arm around me and grabbed a pole with the other hand. Two more people squeezed in and Alex drew me closer, his hand sliding down so his thumb rested in my belly button. Illicit but not crossing the line. I slid him a look. He grinned down at me.

As the train hurtled from stop to stop, he nudged the edge of my shirt up. I stiffened. He ran the pad of his thumb along my waist, lightly sketching my skin. I had to consciously school my breathing and press my thighs together. I waited for him to wander up or down, but he didn't. He did run his thumbnail in a quick diagonal stroke under my ribs. I stifled a gasp. He settled his hand back on my waist.

I waited for his next move. He gave me a smile with a wolfish flash of teeth. I swallowed hard.

The recorded voice announced, "*Prôchaine arrêt, Bonaventure.*"

Alex squeezed my hip. "That's us."

I felt almost sick with longing and the smallest dash of trepidation. It made me walk slower than usual. He led me up the metro escalator and pushed open the awkward plate glass door hinged in the middle. We walked up University Avenue, past the train station and the office buildings and the Eaton Centre. I barely registered the teenagers in tight T-shirts and the stop-and-go traffic, but I did notice a few businesswomen were wearing shorter skirts than me. Alex dipped his head to murmur in my ear, "You look better."

I smiled. I knew why I found him irresistible. When he did it right, he made me feel like a goddess.

I paused at the *de Maisonneuve* intersection for a turquoise Geo, but Alex grabbed my hand and yanked me across the street. The Geo zoomed around us, squeezing back into its lane before an oncoming city bus flattened it. "Now, I know you're from Ontario," he yelled in my ear, once we hit the sidewalk, "but here we walk fast and ignore the cars."

I laughed and shook my head. "If you have a death wish."

He squeezed my hand. "No, the death wish is waiting on the sidewalk for them to stop. You'll die of old age before you get to cross."

I laughed some more. As long as we were talking, I wasn't thinking.

He kissed my knuckles and waved at the blue-and-white bus over his shoulder. "We could have taken the bus, but it wouldn't have been as much fun."

I frowned at him, unsure what he meant.

He said, face serious, "The Côte-des-Neiges bus would have gotten us here a lot faster. But I wanted to give you a chance to think about it."

When I least expected it, he turned into a gentleman.

He grinned at me. "And also time for me to feel you up."

I punched him lightly on the shoulder.

He laughed and ran along the inside of my wrist. "We're almost there."

North of Sherbrooke, the streets narrowed and turned residential. Both sides of the roads were lined with cars. Duplexes, mostly gray or yellow stone, were arrayed behind Lilliputian lawns. Nearly every street lamp had been attacked by posters and packing tape. RAVE, DJ MASTER MIX. *À VENDRE*. WEIGHT LOSS—FAST! On the next post, WANTED: ROOMMATE, LARGE 4 1/2. Above that, LOST: FAT CAT. One apartment's window carried a hot pink sticker proclaiming, VAGINAS RULE.

I swiveled my head away. Not that I didn't agree, but Alex would probably say something embarrassing. Still, I felt at home. I hadn't realized it, but I'd missed living in a university neighborhood. Even though my apartment was only minutes away from U of M, my area felt more sober.

Alex slowed in front of a gray duplex with a cobalt metal roof and a weedy, ratty lawn. An old bicycle was chained to a knee-high, black, chain link fence. A blue recycling bin jammed with pizza boxes marked the curb. I stared at it.

Alex smiled. "I missed recycling day. But at least I tried."

I did not miss, or yearn for, disgusting university boys' pads. Ryan was neater than I was.

Alex draped his arm around me. "Really. It's not that bad. I have air conditioning." He pointed at the little unit hanging in the front window, like a little butt sitting on the windowsill.

Well. That was a plus. It wasn't sweltering today, but a little apartment could get stuffy fast.

He smiled at me. "Unless you'd rather I take you in the subway station?"

It jerked a laugh out of me. He tugged my semi-willing feet past the gate and on to the little concrete doorstep. An white plastic "Ad-Sac" was hung around the doorknob. After a quick glance around, he pressed my back against the door and planted his hands on either side of my head. When I opened my mouth to object, he kissed me.

Deeply and urgently, until I felt light-headed and hypnotized by his tongue, trapped between his body and the warm black door.

While one hand cupped my cheek, his other reached into his pocket. Keys jingled. I both heard and felt the vibration of the lock turning. With a final kiss, he twisted the doorknob and slipped his arm around me for support.

Without the pressure of the door, I took a half step back and was startled when the floor suddenly dropped out from under my foot. Alex held me up until I found my footing again. "Sorry," he said against my lips.

Still in his arms, I twisted my head to check out the dim, cramped hallway and took a cautious sniff. It smelled tolerable, like orange peels and pine disinfectant, which partly covered the deeper reek of cigarettes.

Alex kissed me on the lips, and released me enough to flick the on the light switch. A bare bulb snapped on over our heads. The yellow light warmed his skin. I touched his hand shyly. He smiled and took my hand, turning it over to kiss the palm.

I slid off my sandals on to a bristly welcome mat.

"You don't have to," he said.

I shrugged. It was just my upbringing. The hardwood floor didn't feel too gritty under my soles, which was a relief. Alex kicked off his Tevas, released both our bags, and scooped me up in his arms.

"Alex!" I protested as my skirt fanned open. I grabbed it.

"Stop wiggling and put your arms around me."

His eyes were smoky with promise. I closed my own and wrapped my arms around his neck.

He carried me down the hall and nudged a door on the right open with his toes.

I clung tighter to his neck as I scoped out his bedroom. The shades were drawn and the window closed, so it smelled a little sour, but the smoke smell lessened compared to the hallway. The double bed was neatly made, with an orange, plaid blanket and white sheets. There was just enough room for a desk at the foot of the bed, buried in clothes and paper, and a small bedside table with a lamp, an alarm clock, and some spare change. Alex walked up to the white braided rug at the side of the bed and slowly rotated 360 degrees. "Does it meet with your approval?"

I nodded up at him.

"Good." He lowered me onto the bed. The mattress sagged under my weight, but he stepped back.

I sat up, feeling self-conscious and slightly abandoned. Alex walked to the window at the head of the bed and flicked his fingers though the slats of the blind. The air conditioner rumbled to life.

He adjusted the blinds at an angle so we'd get a little more light without losing the privacy. "It'll cool down in a second," he said, sitting next to me.

Still, he'd damaged the mood. I studied the orange plaid sheets and their pattern of red, yellow, and green stripes. It was cheerful, and nothing like my own sober colors, but I had to wonder if he and Mireille had used these sheets.

Ugh. Maybe we should have gone to my place.

"Hey." He cupped my cheek with his hand. "Stop thinking about it."

"What?" I asked automatically.

"Whatever it is. Probably Mireille." There. He said her name. I tried to detect any suppressed emotion, hints of love gone wrong, but his voice was flat. "That's history. I told you."

I said nothing.

He used his index finger to reach under my bangs and trace my forehead, along the hairline. "I should never have violated the eleventh commandment."

His words rang a faint bell. "What's that?"

"Do not bullshit Hope Sze." He kissed my left eyebrow. His lips were soft against my skin.

I was still trying to work out the reference. "Did you read *Love Story*?"

"Yeah. When I was ten. My sister had a copy." He kissed the bridge of my nose.

I'd picked up Erich Segal's book at a used book sale a few years ago. The final scene never failed to jerk tears from my eyes, but I'd never told anyone that. Certainly not Alex. I tried to push the sentiment away. "Good. 'Cause basically, that's what I want. No more B.S. No more abandonment." My lips trembled a little. "Can you do that?"

He looked deep into my eyes. "Yeah. I know you're having trouble trusting me, but I can do that."

I took a deep breath. I so wanted to believe him.

He kissed my cheek. "Mireille was a mistake." He kissed my other cheek. "I wanted to forget about it." He rained kisses down my neck.

I shivered. My neck is extremely sensitive. But I clung to the matter at hand. "You were the one who said we should drink to truth, Alex. Why did you cover it up?"

"Because when I'm around you, Hope—" He ran his lips down the V of my shirt collar, down one side and up the other, with a hint of tongue that made my stomach plummet—"I'd rather—" A firm kiss at the base of my neck—"just—" Light, butterfly kisses a little higher—"fuck your brains out."

I gasped. He covered my breasts with his hands, over my shirt and bra, but his fingers were everywhere, pinching, kneading, squeezing.

"Alex." But my protest died down to a whisper. The air conditioning seemed to have kicked in, all of a sudden. Goose bumps rose on my arms, and I felt hot and cold at the same time. I arched, pressing myself against his hands.

He grabbed the opening my shirt. The first button resisted, so he yanked the fabric with his fists and tore it open. Buttons pinged and skittered across his floor.

"Alex!" I yelled, leaning across the bed and half-raising myself on my elbows to look for buttons. "I like this shirt."

He pushed me down and opened my front-clasp bra. In less than a minute, he'd rendered me half-naked. I moved to cover myself, but he took both my wrists in one hand and held them above my head.

I froze. I'd had fantasies like this, but I didn't know Alex. What if he hurt me?

Alex laid his other hand on my cheek. "It's okay, Hope." His touch was tender and his grey eyes were clear. "I'd never hurt you."

I sighed and relaxed a smidge.

"Unless you want me to." He dropped my wrists and cupped my breasts in both hands. His thumbs began circling my nipples.

I closed my eyes and gave myself to his fingers, his lips, his nimble tongue. His stubble scratched against my skin, lifting a breathless giggle out of me. And then he flipped my skirt up. My flirty white pleated skirt. I lifted my hips, expecting him to undo the button and zipper at the back, but instead he reached under the skirt and slipped off my panties.

"Alex!" My knees clamped together, trapping the fabric. This was too much.

He kissed me deeply, almost hurting me with his lips. He surged forward, his teeth banging against mine, devouring me with his tongue, until my whole world was us, his hungry mouth, his cedar smell, his stubble marking the skin around my mouth.

He broke off the kiss. We were both gasping. He looked at me and said, very low, "Hope."

I looked back at him. My chest was heaving. I couldn't speak.

He said, "Don't think."

It's my nature to think, to analyze, to extract. But I knew he was right. A sigh escaped my lips. My legs parted. He slipped my panties off the rest of the way and tossed them on the floor.

Then he flipped my skirt up and looked at me. A long, slow look that made me raise myself on my elbows again and clamp my legs closed. He stopped me, with a hand on each knee. And then he touched me gently. And not so gently. And bent his head and drank me in.

It felt so good that I swooned. My eyes strayed up to the ceiling and I felt disembodied with pleasure.

But then my brain started working again. This was my first time with a guy in a very long time. Also the first time I'd been with a doctor. Shouldn't we be using dental dams, those unsexy squares of latex that you, uh, stretch over a woman's privates? Did he have a box in his bedside table? Or if we had to, we could use a condom. Cut one open and spread it over me.

Of course, he wasn't likely to catch anything from me. And I wouldn't catch too much from his mouth except—I stiffened. I couldn't enjoy myself unless I knew. "Alex. Do you have cold sores?"

Alex lifted his head from between my legs, a variety of emotions flicking across his face, settling somewhere between anger and amusement. "No, Hope. No HSV 1 or 2. No HIV, tested last month. No hepatitis, immunized against B, also tested last month." He paused, and with exaggerated politeness, added, "And you?"

I swallowed hard. "Negative."

He stayed there, studying my face. I felt very exposed, in more way than one. This was probably the first time a girl had stopped him in mid-act to give a medical history. He probably thought I was a total geek. Plus I was lying here with my breasts exposed, although my skirt had fallen back down a little. He was still fully dressed. I shifted my hips subtly, trying to get my skirt to fall down further.

I'd shattered the mood. If only I could have let it go. But it was a valid point. Who gets off, thinking about herpes? I'd never had a cold sore in my life. I wasn't going to enjoy having them in my nether region. I shifted again.

"Hope," Alex said, at last.

I nodded, unlocked my throat. "Uh-huh."

He didn't move. The air conditioning stirred his hair. His eyes were the darkest grey, almost black. "I told you not to think."

"Sorry." I squeaked a little on the last syllable.

"You will be." Swift as a snake, he grabbed my thighs and flipped me over on to my stomach. I screamed into his blanket, tried to roll back onto my back, but he lay on top of me, pinning me down and grabbing my wrists again.

I raised my head to scream louder. He abandoned my wrists to clap a hand around my mouth. "It's all right, Hope." He kissed my neck.

His lips were gentle. I calmed a little. My pulse still fluttered in my throat.

Holding my wrists at my waist with a single hand, he ran his fingers down each arm, slowly, lightly. Under my sleeves, the hairs on my arms raised up and I trembled. Then he shifted, kneeling on my thighs and leaning his weight on me. "You are a beautiful woman, Hope."

Ryan never told me I was beautiful. He said I was pretty. And my parents didn't believe in commenting on looks, because brains were more important. It felt very good to hear I was beautiful. I relaxed into Alex's touch. He slid down my legs so he could caress my upper thighs. I arched against his fingers.

"But you think too much." Alex flipped up my skirt and slapped my bare ass.

My entire body went rigid. "Stop—"

He slapped me again, harder. "And you talk too much."

"Alex—"

"What did I just say?" And then he spanked me hard, even though I tried to protest and wriggle away.

When it felt like my bum must be glowing red, and I cried out, he stopped and caressed the skin he had just hit. I quivered.

He turned me over on my back. He studied me once more. I stared back at him. I felt like he had seen me, all of me, the way no one ever had in my life.

Then he bent his head, flipped my skirt up, and ate me until I came once, twice, and begged him not to a third time, because I was too sensitive.

Alex came back up to face level. He was breathing hard. His forehead was beaded with sweat, and his hair clung to his temples. His shirt was ringed with sweat around the armpits. Good. It meant that he wasn't as in control as he pretended.

He kissed me, using his tongue. I flinched. After what he'd been doing—but he tasted musky and sweet. It didn't feel wrong. He kissed me long and deep. Then he pushed the shirt off my shoulders and brushed the open bra aside. He toyed with the button at the waist of my skirt, but then left it alone. "I like it," he said, in response to my questioning look.

I reached for his shirt hem. It was the first time I was initiating something with him, and I felt shy. But he didn't move away, so I lifted his T-shirt up and over his head.

He was thin and pale, after Ryan's glowing brown skin. But Alex was more muscular than I'd expected, with defined arms and the more than a suggestion of abs. Not enough that he looked like a gym freak. Just right. I ran my hands over his shoulders. He had some wiry brown hair on his chest, and even a sprinkling on each shoulder, which made me laugh. He was a lot hairier than Ryan.

Alex kissed me. "What's so funny?"

I shook my head. Talking about exes was verboten. I sure didn't want to hear about Mireille or any of Alex's other conquests—ugh. Mireille.

Alex took my face in his hands. "Don't. Think. Do I really have to spank you again?"

I laughed and shook my head. Trying not to think, I loosened his belt and slid it out from the loops. This was so intimate, even though I'd thought about doing it a dozen times. Unbuttoning his pants and unzipping them was even more scarily intimate. I wanted to close my eyes, but I was curious, too. I'd never seen a white guy before, except for online or a peek in a friend's mother's *Playgirl*.

His erection made a tent out of his black cotton boxer shorts and a wet spot on the front. Again, he wasn't as in control as he pretended. I gave a brief prayer of thanks that he didn't wear a thong before he helped me slip the shorts off his waist.

His penis was redder than I expected—again, the skin tone difference—and, unlike Ryan, he was circumcised. The surrounding hair was russet brown. His penis seemed to strain toward me. A clear drop of fluid beaded at its tip.

I retreated slightly. It was too much. Alex let me draw away but kept a hand on my shoulder. With the other hand, he popped open the drawer on his night stand drawer and handed me a condom wrapped in neat white plastic.

I handed it back to him. I'd sheathed Ryan on occasion, but we usually didn't bother because I was on the pill. And dressing Alex up in a condom was so intimate, you know? Part of me felt like I didn't know him well enough. Ryan and I had been good friends before we became lovers. I wasn't sure what Alex and I were.

Alex laughed and dangled the package in my face. "Come on. You know how to do it. Didn't you do sex ed with kids and cucumbers?"

I laughed, too. "Actually, at Western, we had wooden penises. We only used zucchinis if we ran short. Are you guys so poor at McGill?"

Alex took my hand and placed the condom in my palm. "We've got the real thing."

I chewed my lip. But in the end, I've only ever done one thing with a challenge: face it head on. In more ways than one, I thought, as Alex's cock reared at my face, I took a deep breath.

Alex kneeled on the floor so his lower half dropped out of sight, behind the bed. He drew my head toward him and kissed me gently. "It's okay, Hope."

When I opened my eyes, his face was softer. Tender. It helped. I ripped open the package, careful not to pierce the latex. My hands were steady.

"You're not a virgin, are you?" he asked.

I shook my head and suppressed a laugh.

He wrapped his fingers in my hair, close to my scalp. "It's okay if you are. But I'm glad you're not."

I was, too. I couldn't imagine all this as my first time. It would be like riding around on the carousel for a few years and leaping on to a roller coaster.

Actually, it was still like that. Except I'd had a few turns on the log ride first.

That made me smile. Alex smiled back at me. And I took the condom out and rolled it down on him. His eyes widened at my touch. He arched into my hands and stood up, into my face.

I averted my eyes for a second. When I looked back, his eyes were almost black.

He said thickly, "You're so innocent, Hope."

I shook my head. I'm really not. But he wound my hair around his fingers and said, "I like it. In fact..." His voice lowered even further. "I'm going to pretend that you *are* a virgin."

Oh. Okay. That was more what I was used to. I lifted my chin, expecting gentle kisses and delicate undressing. I was still wearing my skirt.

Alex wound his other hand in my hair and shoved himself in my face. "Suck. My. Cock."

I jerked back, batting his hands away. He made me hot, but if I were a virgin, I certainly wouldn't put up with disrespect.

"I love how your eyes go wide," he said, almost to himself. He knelt down again, so that we were eye to eye. "All right. I'll give you a choice. Either suck me off, or I'm going to fuck you until you pass out." He paused. "Which, given your inexperience, would probably hurt."

I caught my breath. It probably would hurt. It had been almost two years since I'd sex with Ryan. I'd come close a few times, with some other guys. But I was too busy in med school to bother much with dating, and most guys didn't seem worth the hassle. Maybe I should have gotten a dildo? My heart was beating wildly in my chest. I was scared and thrilled and angry and wetter than I'd ever been in my life.

Alex pushed his hips forward. I glared at him for a long, defiant moment. He closed his eyes and extended his neck, his lips parting in a silent snarl.

Seeing him like that, savage yet vulnerable, decided me. I bent forward and took him in my mouth. I half-expected him to try and choke me, but he didn't. He just let his breath out in a shudder and kept very still while I enveloped him.

I smiled inside. Alex talked tough, but he acted with a certain peculiar etiquette in bed.

Tentatively, then with increasing confidence, I experimented with my mouth and tongue until he froze and said hoarsely, "Enough."

I lifted my head. He was red-faced, his eyes glazed with pleasure. His discipline was fraying. I opened my mouth to do more damage.

He dug his hands into the roots of my hair and surged deep in my throat. I held my breath and tried to take it in.

"Oh God, Hope——" He wrested my head away, breathing hard. His eyes raked me head to toe, and then he buried his face in the crook of my neck. "You are so fucking sexy, Hope. You drive me crazy."

I gazed at him from under my lashes. Being a *femme fatale* had its privileges. I started to unfasten my skirt, but he covered my hand with his. "Let me." He took a deep breath and ran his fingers along the line of my cheek. Then he knelt on the floor to unbutton my skirt. He tugged the zipper down slowly, watching me. I shivered—the air conditioning, his hungry eyes, his erection, the wicked improbability of what we were about to do—and he started licking my breasts as his hands guided my skirt over my hips and legs and tossed it on to the floor. Gently, he circled his fingers between my legs, and then inside me, opening me up, until I choked back a scream.

He laid me back on the bed with infinite gentleness, stepping between my knees. He paused here with his hands on my hips. I grabbed his shoulders, hissing, "Yes."

His face darkened. Every muscle in his body was clamped tight, but he tried to take it slow, to take me tenderly. As if I were a virgin. I shifted my hips. He sucked his breath in through his teeth, his eyes stormy, but continued his gradual pace.

I arched up. I grabbed his ass, trying to show that he could go harder.

"Say it," he breathed in my ear, his stubble raking my cheek. "Tell me you want it."

I closed my eyes. It was easier if I didn't have to look at him. "I... want it."

"Beg me for it."

I buried my face in the sweaty crook of his neck. I whispered, barely audible, "Fuck me."

With a growl, he did.

We did.

I did.

I screamed so loud, his neighbours probably called the police.

Afterward, he collapsed on top of me, released my legs, and kissed me soundly. "That was fantastic." The word didn't have the same ring as in the subway, pre-sex.

He pulled out, fumbled down south, and the next thing I knew, a knotted condom sailed through the air and bounced off the rim of the garbage can. He missed.

He looked at me and shrugged.

I pulled my legs away from him. "I'm cold." I felt very vulnerable. Was this what it was like, having sex with someone new? Ryan and I always said, "I love you" afterward. Okay, we did love each other, whereas Alex and I had only met a few days ago, but it made me want to cry. Was this all a giant mistake? Yes, I'd enjoyed myself, I'd gotten laid for the first time in too long time, but I'd done things with Alex that I'd only fantasized about, and now he was playing hoops with the used condom?

And Alex was a colleague. How was I going to act around him at St. Joe's? What if this didn't work out? He'd seen me naked! He spanked me, for crying out loud!

Not to mention that someone at St. Joseph's was a murderer. I still didn't believe it was Alex, but this had to rank as one of the stupidest things I'd done in my life. No wonder Alex told me not to think. If my brain had been functioning, I never would have ended up here. I hated myself, a sudden and furious loathing. I had no one to blame but myself.

I sat up, clutching the blanket to my chest. "I have to go."

Alex grabbed me in a bear hug and pulled me down on the bed.

I stiffened, not fighting him, but keeping my body rigid, even while his legs as well as his arms looped around me and held me tight.

He said, "You know what, Hope?"

"What?"

"You're thinking too much again."

I had to laugh. It was true. If I didn't think at all, I'd just relax and have a grand time with Alex. My body had no complaints. My vaj was still pulsating. If I'd been more of a brainiac, I would have dumped Alex after the café disappearance.

I'd done neither. I was a deeply flawed, fish-fowl, happy-sad, human being.

He kissed my forehead. "What's on your mind?"

Code Blues

"Oh…a few things." Dissing myself post-coitally was not helpful. Neither was talking about the murder. I may have been out of the loop for a few years, but I knew that much.

"Good. Now forget about them."

I laughed again. Alex was so complicated, but in other ways, he was refreshingly direct.

"In this room," he went on, jabbing the air with his index finger, "there are only a few appropriate subjects."

I rolled my eyes. "Let me guess. Sex."

He pressed a big, smacking kiss on my lips. "Yes! That's one of them. Sex is always appropriate. Want to go two for two?"

"Oh, okay." I was a bit sore, but I wriggled against him.

He laughed. "I like the way your mind works. I was asking for other subjects. But you're right." He grabbed my bum. "Who cares about other subjects. Sex all the way, baby."

Now I looked like a sex maniac. I blushed and covered it up by pretending to think. "I'm sure I can do both. Okay, another topic. How wonderful you are."

"Yes!" he chortled and pressed another big kiss on my lips. "You are so smart. You must be a doctor or something."

This was more fun than brooding. I kissed him back and murmured, "Which leads me to even more appropriate, more intriguing subject: how wonderful *I* am."

"Yes!" A kiss with some tongue. "I'm always interested in that subject." He reached down and pinched one of my nipples. I squealed. He said, "Well, if that's the way it's going to be, I may have to get back on to subject number one."

I cautiously reached down and touched him. There was some evidence of life. "Already?"

"Give me a minute. Or better yet, give me more than that." He pressed my hand down on him and kept it there.

As we started to move again, I thought, okay. I guess this is what happens when you have sex with someone that you don't love yet. You don't have the emotional bond. You don't talk about that part, even if you feel it. But you can still talk. And you can laugh. And you can have great sex.

CHAPTER 15

I twisted around to check the clock radio and was astonished to read 10:29 p.m. Night had fallen outside. Alex had turned off the air conditioning while we snuggled under the covers, but it had felt so natural and gradual, I hadn't noticed time passing.

Alex said lazily, "Are you still hungry?"

He'd grabbed a baguette and a jar of peanut butter from the kitchen. We'd slathered smooth peanut butter on torn-off chunks of bread. When I could no longer talk because my throat was mortared shut, he'd grabbed me a glass of lukewarm tap water. It was romantic in a grotty way, a 'jug of wine and thou' sort of thing. I wasn't crazy about the crumbs now littering the bed, but I liked nestling against Alex's warm chest, with his hand on my hip and his legs woven between mine. I wanted to stay here forever. Forget about the time. Forget about murder. Forget about thinking.

When I raised my head again, it was 10:48.

I let my head fall back on the pillow with a sigh. "I have to catch the last blue train. I have a day shift tomorrow."

Alex slid his arms around my middle. "You could stay here."

I lingered against him for a moment. I was glad he'd offered. I didn't know single protocol very well, if I was supposed to take off, wham-bam, or if it was okay for me to spend the first night. But I shook my head. "Do you have any contact solution? I have to take mine out." I flipped around to stare in his eyes. There were no tell-tale circles around his irises. He didn't wear contacts.

He frowned in thought. "I might have some. I never cleaned out my bathroom."

I stiffened. Gross *and* thoughtless. If he thought I was going to use Mireille's old crap—

"Relax. One of my buddies was staying here, and he wore contacts." His face twisted with sarcasm. "Are you ever going to let that go? What's the big deal, anyway?"

"The big deal?" I fought to lower my voice. We'd had such a wonderful little interlude. Well, it was shattered now. If he wanted a fight, I'd give it to him. "That you fucked her and everyone thinks you're not over her, and you still work with her every day? Oh, that's no big. Forget about it."

Secretly, I hoped he'd take me in his arms and tell me I was the only one. He'd understand my jealousy and insecurity and make me see there was no need for it. Instead, he closed his eyes and sighed.

Tears pricked my eyelids. I slid down the foot of the bed, taking the sheet with me. Alex sat up. I ignored him, pawing through our wad of clothes on the floor. I yanked my bra on, but my fingers fumbled on nubs of thread along my shirt. I couldn't even get dressed. He'd ripped off all but three of my shirt buttons. And he was just sitting there, watching me jerk on my panties. They felt cold and icky, but I was too upset to care. Did what we do mean nothing to him?

"Hope, you need a drink. Let me get you one." He stood up, still naked, but I avoided looking at him.

"I don't really drink," I said. Little Miss Muffet from Ontario again.

"Well, I do. Come on." He nudged me in the ribs with his elbow. "We should celebrate, you know?"

I licked my lips and tried to cling on to my anger.

"One drink," he said. "And then I'll take you home if you want. Or you can stay here and I'll buy you contact lens whatever."

I realized that I'd been clenching my jaw and slowly relaxed it.

"Red wine?" he said.

"White?" I said finally.

"I'll see what I can do." He smiled. He pulled open a drawer and dragged a pair of jeans on to his hips without bothering with underwear.

I watched him. I wanted him again.

His smile turned lazy and he eyed me up and down. "After the wine."

"If you can hold out that long," I said. One of my friends once told me about a study on couples that she read in the newspaper. If there's going to be an imbalance, i.e. one of them loves more than the other, it's better if the man's the one who loves the woman more.

Sounds plausible. Harder to implement.

"I can hold out. Barely," he said, and kissed me again, this time exploring my mouth like he was asking me a question. I leaned into it, but when I felt him pause, I pulled away first.

"Good. I hope you can find a good vintage," I said. I smoothed out my collar, which felt semi-ridiculous, when I was still mostly naked and wearing a ruined shirt. But I straightened my back and eyed him, waiting for him to do my bidding.

He laughed.

Not the reaction I had planned for, but I held my pose.

He ran his hand down my cheek. "You're funny."

My heart sank. Not exactly the *femme fatale* I was going for.

"I'll be back in a minute. Don't move."

I glanced down at my naked thighs. The bed sheet lay crumpled on the ground.

"Don't even," he drawled. "I want you just like this. Only more so."

My turn to laugh. I shook my head.

He pointed his index finger and thumb at me like a gun. "Seriously. No wine if you make a wrong move."

"What if I get cold?"

He half-snorted, half-laughed, and flicked off the air conditioning. "There you go." He sauntered out of the room. The jeans almost did justice to his ass.

Then I heard a door close and a toilet ring clank. I turned the air conditioning back on so I wouldn't have to hear any more. There is such a thing as too much information.

I perched on the bed, but the cold air made me shiver. I felt slightly ridiculous, not sexy, waiting for him to come back, and thought of Ryan again. Often we fell asleep with our legs braided together and my head on his chest. If he had to go off, I might lie under the blanket and stare at the ceiling in a pleasant post-coital haze.

Well. Love the one you're with.

I buttoned the three remaining buttons on my blouse. Of course they were the bottom ones, so my breasts still hung out. I'd have to borrow a shirt to go home in. I smiled at the thought.

My smile slipped. Did he have any clean ones?

I slipped off the bed in search of four small, clear buttons. Like I said, I liked this shirt and I might have to wear it home.

I turned on the light and found one in the middle of the floor, but I ended up peering under the bed in search of the rest.

I expected a bunch of dust bunnies and old clothes, but not the long blue box of aluminum foil.

Who keeps tin foil under their bed?

I pulled it toward me and opened it to see your average roll of aluminum foil getting near the end of the roll. I closed the box, but it still bothered me. I could understand used tin foil in your bedroom garbage, like if you were eating leftover pizza and felt too lazy to go back to the kitchen to recycle the packaging. I glanced at his open-mouthed wicker wastebasket and saw a few crumpled balls of blackened aluminum foil.

I frowned. Pizza doesn't turn foil black. And why would he have— let's see—at least four separate black tin foil balls in his garbage?

I hovered around the wastebasket, unwilling to poke through it. Alex was a pretty grotty guy. But maybe I could sift through the rest of his room. Or at least the bathroom, because then I could lock the door. I didn't know what exactly what I was looking for, but—

"What are you doing?"

My head jerked up to see Alex framed in the doorway, two wine glass stems and a corkscrew in one hand and a wine bottle in the other before he slammed everything down on his desk and came at me with both hands open.

"I, uh—I just had to throw something away," I said. "And I was looking for my buttons."

He didn't touch me. His eyes darted past me and fell on the box of aluminum foil now in the middle of the floor. He scooped it up and said, "You find everything you needed to know?"

"Uh..."

"You come here and fuck me so that you can look around here and get evidence against me?"

What? I wasn't the one who'd made advances at the bicycle stand.

But this wasn't the time to stand here and defend my honour. Every instinct screamed at me to get out.

I didn't want to run. Something told me to treat him like a mad dog and just calmly, quietly move away. "You know what? I'm beat. I'll take a rain check on the wine, okay?"

I took three steps and scooped my skirt off the floor. I zipped it up while trying to keep my eyes on him. I refused to turn my back on him. "It sounds really fun, but I've got to—"

Alex's hand shot forward and grabbed my shoulder.

I tried not to scream. His fingers dug into my skin, but not hard enough to hurt. "Hey. Alex."

He didn't speak. His hot breath stank of peanut butter. His eyes were like black holes.

I glanced at the phone lying face-down on the bedside table. No way I could get to it. I still hadn't gotten a cell phone and my pager was in my mini-backpack by the doorway.

I cleared my throat. "Alex. Dude." My voice broke, but got stronger. "I'm just going to head home. The whole contact lens thing, you know?"

He scowled. Slowly, the pressure of his fingers eased, but he didn't remove them.

I backed away, easing off his fingers. "Right on."

His hands fell to his sides, but he didn't blink. His eyes bore into mine.

I took a cautious step back.

He bent down toward my feet. I stifled a scream, but he was scooping his khaki pants off the floor, the ones he'd worn to work, and rooting in the pocket. Without looking at me, he said, "You just crossed the line." He palmed a pack of cigarettes and pinched a lighter between his index finger and thumb.

"Okay." I continued to back out the room door, still keeping my eyes trained on him. "That's fine. I'll leave. See you around."

I hurried to the front hall, jammed my feet in my sandals, and shouldered my bag. We outta here.

As I opened the door, cool air hit my midriff. I kept going anyway and slammed the door behind me.

Once I hit the sidewalk, I looked down at myself. My shirt was hanging open, showing off my bra. I tied the shirt in a quick knot, covering most of my lingerie. I wished I'd kept the white coat on.

I looped my backpack straps backwards over my shoulders, wearing the pack on my front, to cover myself. I did not want to get on the subway like this. But I was alive. I'd take it.

"Wait! Alex's voice echoed down the street.

I waved a cheery goodbye. I would not revisit the apartment of a madman. I started down the street. "See you later!"

A student couple passed me. The woman glanced me up and down. They both looked from me to Alex, and then soldiered up the hill, blank-faced.

"Don't go like this," said Alex, more quietly. He pressed his lips together. I thought maybe his eyes glistened, but it might have been a trick of the light.

"Gotta go," I said, still walking, but slower now.

His lips quirked in a slight smile. "Well, at least take this." He lobbed a plain white T-shirt at me. It fell about four feet short, but I scooped it up. It looked and smelled clean.

"Thanks," I muttered. The couple was now half a block away, so I held my bag between my legs while I twitched the shirt on. It was too big. It hung nearly as long as my skirt. I probably looked like a girl playing dress-up. But I was decent and minorly grateful for it. I turned my back to him. "Thanks. 'Bye."

"Wait. Hope." His hand extended, a $20 bill curved over his index finger.

Did he think I was a prostitute or something? Confused and angry, I shook my head.

"For the taxi," he said roughly.

Oh. Just like that, a kernel of tenderness bloomed in my chest. I tamped it down, but it was there. Alex was my Achilles heel.

He met my gaze. "I don't want you taking the metro."

I hesitated. I have to say, it hadn't even occurred to me to take a taxi. My parents raised me to save and save and save and save. But I kept an emergency $20 in my bag

Alex shook the bill at me. "It's the least—I mean, Hope—"

His Adam's apple bobbed up and down before he said, more softly, "Please."

I hardly recognized myself when I was with Alex, bouncing into bed, running into the street half-dressed, oscillating between seduction and terror.

"No, thank you," I said. "I have money."

Alex said, "Let me call the taxi for you, at least. Please."

I hesitated.

"It doesn't have to pick you up here, if you want."

A woman approached us with a miniature dog on a leash. The dog stopped to root in Alex's pizza boxes. She jerked it away with some difficulty, and glared at me like it was my fault.

"Thanks but no thanks, Alex. I'll see you later." I headed south, where I could hear traffic and see people crossing the sidewalk. I flagged the first taxi I saw.

The black male driver hardly glanced at me in the rear view mirror. He just stared at the traffic while his radio deafened us with information about other pick-ups. Fine with me.

When he came to a stop on Mimosa, I handed him some money and ran down the small, lantern-lit concrete path to my apartment.

I threw the bolt on my door.

What just happened tonight?

When I lifted my phone receiver, the dial tone beeped. I had messages.

Alex, probably.

I threw the phone on the couch and started washing dishes. But then I had to get it over with. Not knowing was stressing me out. I scooped up the phone and punched in the numbers.

"For your—*two*—new—voice messages, press *one one*, now."

My heart hammered.

"First message," said the recording.

"Hope. It's Mom," my mother yelled. I closed my eyes and lowered the volume on her voice. "Where are you? I hope you're not working too hard."

My brother piped up. "Guess who we saw today at Yangtze?" That was our favourite restaurant. "Ryan!"

I choked. They won the "worst timing ever" award. No, wait. Maybe that was me.

Mom said, "I know you said it's, ah, over, but he looked very nice! Handsome. And he was with his family. No girlfriend. We asked his mother."

"Mommy," my father chastised under his breath and added, louder, "Anyway, we were just calling to say hello! We'll call you tomorrow."

The second message was from the moving company, promising that they'd come tomorrow. My temples throbbed. The Zippy company that did zip.

As soon as I hung up, I checked the dial tone in case Alex had just called. He hadn't.

Thank God.

Right?

I walked to the living room without turning on the light. Somehow, the darkness soothed me. The street lamp beamed through the window between tree leaves, allowing me to skirt the few boxes near the doorway and pick my way to my desk. The floor was cool and smooth beneath my feet. I picked Henry up and pressed him against my cheek. "I guess I was better off with you as my boyfriend."

He didn't answer.

"Right. You're the strong, silent type." My voice echoed in my empty apartment. I heard someone scraping furniture across the floor in the apartment above, and felt lonelier than ever. I stretched Henry full-length, his arms above his head, and laid him gently on his stomach.

Tonight, I needed someone more alive than Henry, but just as safe. I opened my laptop and brought up an old e-mail from Ryan.

Dear Hope,

Thanks for coming to my grandmother's funeral. It meant a lot to all of us. I love you....

I tore off Alex's T-shirt, my buttonless dress shirt, bra, white skirt, and soiled panties and launched them in the hall closet. I'd never wear any of them again. Back in my trusty nightshirt, I propped myself up in my sleeping bag, reading Ryan's e-mails until I fell asleep.

CHAPTER 16

By Friday, every minute of my ER shift, my head pounded, hangover-style. My back ached from the unforgiving bedroom floor. My tongue felt thick and furry, even though I'd brushed it, and my breath probably reeked of misery.

I tugged at the sleeves of my white coat, grateful that at least my cleavage was no longer on display for all of Montreal. A girl has to have some standards.

Dr. Dupuis was on. He cast me an appraising glance when I fumbled my presentations, but said nothing until I told him I was leaving for my family med clinic after one more patient. His face seemed to lengthen even more. I could hardly read his eyes as the fluorescent light bounced off his glasses. "Are you all right?"

I shrugged and tried to smile. "As well as can be expected, under the circumstances." It was a loose *Anne of Green Gables* quote.

He eased the last clipboard out of my hands. "I'll take care of this. Go have lunch."

I was too tired to argue. It was almost noon, which was the end of my shift. I'd only picked up the chart because I was trying to make up for my lackluster performance. Until now, I'd been humming along on barbed wire and bug juice, as Jack Nicholson put it. But after Alex, this bug had run out of juice.

I revived my spirits by sipping some literal, apple-flavored, juice from a glass bottle while sitting around the back of the FMC, under an anemic birch tree. I hadn't packed a proper lunch and didn't want to buy one. These calories plus my liver's gluconeogenesis would carry me through the afternoon.

The fresh air and grass under my feet buoyed me slightly, and I strode into my FMC clinic a few minutes early.

Dr. Levine, a tanned, barrel-chested man with bristly brown hair, shook my hand and boomed, "Pleased to meet you, Hope!"

I liked him better than Dr. C. already. Too bad Dr. Levine was no longer our team leader.

"How are you settling into Montreal?"

Until last night, I would have chirped, "Great!" As it stood, I demurred. "It's, ah, interesting. I'm not settled yet. I still don't have my furniture."

"Why's that?" he bellowed.

So then I summarized my saga of furniture-in-limbo, wishing I could pick another story that made me look smart and in-control.

"That's terrible! You don't even have a bed? I'll lend you a futon!" Dr. Levine looked distressed. "My son's home from university. We have some furniture just sitting there."

Tempting, but I didn't want handouts. "It's supposed to come today. I'll let you know."

Stan shook his head. "You should threaten them with small claims court. That'll get them moving."

We laughed at his inadvertent pun. Dr. Levine held out a mixing bowl. "At least have some microwaved popcorn. I didn't have time to bring anything better today."

I laughed. "I'll wash my hands first. Thank you."

He shook the bowl, rustling the popcorn. "Hygiene first. You're off to a great start already."

I shook my head and smiled. Why, oh why, couldn't he have stayed our team leader?

Even fueled by popcorn and a friendly supervisor, I ran a slow-mo, cotton-brained clinic. Dr. Levine prodded and encouraged and eventually sighed, "Have more popcorn" before feeding me the answers.

"Thanks," I said. Now I had an inkling of what the other residents were missing, after Kurt's death. Ideally, the FMC would be a refuge from our other rotations, our chance to learn family medicine and follow patients for two years. Dr. Callendar and the eroding building made it feel more like bamboo shoved under the fingernails. I'd settle for somewhere between the two.

I hid in my room, waiting for my last patient and writing my charts. 76 y.o. male, DM II, HT, COPD. CC: glycemic control. Even my writing was slower and more cautious than usual.

While I was surrounded by other people, I was okay, but as soon as I was alone, I started ruminating about the light in Alex's eyes, his smell of cedar and musk, his nimble fingers and tongue. He felt so *right* in bed and so wrong out of it.

I hated books and movies where women seemed to be punished for premarital sex. Nothing as obvious as a bolt of lightning, but they were still made to feel ashamed and defiled. So why was I living the stereotype?

Oh. Suddenly, I wanted to cry. I bit the inside of my cheek and blinked ferociously. You will not. You will not.

Two sharp raps on my door.

Alex. No. It wasn't his clinic day. I took a deep breath. "Come in."

Tori's face popped around the imitation oak door. Her kind expression made me grip the edge of my wood-veneer desk.

She sank in the patient's chair beside my desk and crossed her legs toward me. "I'm not going to ask you how you are. It's pretty obvious."

I hiccupped something between a laugh and a sob. "Don't you have a patient?"

"Mrs. McNally was my last one. So." She studied me. I cleared my throat and gripped my pen, its plastic edges making ridges in my fingertips. She said softly, "Alex, right?"

I laid down my pen, taking extra care to minimize the noise. "I know you warned me. I know I'm stupid."

She shook her head. "You're not stupid. Alex can be very charming when he wants to be." She hesitated, pressing her lips together. "I wish Kurt was around."

I frowned at her. "I didn't even know him."

"I know." She twisted her only ring, a topaz set in silver. "But he was great with this kind of stuff."

I snorted. "People getting fucked over?" I wanted to shock her, make her sniff and leave me alone.

She didn't hesitate. "Pretty much. Even people you wouldn't expect to open up, like Robin—"

She stopped there, as if regretting her words, but I pounced on them. Lily-white, geek-of-the-year Robin Huxley? "What did he talk to Kurt about? Type I and type II errors?"

She pressed her lips together. "We all have problems."

Well, whip my politically incorrect ass. "Do you know what his were?"

Tori shrugged. "Robin never talked to the rest of us. But Kurt used to talk to Robin, and it seemed to help."

Since I felt so selfish and miserable, I said, "Well, it's too late for me. Kurt's not coming back."

"Yes." Tori's brown eyes were level. "So I'm going to try and step into his place."

I blinked at her. "Why?" I was surprised enough she'd gone to the Jazz Festival with me. She might have been too polite to say no, but she didn't seem to have a stellar time.

She glanced at the closed door before turning back to me. "It sounds silly. But now that Kurt's gone, it's the least I can do for him. His memory."

I eyed her. It was all so strange. I couldn't deny I needed a friend. A real friend, though. Not a pity party. "I'm not a charity case."

She smiled slightly. "No?" She laughed at my injured face. "Just kidding. Look. Kurt helped us all the time, and not once did he make us feel pathetic, like he was too busy for us, or whatever. If he could do that for all the residents and all the medical students, I can handle being friends with you."

212   *Code Blues*

Gee, thanks. But at least she was honest and I respected her. I said heavily, "Okay."

"Okay." She smiled at me.

I smiled back. I did feel better. It feels good to have someone believe in you, even if you don't quite believe in yourself. "Does this mean you'll massage my feet?"

She gave me a strange look.

I laughed. "What, was that something even Kurt didn't do?"

"Not to me!"

We giggled together. I sobered. "Do you have any idea who held a grudge against him?"

She shook her head. "I doubt it's anyone we know. He must have been in the wrong place at the wrong time."

Everyone had their pet theories. Alex and Mireille pointed their fingers at each other. Tucker suspected Dr. Bob Clarkson. But who had an alibi? And how could I possibly ask in a tactful way? "Yeah. What a crazy night. Did you and Tucker and Anu hang out at the Jazz Festival all night?"

"Until midnight," she said, pressing her lips together for a second. She knew where I was going with this, but she was willing to play ball for now.

"Alex and I went out for sushi, but then he took off," I said. "Do you know what the other residents were up to?"

"Well, one of the second years had a party, so a lot of people went to that," she said, surprising me.

"Really?" No one had invited me. Never mind that it had been my first day and Alex had whirled me away on a date. I still felt left out.

"It was sort of a spur of the moment thing, I guess," she said, reading my mind. "Anu and Tucker and I wanted to hang out at the Jazz Festival anyway, so we called you. But Mireille and Robin—"

"Robin Huxley?" Even the town nerd got invited before me?

"Yes." She hesitated. Her head dipped before she met my eyes again. "I heard Alex showed up too."

My head spun. "On Friday night."

"So I heard. I wasn't there."

He ditched me for an "emergency" that was a resident party? If I hadn't already written him off, this would have sent him straight to jail, do not pass GO, do not collect $200.

Tears sprang to my eyes. I blinked them back and shook my head. The guy wasn't worth crying over, unless it was tears of joy that I'd escaped him. "I should make a spreadsheet of where everyone was that night."

She looked pained. "The police will find out."

I shook my head. "Yeah, they've done a great job so far."

"Even so, they've been trained far more than you or I."

"True." I paused. "Uh, did you spend all of Friday night with Tucker and Anu?"

"Of course not." She suppressed a smile. "You want my alibi for your spreadsheet?"

I shrugged, but of course I did.

"Anu went home before midnight. Tucker and I watched Buffy the Vampire Slayer on DVD until we fell asleep."

I didn't like picturing them on the couch together. Clearly, the guy had yellow fever. "So you were together all night?"

"He went home eventually. I didn't wake up enough to check the clock."

I turned to my patient's chart, smoothing the crease down the middle. "Do you do that often?"

"Check the clock?" When I raised my head, she was smiling at me almost maternally. "You're fun to tease."

I flapped the chart closed. "Really? 'Cause I don't like it."

"That's why," she replied. Her eyes glittered with amusement, although her mouth stayed sober. "To answer your real question, Tucker and I both like Buffy. But we've never done what you and Alex probably did. Satisfied?"

I felt guilty. "Do you want to?"

She raised her eyes to the ceiling. "Can I plead the Fifth?"

"We're not American. But I guess I can let you off the hook this time." I toyed with my pen, twirling it between my fingers. I wasn't laughing anymore. "You know how you said Alex was charming?"

She suppressed a sigh and nodded.

Code Blues

"Was that from...personal experience?"

Her eyes were amused and sad at the same time. "No."

It was pathetic, but I breathed easier.

She added, "I have a healthy sense of self-preservation." She stood, smoothing her hemp-colored shorts. "Dr. Levine wants to see you before you go."

My mouth hung open a little. I wanted to tell her I used to have a fine sense of caution and sanity. I used to be a good girl. Just like you!

She touched my shoulder lightly. "Okay?"

She wasn't asking about Dr. Levine. I had to admit, Tori was more tough-love than I'd realized. But maybe it was a good thing. I exhaled. "Yeah. Okay."

It turned out Dr. Levine was dying to give me his son's futon. "Just let me call my wife. We'll work something out. We'll borrow a truck!"

I had to laugh. "The Zippy Moving Company has sworn to send me my things today. If not, I'll call you."

He wrote down his numbers for me. I wondered if he'd always been this helpful, or if he, like Tori, was trying to fill some of the void Kurt had left behind. Not a bad legacy after all.

Tori suggested we go out to dinner. I shook my head. "Moving van time." It was just an excuse. I wanted to see if Alex had left a message. At the very least, I could pull the sleeping bag over my head and leave the world behind.

"I'll walk you home," she said. It was easier to say yes than to keep fighting her. I definitely needed a refill on my bug juice.

We walked to the Mimosa Manor in silence, our feet tapping on the sidewalk. The day had clouded over and the air was heavy. We walked faster. Summer storms could be super soakers.

As we turned down Mimosa, I could see a white van blocking the laneway. I stopped dead. Then I shook my head. The lettering was for a Montreal company, not Zippy.

Tori said, "I bet it's for you." Before I could stop her, she ran up to the passenger side and accosted a van guy in quite good French.

She turned to me with a radiant smile. "Your company gave these guys the contract after their truck broke down. You have a bed!"

The van guy, who was wearing a dirty orange baseball cap over his scraggly blond hair, turned to me and said, "*Appartement cinq? 'Ope Zee?*"

"That's me!" I burst out. Maybe my luck was finally turning. It was a sign. I had an entire wardrobe again. I could sleep in a proper bed. I could brush my hair instead of combing it. My DVD's were back. I clasped my hands together. I wanted to hug this heavy metal moving dude. "Thank you, thank you!"

As he stared at me, nonplused, thunder rumbled in the distance and I felt the first drop of rain on my arm.

The moving guy raised his eyes to the grey skies and summarized our feelings. "*Tabarnouche.*"

Chapter 17

I managed to get through the next few days without seeing Alex, which gave me both a fierce satisfaction and a burning epigastric pain whenever I was at the hospital. I'll never make fun of someone with reflux or an ulcer again, I vowed to myself. It hurts.

Still, I knew Alex would be at Grand Rounds on Wednesday. No matter what rotation you were on, you were supposed to attend family medicine Grand Rounds.

"I wonder what they're going to do for it," Tori had mused to me as she helped me unpack my living room on Monday. "Kurt was supposed to present on partner abuse. He'd been researching it for months. He showed us a stack of articles he'd printed out. He asked if anyone knew graphic design and could help make a pamphlet for the FMC to hand out. Robin told him that child or elder abuse should have a higher profile in our community, but Kurt was adamant. 'This is a still an under-recognized problem. If family doctors don't tackle domestic abuse, who's going to do it? Not the dermatologists or the cardiac surgeons! We're the ones who follow people for years. If you want to do a presentation on child or elder abuse, Robin, I'll be happy to clear some rounds time for you.'" She smiled. "That made Robin very quiet."

I laughed and slit a box open with my Exacto knife. "Really? I'd have thought he'd jump at the chance."

She laughed with me. "That's true. Maybe he was trying to think of some good articles for it."

It was mean to make fun of Robin, but I needed my jollies where I could get them. I sighed. "At least if he was in our group, he'd volunteer to do all the presentations."

She shook her head, a dimple peeking in her left cheek. "Don't worry. Dr. Callendar would never let him get away with it."

"Figures. He wants to spread the pain." I lifted the flaps of the box. Med school notes. Just about useless. I pushed the box under my desk.

Tori just smiled and shook her head. I was no closer to figuring out how she got into that demon's sweet spot. She twirled a screw in my pine Ikea bookcase and made a face at the divots and scrapes. "It's too bad the moving people ruined your furniture. They banged up the front and back, so there's no good side."

I threw up my hands. "I'm so happy to have a bookcase, I don't care!" It made me think of Alex again. I so wanted a boyfriend, I latched right on to him. Did he just seem irresistible because I was desperate?

I remembered the way he touched my breasts and blushed. No. It wasn't just desperation.

Tori clucked her tongue. "Ahem. Do you want medical books in here or regular books?"

I shook my head. "Sorry. Yeah. I mean, medical books. I'll keep regular books in the bedroom."

Her dark eyes were sympathetic. "You know, he doesn't deserve you."

My face looped in a half-smile. "That's what I keep telling myself." I picked up Henry. "Is he more acceptable?"

She tilted her head to one side, considering. "He is rather wooden." She smiled when I giggled. "But I definitely admire his flexibility and his poker face. Yes, he's a keeper."

We laughed as I went to help her figure out how to space the shelves.

On Wednesday, Kurt made the front page of both the Gazette and *La Presse*. The Gazette lamented the belated police investigation as too little, too late. A suspicious death is a suspicious death. They should have erred on the side of caution instead of assuming it was an accidental insulin overdose. *La Presse* did a sort of obituary, talking about how Kurt had tried to overhaul St. Joe's, but really exposing our fleabag quarters. They quoted a patient as saying, "It doesn't inspire confidence when the curtain gets stuck halfway around when you're getting an internal examination." I wondered if it was my patient from Friday.

Funny. St. Joe's FMC was a splintering mess, but I was already getting used to it. After Dr. Levine assisted me with a pelvic exam, I now knew to caution the patient, "The curtain may not work. Sometimes it gets stuck, so I'll knock before I come back. I have to go outside the soak the speculum in warm water. I'll help you on to the table. The lamp may be broken..." Already, I was adapting instead of outraged. I wondered if it was a good thing.

For once, I had the morning off. I checked my e-mail at the hospital, because my high-speed still hadn't been hooked up at home. One of my Western friends sent me her new address. My mother asked if I could make it to Kevin's end of summer school play. Kevin said basically the same thing: HI. COME HOME!!!!

I wrote back to all of them. Then I sat in the residents' room, listening to the buzz of the computer and the occasional footsteps in the corridor. Everyone else was hard at work. It was weird to be here.

The room didn't smell as bad as usual. The trash had been emptied. There were still cafeteria trays and dishes, but it was all stacked on top of the fridge. There was even a new ficus tree beside the computer. I touched the leaves. Fabric, but still. Someone cared. I understood a bit why Kurt had tried. If we all pitched in, we could do something about this place.

Kurt. I looked back at my computer screen. "Click here to return to Yahoo! Mail."

I clicked. Back to the sign-in screen. Instead of using my own ID, I typed in the one from the memo: dr-kurt.

Yahoo was a public webmail system. If I could figure out his password, I could access his e-mail. Of course, if he was at all clever,

I'd never be able to figure out his password. I tried all the usual things: dr-kurt, kurt, vicki, even mireille, under various capitalizations. I dug through my bag for the orientation package and tried his phone numbers. If I knew his birthday, I'd have tried that, too.

No dice.

The police had taken away all his personal papers. The computer had been wiped. But the Internet had been created to survive a nuclear attack. The information was waiting in cyberspace, if only I could reach it.

I wanted to bang my head on the beige monitor. For all I knew, the police had cracked his e-mail and were even now tracking all the people who had met with him and talked to him. But from what everyone said, it was a mammoth task. I just wanted to take a look. See what didn't fit. That was the key in detective books. They're always slipping you red herrings and trying to make you suspect the most obvious person, but I could usually spot the murderer because the person does something that catches my eye. I'm no good at tracking alibis and calculating motives, but I can still finger the guilty party.

The combination clicked behind me. I zapped the screen closed just before Stan Biedelman threw open the door and stared at me. "Hey. What are you doing here?"

"Waiting for rounds."

He gestured at the computer. "I'll go to the library. I can pull a Robin and live there, researching useful stuff like how speed can give you a headache and that's why doctors shouldn't take drugs, even if you've been up for 36 hours."

"No, it's okay. I'm done." I stood up and migrated to one of the couches. "How are you doing?"

He grinned at me. "I only have half a day of internal medicine, and I get free food today. How do you think I'm doing?" He settled down at the computer and opened Explorer. It came up with the default window of St. Joe's hospital.

I laughed, relaxing. "Is the food kosher?"

He waved his hand. "I eat the vegetarian stuff. It's fine. I'm not that observant, anyway. I eat shrimp and lobster." He started typing.

"Oh." I tried not to stare at his *yarmulke*.

He chuckled and swiveled to look at me. "So you're wondering why I wear the funny hat on my head?"

"Oh. No. Nothing like that." I brushed some crumbs off the back of the sofa.

He roared. "Sure you are! It's okay. I'm used to it. My family's more observant. So I do the Friday night Sabbath with them and I wear this." He touched his head. "It doesn't hurt anyone."

I was distracted by the alibi. "You do the Sabbath on Friday nights?"

"Yeah. See, Saturday's our holiday——"

"I know that." At his mock-astonished face, I said, "I used to read these books as a kid about the *All of a Kind Family*. They were Jewish. But the point is, you were celebrating Friday night? All night?"

He nodded, face clearing. "Yeah. So you can count any observant Jews out. It's family night. We weren't out murdering any goyim. So it wasn't me or Dr. Levine." He grinned at my face. "You didn't know? Levine's a Jewish name and he's more observant than me."

"I didn't consider Dr. Levine." I dug my nail into the burgundy vinyl of the couch.

"So who are you considering?"

I didn't want to name Mireille or Alex, but now that he'd mentioned it, they probably weren't Jewish. Certainly Alex didn't have any family here, or a proper alibi after 10 p.m. Every time I uncovered more information, it just opened a new, Costco-sized can of worms. I covered my eyes. Now I'd be spying on them during Grand Rounds. No wonder police did this as a full-time job.

Stan started typing again. "Fine. You're going to crack this case and don't want to share the evidence with me. I understand."

I jumped.

Stan laughed. "Did you hear all the latest shit? How they think it was an insulin overdose, but his drug screen came back positive, so they're not sure?"

I gaped at him.

He cracked up. He even swiveled away from the computer so he could pound his hand on the desk and cackle. "Hey, detective, you should see your face!"

Melissa Yi

221

I shut my mouth with as much dignity as I could muster. "Just tell me 'the shit,' Stan."

"All right, Sarge." He dialed down the laughter. The flush in his face died down, too, and he shifted in his chair. "I guess it's not that funny, but the way you talk about excrement kind of is. You must have a lot of fun with your patients. Anyway, these are all rumors, but the word on the street is that they found GHB and excess insulin in his system and they think the time of death was around 2 a.m, give or take a few hours."

GHB. Grievous Bodily Harm. Street drug of champions. Not. I licked my lips. "I thought they said succinylcholine."

"That, too. But it turns out it's a lot more complicated than they thought. I looked it up. You can test false positive for succ just from background 'noise,' so it's hard to prove one way or another. So they're sending it for more tests. I think the GHB is more solid, though, and they nailed his insulin and C-peptide levels, so it's definitely an insulin OD. Insulin and GHB. Maybe succ."

I licked my lips. "So they still think it's murder."

He shrugged his shoulders. "The whole thing is hard to prove, right? I mean, they'll be searching for needle marks for the succ, but the guy had type I Diabetes. He'd be riddled with them. He could have taken GHB for fun, and then gotten confused when he was hypoglycemic and OD'd on his insulin."

My head spun, but I fought back. "And paralyzed himself with succ while he was at it?"

"The succ isn't a hundred percent, but let's say it is. You know how people get when they're hypoglycemic. Their brains aren't getting enough glucose. They're sweaty, they talk funny, they're confused. Maybe he wandered up around the OR, grabbed the wrong vial..."

I shook my head. "Everything's locked up. He couldn't just 'wander in.' And what was he doing at St. Joe's in the middle of the night, anyway? He didn't even do call, right? Except for taking care of all of you guys who called him for their personal problems. No. I bet someone called him in and asked him to meet them. I bet that's why his pager was missing!"

"His pager was missing?" Stan blinked twice.

"Yeah. You know how we can track back to see who called on the pager? It stores the last few numbers. I bet that's why the murderer took it! We should find the pager!" I paused. "You know how they used to say '*Cherchez la femme*'? We should *cherchez le* pager!"

"What are you talking about?"

I actually didn't know why they used to say '*Cherchez la femme*,' but I was on a roll here. My first instincts had been bang on, just like on a multiple choice test. I flapped my hand at him to make him hush up. "But the murderer took it. So there has to be another way. Phone records? Is there some way I can access phone records?"

Stan stood up. "Hope. I think you'd better calm down."

I leapt to my feet. "Calm down? Not when I could crack this case! C'mon, you were making fun of me, but I just got a serious breakthrough!" I rushed for the door.

Out of the corner of my eye, I saw Stan reaching for me and saying, "Hope, wait a second," but I ripped open the resident room door and nearly barreled into Jade Watterson, the resident on ICU, who still had her hand outstretched to punch the combination into the residents' room door.

"Are you okay?" she called after me. "Rounds haven't started yet!"

What was she going on about? Oh, yes, Grand Rounds, I thought, as I zipped down the stairs with my own breath huffing in my ears. A middle-aged woman in a blue cardigan made a great show of stepping aside for me and I waved my thanks.

Maybe I'd make it to rounds. Maybe not. Kurt had done rounds on physician drug abuse, and people were still talking about it, so it had to have rocked—

I punched open the door on the landing of the bottom floor, but I had to wait for a family with a stroller. The mother lumbered along, obviously pregnant under her long Muslim shift, so I couldn't cut her off even though I really wanted to.

While I waited, my brain ping-ponged. Kurt. Drugs. Was it possible that he'd OD'd instead of being murdered? Well, it was if you thought he'd take GHB, if he was enough of a hypocrite to lecture against drugs and then snort 'em up, or however you took GHB. I personally didn't get why anyone would take a date rape drug for fun, but then, I didn't really even drink, and I'd never tried marijuana, so no one would ever come knocking at my door for a cheap high.

At last, I squeezed by the family of six, more patients with walkers and wheelchairs, and hustled toward locating. I stood in front of their desk while the two women in a booth sat behind Plexiglas and ignored me, white coat notwithstanding.

"*Allo?*" said the plump, middle-aged one with brown curls and glasses, after glancing at her companion. She looked like a librarian, basically.

"Hi," I said in English, giving them my best smile. My French is pretty good, but I figured their English was better and I didn't want to waste time. "I'm Dr. Hope Sze, a first year resident on emergency medicine."

They exchanged a look that said, So?

I concentrated on the librarian, focusing my smile on her while I unclipped my pager from my waistband and showed it to her. "I was wondering if you might have a record of the phone numbers of people who paged me. You know, like I can go through the memory on the pager and find the last three numbers, but before then..."

"We do not keep any phone numbers," said the other woman, with a moderate French accent. She looked 50-something with short grey hair and a jowly mouth like a bulldog.

"Right." I met her eye and beamed at her instead. The bulldog mouth tightened. I wouldn't get too far with this one, but I had to try. "I realize you don't mark them down or anything, but maybe your telephone keeps a log?"

"I don't know why you are asking," said Bulldog.

"I'm just curious," I said. I looked at the younger one, but her eyes slid away. I turned back to Bulldog and made my final appeal. "You know, with everything that happened to Dr. Kurt..."

Her penciled-in eyebrows jerked up in surprise and then settled in grim satisfaction. "We do not know anything. If you have any further questions, you need to speak to the police."

The librarian nodded in agreement.

"Merci," I said as I swung away. I should have realized that they wouldn't go to bat for me. They were probably gossiping about me right now. *Did you know, this crazy resident, la petite Chinoise...*

I couldn't worry about that right now.

I had 24 minutes until Grand Rounds and a police officer to call.

CHAPTER 18

"Rivera."

My hand tightened on the receiver. This was the guy who had interviewed me on the day Kurt died. I'd kept the card in my wallet, but he might not remember me. I glanced around the residents' room, waiting for someone to come in and bust me, but they were probably at Grand Rounds already, snarfing up the free food. I cleared my throat. "Hi, my name is Dr. Hope Sze. We met, um, when you came to investigate Dr. Kurt Radshaw's suspicious death at St. Joseph's Hospital—"

"I remember you. You are the Chinese one."

Yes. That was exactly what I wanted inscribed on my gravestone. I forged on. "You may remember me talking about Dr. Radshaw's pager. I understand that your tests—" Oops, maybe I shouldn't mention the GHB yet. Back to the pager. "—ah, I mean, it seemed innocuous at the time, but I realized that the reason someone may have taken the pager was because it would show the last person who had called him. I bet that someone called him to meet them at St. Joseph's, and if you found the pager, you could see what the number was and who might have called him."

He stayed silent for a long moment. I bounced out of the chair and on to my toes, trying to get rid of my excess energy.

"Why are you calling me about this," he said finally.

"Well, you said to call if I remembered anything else. You gave me your card." I couldn't believe I had to explain it to him. "I thought it would be easier for you to obtain any phone records, since you're the police. If you just got Kurt's pager number, Bell Canada, or whoever, would have to release them to you, right?" I hated the way my voice rose at the end, like I was a little girl asking my daddy for permission.

I wasn't a little girl anymore.

And, by the way, my daddy wouldn't need me to spell it out for him. He would have jumped on it from the get go.

Rivera sighed. "I also told you, no conjecture. No...interpretation." He stumbled a little on the English word.

"But aren't you looking for leads? Especially since he tested positive for GHB, insulin, and succinylcholine?"

His voice sharpened. "Who told you this?"

"Is it true?" I countered.

"This is a matter for the police, Dr. Sze."

So it was true. Score one for the gossip boy, Stan Biedelman.

"If you recall any further facts or circumstances about the day, then I welcome your call. Otherwise, I would advise you to practice medicine and allow myself and my colleagues to continue our investigation unimpeded. Good day."

I sighed and clattered my way through the shadowed front hall of the Annex, past the closed orientation conference room doors. It felt like I was behind enemy lines. I had to follow a little hallway down the left to get to the classroom we used for rounds.

Tile floor, a dusty blackboard, a screen with a tattered white cord attached on its bottom hook, and rows of mismatched blue, orange, and lime green chairs. More importantly, two women I didn't recognize were sitting in the front left hand corner, intent on their plastic plates of food.

Where was my free lunch?

I backtracked into a side room with the same felted grey carpet as upstairs. A wooden coffee table supported giant plastic serving dishes of sandwiches on iceberg lettuce. My choices ranged from triangles of egg to tuna to mystery meat.

I shuddered. For the "gourmet capital of North America," as a real estate agent had described it, the rounds food was frighteningly similar to London. I chose tuna with a side dollop of pasta salad.

At least the desserts were fancier. As I reached for a strawberry cream, I heard footsteps behind me, and a baritone voice said, "Have a chocolate éclair. They're the best."

I whirled around. Tucker's brown eyes met mine. He stepped around the table and pointed out a mini éclair. He was wearing a mustard-colored shirt with the sleeves rolled up past his elbows. "Here. I swear by them. You'll be able to get through Bob's speech, snooze-free, if you have one."

It was the first time we'd spoken since our sausage lunch. I don't know what I'd been expecting, but it wasn't an éclair. His decency made me feel so guilty, I could hardly look at him. I blinked hard.

Tucker seized a pair of tongs and dropped the éclair on my plate, opposite the pasta salad, where it wouldn't get greasy.

"Thanks," I whispered. The plate trembled in my hands.

"Forget it." He grabbed a plate of his own and bent over the sandwiches. "You'll be okay."

My mouth opened. I croaked, "I'm sorry——"

He grabbed my wrist. "I said you'll be okay." His touch was firm but not unkind.

I studied the scratches on the table until I'd gotten my self-control back. My gaze moved to his walnut dress pants and leather sneakers. They were like old Adidas, with the stripes and little lace-ups, except instead of red and white canvas, they were made of medium-brown leather. "Thanks." I cleared my throat. "I like your shoes."

"Good," he said, slowly releasing my wrist. We stared at each other for a long moment.

I wanted to say so many things to him. Like, sorry I misjudged you. Or, what language would you speak to the server if you went to a restaurant and got mystery meat? Or even, hey, did you hear that Kurt's test came back positive for GHB and I just made a fool of myself telling the police to look into his phone records?

Instead, I just stared into his brown eyes and wished I could rewind the clock to June 30th, orientation day.

Footsteps at the doorway clattered to a halt.

I started. My éclair rattled on my plate. I grabbed it to keep it safe before I turned and glanced at the door.

My automatic smile withered as soon as I saw Alex.

His eyes were bloodshot and swollen. He'd shaved, but there was still a dark shadow on his cheeks and a fleck of blood along his chin where he'd probably cut himself shaving. His hair was flat on the left side, as if he'd slept on it.

At least his clothes looked clean: a grey shirt with solid red sleeves, '80s style, dark olive cargo pants, and sandals.

I'd wanted him to suffer, but not look like a total mess. I didn't know if I should yell at him or pity him.

"Sorry. Didn't mean to break up the party." Alex bared his teeth, but his eyes stayed slitted, as if it was too much effort to open them.

Tucker stiffened.

I was already walking toward the door with my food held protectively at my side. When I was three feet away, close enough to get his attention but luckily not too close to smell him, I said, low but clear, "Get lost, Alex." I would have sworn at him, except I didn't want any stray staff to overhear it.

Alex's eyes flickered behind his puffy eyelids. "Hope."

I held my back ballerina-taut. I looked him straight in the eye. "I don't know what's wrong with you, but you're a mess. Go take a shower."

I brushed past him, half-wanting to knock him with my shoulder, but he stepped aside.

Even in the midst of my contempt, I thought, *he doesn't want to touch me.*

"Hope," he repeated, but I lifted my chin and marched back to the classroom, chanting in my head, He's not worthy. You snooze, you lose. So long, sucker.

My whole life, I'd wondered about the bad boy thing.

Now I was pretty sure that bad boy was just a synonym for *loser*.

I could hear Tucker's voice rumble.

Alex answered, "Yeah, well—"

I walked until I found a seat at the far left rear corner, near the windows and as far from the food room as I could get. I could still hear them somewhat. I'd have to plug my ears and hum any minute. I'd forgotten to get a drink, but I wasn't going back in there. No way, no how.

Solution: do what Chinese people do in a crisis, or at times of celebration or, well, any time. Eat.

I sniffed my tuna fish sandwich cautiously. The last thing I needed was food poisoning.

The room started to fill up. Most people sat near the doors, which, as Little Miss Late, is a pet peeve of mine. Leave those seats, so the latecomers can sneak in with a minimum of fuss!

Stan waved at me from across the room. Omar stood next to him. Darn. I'd rather sit with those guys and laugh, even if it put me closer to Alex. I started to gather up my plate.

"Hope." Tori grinned down at me. She'd snuck up the back of the classroom and cut up the aisle next to the windows, surprising me. She'd make a good cat burglar. "Want company?"

"Sure," I said. "If you're going in the lunch room, could you grab me a juice or water?"

"Okay, but—"

"That's enough!" a man's voice resonated from up the hallway. "What's gotten into you?"

Tori sighed and shook her head. "That's what."

Oh. She didn't want to walk into the perfect storm. I was afraid to ask what was going on.

Bob Clarkson popped his head in the classroom. His face was unusually red. "Stan. Rounds will be a few minutes late. Could you tell everyone?"

Behind Dr. Clarkson, I caught a glimpses of Tucker's blond hair and Alex's red, '80s sleeve. Trouble.

"Of course, Dr. Clarkson," Stan said. He sounded like he was enjoying himself. He walked to the front of the room and clapped his hands. "For the one or two people who didn't hear, rounds will be a bit late. If anyone has any wine, now's the time to break it out."

230   *Code Blues*

Laughter rippled around the room. I whispered to Tori, "I guess Alex and Tucker hate each other, huh?" I propped my feet up on an empty chair in front of me.

She raised her eyebrows. "They didn't used to. At least, it wasn't so obvious."

Anu plopped beside Tori. "I'm glad I'm not late. What's rounds on today? Is it still on abuse?" She picked the crusts off her egg sandwich. She sighed. "I miss Kurt."

Her smooth brown face was perfectly serene. It tried to imagine her murdering Kurt and failed. Oh, well, she had an alibi, pretty much. Tori said they'd been at the Jazz Festival until midnight. I realized that just taking people's word for it was not a great policy, but I couldn't run a serious investigation during residency. Or anytime, really.

"I'm not sure who's going to do the main rounds, under the circumstances," said Tori, too polite to add "since the doctor who was supposed to present is now deceased." She continued, "We'll still have the regular teaching afterward."

Anu said, "I suppose they could skip the main presentation, if no one else wanted to fill in on that topic."

"Maybe," I murmured while I straining my ears at the hallway. More people were pouring into the classroom, talking, scraping their chairs on the tile floor, popping their juice bottles. I'd estimate under thirty people, but they made enough noise. No way I could eavesdrop on Alex and Tucker now, even if I wanted to.

"How is everyone today?" Mireille slid into the row in front of us and bestowed a smile upon us. Was I imagining the smugness in the corners of her mouth?

I removed my feet from the seat in front of me. She lowered herself on it. Her plate held only a single mystery meat sandwich. Either she was on a diet, or they'd severely run out of food.

Mireille turned mocking eyes on me. She lifted her sandwich, holding it so delicately that her fingertips hardly indented the soft white bread. "How about you, Hope? Is there anything new in your life?"

Was it possible she knew about the disaster formerly known as me and Alex? The only person I'd told was Tori. I glanced at her, but her return gaze was even. No, Tori was too discreet.

Would Alex tell Mireille? Maybe to try and hurt her. Hey, guess who I fucked today?

Well. I already knew that it had been a mistake to sleep with Alex. And I had no interest in letting Mireille put the screws on me. "Nothing," I said, spearing some pasta salad on the tines of my plastic fork. "My life is very boring."

She paused mid-chew. I smiled at her. Maybe I was getting better at this superficial veneer thing.

Mireille recovered quickly, checking her watch. "I thought we were trying to start the rounds on time."

As if it were a summons, Bob Clarkson strode to the front of the room. "All right, people! Let's get this show on the road!"

Tucker appeared next, disappearing around the back of the room. I was glad he had a plateful of food, but I couldn't tell if he'd gotten an éclair. He leaned against the rear wall and fixed his eyes on Bob Clarkson like an A1 student. No black eye, no abrasions, no obviously swollen knuckles.

Bob said, "As you know, Dr. Kurt Radshaw was supposed to do these rounds today on partner abuse. I know a lot of people were looking forward to it. Unfortunately, due to his tragic death, we've had to cancel the presentation."

Alex sidled in. Nearly all the chairs were taken, so he stood between the door and the garbage can. His arms were empty of food or drink. He had no visible injuries. If anything, he looked better, less dragged out, as if fighting with Tucker had woken him up. Our eyes locked, but with an effort of will, I broke it and faced front.

Mireille lifted her eyebrows at me before turning forward herself.

Bob continued, "Many people have come to my office to express their shock and sadness over his passing. St. Joseph's has lost a friend, a colleague, and a community leader. Could we all please have a moment of silence to respect his memory."

Immediately, we bowed our heads. I closed my eyes and recalled all the things I'd heard about him. Mentor, educator, a revitalizing force. Nothing but good stuff, except for his lust for women. I peeked at Mireille's curls. Her head was bent low. I couldn't see her face.

At last, Bob said, "We all knew and loved Kurt. Instead of doing Grand Rounds, let's take this hour to talk about him, his life and his efforts."

From the somber nods from the nurses and the tight lips of the residents, it was a good idea.

Bob went on, "Tensions are high. We're all feeling it. In fact, I just had to break up an argument." He paused to give the evil eye to Tucker and Alex. Tucker looked impassive, but Alex stared right back at him. Bob Clarkson shook his head sorrowfully. "This is not the St. Joseph's we all know and love. This is not the St. Joseph's Kurt would have wanted, and which we are all striving to achieve. Since my first days as chief, I have worked very hard for a consensus, so St. Joseph's can light up the twenty-first century as a leader among community hospitals." He brought his hands together in a circle.

Heaven help us. This was turning into a vote for Bob Clarkson speech. I glanced at Tori. She appeared to be listening. I took a bite of the chocolate éclair. It *was* good. I started nibbling around the edges. It was more interesting that Bob Clarkson.

He finally wound down. "Now, if anyone else would like to say a few words, the floor is yours. If it's too painful to speak in public, I understand."

Mireille's hand stretched in the air. "I would like to talk."

A startled sigh rippled through the crowd. Mireille tucked her plate under her chair and rose up. She had excellent posture.

Bob said, "Ah, Mireille, you can just speak from where you're sitting."

"It's all right, Dr. Clarkson. I would like everyone to hear." Instead of turning to her left so she could cut along the wall, she chose to walk down the row, forcing everyone to turn their legs aside and clutch their plates. Maximum disruption. I watched Alex watch her. His expression seemed neutral. His eyes flicked toward me. I looked away, but the skin on my arms tingled. Damn it.

Mireille planted her feet at the head of the classroom. She clasped her hands behind her back. She was wearing a demure, short-sleeved black dress with tiny blue flowers which fell to just above her knees. She looked perfectly at ease, more so than Bob Clarkson, who seemed to be muttering at her under his breath. She ignored him, raising her voice to the crowd. "Kurt Radshaw was a wonderful man, doctor, and human being. I hope they catch whoever killed him."

Another group murmur. She smiled. "I know that was not what you expected me to say. But it's true. I loved him. I want his murderer brought to justice."

The room went silent. Bob Clarkson's face froze in a rictus, but he managed to force out, "Ah, Mireille—"

She stepped forward, away from him. "There have been a lot of rumors about him and me." She looked right at me. "Some of them are true." She smiled again, a flash of teeth. "I loved him. I would never have hurt him."

Bob Clarkson cleared his throat. "Well, Mireille. That is certainly—interesting. I thought we'd talk about Kurt's life, and how St. Joseph's can move forward from this."

Mireille talked right over him. "I even have an alibi. I spent most of Friday night with people from St. Joseph's before I ended up with one in particular." She didn't look at Alex, but the rest of us did. His lips had gone white.

I felt sick. So she was Alex's "family emergency" before he hopped in bed with me. What kind of guy did that make him? What kind of person did that make me?

I hadn't eaten much, but I felt nauseous. Tori pressed a quick hand on my wrist. I took a little comfort from her cool skin. Thank goodness no one else really knew about me and Alex. If nothing else, I prefer to be humiliated in private rather than public.

Bob's hand pressed into Mireille's shoulder. "Thank you, Dr. Laroque. Does anyone else want to speak?"

A black nurse in a lab coat stood up at the end of the front row. "I was the nurse on Dr. Radshaw's team, and he was wonderful to work with. He was always teaching, always willing to stay late or to lend a hand. We'll miss him."

An appreciative ripple through the audience.

"Thank you," Bob said, obviously relieved. "That was very appropriate, Anne. Please sit down, Dr. Laroque."

A rebellious expression crossed Mireille's face, but after a long moment, she glided back to her seat, making sure to cut back through the row of people.

Tucker said, from the back, "He was a leader. That's what I liked about him. It's easy to complain about all the problems, but he worked to find the solutions. He didn't just talk about it, either. He did it."

Bob said, "Excellent point, Dr. Tucker. Thank you." His bland face showed no recognition of any jibe on the talk vs. action score.

Tori made noise in her throat, lower than a sigh.

A secretary said that Dr. Radshaw always made her laugh, even on the most hectic days.

Omar put up his hand. "He was a good teacher and very kind."

"He always had his pager on," added Stan from his seat by the door. "Isn't that what most of us will remember? Whenever you were reviewing a case, his pager would go off, or the phone would ring for him, or one of his patients would have a crisis only he could answer."

Some people laughed. A woman behind me said, "So true, so true."

"And somehow he'd manage everything at once," Stan finished. "He didn't get flustered or impatient. He just dealt with everything. Actually, if it was quiet, he didn't like it. He'd jump up and point out an article he'd just read, or tell us about an interesting case he'd seen. He was always moving."

Mireille was smiling and shaking her head. I saw the same look around the room, of affectionate recognition. Stan let them enjoy it before he added, "There's one other thing we'll never forget about Kurt."

We all leaned toward him.

Stan waited a beat. Then, with a twinkle in his eye, he said, "His moustache."

We laughed, and a few people even applauded. I grinned at Stan. He knew how to liven up a party.

He looked ready to go on, but Robin spoke up behind him. "I try to remember him as a human being."

He looked paler than usual, if that were possible. His blue pop-eyes were trained on Bob. "He wasn't perfect. But he was a very good teacher. He always tried to be evidence-based. He was the only doctor who brought in recent articles for us to read, and who asked us to follow the guidelines. I respected that."

We waited, but Robin settled back into his chair as if he'd said everything. Maybe for him, he had. Some booky classmates of mine from med school were like that. They lived for learning and thought everything else was beside the point. Usually, they went into internal medicine. I wondered why Robin had chosen family medicine and, more interestingly, what Kurt had to coach him through.

"Ah, that's a good point, Robin," said Bob. "We often lionize people after their deaths. But no one is perfect. We're all imperfect 'human beans.'" He chuckled at his own joke. A few people chuckled, probably out of sympathy. "Also, we pride ourselves on our teaching at St. Joseph's. We do our best to be evidence-based, to train the next generation of physicians..."

Man. I remembered what Tucker had said, about Bob Clarkson being jealous of Kurt. Certainly, Bob seemed to want to turn everything into "St. Joe's forever!" Still, it was a stretch to get from there to murdering his rival.

To my surprise, Dr. Callendar said, "Kurt was a good friend and a good doctor. I'll miss him."

Simple, but to the point. I found myself nodding. Maybe the guy was gruff because he was in mourning. Then I remembered, no, he was mean to me when I first met him, on Saturday morning.

Dr. Callendar was sitting in the middle of the first row. I tilted in my chair until I had a good angle on him. He had black hair which, under the fluorescent lights, was studded with silver. A sharply defined nose, arched eyebrows, ears that curled under at the tops like they'd been overheated on a stove. He was the only staff doctor wearing a white coat. It couldn't have been because he needed to look older.

Just then, Dr. Callendar's head swerved to glare straight at me.

Affecting casual disinterest, I turned my eyes back to Bob. But my heart was pounding. The man was freakishly attuned to my moves.

It was paranoid to suspect all the doctors and residents of murder. Tucker had pointed out it was just as likely to be a nurse or RT. Maybe I should talk to him, see if he'd found anything else out on that score.

Bob concluded, "Thank you. We'll miss Dr. Kurt Radshaw and we will never forget him. If you need to talk about him some more, please make an appointment to come by my office. My door is always open." He clasped his hands and gave us a sorrowful look, like a bad funeral director. "We'll take a ten minute break before our talk on peripheral neuropathy. Ten minutes, folks. We want to start on time."

People muttered and rose to pitch their plates in the already-overflowing garbage. Now that I had my kitchen boxes, I should unearth some Tupperware and use it instead of disposable plates.

Tori said, "Do you want to go for a quick walk?"

"Sure." I glanced at the doorway. Alex had already disappeared. He was good at that.

We brushed past the people waiting for the bathroom and the huggers in the front hall. No one wanted to leave yet. A good third of the women were crying. Bob Clarkson's break was unlikely to fit into ten minutes. I wondered if Tori wanted to escape from all the emotion.

After we descended the front steps, I let Tori take the lead. If we turned right, there was a parking lot, a church, and the metro station; if we turned left, there was another parking lot and the hospital. Straight ahead was an empty picnic table.

Tori aimed toward the church. "That was heavy," she said.

"Yeah." People spilled on to the front porch behind us. I had to lengthen my stride to keep up with Tori. I glanced around and lowered my voice. "Was Dr. Callendar always, ah, so hard to get along with?'

Tori glanced up at me. "Yes."

"Oh." Yet another dead end.

Her eyebrows quirked. It seemed to be her substitute for a small smile. "Why do you ask?"

"I wondered if his personality had changed since Kurt died."

She shook her head. "He's notorious. The med students try to avoid him. If you get along with him, he's okay."

I knew that. I just had no idea how to get along with him. I kicked a stray piece of gravel. We watched it skitter across the parking lot and roll to a stoop under a Jeep.

"Don't worry about Dr. Callendar." Before I could ask why, she glanced at her watch. "We'd better head back."

It seemed like we'd only just escaped. I lagged behind, noticing for the first time the rusted, deformed bike rack beside the disabled ramp at the front of the Annex. The covered front porch was jammed with residents. I could see Mireille's brown curls at the centre of the crowd. A few stragglers squeezed by the residents, but they were too intent on their own conversation to notice.

As we mounted the stone steps, Mireille abruptly switched from French to English and faced us. Her cheeks were cherry red, like I'd imagine in carbon monoxide poisoning. Her eyes glittered. She said, "My sister just called. The police have called Vicki in for questioning again. They think she killed Kurt."

CHAPTER 19

One of the second year residents, Sébastien, whom I didn't know well, shook his head. "*Impossible.*"

"Why not?" Mireille returned, in English. "I've read that it is often the spouse. A crime of passion. Of course, in this case, she was not the spouse yet and would never be."

A soft snort escaped my lips. Everyone else had said Vicki was the fiancée. Tori shot me a warning frown, but it was too late.

Mireille whirled on me. Her mouth twisted. "Oh, you don't believe me? Too bad. Really, a shame." She threw her arms in the air. "They found the killer. Thank God."

She was more volatile than ever. Some people have said this of me, that I hum with energy, that I seem angry or anxious when I'm really just at my baseline. Observing Mireille, I could see why. She was off the charts. A volcano. She made me look like a Zen monk.

A white guy with dreadlocks, whom I hadn't met yet, said to one of the second years, "Did Vicki have access to insulin and succ?"

Mireille stamped her foot on the wooden slats. "Of course she did."

The guy held up his hands. "Look, Mireille, I'm just asking. She's an OB nurse, right?"

"Yes, but we all know how easy it is to get drugs," Anu, of all people, piped up. Her face shone like an eager student's. "They always draw up extra morphine and throw it out. Plus on OB, they do spinal blocks and epidurals. A narcotic would be no problem and they don't even count insulin."

The dreads guy nodded slowly. "Or she could just take Kurt's extra insulin and swipe succ off the crash cart. Okay. But I still don't get the motive."

Mireille said triumphantly, "Simple. He was going to dump her and come back to me."

We all stared at her.

"That's what he told me. Friday night. The night before he—" Her voice shook for the first time. She took a deep breath. "Before she killed him."

The main door creaked open. We all jumped. Stan called, "Time's up, folks. Dr. Lieberman is ready."

Mireille said under her breath, "She was at the top of my list. I hope she rots in hell."

My eyes widened at the venom in her voice. *Do not cross this woman.* She turned and smiled at me, then cut in front of Robin, so she could be the first one through the door. Even in her grief, she was as bossy as ever.

While Dr. Lieberman tried to educate me on peripheral neuropathy. I pondered life and death. If Mireille was telling the truth, and Friday night was a joyful reunion with Dr. Kurt, how had he ended up doing a face plant in the men's locker room by 2 a.m.?

If Kurt was the person from St. Joseph's she'd spent most of Friday with, that wasn't an alibi. He was dead. Unless they'd been in public, with witnesses.

I tried to ignore the little voice that whispered, If Kurt was her "one person from St. Joseph's in particular," then she didn't spend Friday night on a sleepover with Alex.

And Alex wasn't a complete liar. Maybe he *was* getting over her. The thought warmed my cold, cold heart.

I glanced at the door. Alex hadn't returned for the small group lectures, but neither had at least half the group. It seemed like everyone showed up for Grand Rounds and ate. Then the attending staff and nurses left. Only the residents remained for the next speakers, and I bet attrition took its toll over course of the afternoon.

Code Blues

I doodled on the handout, which was filled with differential diagnoses and clinical tests I'd never heard of.

I was no detective. I'd never really suspected Vicki.

Chairs scraped around me. Everyone was filing toward Dr. Lieberman. I cast a glance at Tori.

She whispered, "He's showing us how to test for motor weakness in carpal tunnel."

Belatedly, I stood to join them. Naturally, Mireille was the first to push on Dr. Lieberman's thumbs. "Did I do it right? Let me try again!"

He shook his hand and grinned. "Very good. But try not to be so, uh, vigorous with your patients."

She giggled. I'd never seen her so giddy. She was loving it. Her face was flushed, her shoulders down, a new ease in her movements as she moved back to her chair.

Maybe I could turn her happiness to my advantage. It was the best time to ask her questions. But not alone, after the last time we talked one-on-one. I'd try to keep Tori close and, if possible, Tucker.

But at the end of teaching, Tucker zoomed out of the room à la Alex, with a quick, embarrassed wave at me. I didn't have time to thank him for the éclair, let alone ask if he'd help interrogate Mireille. But he was probably embarrassed enough after Kung Fu fighting with Alex.

Too bad.

Most other people had regrouped around Mireille. She tapped her cell phone. "We can call my sister if you don't believe me. In a few hours, it's going to be on the Web and in the newspapers. I bet they'll hold a press conference. The police want to find the killer ASAP. It makes them look bad, too, because they didn't think it was murder. But I knew. I always knew."

Tori and I hung at the sidelines after I had whispered my plans to her. I wanted Tori to be the one to invite Mireille for coffee, but she just nodded along with the rest of the group like Mireille was the new Moses.

Finally, I took a deep breath. "Anyone want to go to a *térrasse* and talk there? It's a beautiful day." I was taking a chance. If the whole gang came along, Mireille would keep singing the same song. On the upside, it was less likely she'd brain me in front of all our colleagues.

The tone of the room faltered. "Ah—no—sorry." One by one, they checked their watches and scattered. In residency, it's all-too-rare to get home before sundown. They had banks to go to, people to do. I waved off their apologies. "Next time, okay?"

Robin was the last to leave. He said solemnly to Mireille, "I'm sorry about Kurt. He was a smart man. He had a lot of good advice. Not all the time—no one bats 100 percent—but most of the time."

I waited for him to go into evidence-based medicine mode, but thankfully, he restrained himself for once.

Mireille glared at me for breaking up her flock. Tori stepped in quietly. "It's too bad we never go out after teaching. Everyone is so busy."

Robin flapped his shoulder bag closed and fled. We could hear his dress shoes hastening down the hall. The three of us were the only ones left in the room. Tori continued, "Would you like to be alone, or would you like some company? Hope and I were going to have coffee."

Mireille's shoulders tensed. She didn't look at me, but it wasn't because of Tori. She said, "Well..."

She wanted me to beg off, but I'd hold my breath and turn blue first.

Tori simply waited. She had such a calm energy, like a pond with water lilies. In comparison, I was a raging river and Mireille was Niagara Falls.

Mireille pressed a hand against her eye and stared at the floor. "We could go to the *Brûlerie St-Denis*."

I remembered seeing their sign on Côte-des-Neiges: black lettering surrounded by drawings of coffee beans. "Sounds good to me," I said, even though I don't drink coffee.

We cut through the mostly-deserted parking lot to the metro station. Mireille took a deep breath, her face tilting up to the blue sky. "I really like the coffee at the *Brûlerie*. Kurt and I used to come here—" She stopped.

Tori said, "It's all right. You can talk about him. We knew him, too."

I nodded vigorously.

After a long minute, Mireille said, "Yes. I *would* like to talk about him." But she bit her lip and took a deep breath and stayed mum until we reached the *Brûlerie*.

The *térrasse* tables were taken. Everyone from a bald guy with a terrier to a bunch of laughing university students had already staked their claim. Not unexpected on a sunny summer day, but a bummer nonetheless. Tori said, "I'm sure there are tables inside."

Mireille frowned.

Please don't make a scene, I thought. Just then, two girls jumped up from a little round table next to the building. They'd left their trayful of empty coffee cups and lipsticked napkins, but Mireille rushed to plop her notebook on the nearest seat.

"It's like circling the block five times, and then a parking space opens up right in front of you," I said.

Mireille gave me a genuine smile. "Exactly."

Tori offered me the one other chair, but I borrowed one from another table. The terrier wasn't using it.

The building's shade felt pleasantly cool. A server, a young woman in a visor, cleared away the old tray and handed us menus.

Kurt, Kurt, Kurt, I mentally urged Mireille, but they scouted the menus before settling on coffee for Mireille and a mochachino for Tori. I asked for a banana-raspberry smoothie.

When the server left, Tori said simply, "I thought Kurt might change his mind."

Mireille's face transformed. Her eyes glowed and her expression softened. "You did? Why?"

Tori's eyebrows quirked. "I knew what the relationship meant to you."

Mireille touched Tori's hand. "Ohhh, Tori. It makes me so happy to hear this. Yes, I loved him more than—anyone. He said I was his little star."

I shifted in my plastic patio chair. Little star?

"That's beautiful," said Tori. They looked at each other intently.

Their connection completely bypassed me. I could've been the terrier at the next table. I tried to tell myself it was a good thing. Mireille was more likely to confess if she forgot all about me.

"Yes." Mireille smiled. "He was proud of me, both personally and professionally. He encouraged me to present at my first surgical conference. He couldn't come with me, but we talked the whole time." She patted her white bag, indicating her cell phone. "He was right. I was glad I went. Everything was perfect. We were true equals. Soul mates."

So why did he dump her?

Tori laid her hand on Mireille's. Mireille smiled, but her eyes were glistening.

The server appeared with a red plastic tray. She clicked our drinks on the table and swished off.

My smoothie was a little thin, but otherwise quite tasty. I played with the straw to give me something to do. I felt uncomfortable with Mireille's emotion. It was easier to think of her as a charging rhino than a wounded woman.

Mireille ripped open a pack of sugar and stirred it into her coffee. Her metal spoon clinked against her ceramic cup more than was strictly necessary. She said, matter-of-factly, "That woman preyed on his weakness."

I set my smoothie back on the table. Tori pressed her knee against mine for a second. I got the code: *shut it.*

Mireille gave a hard laugh and released her spoon, letting it clatter on the edge of the cup. "It's quite simple. Kurt loved to help people. He couldn't resist it. That was why he loved family medicine, why he worked in a teaching centre, why he chose St. Joseph's. The more trouble people were in, the more irresistible he found them." She glanced at me for the first time. "His cell phone and pager rang at all hours. I told him, 'Look, Kurt, I'm only a medical student, but I know this. You have to set limits. This is what all our professors are telling us.'"

I couldn't speak. I heard a high-pitched ringing in my ears. I knew she was telling the truth right here, right now.

"But no. He wanted to be the hero. He wanted to be available. Even to his patients who quit smoking, he told them to call if they were thinking of smoking!" She flapped her hand, and not just because at least five people had lit up around us. "This was quite apart from all the residents and medical students. Bob Clarkson continually asked for meetings. It was too much." She shook her head and repeated, more softly, "Too much."

"Did he cut back?" Tori asked softly.

Mireille's lips tightened. "No." The syllable was clipped. "He went back to a woman who told him that everything he did was perfect. But in the end, he chose—" Her voice broke. She pulled her spoon out and dropped it back on her tray. She swallowed her coffee. After a minute, she said, almost steadily, "He was coming back to me. I know he was."

Chapter 20

In parting, Mireille pressed kisses and a hug on Tori and even a peck-peck-shoulder squeeze on me. I forced myself to hug her back, feeling more awkward than ever.

Back in my apartment, Tori helped cut open a box of CD's. I said, "So, do you believe her?"

Tori shrugged. "It's difficult to know what to believe."

I made a face. "Can't you just say yes or no?"

She laughed and cut open a box with an Exacto-knife. "I'm sure she believes what she's saying."

"So what?"

She shrugged. Another non-answer.

I pulled a handful of CD's out. I couldn't bear to sell them, even though I only listen to MP3's now. "You know what, maybe we'd better leave these until I find my CD rack. I know it's somewhere."

Tori moved on to the next box, labeled Medical Books, and applied the blade.

I said, "Actually, you know what bothered me the most?"

She murmured, "What she said about Kurt."

"Exactly. About him being a martyr, basically. You think it's true?"

Tori hesitated. "He enjoyed it. But yes, it was true. He was always available." She ripped open the flaps of the box.

"Yeah. It made him a great doctor and a great teacher. But I bet it didn't make him the world's greatest boyfriend. I'd need someone who was more there *for me*. And not just helping me with my poster for a surgical conference." I peered inside the box. "Oh, those are more notes from med school. Damn, I wonder where my ACLS went."

I spun *The Best of Miles Davis* on my CD player, which was sitting in the corner behind some boxes. Miles's melancholy tones hit home today. Kurt had been universally loved and lauded for giving so much of himself. That was the way doctors used to be, available 24 hours a day, 7 days a week, for births, deaths, fevers, sore throats, and things that went bump in the night. Everyone loved and respected the town doctor.

Things changed. I wasn't sure where, exactly. But now, there were walk-in clinics, academic physicians who worked in research centres, and ever-fewer old-fashioned family docs. The public had lost respect for us, the money wasn't as good, and, perhaps as a consequence, our generation of doctors were not as willing to sacrifice their whole lives to medicine. Surgeons were still hard core, especially during residency. But most physicians wanted to live, too. We usually banded together in call groups to arrange time off. At St. Joseph's, the doctors took turns backing up the resident-on-call for the FMC. There was no need for Kurt to be on call 24/7.

So what did you do, if you were the old-fashioned type, medicine *über alles*, and you went into family medicine, which is looked down upon as a more slack field? Kurt could have gone the rural route. Instead, he chose to stay in Montreal, but he selected the most derelict hospital he could find, and advertised far and wide that he was there for everyone. All the time. He was going to be the St. Joseph's Superman.

I'd never known the guy, and I couldn't really guess what motivated him to work like that. But it finally made sense to me. I'd been wondering to myself why anyone killed him, when everyone seemed to love him. Like I said, in fiction, it's always the biggest stinker who gets knocked off, and no one knows who did it, because everyone else plus the cat has a good motive. But for the first time, I thought the very quality that made Kurt the best-loved doctor was what broke up his personal life and, maybe, made him vulnerable to a murderer.

How depressing. I'd chosen a profession that would consume your soul, if I let it.

Tori's raised her voice above Miles's trumpet. "Are you all right?"

I realized that I was sitting on the living room floor beside the boom box, barricaded behind boxes, with my arms wrapped around my knees. I said, "Yeah."

She perched on the lumpy green cushion of the futon I'd managed to assemble. "What's wrong?"

"Is it worth all this? To become a doctor?" I gestured at my tornadoed room, but I really meant all of it. The work, the crap pay, the rocked relationships, moving across the country because the Match said so, sleeping on the floor for a week.

Her dark eyes were kind. "Why did you go into medicine in the first place?"

"I wanted to help people." The traditional answer, but true. I added, "And I thought it would be challenging and fun."

Her eyebrows lifted a touch. "And is it?"

I nodded. "Most of the time."

She waited. I conceded, "I guess I like it. When I don't have to work with Dr. Callendar."

She smiled. "You'll live."

"I guess." I hadn't thought about Alex for an hour, and it felt good. But remembering Alex now felt like ground glass in my stomach. "Do you think Alex was with Mireille Friday night? When Kurt was killed?"

Tori hesitated. "It's hard to tell when either of them is telling the truth."

I bowed my head again. The drummer tapped his cymbals, the pianist played background, and Miles's trumpet blew across them both.

A breeze rustled the tree leaves outside my living room window. Tori turned her face to it and closed her eyes. "But Mireille insists she was with Kurt that night, for at least part of the night. " She hesitated. "It would be a lot to make up."

We'd never grilled Mireille about her alibi for the rest of the Friday night. Tori read my mind. "I wasn't going to ask her for an alibi. I want her to trust me." She smiled a little.

"You want me to be the bad cop," I said.

She shrugged. "I want the cops to be the cops. But yes, if you insist. I don't want to alienate Mireille in an attempt to investigate her."

Pah. I still thought there were more holes in everyone's story than Havarti cheese, a product I'd recently discovered in the Montreal supermarkets. No one was willing to play Kinsey Milhone with me. I tried to needle her. "Okay. Are you willing to alienate Alex?"

Tori laughed. "I'll leave it to you." Her hand flew to her mouth. "I'm sorry, Hope. I wasn't thinking."

My eyes smarted, but I tried to smile. "It's true." A pain twanged in my chest around my heart. Maybe I could have aortic dissection and get it over with.

Tori shifted on the futon. She traced the white piping of the cushion with her index finger. "All I know about Alex is, he seemed very disturbed about his past. He used to talk about it a lot with Kurt—" She stopped abruptly.

I clicked through what I knew. He was from Kitchener. He might be a Mennonite. What could be so traumatic about buggies and plain clothes? Or in his case, forsaking buggies and taking up zippers? Wait, maybe that was the Amish. "What about his past?"

Tori shook her head. "I'm not sure. Alex used to joke about it a bit. You know, if someone asked him why he talked to Kurt, he'd say, 'Blast from the past.' But he never said any more. And of course, Kurt kept all our talks confidential."

I knew very little about Alex's past. I hadn't thought it mattered. We were here, we liked each other. If he rejected me, one of us had done wrong. But there might be a third factor holding him back, in addition to Mireille. His family, somehow.

Some white people make a big deal about my race. Their favourite question is, "Where do you come from?" That means that I'm from elsewhere. I like to shoot back, "Where are you from?"

"Oh, I'm Canadian," they say, laughing.

"So am I."

"No, where are you *really* from?"

This can go on forever.

Others ask, "How often do you go to China?" They're astonished that I've never been there, and want to regale me with descriptions of their own trip to China in 1989. So their question was a cover for a travel monologue.

I've come to realize people's questions about my race reveal a lot more about themselves than it does about me.

On the other hand, in the last few years, I've figured out how much my family has subconsciously influenced me. Although I've been educated as a scientist, I'm very superstitious. I'm 26 years old, and I still don't step on cracks in the sidewalk. Just one of my quirks, I thought, until my mother told me four was an unlucky number because in Chinese, it sounds like the word for death. I'd never thought much about the number four, but I started avoiding it. Just in case. I even counted the leads in my mechanical pencil before each exam and made sure there were seven or eight but never four.

I rejected the stereotypes—ah, Asian girl, therefore, must be a rich math whiz with good legs—but clearly, culture had influenced my personality. Because Alex didn't talk about it, because he dressed and acted and spoke like an average guy, I hadn't thought culture was a big deal to him. From Tori's comments, it was probably the opposite.

"Huh," I said, finally.

She flicked her eyebrows at me with her trademark economy of words.

"It's just not me," I said. "Keeping it all bottled up inside. I've tried it. I just end up obsessing and, uh, exploding." Compared to her silence, it seemed immature. Cultural differences again. To change the subject, I peered into a box by the wall. Even though it was marked "Study," it was filled with interview clothes. "Geez, that's useful," I said.

Tori checked her watch. "I should go soon." She surveyed the room. "I wish I could help more."

"That's okay. You've done enough slave labor. We'll have to do something fun next time."

She smiled wryly as we waved goodbye.

I was overwhelmed by the chaos when I returned to the living room. The bedroom wasn't too bad. I'd unpacked some day-to-day clothes, and left the other boxes to be dealt with later. The bathroom was in order out of necessity, and boy, I was glad to have all my face-cleaning solutions and choice of hair conditioners again. The kitchen I was mostly deferring to that nebulous tomorrow when I'd have free time. As long as I had the basics, like some cutlery and dishes, a milk pitcher, and a can opener, life was pretty good.

However, the living room suffered from the "dump everything here and start unpacking" syndrome. Three walls were stuffed with boxes, with tunnels to my desk and futon. The desk had become a collecting ground for fragile things like flower vases and jewelry boxes, as well as important papers and my laptop. I could hardly see Henry.

I liked working with my hands. Medicine is mostly mental work. You can spend all day crouched over a book, and by the next morning, at least half the knowledge has leaked out and you have to learn it all over again. But a bookshelf doesn't usually tumble down unless you're a mighty poor builder.

I levered the frame upright and screwed in the centre shelves. The bookshelf was now much more stable. I filled it with medical books. Get thee away from me, chaos!

I'd managed to empty four or five wine boxes. I collapsed the boxes for recycling. We only had two lousy blue recycling bins for two entire apartment buildings. Last I checked, the two bins, each about the size of three milk crates, were overflowing with plastic jugs and, yes, cardboard boxes. With everyone moving July first, there was a ton of garbage.

I shoved the boxes under my arm and trundled down the stairs, through the main foyer, and down a second, short, set of stairs to the basement.

I pushed open the double doors, both of which were covered in flaking, gunmetal grey paint. A bare fluorescent light bulb glowed above my head. Cars had pulled up snugly to the concrete wall. The concièrge had told me to park as close as possible, to minimize the chance of another car taking off my bumper.

Someone had left the garage door on my left yawning open again. I had complained to the concièrge about the unlocked, often gaping, garage doors. He'd pointed out the foot-high white letters spray-painted on the inside: *FERMEZ SVP*, CLOSE THE DOOR! I conceded that the one on the right, underlying the adjoining building of the Mimosa Manor, was usually closed. Perhaps only half the people here were literate.

Evening had fallen. Through the open door, I could see the fuzzy outlines of pine trees, black against the grey-blue sky. At least the breeze dampened the smell of rotting food and damp cardboard.

I advanced on the three garbage cans and two recycling bins next to the open door, and tucked my own cardboard between the overflowing blue boxes and the wall. I brushed the dirt off my hands and stepped toward the garage door, my hand already outstretched to pull it closed.

A shadowy figure appeared in the mouth of the garage. "Hi Hope," he said.

I screamed.

Chapter 21

"It's me, Alex!" the shadow exclaimed. He stepped closer to the 60-watt bulb, illuminating his forehead and his shaggy chestnut hair.

It looked like Alex. It moved like Alex, with a casual, shambling gait. It sounded like Alex. My heart slowly re-entered normal sinus rhythm. "You scared the hell out of me!" I yelled at him. "Why can't you just ring the doorbell like everyone else?"

He took a half step back. "Yeah, I see that." His hands remained outstretched, but didn't touch me. Although he smiled, his grey eyes were wary. "I just wanted to talk to you."

I eyeballed him until he stuck his hands back inside his pants pockets. I asked, more normally, "Why didn't you go by the front door?"

He sighed. "I did. But I saw you through the window. You were heading downstairs, so came down to meet you."

Plausible but pat. "You shouldn't tell me it's a bad neighborhood, and then sneak up on me in the dark."

"Okay, okay. *Mea culpa*. Walksafe. Take back the night."

I had to laugh then. So did he. He gestured at the garage, encompassing the oil spills on the floor and the junk along the walls. "Clearly, I was wrong about your neighborhood. A fine ambiance. Who said romance is dead?"

I laughed again. "Don't push it." I cocked my head to one side. "I think they said *chivalry* is dead." I gave him a significant look. "I see no evidence to the contrary."

He narrowed his eyes. "You just want me to kiss your feet again. I would be delighted."

I giggled.

"But first..." He backtracked and reached for the cord on the handle of the garage door and yanked it down. The door rumbled shut. He waved at it. "Chivalry."

The enclosed garage suddenly felt quieter and more intimate. I was conscious of how close he was standing to me. His grey eyes were intense. His breath warmed my cheek. I tried to tell myself I was intoxicated by the smell of putrefying fruit in the garbage bin. I turned away.

"Hope." A note of such yearning rang in his voice.

It made me want to throw myself in his arms. I dug my nails into my palms. Just say no. You can do it, Hope. Café. Mireille. Bad boy. Bad boy.

I didn't touch him. But I heard myself asking, "You want to come up?" Knowing it could spell doom.

He stood so close, I could almost feel him nod.

I walked faster, twitching open the first door. He grabbed it mid-swing and opened it fully. "After you."

He made sure to beat me to the second door, too. I took a deep breath. Ryan used to open doors for me all the time. It wasn't such a big deal, but with Alex, every move felt seductive.

Café. Mireille. Run away. I could make a poem out of this. Resist, resist. I could feel his eyes travel down my body as I mounted the stairs to my apartment. His hand trailed near mine on the banister. He wasn't even touching me, but my nipples were hard.

No. Resist. Take a cold shower. But it made me think of Alex with me, his hair plastered to his head, rivulets of water coursing down his skin, his eyes bright with love for me.

Aside from the sex, I just liked *being* with Alex. He made me laugh. He made me think.

Code Blues

Some people, like Mireille, make the hair stand straight up from my head. I liked Tori, but she was so quiet, it was a bit of an effort to communicate.

Alex struck just the right chord. When he wasn't running off or mentioning Mireille, that is.

Alex leaned against the doorway as I fumbled with the lock. My keys jangled into the silence. I threw open the door, hitting the light switch on the left. "Sorry it's such a mess."

"Sure is." He raised his eyebrows.

"Thanks a lot!" I snapped. He was one to talk.

He shook his head. "Hope, you were the one who said it."

I slipped off my sandals and crossed my arms. If we were fighting, it was easier to stave off the attraction. "Yeah, I know. But it takes one to know one."

He inclined his head. "Guilty."

Now I was even more embarrassed, remembering his apartment. I'd basically never made it out of the bedroom.

His grey eyes were steady. "Anyway, I came to apologize."

I stiffened. "Well, okay. About what, exactly?"

He ran an aggrieved hand through his hair. "Sorry I freaked out that day."

I waited.

He shifted from foot to foot. "You don't know me very well, but I hate people looking through my stuff. It makes me crazy. But"— he shot me a smile—"when I cooled off, I figured it was probably a mistake."

"Probably?"

"Definitely a mistake. Sorry for going ham on you. Like I said, I'm ready and willing to kiss your feet or do anything else—"

I shook my head. "Going ham?"

"Going ape on you. You know. MC Hammer style."

I didn't know anything about MC Hammer except "Can't Touch This" and the unforgettable pants I spotted on YouTube. I changed the subject. "You and I both think the problem is I don't know you well enough. So teach me about you."

He leaned in close, his voice husky. "I thought you'd never ask."

I took two steps away and bumped into a box, but evaded his steadying hands. "Not like that."

"Like what, then?" His face curled in irritation. "Can I come in, at least? Or do we have to do this standing in your front hall?"

I shrugged. "Hey, you thought the garbage basement was romantic." For once, I felt like the one holding the aces. It made me more relaxed. Alex wasn't that good-looking. His nose was a bit long. He was shorter than one of my towers of boxes. He got by on charm.

But I was building an immunity to it. I hoped.

"Fine."

He exhaled and crouched on a bare patch of floor. He rested his back against the door and extended his legs, still wearing his Tevas for a quick getaway. "Shoot."

"Tell me why you left Kitchener."

His eyes widened briefly. "Who told you about that?" He ran his hands down his thighs. "Mireille? Shit."

I stayed standing. "No shit. That's the whole point, Alex. Drop the guessing games and tell me yourself."

He sighed and closed his eyes, resting his eyes against the door. "Ah, man. You know how to go for the jugular, don't you."

I waited. Silence worked on Alex. He was too fidgety to hold back for long. I crossed my arms. I could hear the clock ticking in the kitchen, and two kids pounding down the hall, giggling while their mother called after them.

Alex cracked an eyelid at me. "Are you going to sit down, at least?"

I leaned against the door of my hall closet. It bounced but didn't close—one of the feet from my ironing table in the way, propping it open.

Alex snorted. "It's a sign. Come on. Sit. It's not something I like to talk about, okay?"

Finally. No *petit-fours* and no B.S. Just us.

I dropped to the floor, leaning against the bouncy closet door and sitting cross-legged.

He closed his eyes and exhaled, exposing his pale throat. "I can't believe I'm telling you this. I never told anyone here except Kurt. But what the fuck. It's therapeutic, right?"

I tried to quiet my breathing, keep as silent as possible. It was stuffy in the front hall with the bedroom door closed.

He laughed bitterly. "It's like this. I'm not even from Kitchener. I'm from a little town outside it you've probably never heard of." He ran his hands down his thighs again. "A real shit-kicker of a place." He stopped there, his Adam's apple bobbing.

My heart dropped into my lap. I remembered another news story, buried deep in my subconscious. I hadn't thought much about Mennonites or Amish communities beyond their charming buggies and pioneer clothes, until one such prairie town was recently busted for child abuse. Some elders of the community took turns beating children, often girls under the age of twelve. Sometimes it was their own daughters or granddaughters. This abuse went on for years, for generations, before the RCMP busted it up.

I hoped to God Alex hadn't gone through the same thing. If he'd been abused, I could try, but I probably couldn't help him. If he was an abuser, I could not forgive him.

Alex said abruptly, "Did you ever hear about the smuggling?"

"What kind of smuggling?" My voice was Ginsu-sharp. Child smuggling?

"You know. Across the U.S. border. With the cheese."

"No." It sounded like a strange game of Clue. Instead of Mrs. Peacock, in the library, with the candle stick, it was smuggling, across the border, with the cheese. It did not sound like abuse. I relaxed a little.

He crossed one of his outstretched legs, bringing his left foot closer to mine. I didn't move away. He spoke to his sandals. "You probably did. It was on *60 Minutes* and everything. The Mennonites used to be able to ship things across the border without being searched. Furniture, tools, whatever. But then the border guard cut open a wheel of cheese and found cocaine. The RCMP came. They investigated a few of towns, but they hung around ours a lot. Charged a few people but dropped the charges. The case is still open."

Alex started talking faster. His eyes darted from side to side. "So no one was convicted officially, but unofficially, everyone thought it was my family. We had to leave. We sold the farm at a loss, and moved to Kitchener. But there were still rumors." He made fists out of the material in his pants. "It was almost worse that way. We had no trial, no way of defending ourselves. It was hell. People wouldn't talk to us, wouldn't sell us things in the store, and at school—" He swallowed hard. "I left."

His words hung in the air. His pain felt like a living presence in the room, a cloud of purple and black invading my nostrils and choking down my throat.

I had to break the silence. "I'm sorry."

He took a deep, shuddering breath. "Yeah."

We sat there, my toes nearly touching his. I wanted to draw him into my arms and tell him everything was going to be all right. I wanted to stroke the hair out of his eyes and kiss his temple. And I wanted to ask more questions.

Like, did his family really smuggle the cocaine? Did he do it? He was vague on the time, but it must have happened before he'd come to university at McGill.

Or was someone just duped by a wiser dealer? Hey, I like how you churn your own butter and sew ruffles on your dresses. Could you do me a favor? Wait, that was probably the Amish again.

Alex hadn't been exactly trustworthy, but he'd never acted like a criminal. I wanted to give him the benefit of the doubt. Like Kurt did. That's what we often do in medicine. Patients say, yes, I'm going to quit smoking, or hey, I really need you to fill out my disability form, and for the most part, we take a chance and say okay. I took a deep breath and said it now. "Okay."

His gray eyes swept up to meet mine, wary and angry but with a spark of wistfulness. "Okay?"

I had to hide a smile. "Okay."

He grabbed my left knee and shook it.. "God, I've missed you, Hope."

I laughed as my leg jiggled under the force of his enthusiasm. "We just met."

He grinned. "Yeah, imagine how bad it'll be after we've known each other a whole month." He got up on his hands and knees and crawled toward me, pressing a tender kiss on my lips.

His lips were smooth, but the unshaved stubble around his mouth marked my face as pressed more deeply, more hungrily. His hands grabbed my shoulders. He spread his lips, straddling my hips.

I tried to break the kiss. He reached up to cup the back of my head. I had to wrench my lips away. "Alex."

He pressed kisses along my jaw line, down to my chin. "I've never told anyone before. Anyone except Kurt. You're the best, Hope. You fuckin' rock."

I had to laugh. "Alex."

"Sorry. I mean, you're amazing, you're superb—" He ran his tongue along my ear.

"I liked fantastic," I offered, a little breathless.

"That too." I could hear the smile in his voice.

"But, uh, I don't want to fall into bed again."

He went very still. Then he said, "Okay. You seem to like this hallway. I'm game." He slipped his hand under my shirt, running up my back.

"Alex!" I pulled away so we were face-to-face, even though he wouldn't let me out of his arms. "We were talking."

"Right. I talked. You listened. Now you know all about me. We're square, right?"

Right. I wanted to say it. I wanted to inaugurate my front hall and let him sweep me away. But I shook my head.

He closed his eyes. "What the hell do you want from me, Hope."

I laid a finger on his chin. "I know it was hard for you to tell me."

"Damn straight."

"But it's hard for me, too." Hesitantly, I curled forward and laid my head against his chest. His hands rose to circle my waist, so he wasn't irretrievably angry. "Yes, I'm happy you told me. But it's like there's a skeleton in your closet, and you gave me a glimpse of the ankle bone and said, 'See? Now you should understand everything. Let's do it.' But I don't understand, Alex. Not even half of it."

He withdrew, dropping his arms. "So what you're saying is, not good enough."

I grabbed at his hands, tried to catch his eye, but he was already rising to his feet. I said, "No, Alex, I'm saying, thanks for the ankle bone, it's really good, I just need—"

"What?" he spat at me. "You need to study the skull, the pelvis, the clavicle and humerus? You'd like to probe my internal organs? You'd like to drip fluorescein on my eyeballs or do a rectal exam? I've already given you everything, and it just isn't good enough for you?"

I drew myself to my feet. "Alex—"

He threw open the bolt on the door. "Hope, I'm sick of playing by your rules. 'Earn me.' 'Tell me.'" His eyes glittered. His cheekbones were sharp under his skin. "I'm never good enough. Well, fuck this noise. If you want me, *you'd* better come earn *me*." With that, he slammed the door shut behind him.

CHAPTER 22

When I woke up, grey light filtered through my white blinds. It was morning. I threw off my fuzzy yellow blanket, grabbed my phone receiver and listened to the dial tone hum steadily in my ears. No messages.

I'd slept fitfully the whole night. I'd called a med school friend, Ginger, to ask what she thought of the whole mess. She was doing peds at Western. I caught her post-call and explained, "It's just, I don't trust him. I'm glad he told me his secret, but I still remember how he kicked me out and lied about Mireille." I sighed. "Maybe I should give him another chance. I always blow up at people too quickly and then carry grudges. I should have been more sensitive about his story, I guess. I should have been happy he'd told me part of it. I should have been satisfied with the ankle bone."

She yawned. "That was the strangest thing. I expected you to say 'Medial or lateral malleolus?'"

"Yeah, well. What do you think about me and Alex?"

She sighed. "I'm too fried to think. Look. If it'd been me, I would have dumped him after he took off in the café. But you didn't. You hung in there, even slept with him. It's not like you."

"Yeah, I know. He brings out the worst in me."

She laughed. "I don't know about that. You were past due."

"Ginger!"

"It's true. I'm sorry. No great insight from me. I'll call you tomorrow, okay? Are you off tomorrow?"

I was so disappointed, my chest hurt. "Yeah. I'm on evenings."

"I'm doing the ward days. Crap. But I'll call you." She digested my silence. "Hope, I'm no relationship guru. But you know what I think? It's like what we tell women in threatened abortions. In a few days, it will declare itself."

Great. Just great. When pregnant women come in bleeding during their first trimester, we examine them and do a blood test and an ultrasound, but basically, within a few days, either they'll lose the fetus or they'll keep carrying it. It will declare itself. "Thanks a lot. Do you really say that to your patients?"

"Of course not." She sighed. "I'm terrible company right now. But I don't think it's so bad, Hope. Really. I've dated worse. Remember Rick?"

I sighed. We all remembered Akido Rick. It was small comfort not to have a pregnancy scare and have my martial arts boyfriend dump me. I let Ginger go to sleep and tried to follow her example.

When I couldn't, I turned on the radio. Vicki had been questioned and released. The homicide squad had no comment at this time.

I started an Excel sheet on my laptop, listing all the residents and staff at St. Joe's, and their alibis and motives. It was a pretty thin list. I was a terrible detective.

Something was bugging me, though. About Kurt's office. It was all sealed up now, as per homicide procedure, but I'd gotten a peek inside. I had the feeling I'd missed a clue.

My clock blinked 11:20 p.m. I wanted to go online and look up all the details of Kurt's murder, but my Net access wasn't up for another week. I'd have to go to the hospital.

The temperature dropped at least ten degrees at night, so I slid on a pair of jeans and a light pink T-shirt. One good thing about not having a functional kitchen for ten days, I'd lost weight.

St. Joe's felt much quieter at night. I found a parking spot right on Péloquin. No one was on the street, but I could peep into people's lighted rooms in their duplexes. The hospital's brick face was clothed in darkness except for spotlights highlighting its name. The wind rustled through the trees and crickets whirred. I ran across the street and cut through the flowerbed hill in front of the hospital. My feet sank into the dirt.

The main doors were supposed to be locked at night. Everyone had to go through emerg and pass the guard, but as I neared the main doors, a woman in pink scrubs pushed a door open and held it out for a colleague, so I stepped inside.

The murderer could have slipped into St. Joe's undetected. Sure, a guard hung out behind the counter, but tonight he was chatting with a friend and didn't look particularly alert or watchful. There might not even have had a guard by the door on June 30th, before Kurt died and the newspaper editorials questioned St. Joe's security. The murder might have been an outside job.

I was able to walk down the main hall, past the elevators and up the stairs, without running into anyone else. Most visitors and staff were in the next wing, for the ER, or ensconced upstairs, on one of the wards.

This must have been how the murderer came in.

The second floor looked and felt deserted. The white tile floors, the cavernous white halls, and the white ceilings gleamed under cold fluorescent lights. I couldn't hear or see another breathing organism. The office bureaucrats had long since departed for the day, the cafeteria was closed, and the library never had traffic at the best of times. I suppressed a shiver and clicked open the combination of the residents' room.

The room smelled of day-old chop suey. As usual, someone had left the remains on the table behind the computer. A medical student was watching the news, his feet propped up on the coffee table. "How's it goin'," he said, barely turning from the TV.

"Good." My premonition of danger fled in the face of such mundanity. "What are you on?"

"Medicine," he said. His pager went off. He groaned and walked across the room to the phone. "Hi, are you paging—? Yeah. She fell? An incident report? Uh, okay?" He hung up and cast me a quizzical look. "They're calling me from the eighth floor. Mrs. Bruyère fell."

"You just have to check if she's okay," I assured him, even though I hadn't fielded many of these calls myself.

He grabbed his stethoscope from the coffee table. "Okay. See ya."

For me, the timing was Hollywood-perfect. Before the door clicked closed behind him, I sat down at the computer. Someone had changed the background to a sunset with palm trees. I brought up Yahoo again and tried to crack Dr. Radshaw's password.

I had an idea. After a few permutations, "stjoes" made the login screen blank out. I held my breath.

I was in. "Inbox (66), Bulk (191)..."

I clicked on his Inbox first. It was mostly junk. Spam, solicitations to attend conferences, Aeroplan. Bob Clarkson had sent a few nondescript memos. Robin had replied to a forwarded article on partner abuse with "Can we talk about this?" More comments from Robin on stalking articles: "I don't believe the methodology was valid." "Observational study." "Does not generalize to the Canadian population." "Is abuse in gay populations statistically significant enough to warrant mention?" What a brown-noser. He'd even sent back some articles on drug abuse. I started ignoring the Robin e-mails. They were legion.

Dr. Callendar, whose first name appeared to be Morris, wrote on June 29th, "Need to talk to you." Vicki had written on the afternoon of the 30th, "Thinking about you. I love you." And Mireille had written on July 1st, "I can't wait. xo xo xo Mireille."

I kept glancing over my shoulder to see if someone was coming in, but I should hear their footsteps and the lock click first. I marked each message as unread after I read it, but I knew if they were checking, the police would soon discover someone had logged into Kurt's account.

He had an entire folder called "abuse." I clicked on it. Articles and references on partner abuse. Nothing personal.

I went to "saved mail." A bunch of names I didn't recognize. I clicked on one with no subject. "Dr. Radshaw, can't stop smoking. Can you help me????? You're secretary won't give me an appointment. R."

Obviously a patient with a smoking addiction and an imperfect grasp of grammar.

I went to the folder marked "Personal." Most of the messages were from Vicki, all along the lines of "Tell me if you can't make it to the restaurant tonight. I love you. Bye." Not great love letters. I wondered why he saved them. Paging back, I found one from Mireille. No salutation, just

"I can't talk to you. It hurts too much. Don't call me. Don't email me. I can't be friends with you right now."

It was dated May 13th.

I heard steps in the hall, signed out, and shut the window just as the combination lock clicked and the knob turned. I turned, trying to appear casual. Mireille's large figure stood framed in the doorway. Her eyes bulged at me. "What are *you* doing here?"

"Nothing." I stood up, knocking the chair back with my knees. I felt like a thief. I'd read her private e-mail. "Just leaving, actually."

She advanced on me. "Checking your e-mail?"

I nodded. "Nothing good, though. I guess everyone's busy." With any luck, she didn't pick up the slight tremor in my voice.

Her hands settled on the chrome back of the chair. Her hands were meaty. "Well, if you're done, I'd like to get on there."

"Sure thing." I ducked around her with a tight smile and strode toward the door. "See you!"

My hand was already on the cool metal of the doorknob when she called me back. "Hope."

I spun on my heel, my hand still resting on the knob. "Yes?"

She recovered her own smile. Her cheeks were plump with satisfaction, her slitted eyes were unreadable. Only her hands, gripping the edge of the desk, revealed a trace of uneasiness. "I heard you're investigating Kurt's death."

I searched for my vocal cords. "Well. Who told you that?"

She blew her breath out through her nostrils. "It does not matter. I have only two words for you: don't bother."

Technically, it was three words, including a contraction, but I was in no mood to quibble. "Yeah? Why's that."

Her smile widened. Her teeth gleamed. "Because I am going to solve it."

I struggled to keep my jaw from dropping. She laughed outright. "You like that? After Alex had accused me? Well, it's true. I loved Kurt. He was *mine*. No one else will bring his murderer to justice. Not the police. Certainly not *you*."

Contempt and anger warred in her voice. I fought back my own retort. Let her talk.

She tilted her head in amusement. "I already know who did it."

"Yeah? You thought it was Vicki. The police don't seem to agree."

She rolled her eyes. "Of course it was not Vicki. Still, I enjoy them questioning her."

She was the one siccing them on Vicki? My head whirled.

She shook her head. "You poor lamb." Her voice oozed with false sympathy. "You have no idea. The murderer is much more intelligent. Cunning, I would say. However, he may have been lulled into a false sense of security."

I pointed at the phone. "If you know who did it, you should tell the police. They'll take care of it."

She laughed and propped her behind up on the desk, watching me. Her French accent had grown more pronounced. "I have no doubt they would figure it out eventually. But after all, what is one doctor to them when they have biker wars and gangs to fight? This is my work. My revenge."

I shook my head. "You're being a vigilante. If you have evidence, you should turn it over to the police."

Her laugh was like shards of glass. "I don't have concrete evidence. When I do, the police will be the next to know." She waved her hands in dismissal. "I'm sure you have something more important to do. Alex, perhaps?"

A low blow, but I shook it off. "Mireille, I know why you're doing this."

Her lips drew back in a snarl. "Because I loved him."

I nodded. "And because you couldn't have him in life."

She slammed her hand on the desk, rattling a cafeteria tray and upending a plastic tumbler. "Spare me your amateur—"

I kept talking. "I understand that. I really do. But don't risk your own life, Mireille. Just turn the guy in. That's what I would do."

She raised her chin, "I, Am. Not. A coward."

In a way, she was right. I have almost always played it safe. And in the end, I didn't have as much invested in Kurt's death. "Insulting me won't bring him back."

Her mouth worked.

I said, "At least tell someone else what you're thinking. It doesn't have to be me. Just tell someone, okay?" Her mouth opened, but I knew it would just be more slagging. I twisted the doorknob and let myself out.

CHAPTER 23

So now it was morning and Mireille preyed on my mind even more than Alex. I called Tori and left a message on her machine about Mireille's intended one-woman show. "Maybe she'll listen to you." There was no love lost between me and Mireille, but I didn't want her dead, either.

My head ached. I tried to think. Who was the murderer? Who was she referring to? Intelligent. Cunning. It didn't sound like Bob Clarkson, but he could play the fool for us and mastermind behind the scenes. Alex? I had sex goggles on when it came to him. I didn't have confidence in my own judgment on Alex.

I could call the police myself and tell them Mireille thought she had solved the case. But it sounded ludicrous. I'm sure a lot of grieving partners fancy themselves detectives after a murder. She wasn't necessarily in danger.

I rubbed my forehead. I understood Mireille better, anyway. She was single-minded and loved the spotlight. No wonder she hosted a party right after Kurt's death. She wasn't just holding a wake, she was questioning people. At Grand Rounds, she had publicly announced her intentions. And now she wanted to shove it in my face: I know, you don't.

She certainly had the advantage of knowing all the players. Hell, she'd slept with at least two of them.

268

I turned on the radio as I brushed my teeth. No news on Kurt. My evening shift was from 5 p.m. until midnight. The empty day stretched ahead of me.

I wandered back to my living room. It looked even more disastrous in the clear light of day. At least the bookshelf was up and ready to go, so I started shelving more medical textbooks. When I had the extra-heavy, red and white Tintanelli ER tome in hand, I paused. I knelt on the floor and flipped to the section on domestic violence. I didn't see a lot of new information, although I liked the headings "Why does she stay?" "Why doesn't she tell?" Under "Men Who Batter," it said the men didn't fit any neat profile. Any economic, racial, religious, or educational background. They were more likely to have personality disorders, but no one such disorder in particular. They were controlling. They used denial. They minimized the damage they'd done. They blamed others for their actions.

I wondered why Kurt had chosen this topic for Grand Rounds, besides its relevance to family medicine. Now we'd never know.

I decided to take a single leaf from Alex and stop thinking. I turned up the volume on my stereo. When I got tired of Katy Perry, the Black Eyed Peas and Sean Kingston burning up the dance floor, I turned to good, old-fashioned CBC Radio. I hung up my clothes, cheered to see my outfits again, even if they severely needed ironing. I couldn't compete with the French girls yet, but now I had more ammunition.

Making order out of chaos was more satisfying than I'd expected. I assembled two more bookshelves and threw volumes at them. I unpacked my pots and pans and arranged my spices in the sticky white shelf above the stove.

By the time I sailed out the garage on my bike at quarter to five, I was in a fine mood. I was even going to be on time. Life was good.

Except my brain started clicking again. Just riding my bike made me think of Alex and our foreplay by the bike rack.

No. I pedaled faster, dodging a double-parked car, four-ways flashing, while a car roared around me and an oncoming car in the opposite lane slammed on its brakes and its horn.

Even a near-death experience couldn't stop my thoughts. Who had paged Kurt the night of his death? The police must know it was a vital clue. Had they recovered the pager, or at least the numeric messages? What about his cell phone? Had Mireille used the numbers to track the murderer?

I rode up the exit side of the parking circle. Instead of dismounting and walking my bike up the sidewalk curb, I jerked my steering wheel upward. I hit the curb and bumped over it. All the saliva had dried out of my mouth. My heart pumped hard.

If Mireille could solve this, so I could I. I just needed to ponder it more. I locked the bike and tossed the keys in my backpack.

When I got on, Dr. Dupuis was working the acute side. Double bonus. I smiled and headed straight toward him, barely registering the ambulatory side until a man raised his voice. "No. It would be ridiculous to start in the emergency room, without any follow-up. The man needs a family doctor. Have him follow up with the FMC."

I paused and turned. Sitting behind the long, white counter, yelling at a medical student, was my man, Dr. Morris Callendar. My heart sank. I'd have to forgo Dr. Dupuis. Dr. Callendar was one of the main players. If I wanted to talk about Dr. Kurt's final night, now was a good time and here was a good place.

Dr. Dupuis had come outside the nursing station to see a patient in a gurney lying between the ambu and acute side. He waved at me.

I crossed to his side and gestured at the walk-in area. "I'll work here for a bit, and then I'll join you, if that's all right with you."

"Sure." He gave me a strange look. He knew I'd never chosen the ambu side before and had been previously allergic to Dr. Callendar. "It's up to you. I'll pull you over if there are any interesting cases."

"Thanks." If my luck held, I'd get to pump Dr. C. and join Dr. Dupuis immediately after.

"Sure." He strode off to take care of another mini-crisis. He seemed unflappable. Then I remembered his red face when we found Kurt's body. No, he was flappable.

Dr. Callendar grunted when he saw me, and gestured at the charts. In addition to the ones who were already in rooms, the clipboards hung on the walls with blue numbers affixed in order of priority. There was also a long trail of charts snaking its way down the counter between triage and the patient rooms. He ducked around the other side to check an X-ray.

I nodded hello at the medical student. "I'm Hope, an R1. Who are you?"

He mumbled, "William York." He was a skinny white guy who'd buttoned his white coat all the way up to his neck, with just the knot of his brown tie showing.

Poor guy. He reminded me of Robin—must have been the tie—with no articles to back him up. I wanted to tell him he'd get used to Dr. C., but then the man in question sailed back around the corner. "Hope, William, we're not paid by the hour. Let's get a move-on!"

Grr. I wished he was the murderer, but I couldn't see how he'd manage to sneak out of a busy ER, kill his buddy, and make it back down undetected. Even if he just let the charts molder on the counter.

I picked up the first chart. Someone had scrawled a Post-it note that said "Computer flashed 'drug.'" The case was a 31-year-old woman with dental pain.

When I emerged from the room, Dr. Callendar and the medical student were occupying the only two chairs, so I leaned against the counter and waited my turn. Dr. C glared at me throughout my entire presentation, then snapped, "Does she have a fever? Is there any evidence of an abscess?"

At least leaning on the counter, I got to literally look down at him. I shook my head. "I don't see anything. But she says the only thing that helps is Demerol."

He stood up. "I don't put up with this kind of nonsense. Come with me." He turned and gestured at the medical student. "You too!" William sent me a wide-eyed look and followed us. Dr. C. threw open the door of room 3 without knocking. "Hello, I'm Dr. Callendar, how are you?"

"Oh," the woman moaned, "My tooth is killing me. I had a cavity here—"

"Open up." He grabbed a flashlight and tongue depressor from his pocket and tapped on her tooth. "I don't see anything."

"But it hurts. It's killing me. You gotta—"

"If there's no infection, there's nothing to treat. See your dentist tomorrow."

"I did. He—"

"Good-bye, ma'am. Come back if you have any fever, swelling, redness, or difficulty opening your mouth." He was already halfway out the door, William hot on his heels. I shrugged helplessly at the patient.

She slid off the examining table, her hands bunched on her considerable hips. Her face was bright red. "That's *it?*"

"Uh, I guess so. Sorry."

"What about my *Demerol?*"

"Uh—" I glanced at the door again. No cavalry. "I guess you don't need any. Goodbye." I slipped out.

She yelled at my back, "I'm not leaving until I get my Demerol!"

When I reached the desk, Dr. Callendar was writing up another chart and talking to William, unperturbed. "She's a drug-seeker." He pointed at the Post-it note. "We keep a record on the computer. It came up when she registered at the front desk."

"Oh. *That's* what it means." Of course, I knew that people came to emerg for drugs, but no one in London had ever asked me for them. I thought the note was something about the computer!

More shouting from room 3. The nurse tapped Dr. C. on the shoulder. "Morris, you'd better come talk to her. She won't leave."

"She will." He stood up and tucked the chart under his arm. "Both of you. See more patients."

It was machine-gun medicine, seeing and reviewing patients rapid-fire. Asthma exacerbation, sore knee, sore throat, urinary tract infection, atypical chest pain. I despaired of getting a chance to ask Dr. Callendar about Kurt's last night.

The med student took an age to see each patient. He was only in second year, so this was a trial by fire for him. Strangely, Dr. Callendar seemed more mellow with him. "What do you think this is?"

"Uh," William said, "I think she has a cold."

"Do you have a differential?"

William shook his head. His fear and subservience seemed to endear him to Dr. Callendar. Meanwhile, the same doctor would snap at me, "Is that all? Don't you have a plan? You should know what to use for strep throat on pen-allergic patients. Is it a real pen allergy? You didn't ask what his reaction was? Well, what good are you, then?"

He sure knew how to charm the ladies. I started tuning him out. There was something I was missing about Kurt. Something Mireille had noticed. Her e-mail to him in May—the "Don't call me" message—could have been evidence of harassment, but I didn't think so. She wrote, "I can't be friends with you." Kurt, as usual, trying to be all things to all people, must have been trying to maintain friendship with his ex. Still, sometimes the line blurred. He might have been persistent to the point of harassment. Maybe that's why he chose the topic for Grand Rounds. Physician, heal thyself.

I pictured his body again in the lounge. Mottled face, staring eyes. No pager. No cell phone. The last two still seemed significant. The killer must have contacted him and asked him to meet him in the middle of the night.

While Dr. Callendar battered me with words, it clicked. I knew what had bothered me about Kurt's desk. There were no articles on abuse. There were articles on vaccination, but nothing on abuse at all, even though Tori said he'd printed out a stack of references. And the computer didn't work. Not just because it was a St. Joe's special, but maybe because someone had already reformatted the hard drive.

Maybe the killer had not just confiscated the pager and cell phone, but cleared the office of any articles or references on abuse.

My mind made the leap.

The killer was an abuser.

How had Mireille figured it out? And how was she going to obtain hard evidence for the police? I closed my eyes, remembered every time I had seen Mireille and what she had said. The party. Coming to my house. Hanging around with her former surgery comrade. I figured she was the one calling me and pretending she was Vicki. Every time, she had been on a mission. Collecting evidence. Intent on revenge.

Until last night, when she had told me to stay away.

My mind made another leap. She was going to confront the killer.

And I finally knew who he was.

I said, "Dr. Callendar. I'm sorry. I have to go to the bathroom."

He halted mid-diatribe and glared at me. "Well, go on, then!"

I escaped to the back hall, pausing to grab the yellow stick with the key to the emergency resident's room. Forget the toilet. I had a phone call to make.

I popped into the resident's room and called Agent Rivera. It rang and rang, and finally an irritated Frenchwoman answered and told me he wasn't there, could I leave a message.

I did, stumbling over the French, explaining my theory on Kurt's murder.

"*Bon*," she said tersely. "I will pass on the message. *Au revoir*." She hung up.

I stared at the black plastic receiver. When would she pass on the message? Tomorrow morning? It might be too late.

CHAPTER 24

I punched zero to page Mireille through St. Joe's locating. "Who?" said the operator.

"Dr. Laroque! She's on family medicine."

"She's not on call."

"I know! I need to speak to her. It's urgent."

"The resident on call for family medicine is Dr. Fabien. Would you like to speak to him?"

"No! I need to speak to Dr. Mireille Laroque!" If only I'd downloaded the entire list of residents' pagers.

She heaved an enormous sigh. "Well, okay..."

"Thank you."

Three minutes ticked by while I tried to log into my email from the break room's ancient computer. Some bright light had turned off the machine, so I had to boot it up and wait for Windows to load, before I could log in, click on the Explorer icon, and slowly, painfully, bring up my webmail and view Sheilagh's messages.

Dr. Callendar must be frothing at the mouth by now. I couldn't wait any longer. I called locating back. "This is Dr. Sze. When Dr. Laroque calls back, could you ask her to call me through the emergency room? I'm on the walk-in side."

"The emergency room?"

"Yes! On the walk-in side. Please!" It was a miracle anyone managed to get a hold of any individual through St. Joe's locating.

I called Tori, but there was no answer. I left a message explaining who I thought the killer was and my fears Mireille might confront him. I needed to scatter my eggs in as many baskets as possible.

When I returned to the walk-in side, the med student was slaving over a note. Dr. Callendar was nowhere in sight. I grabbed the chart for a sore shoulder and sent him off to X-ray.

Dr. Callendar reappeared and opened his mouth, but I struck first. "You know, I met you here on the morning of July first. You had worked overnight."

He kept his black head bent over his chart. "Yeah. So?"

"Was there anything unusual about that night?"

He looked at me then, his brow furrowing. "You mean, clues that my colleague was being murdered upstairs?"

I nodded, holding my breath.

"No."

Damn. "Did you see him that night?"

"No. I was working. It was busy. There was a code pink—" He exhaled impatiently at my blank face—"a neonatal code on the floor."

I asked if he'd seen the man I now thought was the murderer.

"No. I understand he was at a party, not that it's any of your concern."

A party. Interesting, especially considering the GHB.

He pulled the clipboard right out of my hand. "Back to business. Tell me about your patient."

For the rest of the night, I was unable to escape Dr. Callendar; Dr. Dupuis didn't signal me for any interesting cases. I kept an ear out for Mireille's call back, wincing every time someone used the phone to answer or place pages. Come on, Laroque. I paged her twice more directly to the phone line at the walk-in desk.

I ended up spending seven hours with the Big C. Cancer patients sometimes call their disease the Big C. Although it was petty of me, it seemed fitting. My shift was supposed to end at 11 p.m., but the Big C. said there were still patients to C.

Clearly, I was losing my mind.

When he finally muttered, "You can go now," it was almost midnight. Damn Mireille. Should I page her from home?

The black phone burbled. I lunged, but the Big C. was closer. "Yeah," he barked. "What? Hang on."

I grabbed it. The receiver was still warm from his hand. "Hello?"

Thank goodness, it was Mireille. "Quit paging me."

I turned away from Dr. Callendar, stretching the cord as long as it would go. "Mireille, I know who it is. I told the police."

She didn't speak. I heard the faint, tinny sound of MuchMusic in the background. Then her breath whooshed out. "*Tabernac.* Fuck off!" She slammed the phone down.

Dr. C. stared at me, his lips twisted in amusement. He'd obviously overheard at least the last part. "Making new friends?"

I hardly paid attention. She didn't want me paging her. She hadn't answered me, but she finally did because she didn't want me to disturb her.

Why did she need to be left alone?

She was confronting the killer. Imminently.

Where?

MuchMusic could have been playing anywhere, but I bet they wanted somewhere quiet. Neutral ground, but out of the way.

If Mireille was smart, she wouldn't agree to anywhere too isolated.

The residents' room.

CHAPTER 25

I ran just as fast as I had for the Code Blue. Faster, because this time I knew I could save a life.

I nearly collided with Jade Watterson, the ICU resident, on the stairs. She held her giant plastic coffee mug above her head. "Whoa!"

I snapped over my shoulder, "I think Mireille's in trouble. Get help! Residents' room."

I slammed open the doors at the top of the stairs, skidded around the corner on the freshly-waxed floors, and punched the code. I turned the knob, but the lock didn't open. Damn! I punched the code again. This time, the door swung open half an inch before crashing into a barrier. I spotted someone's arm in a white coat in the far corner of the room, against the wall.

"Mireille!" I hollered. "Mireille!"

I rapped on the door.

Someone grunted and I heard and felt a thump through the wood as something crashed against it, sealing it shut again.

"I can hear you!" I shouted. "Let me in!"

I banged with one hand while I punched the code in with the other. The door handle turned, but banged into something again.

I started bashing the door against the barrier. I'd break it if I had to. If nothing else, I'd provide a distraction.

Slam.

SLAM!

The barrier held, but I'd gotten another half inch.

I slammed the door, yelling and cursing until my throat grew raw. The door moved another inch.

I screamed in victory. Then I realized that the door was moving more easily, and someone was talking. A male voice was saying, "Just a second."

The door swung open. At last, the dark blond figure in the white coat advanced on the door. A protuberant blue eye peered at me through the opening slit. "Oh. Hello, Hope."

I heard some thumping and the sprong of a chair removed from under the doorknob. He drew open the door and started to block it with his body.

I squeezed by him. "Where is she? What did you do with her?"

Robin surveyed me mildly. "Who?"

I cast about the room. Fridge, two couches against two walls, TV, table with cafeteria trays, desk with computer, phone, ficus tree. Where was she? I ran to the computer and threw the chair away from the desk, but there was no Mireille. Just a filing cabinet under the desk with some blue boxes filled with juice bottles and crumpled paper. The desk chair rolled to the middle of the room and stopped. Where was she?

I turned on him. He stood on the other side of the roller chair, his head tipped to one side like I was a particularly interesting specimen. I said, "Robin. I know it was you. You're here to meet her. What did you do with her?"

He raised his taffy-coloured eyebrows. "Who?"

"Mireille. Mireille Laroque! Who else do you think?"

"Why would I do that?" He smoothed down the front of his white coat. The pockets seemed to be empty. He wasn't wearing a tie today, just a cream dress shirt buttoned all the way to the collar and some '70s brown dress pants. He looked perfectly presentable. An A+ student murderer.

"Because you killed Kurt and she figured it out!"

"I did?" His brow furrowed, turning his eyebrows into a single furry caterpillar. He looked so *normal*. But I realized he had placed himself between me and the door.

I started walking toward the exit. "Yeah. You did. Pretty smart, Robin. I have to congratulate you." I skirted between the round table and the wall with the ficus tree.

He took a step toward me. "Why do you think that?"

I circled away from him, keeping it casual, keeping the five-foot diameter table between us. Now I was between the table and the computer desk. If he kept following me, he'd end up between the table and the wall, and I could make a break for it. "Well, I think it must have started with your wife."

"What about her?" But his eyes widened a millimetre before he forced a laugh.

I kept my tone light. "I guess you don't know what's going on with her, huh? Did she leave you?"

"*She never left me!*" He grabbed the table and flipped it at me.

The fake wood-grain tabletop tumbled toward me. I screamed and threw myself under the computer desk, between the filing cabinet and the blue boxes. Then I realized it was exactly the wrong place to be. The overturned table blocked off my route. I was caught between the table, the wall, and Robin's legs.

I was breathing hard. Almost panting. My life could not end this way. It could not.

But I couldn't think of a good way out. I stared at Robin's neatly polished brown dress shoes. He even double-knotted his laces.

"You bitch," he said. "You had nothing to do with this. Why couldn't you just leave it alone?" As his pale hands reached for me, he said, "This is all your fault."

My first instinct was to block his hands. Instead, I screamed and dove for his ankles. I wanted to topple him, pull his feet out from under him, throw him to the ground and run past him.

Instead, he shook off my grip and kicked me under the chin, snapping my head back.

Pain. Searing through my head, tearing down my neck.

For a second, I couldn't focus.

I felt something warm drip down my face, toward my mouth. Smelled iron. Blood.

He kicked me in the chest. The new pain exploded in spirals, but it gave me something to bite down on. No. I would not die like this. I huddled in genuine agony, but as he paused to smile, his glasses still in place, his chest barely heaving, I grabbed a recycling bin and launched myself at him.

Instinctively, he shied away.

I tripped on a table leg. Paper went airborne. A bottle crashed to the floor but didn't break. I landed on my knees, hitting the bin lid with my chest.

I saw his hands flash. I whimpered, but he was grabbing the bottle.

"Okay. That's enough, Hope," he said, returning to that eerily calm voice.

I heard a smash just as I flipped myself over and scrambled to my feet, grabbing the blue box like a clumsy shield.

Robin held the jagged remnant of the bottle up to my face. His hair was damp with sweat. His mouth made a straight line. "I didn't want to do this."

I brought the box up from underneath, striking his arms upward. The glass soared and shattered behind me.

I snarled in triumph, but he smashed the box out of my hands. It crashed to the floor. Before I could dive for it, his hands closed around my throat.

Suffocating me.

I tried to tear his hands away. He was fiendishly strong. His face was flushed. Dimly, I remembered an Akido move Ginger had showed me, and shoved my arms between his, trying to break his hold.

He squeezed tighter.

I reared back and kicked him.

He grunted, twisting his hips away. My foot made solid contact with his thigh.

He grip only tightened.

The room was ringed with darkness. I couldn't breathe. I couldn't breathe! I made one last, desperate swipe at his head.

And the world went black.

CHAPTER 26

Carpet. Flat grey carpet, nubby under my hands. A woman's voice, screechy with panic.

Blackness.

A long face. Long nose. Round glasses. Green eyes. Thin mouth, starting to smile.

Dr. Dupuis.

I sagged into the—mattress?—clutching at the white sheet lying over me. The ceiling was covered in white acoustic tile. A clear plastic mask sat on my face, augmenting the sound of my every breath. A heart monitor beeped in my ears. Stickers on my chest. Wires all around. Something around my left arm. A soft gray plastic probe on my right index finger. My bed was surrounded by metal railing on three sides.

I was in resus. It was like being in an adult-sized crib in a very scary nursery.

I lifted my right hand, stared at the IV embedded on the back of it, attached to clear plastic tubing.

"You have good veins," said Dr. Dupuis.

It was uncomfortable to bend my wrist. It made the catheter shift a little, even though it I had what felt like an entire roll of tape on my arm, securing it. I let my hand fall back on to the stretcher.

"You're okay," Dr. Dupuis said. "I'm going to check on Mireille."

I fought to sit upright. My monitor started beeping, but I ignored it. My voice rasped, "How——?" I had to grab my throat. It hurt too much.

"She's okay. Dr. Trigiani's looking after her in A," he said. His eyes darkened. "I guess Robin was in the middle of attacking her when you came around. He dumped her behind the couch, tied up and gagged."

I gasped, my eyes darting around the resus room. My monitor beeped at high pitch, at the same tempo as my heart.

Dr. Dupuis grasped the left bed rail and leaned toward me. "It's okay, Hope. Robin's not here. The police took him away."

I shuddered. Then I couldn't seem to stop shaking. My arms and legs trembled. My teeth chattered loud enough for him to hear them rattle, but I couldn't control it. My body jerked under the white blanket like I was having mini-seizures.

Dr. Dupuis called, "Andrea? Could you bring her some warm blankets?"

A nurse in pink scrubs, with a neat brown bob, draped two blankets over me. They were pre-warmed and felt like heaven. I tried to croak my thanks.

Dr. Dupuis put his hand on my arm. "Don't talk. Your throat is too sore."

Well, I knew that! My trembling slowed and almost stopped.

He laughed. Andrea handed me a pen and a clipboard, the same kind we used for patient charts, but with a blank sheet of paper and pen. I smiled at her and wrote THANK YOU.

"You're welcome," Dr. Dupuis said promptly. "Just doing our job. You're going to be fine, Hope. We'll observe you for a few hours. I think your airway will be fine, just some soft tissue damage, but this way, we'll all feel better."

Andrea patted my shoulder.

I smiled at her, but as my relief wore off, another feeling built and accelerated under my breastbone. Rage. My fingers tightened around my pen. I wrote, carving into the page, "I HATE HIM."

Dr. Dupuis and Andrea exchanged a look. He said, "It's understandable. Do you want to get some rest?"

Code Blues

I shook my head and wrote, "I want him dead."

Dr. Dupuis smiled crookedly. "Well, we don't have the death penalty in Canada, but if it's any comfort, they'll probably put him away for a long time. Jade and the guards caught him choking you—"

My eyes widened.

He said, "You didn't know that, huh? Jade said she ran into you on the stairs before you went to play Call of Duty. She listened at the door before sprinting for security. It took two guys to pull him off you."

I sagged into my pillow. Thank God I'd done what I told Mireille to do, call for backup. Thank God I'd called someone who listened.

"While we brought you in here, your pager started going off. Tori was worried about you, too."

Tears leaked from the corners of my eyes. I was too tired to fight them off. Andrea stroked my non-IV hand. I looked at her, mute with gratitude.

"I'm going to let you rest," said Dr. Dupuis. "You did a good job." He started out, then stopped.

Jade hovered in the doorway. She shoved her hands in the pockets of her white coat, her dark eyes darting between me and Dr. Dupuis. "Just wanted to make sure you were okay."

"She wanted to do a CT of your neck," said Dr. Dupuis, with a smile. "But I wanted to keep you in resus. If we have to tube either of one of you, I'd rather do it here than in the CT suite."

I held out my hand toward Jade. She walked to my right side. While Andrea lowered the bedrail, I grabbed Jade's hand. Clumsily, with my left hand, I circled the THANK YOU on my board several times.

She laughed, trying to tug her hands away. "I just did what you asked me to."

I wrote, "You saved my life." My eyes were leaking again. Jade squeezed my hand, her own eyes downcast.

Dr. Dupuis said, "You saved Mireille's life. It all works out. Now, I want you to rest."

I was still clutching Jade's hand. Now I knew how my elderly patients felt when they wouldn't release me; they didn't know how to properly express their gratitude. I felt the same. But her fingers wiggled uncomfortably and I let her go.

Jade leaned over and whispered in my ear, "You're bad luck for me when I'm on call."

I giggled almost soundlessly, my breath rattling in my throat. I wrote, "You're good luck for me. All of you."

"Now we're getting sappy," said Dr. Dupuis. "All in a day's work. Get some rest. Dr. Trigiani will check on you in a bit." He saluted me.

I touched my neck. It felt okay. More swelling than usual, but I could still make out the base of my trachea and, to a lesser extent, my thyroid cartilage. I listened to my own quiet breath whoosh in and out. No stridor.

Dr. Dupuis smiled, reading my mind. "Like I said, we'll observe you, but you'll probably be fine. We can take off the oxygen."

I pulled off the mask with relief. While Andrea shut off the oxygen, I lifted my pen at Dr. Dupuis to indicate I still had something to say. He stopped at the foot of my bed. I wrote, "I don't want to go home tonight."

He nodded. "You don't have to."

Tears sprang to my eyes. Relief, I guess. The last thing I needed to do was head home at 3 a.m. and lie awake in my black bedroom, with only Henry for protection. I pointed to the resus room floor. I wanted to stay here, not go to a creepy call room by myself.

Dr. Dupuis shook his head and grinned. "You're a glutton for punishment. Okay, we'll find you a room at the inn."

I tapped the "THANK YOU."

He thumped the mattress below my feet. "You're welcome. Now get some sleep." He marched out of the room, his shoulders shifting under the stiff fabric of his greens.

Jade hesitated. Her brown face was uncertain. "Call me."

I nodded. I'd text her in the morning.

Andrea offered me a throat lozenge. I unwrapped the clear, crinkly plastic. The lemon flavor burst into my mouth. I closed my eyes, savoring it.

I was alive.

A woman's voice called from the nursing station, "Andrea. Phone call."

She tucked the blankets around my neck. "I'll be back in a minute."

I closed my eyes. It was heaven to relax again, an almost physical weight lifting from my lungs.

Andrea reappeared, perturbed. She was holding her hand over the mouthpiece of the black cordless patients' phone. "I know you can't talk, but Dr. Alex Dyck is very insistent."

I bounced up, my muscles tense, my heart monitor beeping frantically again. She reached for me. "Whoa, whoa, whoa. I'll tell him you'll talk to him tomorrow."

I shook my head frantically. I wanted to hear from him.

She hesitated, her eyes moving to the doorway. I knew she wanted to talk to Dr. Dupuis or Trigiani. I held my hands out, imploring.

She sighed. "Just for a minute." She repeated it, sternly, to Alex, and handed me the phone.

I cupped it to my ear. Tried to say his name. Couldn't make it past the first syllable.

"Hope." His voice broke. "I am so sorry."

I made a sound low in my throat.

"That's all I wanted to say. I'm so, so sorry." His breath hitched. "It's all my fault."

I tried to speak, but Andrea grabbed the phone. "You said you weren't going to upset her! That's enough, Alex!" She marched out of the room, still telling him off.

When she returned, she pulled the blankets above my neck, her movements brisk. "I knew I shouldn't have let him."

I reached up from under the covers, grabbed her hand. I let her know with my eyes it was okay. I took responsibility, even if his words swirled through my head. Sorry? For what? Why was it his fault?

She softened. "You should rest." The lines around her mouth faded. She made sure the call bell was still clipped to the bed rail. "We're here if you need us."

She turned off the fluorescent lights. There was only the faint glow from the street lamps through the window and my monitor's gleam. I heard her footsteps recede.

Robin's hands seemed to lace around my neck. I bit back a scream. No. He wasn't here. I forced myself to feel the blanket lying over me, listen to the murmur of voices from the nursing station, watch the pale glow of the pockmarked tile above my head, taste the faint lemon residue in the corners of my mouth.

I was alive.

CHAPTER 27

Tucker pointed out the bright side when he and Tori dropped by my apartment the next day. "At least you get to skip your weekend night shifts."

I nodded agreement. I wrote "Mireille?" on my notepad.

"He bashed her on the head, tied her up and used his tie to gag her," said Tucker. "But she's okay. Better than you, I think." His brown eyes flickered. He stared at my pine headboard. "I could kill him."

I nodded. With every twinge in my neck, I hated Robin.

Tucker looked at my face. The muscles around his eyes tightened. His hand stirred, but he let it fall back on my fuzzy yellow blanket. He took a deep breath.

Tori cleared her throat. She was standing at the head of my bed while Tucker sat at the edge of my mattress. "Robin's in police custody. You don't have to worry about him anymore."

Yeah. Only in the way I jumped every time the phone rang, even if it was in the next apartment. Only in the way I woke up with my heart pounding, a scream locked in my throat. Only in the white plastic bottle of Ativan that lay on my night table, untouched. For now.

Tori pointed to the bouquet of daisies beside the pill bottle. I hadn't unpacked any vases, so the flowers stood in a white plastic juice container. The petals bent under her finger. "I hope you like them."

I did. I liked their get well card, too. It was a cream-coloured card, with a heavy border and a tiny drawing of a daisy in the corner. Still, I wished Alex had come instead.

Tucker tried to smile. "I have to hand it to you. Mireille said she heard about Robin stalking his wife by talking to some guys at the Jewish. But we're still not sure how you figured it out." His eyes rested on my bruised and reddened throat. "I know you're just pretending you can't talk so you can keep us in suspense."

I cackled a little laugh. I could speak now, but preferred to conserve my voice. I had typed out a statement for the police. It was nothing solid, nothing a linear mind might have pieced together, just a confluence of clues. One, the absence of the pager and cell phone meant the killer was trying to hide Kurt's pages, although it turned out Robin had been canny enough to call from within the hospital most of the time. We all knew Robin was the most intelligent person in our year.

Two, the lack of abuse articles told me the killer was an abuser.

Three, Robin talked about Kurt in a depersonalized way, still minimizing, still denying.

Four, Robin's wife was pretty classic, if you knew what to look for, but none of us had been looking, except Kurt. Probably he'd stepped it up when he was researching the Grand Rounds presentation. Maybe he'd even reached out to Robin's wife.

Tori shook her head. "We had no idea Robin was... unbalanced."

"The guy was a complete wing nut," said Tucker. "I hear he planned to take away the pager and cell phone. He even came in on Monday and wiped out Kurt's hard drive, just in case the abuse articles tipped anyone off."

Ah. Just as I thought.

Robin must've confessed in great detail, meticulous to enumerate each point. I wondered if he finally smiled while doing so. If he was going to be convicted, it would have to be evidence-based. It was only fitting.

My neck seized up. I still hated him.

Tucker sighed and stretched out his long legs. "He was always such a smart guy. The gold medalist in our class. So when he planned to kill Kurt...I heard he brought his own pair of gloves and two paper cups of coffee." Anger and admiration warred in Tucker's voice. "He called Kurt to meet him in the OR lounge and spiked Kurt's cup with GHB. When Kurt went unconscious, Robin dragged him into the men's change room to inject him with succ and insulin."

I shuddered.

"Then Robin put Kurt's empty coffee cup in his own, tucked the gloves and the needle in the top cup, and walked to another floor so he could throw the gloves away and toss the needles in a sharps container. He walked out wearing Kurt's pager and cell phone and junked them later. He was only gone from the party for thirty minutes. It was *genius*." Tucker glanced at my throat again. "Evil genius."

"Do you think he could get out on a medical defense? Criminally insane or, what is it called now—" Tori tipped her head thoughtfully to one side. Her shiny black hair traced the line of her jaw. I mouthed the answer, but she already remembered. "Not criminally responsible. Robin's wife was planning to leave him, and now Kurt was telling him to get help, threatening to ruin his career, well—"

"No," I croaked. I evaded Tori's touch. My body was as taut as a piano wire. I could not feel compassion for Robin now. I wasn't big enough.

Tucker shifted, denting the mattress. "Yeah, I know what you're saying. Both of you. It sucks for Robin, but he was a murdering bastard. He should rot in jail."

Tori closed her mouth and nodded. "I'm sorry."

I relaxed a smidge. I wrote, "Sorry. I'm uptight."

"Yeah," said Tucker. "I wish I could help."

I patted his hand. He squeezed mine back. I thanked Tori with my eyes.

I was so glad they were here. But I still wanted to see Alex.

He'd shoved a card under my door while I stayed in the emerg overnight. The front was a picture of flowers spelling out "Get Well Soon." Inside, he'd scrawled "Alex." Nothing else.

Three days later, when my throat felt decent, I chose to come back to work. I could talk again. I was tired of my apartment, which was still only half-unpacked. I didn't want to take any more sick days. And I wanted to see the guy with the messy chestnut hair.

I was eight minutes early for the FMC clinic. I beat Dr. Callendar there, but not Tori. She greeted me with a loose hug. "Are you sure?"

I nodded. My motto: *do what you're afraid to do.*

Her brown eyes were troubled when she released me. "You're the first one back. Mireille is still away. So is Alex. Sheilagh said she doesn't know when he'll be back. Stress leave."

My stomach plummeted. I tried not to show it, but I must have, because she hugged me again, wordless.

Physically, Alex must be okay if he slid a card under my door. But he never called or texted or even e-mailed after that first night in the hospital.

I hugged her back. I was glad to have at least one uncomplicated friend in Montreal.

Stan called from the doorway, "What are you doing here? You should be at home eating bon-bons! I was going to bring you some!"

I laughed and broke away from Tori. He gave me a big bear hug, reaching down to envelop me. "Good to see you. Glad you're okay."

I hugged him back, and he said, "I guess my wife and I will eat the bon-bons then."

Some things were back to normal.

Omar pulled my chair out for me. "You were very brave," he said simply, but it sounded like a benediction. I smiled at him.

Dr. Callendar dragged his chair across the linoleum floor. "All right, everybody. Glad you're all here." He didn't quite look at me. "I saw some patients waiting already."

My face flushed. What a bastard. Couldn't even manage a "well done." And where was he, after I got choked? Running home? Doing his billing in the staff room?

I turned on my heel and called in my 18-year-old patient with panic attacks.

I decided to write some Ativan for my patient. He only got panic attacks a few times per month. It didn't seem worthwhile starting him on a daily medication. When I reviewed the case with Dr. Callendar, my eyes dared him to contradict me.

His Adam's apple bobbed. He looked away first. "Fine, good," he said. Paused. Muttered, "You all right?"

I nodded, hiding a smile. It was like not finding the abuse articles in Kurt's office. The absence of criticism was significant.

Dr. Callendar turned to the doorway and beckoned Omar to his side. "What do you have for me?...No, no, no! That patient has type ONE diabetes!"

Omar said, "Yes, sir," but when he glanced up at me, one eye flickered in a wink.

Yes, things were back to almost normal. A fledgling love and gratitude for my new life in Montreal unfurled in my heart.

Still, Alex churned at the back of my mind all day. Every brown-haired guy made me jump. The sight of a water bottle, a miniskirt, an *Au Pain Doré* bag, or a bicycle all reminded me of him.

It was an obsession.

I had to talk to him. Sort it out one way or another. If we ended up in a passionate embrace in front of the sunset, great. If not, probably even better.

Alex and I were on a weird relationship see-saw. Every time I was up, he was down, and vice versa. We could never find an equilibrium. Or rather, we only did once, that night at his place.

I took the 5:35 Côte-des-Neiges bus to his apartment. I had to stand, clinging to the silver rail, pressed between a group of schoolgirls in uniform and a black guy in sunglasses. I rested my backpack on my feet so it wouldn't abrade someone's face. I peered through the forest of arms, trying to figure out the closest stop.

Alex was right about one thing. The bus was a lot faster than the metro. I didn't have time to change my mind. I strode down the remaining slope of the mountain and turned east along Sherbrooke. With half a mind, I enjoyed the "Golden Mile" stores of Versace and Holt Renfrew, with their elegantly-dressed, beheaded mannequins. Several limos had pulled up in front of the Ritz Carleton, so the white-gloved, navy-uniformed and -capped butler types at the brass and glass doors didn't so much as glance at me.

I probably looked like a tramp in my knee-length hemp shorts, white tank top and ginormous backpack. Maybe this wasn't the best look for a truth and (possible) reconciliation commission. Ryan once said my Mountain Equipment Co-op bookbag weighed more than I did. Not sexy.

Of course, my backpack didn't stop Alex the last time. I had to smile.

I turned south on Peel and headed through the McGill ghetto. All the lampposts sported new signs. More waves of packing tape and photocopying. "For sale: Ikea bed. Like new!"

"Roommate wanted. Large apartment in 5 1/2."

"Le plus gros party de l'été!"

I barely registered the passers-by except to check if they were Alex. I hadn't called. Hadn't paged. I just wanted to know if we could try again. If he wasn't home, well, that was another sign.

Not that I'd give up if he was out, but I'd give it a rest for tonight.

I found myself standing outside Alex's duplex. The pizza boxes were gone, but the wrought iron gate was crooked and the lawn ever-weedier. I was glad to see the bike still chained to the fence. Maybe he was home.

I picked my way along the cracked concrete path and knocked on his wooden door. A small circle of a window was inset at head-level, but it was too dim for me to see inside. A white plastic Ad-Bag hung on his doorknob.

I heard no footsteps. Belatedly, I spotted the doorbell on the left. Its one-note electric tone echoed down his halls.

I took a deep breath. Okay. Alex wasn't home. I should have called. I turned back to the street and adjusted the straps on my backpack.

Footsteps padded in the apartment behind me. Heart pounding, I revolved to face him.

I heard the chain rattle. He threw the bolt and opened the door.

His bloodshot eyes were slitted against the afternoon light, making them small and bear-like under his overhanging forehead. His stubble had filled out into a straggly beard. He smelled like he'd been lying in a rancid bed all day, and he was only wearing a ripped white undershirt and tan drawstring pajama pants.

I choked back a gasp.

He ran a hand through his rumpled hair, his eyes daring me to comment.

I swallowed hard. My fists were knotted, but I stood my ground. I'd come this far. I'd see it through.

He stepped aside, wordless.

He hadn't bothered to switch on the hall light. The entrance was dim and smelled like stale smoke and bedhead. I tried to breathe through my mouth.

Alex kicked some shoes off the welcome mat, making room for mine. I supposed it was his gentlemanly move of the day. I stepped inside, my toes curling inside my sandals. But I'd been raised to take off my shoes indoors, so after a second, I did. I tried not to grimace when my bare soles made contact with his gritty floor.

He pulled the door shut behind me, making sure not to touch me as he cut off the last vestige of sunlight.

Neither of us had said a word.

This was not at all how I'd imagined our reunion.

He beckoned me into the room on the left with a white love seat and battered wooden coffee table. The TV against the wall was playing a Dentyne ad on mute. The fresh-faced, laughing couple seemed at odds with our own mood. Alex clicked it off.

I perched on the end of the saggy loveseat. Alex glanced at the empty spot beside me but ended up dragging an orange beanbag chair out of the corner and dropping down in front of the TV.

I stared at the crumb-covered plate and empty glass on the edge of the coffee table. I wasn't about to speak first.

He did. "Hope."

Our eyes met over the coffee table. He lowered his gaze to his knuckles. "I'm sorry."

"For what?"

He exhaled. "Every fucking thing."

I tried not to wince. His words seemed to reverberate off his empty walls.

He grabbed the edge of the coffee table. It was an old '70s number, the wood grain dyed a thick, unflattering black. "Are you okay?"

I nodded. *Take me in your arms. After you take a shower and brush your teeth.* "My throat hurts. But I'm okay. How are you?"

"I'll live." He released the coffee table and began spreading his fingers on the floor, pumping his hands up and down like they were pale spiders doing pushups.

I cleared my throat. "Thanks for the card."

His gray eyes shot up. "No."

I stared at him.

He jumped to his feet and began pacing around the card table on the opposite side of the room. He faced the opposite wall and said, "Don't."

I stood and cautiously made my way toward him, but left a meter of space between us. "Alex. What's wrong?"

His gray eyes burned. He was a lean guy, but his now-puffy face made him look older, more corpulent. "You should go."

I shook my head, planting my hands on the back of a folding chair. It rocked under my weight. "No way. Not until you talk to me."

One corner of his mouth twitched. "Why?"

"Because—because—" I wanted to throw the chair at him. I forced myself to release it. It tipped but stayed standing. "We solved the murder! Mireille and I!"

"I know," he whispered, gazing at his grotty floor.

"Isn't that what's been hanging over you? Freaking you out? Robin's gone, okay?" My throat ached, but I wouldn't stop. "So what's with all the...mystery and angst? Let's celebrate!"

He squeezed his eyes shut. "I wish I could."

"God!" I stomped back toward the loveseat. "Why? I don't get it, Alex. You told me your sad story about being ostracized. I almost got killed putting Robin away. Drop it already!"

"I can't," he ground out.

The pain in his voice halted me. It sounded genuine.

He picked his way in front of me, blocking the window. "You don't want anything to do with me."

I met his eyes. "Don't tell me what I want."

I saw something in his eyes. Sorrow. Stubbornness. And something deeper. Longing.

My lips parted. I reached for his hand.

He jerked it away. "No!"

We stood in silence, breathing at each other. A dog barked outside.

He muttered, "I'm no good to you. I'm no good to anyone."

"Alex—"

He shoved his face in mine. I could smell his rank breath, nearly count the hairs on his face, but his charcoal eyes fixed me in place. "Do you know where Robin got the GHB?"

Suddenly, I didn't want to.

Alex enunciated at me, "I told him where to get it."

My mind balked and restarted. "Alex. You couldn't have."

His mouth shaped a laugh, although his eyes looked like they were on a tour of duty of Vietnam. They told me the answer even as I fumbled to talk. "You gave him a date rape drug? When you knew he was abusing his wife? No way. That would be—" Criminal, my mind whispered.

Alex finally backed off, laying his hands on his loveseat and staring out the window. Two women jogged by, their laughter muffled by the glass. As if it were an ordinary day. For them, it was.

Alex said, "I didn't give it to him. About a month ago, I told him where he could get it. I didn't know about his wife. He said he wanted to try it. He was sick of hitting the books. He wanted to try oblivion. Just for one night." His voice dropped.

I snorted. "He said he wanted to use it on *himself*? And you bought it? Who would—"

Alex swung around to face me, unsmiling.

A chill ran down my arms. His hair curtained his eyes. He smelled fermented. And now I knew he did GHB. He seemed so far from my light-hearted lover, I could hardly believe it was the same person. My T-shirt clung to my sides. His small apartment was suddenly stifling. "Okay. I didn't know—I mean, how did you know about that kind of stuff?"

Alex's face didn't change.

I backed up, inching toward the doorway. "Yeah. Okay. Well, I'd better go. Tori's waiting for me." Total lie, but he didn't have to know that. "I'll, uh, see you around."

"See you in hell," he muttered.

I chose to believe it was his code for St. Joseph's. My shoulder bumped into the plaster doorway. I felt my way back to the door rather than take my eyes off him.

Alex reached for me. "I'd never hurt you, Hope."

I squeaked, evading his touch.

His hand dropped. "Yeah. That's what I thought."

If I were a real forgiving type, I could look beyond and say it wasn't exactly his fault. But I did think he shouldered part of the blame. He gave Robin his secret weapon because he didn't know or care enough to check before handing out references to local dealers. Obviously, Alex agreed, because he was consumed by self-hatred.

I needed to escape. Fast.

I stumbled over a stray pair of shoes, caught myself, and shoved my feet into my sandals. The straps snared under my heels, but I didn't bother to pull them up. I just grabbed his doorknob and twisted. "Good-bye, Alex."

I heard the ring of finality in my own voice. His doorstep was cast in shadow. The early evening air was cooler than I expected.

In answer, he slammed the door shut. The frame reverberated. He threw the bolt.

That hurt my feelings more than anything. He didn't have to lock me out.

But I knew, in a way, he'd locked me out all along.

I closed my eyes, recalling that afternoon we'd spent, the subway foreplay, the sun through the window blinds, how Alex had kissed me and made me taste myself, musky and sweet.

For once in my life, I'd taken a risk and gambled on a sexy, shady guy, who made me crave things I'd kept double-locked in the depths of my brain.

And who inadvertently helped kill his mentor, then asked me to look into it.

Something was building inside my chest. I took a deep breath and tasted it at the back of my throat.

Rage.

I hated Robin. That made sense. He'd tried to kill me.

But part of me loathed Alex even more. A user in every sense of the word.

I stepped into the sunshine. The heat was like a caress on my skin. A trio of students with gym bags strode past me. A woman chattered on a cell phone across the street. I started walking south, passing an old man with a very small dog. I'd never liked small dogs, but this Chihuahua, with its round, peaked ears and tiny feet, cranking along at its top speed, was comic relief. I ground out a laugh.

The man picked up his Chihuahua and hugged it to his chest, glaring at me.

I laughed harder. My ribs hurt with the force of my giggles. The Chihuahua stared at me with black circles for its eyes.

Suddenly, it didn't seem so funny anymore. I hurried down the street. I had to get away. Alex was probably watching through his window, judging me.

I had to get home. I had to lick my wounds in private, before I really did crumble. I tightened the straps on my backpack. The contents jostled with every quick step.

I stopped short at the end of the block. What I needed to do was take the bus home, not the metro. Tori had mentioned the 129 bus stop near the Air Transat building. I scouted for the high-rise with the tell-tale navy sign and aimed toward it. Ten minutes later, I had zigzagged my way to its side, right on Parc.

A blue and white STCUM bus barreled north. Its pixilated yellow sign in the back said *129 Côte-Ste-Catherine*.

I scampered toward the bus's rear end, waving. It didn't stop. In fact, it might have sped up. A passenger in the back seat gaped at me through the window, making no apparent effort to call to the driver.

The more things change...

My hands curled into fists at my side. Goddamn this city. Goddamn everything.

According to the schedule posted on the street lamp, the next bus wasn't for another half hour. I was tempted to walk home in that time, but I knew I was being ridiculous.

One block south, there was a little green-roofed mall with a sign for Cinéma du Parc. I rushed inside its glass doors to call Tori. Unshed tears were a pendulous weight in my chest.

The phone rang and rang.

"Bonjour. Vous avez bien rejoint la boîte vocale de Tori."

One thing I never understood is why so many anglophones started off in French on their machines. My parents would be confused if I did that. A smile touched my lips. I was able to say in a quasi-normal tone, "Uh, meltdown with Alex. Can you call me? I have my pager, but I'm on my way home. Just waiting for the 129—" My voice broke. I struggled to contain it. "Next to Air Transat—"

I was going to cry. So I hung up.

I poked around in the boutique near the main entrance. I admired a pair of chopsticks in a cloth case with a wooden clasp carved in the shape of an elephant.

Even as I did this, rubbing the soft navy cloth, running my finger along the sanded wooden chopsticks, smiling at the elephant—it hit me again.

Rage, so strong it seemed to burn through my sternum and boil up my throat. And not just at Robin and Alex, but at myself.

I'd been so fucking stupid. I'd almost died.

I'd poked my nose into their nasty, incestuous business. I'd slept with a user. Yes, I'd saved Mireille's life and been lucky, but I despised myself more than anyone else.

All my life, I'd played it safe, worked hard, made my parents proud. I'd built myself a charmed life.

I'd almost torched it in less than three weeks.

And for what? For Alex? No guy was worth that much.

For my pride? Probably closer to truth.

Plus some anemic sense of justice for a man I hardly knew.

I forced myself to lay the elephant chopsticks back down, but in my head, I saw myself taking a broken piece of glass and carving

Code Blues

bloody wounds into my face. Then everyone could see what I was feeling.

No! I must be more unhinged than I realized. I shouldn't have come back to work so soon. I shouldn't have gone to see Alex. I shouldn't—

The breath seemed to get vacuumed out of my lungs. My hands fluttered helplessly in front of my chest. My heart beat against my ribs like it wanted to kick its way free. My ears roared in one solid ocean wave. A black veil settled over the periphery of my vision.

It felt like Robin was strangling me here. Now. Again.

People walked by with shopping bags looped over their wrists. Their eyes slid past me. One woman was so close that I could smell the coffee in her paper cup. She checked her watch and strode on.

I

can't

breathe

!

I closed my eyes and grabbed the edge of the display box. Its smooth, painted MDF surface was soothing. I ran my thumb the length of the box and pushed on the outer corner so it dented my thumb pad.

Pain. A blunt sort of pain.

Good. Anything was better than my own thoughts.

Focus. You have to get out of here.

You survived Robin. And Alex. You will not break down in front of the elephant chopsticks.

"Hope?"

A quiet voice. A familiar baritone.

Alex? My heart leapt, even as I whirled around to see a wheat-blond flattop and sympathetic brown eyes shaded by long lashes.

Tucker. I covered my face with both hands.

"Hope." He laid his hand just above my elbow with a light pressure. A "good doctor" pressure, empathetic but not cloying. "Are you okay?"

I nodded. My chest was still heaving, but I was getting some air in. I released the display box, to the relief of the East Indian storekeeper who had come to stare at me. My heart downgraded from jackhammering to hammering. I could feel a sheen of sweat on my forehead.

So stupid. A panic attack. That was what psych people got. I answered Tucker through chattering teeth, "Need—fresh air."

Tucker steered me outside the glass doors, through the paving stone patio, and up to a thigh-high concrete wall bordering the sidewalk.

The sun felt good on my arms, even though I could smell the cigarette smoke drifting from the restaurant *térrasse* around the corner. People sauntered by, hardly glancing at me, but this time, I found their indifference comforting. Nothing to see, folks. Keep moving, keep moving. I took a stab at normalcy. "So what are you doing he-here?" I choked back a sob, but tears welled in my eyes. I rubbed them back. They still spilled over my eyelashes.

No. Do not cry. I tried to concentrate on something else—the pits in the concrete sidewalk, the laughter of the people on the *térrasse*, Tucker's hand resting on the wall beside my leg.

His hands were tanned a light gold. His fingers were long, with endearingly knobby knuckles. No rings, just light cover of blond hair that gleamed in the fading sunlight.

His hand clenched the wall before he forced it to relax. He said, "It doesn't matter. You're okay."

It was such a humane thing to say, I sobbed.

I did not want to cry. But I couldn't hold it back any more.

I wanted to launch myself at his chest and weep against his shoulder while his hands caressed my hair.

I wanted him to fly away so he wouldn't witness my humiliation.

I didn't know what I wanted anymore.

I stood up. "I have to go. Thank you," I said, even though tears were still spilling down my face like they wanted to supply a water bottling plant. "I'm better now."

"No, you're not." Tucker's hands reached forward, as if to hold me back, but stopped an inch short of my shoulders. "Just stay here. You don't have to talk to me."

It was exactly the right thing to say. No judgment, no questions. He was just there for me. So there for me, in a way that Alex had never been and never would be. Tucker was so great, but every compassionate move felt like a vice around my chest. More evidence of my idiocy, that I didn't even *like* Tucker.

I started to bawl. My shoulders shook. My hands grew slick with mucous and tears as I covered my face.

I heard Tucker stir. So he wasn't so enlightened after all. He was ditching me for being the weeping wall. I felt something detach inside my chest. Fine. This was what I learned, after all. I had no one to count on but myself.

His hand brushed the side of my shoulder. "It's okay, Hope. Sit down. Please."

He waited until I sank back down on the wall.

"Back in a minute. Okay, Hope?"

What else could I say? I nodded from behind my hands. All told, it was a relief to cry. I'd always avoided blubbering in public, even when I was younger. Now I was doing it in full Technicolor and yet I would survive.

His shoes padded away. I allowed myself some full-frontal sobbing. A mother towed her two kids past me while they craned their necks, hanging back to goggle at me. I swung myself around so my back was to the sidewalk. Now the guy cleaning out the garbage cans outside the mall cast me nervous looks. Maybe they'd arrest me for disturbing the peace.

The thought made me smile a little. There is some comfort in hitting rock bottom. You know it can't get any worse.

The green glass doors punched outward. Tucker's face cleared when he saw me still perched on the wall. He flew toward me. When he skidded to a halt, his leather sneakers kicked up a stray piece of gravel. He was slightly breathless as he shoved some white paper Subway napkins under my nose. "Here."

Jesus. I grabbed one with a watery smile. I blew my nose. It was so clogged, I had to blow twice. I searched for a dry corner to wipe my face.

Tucker plucked the napkin out of my hand without wincing at its condition and pressed some new ones on me. He wadded the used one up in his fist and held slightly behind his back, out of sight.

Wow. He didn't even run to the garbage with it. He held on to it because he'd rather stay by me. And he didn't say a word.

I tried to imagine Alex holding a snot rag for me and I couldn't. That meant I was well rid of him.

Okay.

I gambled on Alex. I lost. I lived.

I tried to save Mireille. We won. Robin lost.

I took a deep breath. Blew my nose one more time. Then I said, "Okay."

Tucker held out his hand, folding the rest of the napkins under his arm as he helped me up. He still held the soggy one behind his back. I smiled at that.

A few steps north on Parc, at the glass and red metal bus shelter, we paused by the garbage bin. We both tossed our used napkins. I gave a watery laugh.

Tucker looked pleased. He handed me the remaining napkins.

I laughed. "I don't need that many! I'm okay."

He shook them at me, the white ends fluttering in the breeze. "Just in case. You never know. Someone else might need them."

"Yeah. Lots of crying jags on the bus."

He nodded, drawing his eyebrows together in mock seriousness. "Or you could use them as a pressure dressing."

I laughed some more. "Okay." I slid off my backpack and unzipped it. He tucked the napkins in the front section.

When we straightened, we were standing quite close together. Only my bag separated us. His brown eyes were very fine, with a golden light in them, reflecting the sun. I could see his chest rising and falling under his black T-shirt. I had the urge to touch the bow of his upper lip.

But I didn't. I couldn't trust my judgment anymore. Alex was still a third degree burn across my heart. We stepped back at the same moment.

A faint flush rose in Tucker's neck, but all he said was, "So you were taking the bus?"

"Yes." I sniffed hard. "The 129."

"This way."

We continued north. When there were too many people on the sidewalk, he stepped behind to let me precede him. Then he rejoined me. Our shoulders brushed occasionally. We didn't speak.

Back in the shadow of the Air Transat building, a lineup of people climbed on the number 80 bus. Mine should get here soon. I sighed and slipped off my backpack to root in the front compartment for my wallet. Tucker cleared his throat and held a paper ticket under my nose.

I straightened and shook my head. "You've been too nice."

He shook his head. "It's what, two bucks? I can afford it."

I hesitated. He shook the ticket at me.

My fingers closed around it. "Thank you."

"You're welcome."

Our eyes locked.

I heard a buzzing noise. Tucker's hand clapped to his pants pocket and unfolded his vibrating cell phone. "Hi. Yeah. She's right here. Okay. Sure. Meet us at the Mimosa Manor." He smiled at me. "Yeah. Okay. Yeah. No problem. Thanks, Tori."

Tucker hung up and pocketed his cell phone. "You're on your way to Mama Tori," he said.

I nodded blankly. That sounded like an Italian restaurant. I knew I should be glad they were taking such good care of me, but it made me feel guilty.

Tucker lightly grasped my elbow and arm waited with me by the bus stop. Three more number 80 buses rolled by, but no 129's

At last, a bus pulled up. Its sign flashed "129" and then "Côte-Ste-Catherine."

I turned to Tucker. For the first time, I noticed that his brown eyes curved down at the corners, giving him a rueful air. He had to raise his voice over the rumble of the bus engine and swishing of passing cars. "Tori will meet you at your stop if she beats you there. Or if you get home first, she'll buzz you." He hesitated.

The bus doors folded open. An old lady began mounting the steps, her cane digging into the black rubber floor.

Tucker added awkwardly, "You'll be okay."

I nodded. I was already better. I closed my eyes.

I felt a light touch at my forehead. Tucker brushed a stray hair behind my ear, his fingers barely sketching across my skin.

I opened my eyes. Tucker waved me on to the bus, where two teenaged guys were hopping up the steps, flashing their Opus cards at the bus driver.

I didn't want to leave him there. I leaned forward. "Aren't you going to—"

He shook his head.

I hesitated. I'd imposed on him too much, but it didn't seem right to just cry on his shoulder and run away. "Thank you."

"You're welcome." He smiled down at me.

Out of the corners of my eyes, I saw the bus doors twitch. I yelled, "*Non, non, attendez-moi!*" and leapt on, shoving Tucker's ticket in the silver fare box. The bus driver grunted and shot the bus into gear, throwing me off-balance.

The light had just turned red, but we barreled through on the tails of the car in front of us. Clinging to the hand rail, I swung around for one last glimpse of Tucker through the wide panes of the bus window. He never took his eyes off me.

AUTHOR'S NOTE

If you liked this book, would you consider signing up for my mailing list at www.melissayuaninnes.com? I occasionally send out special deals and behind-the-scenes info about Hope.

And if you could write a review, even it's only a line or two, it makes all the difference for a new author.

Now, an enormous thank you to everyone who helped me with *Code Blues.*

My friends from Montreal to Vancouver got me through medicine and now support my scribblings.

Bruce Kahn is a Montreal police officer who poked holes in my plot and helped me fix them.

For edits, I'd like to give a special shout out to Camden Park Press, Andy Rorabeck, and Alberta's Dr. Greg Smith. Much gratitude to the Oregon Writers Network, most especially Kris Rusch and Dean Smith. Couldn't have done it without you. Or actually, I could have, but it wouldn't have been half as fun or look one tenth as good.

Speaking of fun and looking good, my husband Matt always encouraged my writing. Max and Anastasia are my little wonderwalls. My parents really did call and bring me food.

Once again, this is a work of fiction. All names and details have been changed or invented. If you are a doctor and want to make fun of the medical errors, bring it on, but remember, Hope's just a resident. Go easy on her and her creator.

Please note that this book is set in 2011, but I have altered some of the dates as an artistic liberty. The spelling may also seem like a Choose Your Own Adventure™, but it's Canadian, which is a luscious hybrid of British and American spelling.

ABOUT THE AUTHOR

Melissa Yi is an emergency physician trained in the crumbling corridors of Montreal, Canada. She now runs codes in Ontario.

A preview of Hope Sze's next adventure

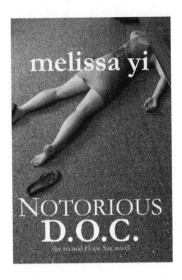

melissa yi

NOTORIOUS
D.O.C.
the second Hope Sze novel

I'd avoided St. Joseph's emergency room for the past week, but it hadn't changed. Stretcher patients lined the wall and spilled into the hallway. Fluorescent lights turned everyone's skin yellow, even though most of them weren't Asian like I was.

I smiled at a nurse who squeezed my arm and said, "Welcome back, Hope!" just before a patient's wrinkled mother waved me down. "Miss. We need a blanket!"

Home, sweet home.

Well, sweet except for the smell of stool drifting from bed 12.

I nodded at a few fellow medical residents. Officially, we're doctors in our first post-graduate training year, formerly known as interns. Unofficially, we're scut monkeys rotating from service to service. Last month, I'd done emergency medicine and tracked down a murderer; this month, I was on psychiatry and opting out of any drama.

I just needed to see one scut monkey in particular. A blond dude. A guy who appreciated sausages and beer and me, not necessarily in that order. A guy I'd overlooked when I first came to Montreal for my residency, but I wasn't about to make that mistake again.

Sadly, no matter how casually I glanced out of the corners of my eyes, John Tucker did not appear.

Since I was officially starting my psychiatry rotation a week late, duty called first. I perched on the chair in the psych corner of the nurses' station, near the printer, and grabbed the chart lying on the table. Normally the psych nurse would occupy this chair, but she was probably talking to the patient whose chart I was holding, Mrs. Regina Lee.

I pretended to read the triage note, my skin still electric at the possibility of seeing Tucker. Was that high school or what? I might be 26 years old, with an M.D. behind my name, but I still got rattled thinking about A BOY.

My favourite emerg nurse, Roxanne, paused beside me and shoved a pen behind her ear. "Hope! Nice to see you. Are you doing okay?"

I nodded. We hugged. She smelled like Purell and she was built like me, skinny but strong. Once she told me her Italian grandmothers practically cried when they saw her, they found her so emaciated-looking. Of course, that didn't stop me from complaining about my thighs on a bad day.

Roxanne glanced at the blue plastic card clipped to my chart. "Oh, no. You got Mrs. Lee. Is it Fall already?"

I frowned. "August fourteenth?" After sitting in school 20-odd years of my life, including most summer vacations, I hate when people call autumn prematurely. As far as I'm concerned, it's still summer until the snow hits the ground. I don't even like to see the leaves change colour. Call it denial if you want. Whoa—I was in psych mode already.

Roxanne shrugged. "Close enough. She always comes here. Especially around now. It's very sad."

"Why?"

"Did you know Laura Lee?"

I hesitated.

She shook her head. "You're too young. Anyway. She was a resident here. Star of her year."

A resident, just like me. "What does that have to do with Mrs. Lee? Are they related?"

Roxanne pointed to the clipboard. "I'll let Mrs. Lee tell you. It's her favorite story."

Strange. I strode through the open door of room 14, the designated psych room. The stretcher and its five-point restraints stood empty, but a woman sat in a chair by one indented white wall. "Mrs. Lee?"

She clutched the clunky leather purse in her lap as she turned to face me. Her permed black hair was streaked with white, but I noticed her strong cheekbones and her skin, still enviably smooth considering her 64 years. Although her lips parted, no sound emerged.

"Hi." I held out my hand.

She didn't take it. My hand hovered in the air until I shoved it back in my lab coat pocket. I belatedly remembered I was trying to improve my body language and dropped my hand to my side instead. The smell of bloody stool wafted toward us from room 12 and we both winced before I changed the subject. "My name is Dr. Hope Sze. I'm a resident from psychiatry. Could we—"

She was staring at me with such intensity, I faltered.

Her eyes filled with tears.

Oh, dear. She really was depressed. The psychiatric patients who come to the emergency room are usually depressed or psychotic. I set her file down on the desk and scanned the room for tissues. They always kept a box handy on psych.

She said something in Chinese.

"I'm sorry. I don't speak Chinese. But I could get a translator if you like." My parents thought we should be Canadian and always spoke English to us.

She reached a hand toward my face, gazing at me like she was in a dream.

I flinched, not wanting to jerk away, but mildly freaked. Who *was* this woman?

She checked herself. Her hand dropped to her side, and she tried to smile. "Excuse me," she said, in perfectly good English. "It's just that you look so much like my daughter."

I relaxed a little. "Oh. That's nice. Is your daughter, ah, here with you?"

"Not anymore." Her brown eyes met mine, direct and level. "She's dead and somebody killed her."

My shoulders tensed. It's an answer you never expect. And, even though I tried not to be superstitious, I found it eerie that her dead daughter was a resident who looked just like me.

She blinked. The tears already shining in her eyes dripped on to her cheeks. She ignored them, still staring at me. "I'm sorry," she said. "You must think me very foolish."

"Not at all."

She dabbed her eyes with a tissue she extracted from her purse. "I know you're not Laura. I know she's gone. It's just that I've been without hope for so long."

I twitched. My name, Hope, is a constant sore spot for me. When people mention the concept, I always feel like they're talking about me, although Mrs. Lee was the most poignant example.

She shook her head. "I know what they say about me, that I can't accept my daughter's death. They think it's tragic but I should move on after eight years."

Although the emerg nurse, Roxanne, hadn't rolled her eyes, I could certainly imagine others would, and Mrs. Lee knew it. To use psych lingo, Mrs. Lee had insight, meaning that she understood her condition. A lot of psych patients don't. They think you're the nutbar who doesn't receive the secret messages from the Cadbury commercial and they're perfectly sane.

So far, Mrs. Lee didn't seem crazy, just sad.

Somehow that was worse.

Her mouth twisted with what might have been humor under different circumstances. "They even think I should move 'so I'll make new memories' and, not coincidentally, remove myself from their sector."

I nodded. I only knew about sectors because Tucker, who did psych last month, had explained them to me. The Island of Montreal was carved into psychiatry "sectors" according to postal code. If you had mental health issues, you had to go to whatever hospital sector you belonged to. No exceptions, even if it made no sense. We had patients who were literally born at St. Joe's and lived across the street, but they had to get downtown to the Montreal General for their psychiatrist.

Mrs. Lee already knew this, which was a little scary. She was a highly intelligent woman who'd been grieving for eight years. What was I going to do for her? I'd better steer her away from the subject of her daughter's death, even though I really wanted to know how she'd died. Curiosity not only killed the cat, it lured me into medical school and into fighting crime, although I was hanging up my magnifying glass after my first and only case last month. "I'm very sorry for your loss. Maybe we should start at the beginning. How would you describe your mood, on a scale of one to ten——"

She waved her hand, cutting me off. "I already have a psychiatrist. Dr. Saya is happy to prescribe me medication or let me run off at the mouth, but I don't want to talk about it anymore. I want justice."

Justice. I knew I should get back on track, asking her about depression, but I couldn't resist. "Have you talked to the police?"

She laughed and tossed her tissue in the garbage. Two points. "They know me well. They say I don't have any proof it wasn't an accident. It was a hit and run, you see."

Well. Maybe it really was an accident. I crossed my legs. "Do you have any proof?"

She leaned forward and placed her hands on her knees, eyes suddenly sharp. "You believe me, don't you?"

I hesitated. I yearned to say yes, even though my logic and medical training shied away from her.

She shook herself. "How silly of me. Of course you don't, yet. But I could show you what I have. I have an entire file on Laura."

I had to draw the line at sorting through Laura's gap-toothed elementary school photos and stellar report cards. "I'm sure you do, Mrs. Lee, but——"

"Not that kind of file. Evidence. The police reports. The autopsy." She paused. "I used to carry it with me, but most people here have seen it already and don't take it seriously. I couldn't bear that."

How many mothers could say "autopsy" without breaking down? On the other hand, she'd had eight years to acclimatize to the word. I had to admire her drive, still searching for justice.

But it wasn't my place. The fact that I reminded her of Laura made it even more unprofessional. "I'm sorry, Mrs. Lee. I do know one or two people at the police department. They might be able to help you with...justice." The word tasted foreign in my mouth. I hurried on. "In the emergency room, we deal with medical problems. You seem quite stable. Are you feeling more depressed lately?"

She shook her head. "I feel much better now that I've met you."

I closed my eyes. I couldn't save this woman. I could hardly save myself.

"Please, Dr. Sze. Just have a look at her file. That's all I'm asking."

I had to say no. I took a breath.

One of the things I never liked about psych was, when you interview a patient, you're not really an ally. You're mentally critiquing what they say and how they say it while trying to categorize them. It sounds harsh, but a gazillion people came to the ER and said, "I'm depressed." Very few of them were truly suicidal. Some of them were trying to manipulate you. Some of them just wanted attention. Of course, this happened in emergency medicine too, which was what I planned to specialize in, but I generally wanted to be on the patient's side instead of inspecting them from behind glass.

This time, though, I should keep her behind glass.

I knew what my supervisors would say. I knew what I should say. I forced the sentences into the air, creating a barrier between us. "Mrs. Lee, please, let's concentrate on you. Have you thought about hurting yourself?"

She sighed. "No, I am not suicidal. Naturally, after Laura was killed, I had days of despair, but I never attempted to kill myself. I have never tried to hurt anyone else. I am not hallucinating. I do not have a special relationship with God or Satan. I do not drink or take any drugs except an occasional Ativan to help me sleep, and even then, I only take half a milligram. I know I am at St. Joseph's Hospital in Montreal, Quebec, Canada, and that it is August fourteenth in the year 2011."

I stared at her, wide-eyed. She'd just encapsulated a psych interview better than I could have done.

She smiled. "It's just practice, Dr. Sze. I've had many, many of these interviews. I could go on if you like. But I am not crazy. I am not going to hurt you or anyone else, including myself. I already have a doctor and I'm not asking for any special treatment. All I am asking is for you to read my file on Laura. You don't even have to meet with me. I could leave a copy in your mailbox."

"Mrs. Lee." I should say no. I should concentrate on medicine or even on Tucker. *Curiosity killed the cat.*

Satisfaction brought him back.

At last, I looked into her steady brown eyes and said, "All right."

Notorious D.O.C.
Hit. And Run.

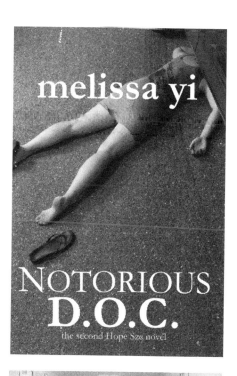

melissa yi

NOTORIOUS
D.O.C.
the second Hope Sze novel

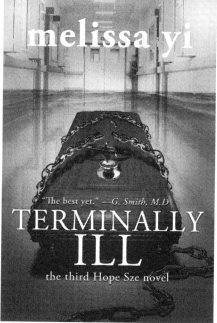

melissa yi

"The best yet." —G. Smith, M.D

TERMINALLY
ILL
the third Hope Sze novel

Made in the USA
Charleston, SC
27 July 2014